Praise for *FOREIGN BODIES*

"He is as strong a storyteller as anybody—as uncomfortable as some of this is, it is likely to get you turning pages."
—Analog

"Dedman can turn a phrase as neatly as any hard-boiled writer. Dedman is one of the writers we might expect to join the likes of Greg Egan, George Foy, William Gibson, Peter F. Hamilton, and Melissa Scott in producing entertainments with the combination of smart extrapolation, satiric edge, noir atmosphere, and tough-guy attitude that bring Dashiell Hammett, Raymond Chandler, and John D. MacDonald into the new century."
—Russell Letson, *Locus*

"*Foreign Bodies* is a fast-paced SF adventure through a dystopian future criticizing the intolerance of many current religious and extremist groups and where this tendency might take us. Dedman manages to weave a social conscience through the novel, without making the message the point of the book—or slowing down the plot."
—Lawrence Schimel

Praise for *THE ART OF ARROW CUTTING*

"What a wonderful novel! Stephen Dedman's *The Art of Arrow Cutting* is a very auspicious debut—a gritty tale, beautifully understated, with finely drawn and convincing characters. You'll be pulled into his world—a world just slightly skewed from our own—and will find the pages turning themselves."
—Robert J. Sawyer, author of *Calculating God*

"An agreeable blend of oriental fantasy and noir-ish sleuthing: a polished, well-organized debut, complemented by Dedman's nice light touch on the tiller."
—Kirkus Reviews (pointer review)

"Dedman's first novel is very well written and the author has a knack for developing fascinating, if somewhat unlikely, characters. This novel should appeal to readers who enjoy urban fantasies of the sort made popular by Charles de Lint, Megan Lindholm, and Emma Bull."
—Publishers Weekly

Tor Books by Stephen Dedman

THE ART OF ARROW CUTTING
FOREIGN BODIES

FOREIGN BODIES

Stephen Dedman

A TOM DOHERTY ASSOCIATES BOOK   TOR®   NEW YORK

This is a work of fiction. All the characters and events portrayed in this novel are either fictitious or are used fictitiously.

FOREIGN BODIES

Parts of this novel were previously published in *Aurealis: The Australian Magazine of Fantasy and Science Fiction.*

This book is printed on acid-free paper.

Edited by James Frenkel

Book design by Jane Adele Regina

A Tor Book
Published by Tom Doherty Associates, LLC
175 Fifth Avenue
New York, NY 10010

www.tor.com

Tor® is a registered trademark of Tom Doherty Associates, LLC.

Library of Congress Cataloging-in-Publication Data

Dedman, Stephen.
    Foreign bodies / Stephen Dedman.
       p.   cm.
    "A Tom Doherty Associates book."
    ISBN 0-312-86864-2 (hc)
    ISBN 0-312-87259-3 (pbk)
      1. San Francisco (Calif.)—Fiction. 2. Twenty-first century—Fiction.
3. Time travel—Fiction. I. Title.
PR9619.3.D387F67   1999
823—dc21
                                        99-055808
                                        CIP

First Hardcover Edition: December 1999
First Trade Paperback Edition: November 2000

Printed in the United States of America

0 9 8 7 6 5 4 3 2 1

To Bill,
for many years of friendship,
and to Elaine,
for putting up with me while I finished this book

Thanks to Richard Curtis; Jim Frenkel, his family, and his team; Anna Hepworth; Stephen Higgins and Dirk Strasser; Alexandra and David Honigsberg; Laurton McGurk; Jim and Sondi Minz; Mary Anne Mohanraj; Chris Muncy; Robin Pen; Dorothy Taylor; and Dean Wesley Smith, Sue Isle, and my wife, Elaine, for wanting to know what happened next.

"It's an odd thing, but anyone who disappears is said to be seen at San Francisco. It must be a delightful city, and possess all the attractions of the next world."

—OSCAR WILDE

"Fex urbis, lex orbis."
("Dregs of the city, law of the world.")

—SAINT JEROME

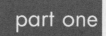

part one

FEX URBIS

1

MIKE

I woke just before dawn (not by choice: All the springs in my biological clock wore out last century) and Swiftie was sleeping on the balcony. She was there about one morning in three, lately. I lay there, looking past her to the sky, trying to remember whether the weather was turning wetter, or colder, or whatever. I'm supposed to know these things.

Swiftie rolled over, her eyes closed, her face mobile. Whatever she was dreaming wasn't fun. I considered waking her but decided she wouldn't thank me; her days probably weren't much fun either. I tried to get back to sleep but that didn't work, so I hauled myself out of bed and careened into the shower before remembering that there wasn't enough sun yet to run the purifier. I sat on the toilet for a moment, then found my way to the kitchenette and fired up the percolator. I carried two mugs back to the bedroom, watched Swiftie for a moment, then opened the French window and placed one mug near her face. Her nostrils twitched; then, a moment later, her eyes opened slowly: She stared through the window at me, and then reached for the coffee.

Swiftie was too skinny to be pretty, her hair needed a gardener, and you had to look at her face just to be sure she was female. But her eyes were—open, I guess. If you've seen statues of Buddha—bald, bulging belly, boobs, eyes closed serenely . . . well, Swiftie was the opposite, an anti-Buddha, half waif, half wraith. I didn't know where she was from, but her skin seemed to be brown beneath the usual stripper crust, and her eyes and cheeks looked Asian. Amerindian? Arab? Filipina? All of the above? Bangkok had been mostly under water for years, and a lot of islands were disappearing. All those people had to go somewhere, and a lot of them came here.

"Thanks," she rasped warily. Her voice was like black BritRail coffee, no sugar, late at night. I wondered why she picked my balcony so often. I lived on the second floor (or the first, in Australian), and while I didn't keep bees or cacti or a muteweiler, I was sure there were other, equally desirable squats nearby. Maybe strippers like to call someplace—well, a few places—home too. Without sitting up she reached for the mug and took a cautious sip. I'd made it light, with two sugars: I figured she could use the nutrients.

"Now what?" she asked when she'd finished. "You want me to eat out of your hand or something?"

I shook my head.

"Charity, hah?"

When did "charity" become a dirty word, at best a euphemism for "tax evasion"? I'd done a lot of volunteer work for Amnesty and Greenpeace and other organizations when I was younger and single, before the ICE Age, but I no longer mentioned it to anyone; they tended to assume I was either a sucker, a fanatic, or a spy. I said nothing.

"Don't panic," she said, making a good guess at what I was thinking. "I won't tell anyone. Hey, this is a nice place we've got, right?"

I shrugged, and smiled. I'd certainly lived in worse; I'd even done some squatting once or twice. "Squatter" has a different connotation in Australian: It was originally a farmer who couldn't afford to buy his land, and later came to mean farmers in general. "Stripper" meant something else when I was young too, but now they call them exotic dancers, and how many times a day could you say "streetperson"?

We watched each other for a few minutes, and then she sat up and stretched. If it was meant to show off her figure, it failed. "What you do for ice?"

"I run a bucket shop."

"Hah?"

"Travel agent and courier broker. I sell cheap airfares."

"How cheap?"

Okay, so there's no such thing as a cheap airfare anymore, even by zep. "Depends where you want to go."

"Anywhere."

"Here to L.A. is—"

"Not L.A."

I agreed with her. I didn't mind wearing armor, but I refused to drive it. "Seattle? New York?"

She shook her head. "Canada?"

"Vancouver? A thousand ice, but you'd need a passport—which means a Worldwide Identification Number. Montreal's twenty-five hundred ice, a passport, a visa—and a literacy test in French. *Parlez-vous français, mademoiselle?*"

She smiled sourly. "A few words, but I can't spell 'em for *merde*." She stood, grabbed the bulging bag she carried everywhere, and looked over the balcony. "Hey, I gotta get to work 'fore the trashman cometh. See you 'round, winner."

I felt like telling her that I'd done some Dumpster diving myself, back in the eighties, behind the Club Med in Eilat; but what the hell, for me, it'd been because of a temporary setback and something of an adventure, not a way of life. Besides, it was probably 'fore she was born.

In case you ever wondered, being a travel agent wasn't exactly a high-pressure job, though I was probably busier than most: If you wanted the best prices on a one-way ticket, you came to me. Besides, I had itchy feet up to my armpits, and I speak bits of seven languages and twenty-some accents. Like Shakespeare said, who's gonna hire a skinny cook?

I'm qualified, too, of course. Cheap travel gets a lot harder when you turn thirty, thanks to visa restrictions and similar bullshit, so I tried settling down, married Angela, took an agent's course, and, having a green card and an American prefix on my WIN, got a job with the Australian Tourist Bureau here. We moved around the country every time Angela found a better job, and when we split up, I tried going back to traveling and teaching, but by then I was forty-two, most of Asia and South America and Africa had been hit hard by the greenhouse effect and the economic downturn, the UN was bankrupt, and work overseas, even volunteer work that only fed and housed me, wasn't easy to find. I hadn't gone far before I decided to turn around and come back to San Francisco. Now I owned my own business, and a mortgage, and it looked like I was stuck here.

Two mornings later, Swiftie was on the balcony again. This time, it was the alarm clock that woke me; Swiftie was already awake, attacking a burned loaf of bread with a switchblade. I thought of offering her another coffee, but that would have meant letting her in, and that—well, if the cops found out you'd had strippers in your house, you could forget about Victims' Aid or insurance payouts. So could your neighbors. Legally, it's sort of like inviting a vampire to visit. So I left the window one-way and soundproof, and stomped off showerward.

I wondered, as I walked to work, just how many strippers there were in the city, what percentage of the population. I couldn't find any official figures, and I'm not sure I'd have believed them if I had. Where do you look for an answer? Walk down the Haight or Market and you see more strippers than citizens, but how much time do citizens spend on the streets? They telecommute, on average, four days out of six; they only socialize with people inside their building, or via computer; everything they need and most of the things they know or think they want are delivered to them. Some don't leave their homes anymore; they live in what used to be one of the most beautiful cities on Earth, and probably still is, but they never see it. Nihonmachi was sealed so tight it looked like Stonehenge, and Nob Hill was more like a mountain fortress.

Christ, I must be getting old.

"How was work?"

"Okay. What'd you do with *your* day?"

"Went to Saint Vincent de Paul's. They let you read the old books free, unless you're a winner." She chuckled. "Course, I had to hit the Mission for a shower first. I feel like a salted herring."

I laughed. "You read a lot?"

"Got fuck-all else to do, and those places are *warm*." She sipped at the cup of coffee I'd given her. "Did you ever read a science-fiction story where the future got so bad everyone went to hide in the past?"

"Probably," I said after a moment's thought. "It's an old idea; they even used it on *Star Trek*."

"What about if we never really left Earth, but invented time travel instead?"

"Uh-huh. *The End of Eternity*."

"What if time travelers couldn't take their bodies with them, but had to borrow them?"

I had to think about that one. "*All the Time in the World*? Arthur C. Clarke?"

"What if the bodies they borrowed had to be dead? I mean, just dead—taking over the bodies at the moment of death."

"No," I replied a moment later. "I don't think I've read that one."

She grinned. "Then I guess I'd better hurry up and write it."

I blinked, then nodded. Writers had been starving on other people's balconies for centuries: I guess if you had to starve on a balcony anyway, you might as well convince yourself that you could be a writer.

She astonished me by actually beginning to write the piece, using an unreliable ballpoint pen found in the street and the backs of assorted handbills. She read it to me through the window. It was set a few centuries from now, but there had been few major scientific breakthroughs. There'd been no contact with aliens, spaceships still traveled much slower than light-speed, most guns still fired bullets instead of rays, and her time-travel mechanism had been a spin-off from the space program: a braintaper that could download a human mind into a brain that had been flat-lined by their suspended-animation process—or, it was later discovered, into any other recently dead but undamaged brain, as long as they knew the precise time of death. Longevity was cheap, and near-immortality possible, but most people on Earth seemed too bored to bother with much life extension. Life on the outer worlds—enclosed bases in this solar system, new settlements farther away—was shown as more tightly regimented and less physically comfortable, but exciting. Space travel, unfortunately, was still expensive, and the offworlders accepted only those they needed. It seemed a pretty bleak future for most, despite its material comforts, but Swiftie assured me the story had a happy ending. I commented that this would make it more salable—most published SF is obscenely optimistic—and she laughed. "*Sell* it? How?"

"Well, you'd need to finish it, and wurp it—"

"Where would I get a wurpressor? I was lucky to find this fuckin' pen!"

"I have a computer. If you finish it, do a draft I can read—"

"And how do I get paid? I don't have an ICEcard, and I can't get one without a WIN."

"I'll get it put on my card, and you tell me what you want bought."

"You can do this?"

I doubted it'd ever become an issue—they say more people write short stories than read them—but what the hell. "Used to do a lot of it. When I was a lot younger, even when cash was legal, you could hardly ever get *paid* in cash. Then it started getting harder to find a job—even a few days' picking fruit—without some proof you were a citizen. They called 'em Social Security numbers here and Canada, Tax File numbers back home—"

"Home?"

"Oz. Australia. Anyway, these numbers were the ancestors of the WIN. So first time I bummed around the States, I only took jobs that paid cash and didn't ask too many questions. Got paid half the going rate, and half the time I didn't even get that—I mean it wasn't like I could go to the cops. Next time around, things were tougher, so I borrowed a Social Security number from a friend of mine, and he cashed the checks for me."

"Nobody wondered why he was getting all these checks for different jobs?"

"He was a writer, and a part-time vagabond himself. His income was sort of Heisenbergian: unpredictable, but not statistically significant. The IRS didn't hassle him much."

Swiftie smiled. "What about you? You a writer?"

"Nah, not really. I used to do travel articles, wrote stuff for some of the guidebooks. Didn't pay much, but it scored me the occasional free feed." Suddenly I wondered what I was letting myself in for. I'd never heard the term used in America, but "swifty" is Australian for a trick, a fast one. "But I think I still have some writing paper somewhere, if you want it."

We e-mailed the story off a week later. We had a small disagreement on the title: She'd called it "Refugee," which is the second most frequently used title in SF, so we changed it to "YesterDei."

Apart from that, I edited it very slightly—her spelling was consistently bizarre—but we'd agreed that it was going to be *her* work, even if it was my WIN on the title page. I wanted to use her name for the byline, but she wouldn't tell me what it was. "We could pretend I'm half Vietnamese, half Sioux," she suggested. "Call me Hai-Lee Ill Eagle."

I would've thrown something at her if she hadn't been on the other side of a shatterproof window. In the end, we compromised on the safely neuter Lee Bird.

Swiftie celebrated by bringing a girlfriend "home." It took me a few minutes to realize what was happening: All I could see, at first, was Swiftie's army-blanket poncho and motley jeans, a mop of Manhattan-sunset-colored hair, a black coat, and a recycled beach umbrella. Strippers, it seemed, never completely removed their clothes, for fear that someone might steal them.

Swiftie poked her head up and looked straight at me, grinning, even though she couldn't have seen or heard me through the window. Watching the women feasting on each other, I realized how little I actually knew about Swiftie. I still didn't know her name, how old she was, where she was from. I mean, I'd slept with a few girls I hadn't known any better, but Swiftie and I had been talking for *months*.

Swiftie brought four different women home that fall—or maybe it was more, wearing four indistinguishable costumes. They were all skinny, at least from the waist up, with thin, scratched arms and mud-wrestler's legs, and hair apparently cut with a Swiss Army knife—one with saw, file, toothpick, and wire-stripper blades. One was tiny, as flat-chested as Swiftie herself, and probably even younger; one had jagged scars across her belly, and breasts that looked like dirty socks; one had been badly shaved and was growing out blond; one was chunky around the hips, with a broken nose but all her teeth; the youngest-looking had bright blue eyes and breasts like little fists, and the improbable name of Cannon.

On nights when she was alone—by now she was sleeping on the balcony two nights out of three—Swiftie would sit there and . . . masturbate. She seemed fascinated by her own breasts, small as they were. I suspect this was, at least partially, an act for my benefit. Actually, I stopped watching after a few weeks. This sort of teasing had never really grabbed me; if it had, I would've subscribed to AdultCheck. Besides, I had a daughter about her age. I also stopped watching her with the women, except sometimes for Cannon, who, unlike the others, seemed to know she was being watched, and who also seemed to be Swiftie's favorite. She reminded me of a girlfriend I'd had when I was teaching in Korea; she had been skinny enough to be the Grim Reaper's daughter, and I was dumb enough not to realize at first that she wasn't doing it to be fashionable. She died in a student protest a couple of years later, when I was in Bangkok. Anyway. Cannon wore a collection of patches that had once been held together by denim dungarees, a costume more honored in the breach than the observance. One night, I tried on some of my old jeans and discovered that I'd put on some weight. Correction: some fat. So I went through the closet and found outfits for Swiftie and Cannon. I mean, winter was coming, and they needed them more than I did.

"Mike?"

"Yeah?"

Swiftie had spent the night alone again. I didn't ask where Cannon was. "You said 'Refugee' was the second-most-used name for SF stories. What was first?"

" 'Homecoming.' " I used to wonder what that said about SF writers; then I started to wonder what it said about the SF readers. I never did think of a good answer. Swiftie nodded, and then asked. "Why don't *you* go home?"

"Never been there."

"Hah? What about Australia?"

"I don't know." I sipped at my coffee, reminiscing. "This town isn't my home, but I like it." I looked across the street and nodded at one of the old "painted lady"–style houses. "I can't afford to live in one of those—wish I could—but at least I can look at them. Beautiful buildings, kept up just because they're beautiful, even though it'd be more economical to tear them down and build high-rises, earthquake zone or no. Even the new buildings are being designed to blend in with those—okay, they're imitations—but at least they *try*, they *care*."

"I don't understand."

"My mother lives in a place almost exactly like this, in Fremantle,

Australia. My father lives in another, in Belfast. My ex-wife lives in New York, in—"

"I think I can guess," she said dryly, "but I still don't *understand*."

"Vagabondage," I explained. "I was a traveler, a tourist; wherever I was, I always had to be somewhere *different*. And now there's almost nowhere that's different, where you can wake up and look out the window and know where you are." I stared into my coffee, as though there were some answers in it. "For most people, I guess, home isn't a place at all. It's a time. What about you?"

"Hah?"

"Where's your home? Here?"

She turned, looked out toward the park, and shook her head.

"Don't want to talk about it?"

"Some other time."

We received a contract for the story two days after Thanksgiv-ing: Payment, they assured us, would be on publication, some time in the next eighteen months. They paid six cents a word, the same rate as twenty years ago. Swiftie was delighted, and I offered to give her the money immediately. "How do you want it? Food? Clothes? A sleeping bag?"

"Electronics."

"*What?*"

"Electronics. Chips, wires, that sort of crap. I'll tell you what I need."

"*Electronics?*"

"It's a hobby."

I stared at her, and then noticed that bag she carried everywhere. It was bulging more than it had in summer. "What are you making?"

Swiftie shrugged, and looked away.

"Remote control? Lock pick?" No answer. "Icebreaker?"

"What if I am, hah? What're you going to do?"

What *was* I going to do? I mean, reprogramming the ROM on an ICEcard should take more than a few scrounged circuit boards and Laser Shack LCDs, right? And, even if she succeeded, the International Credit Exchange wasn't exactly a bosom friend of mine.

But what if she failed? Seven-to-ten planting trees or cutting kelp? "What is it, Swiftie?"

"A new life. Okay?"

I backed down. "Okay, okay. Tell me what you need."

Winter hit the city like a soggy sponge, and I found myself staring into the double-barreled horror of Christmas and my forty-ninth birthday. I hadn't seen much of Swiftie since I'd bought her the stuff she'd asked for, and I started to wonder what *she* might be hiding from.

Christmas morning woke me with one hell of a thunderstorm, and I rolled over to watch the fireworks. Swiftie was huddled on the balcony, becoming drenched by the rain, sheltering her bag with her skinny body. I stared for nearly a minute, then draped a kimono around myself and got up to open the French window. She looked up at the sound, and I stepped aside to let her in. She hesitated, and then dashed in before either of us had a chance to change our minds. That done, we stood on opposite sides of the room, tensed, waiting.

"The shower's through there," I said at last. "Should be some warm water . . ."

She left her clothes hanging over the shower stall, and emerged with a towel wrapped around her waist. We tried to talk, and failed, which I guess is how we ended up in bed.

It was the worst sex I'd had in years. It wasn't a rape—she kept telling me *not* to stop, and if anyone was in control at all, it was her. She was reluctant to touch me, let alone kiss me, and she wouldn't let me touch her anywhere but her breasts and between her thighs. She squirmed when I went down on her, and her body seemed to come several times without it reaching her head. I rolled over, reached for a condom, checked that it wasn't past its "use by" date (I hadn't needed one in a while), and suggested she get on top. She knelt over my cock and barely kissed it with her labia, squirmed around a little until the head slipped in, gasped, and then backed away from it, not looking at me. It occurred to me that this might be her first time with a man, at least voluntarily, and I murmured something that I hoped sounded soothing. My erection dwindled, and I suggested we quit. She did.

I lay there for nearly a minute, clammy with sweat and tense in all the wrong places. She rolled over and grabbed her bag.

"Is it finished?"

"Yes, it's finished." She paused, and said, "Mike . . ."

"Yes?"

"You still want to know about my home?"

"If you want to tell me."

"I've already told you most of it. You remember the story?"

"The . . ." I found the strength to turn on my side and stare at her. " 'YesterDei'?"

"Yeah."

"What about it?"

"It's true. Some of it, anyway. That's my home. I'm a refugee."

It had to be a joke. I didn't know Swiftie well, but I didn't believe she was deranged. Or maybe she was a refugee from somewhere that had been exaggerated into her version of the future—Brazil, maybe, or Burma. Sure, writers and good would-be writers have pretty twisted imaginations, but they know fantasy from reality: they have to. "And you came *here*?"

She smiled. "That was a glitch, a miscalculation. Remember that we could only take over a body when it died but was still sound? My, ah, destination was supposed to die on the operating table, but they must have recorded the time wrong—only a few seconds one way or the other, but the Earth *moves* in that time. . . .

"I found myself in this body, in the back of a van. Somebody had flat-lined this woman's brain; they must have been gutleggers, hoping to sell her organs. I didn't know that at the time—oh, I knew that happened in places like Brazil, but not *here*—that wasn't in the history texts. Fortunately, it wasn't too difficult to get out of the van and find a hiding place, and they drove away a few minutes later without checking on me. They obviously hadn't expected their victims to be able to escape.

"I had to learn survival skills I'd never even *dreamed* about. If I'd been a citizen, I could be filthy fucking rich by now: I was only a technician in my time, but hell, what I know about the stuff you'll blunder across in the next few decades—controlled fusion, high-temperature superconductors, monofilaments, braintaping. . . .

"Fortunately, I also know how to transfer bodies." Her smile was becoming wider by the second, hungrier, but she still didn't seem crazy.

"And one thing about my home I didn't tell you . . ."

She reached into her bag, and I had a sinking feeling that I'd just been outmaneuvered. She might be faster than I was, but she certainly wasn't as strong, and she hadn't been armed—until now. My breath caught as she removed something that resembled a huge camper's flashlight with built-in radio, and probably had been before she tampered with it. "What?" I croaked.

She pointed what seemed to be the business end of the device at me. There was a flash of light so intense I could almost hear it, followed almost immediately by deep darkness, but I'm sure I heard her say, "I was male."

2
MIKE

It was still dark outside when I opened my eyes again, tried to look around, and found that I couldn't; something was holding my head fixed in position, and I could feel the tackiness of duct tape and the cold of metal on my skin, as well as something in my mouth that I couldn't spit out. I tried moving my arms, but they were so weak that it was several seconds before I realized that my wrists were tied too. With towels, judging from the feel. Same with my ankles. At least I could see enough of the room to know that I was in my own bed. I heard myself say "Ah, you're awake" and was almost ready to answer before I realized that it hadn't come from inside my own head, but from a few feet away. I tried to speak anyway, and I—no, someone else who only *looked* like me—came over and removed the wooden spoon from my mouth. "Don't try yelling," he advised. Did my voice really sound like that to other people? I'm *sure* that wasn't my accent. "The windows are closed, and you don't have the strength. I'm going to ask you a few questions, though, okay?"

I glared at him, and tried wiggling my toes, my fingers; it took time, but eventually I satisfied myself that they were all present and accounted for. "What's your name?" he asked.

"Michael Byron Galloway," I replied. "And you are?"

"I can't answer that," he said. "When were you born, Mike?"

"December twenty-first," I said. "1965. You?"

He shook his head. "I suppose I could tell you that, but it wouldn't mean anything to you; we don't use the same calendar. Any children?"

"Why?"

"I just want to make sure you haven't lost too much memory. You probably haven't; memory's holographic, it—you know about holographs?"

"A little."

"What happens when you cut a holograph in half?"

I had to think about that one, but I soon remembered it. "You get the whole picture, but not as clearly focused—less detail. The smaller you cut it, the fuzzier it becomes, but you still get the whole image."

"Good. Any children?"

"Only one—Belinda. She's seventeen. Wants to be a teacher, last I heard, but she'll probably grow out of it."

"Her mother?"

"Angela. Remarried five years ago. Lives in New York. *Why do you look like me?*"

"Because I need to," he said. "I came back to this time to do a job, and I'm behind schedule—I may already be too late. I need a WIN, some ice. I can't tell you any more about it, but believe me, if any of your descendants are still alive in my time, they'll thank me for it. And that's all I can say."

"I can help you. I can—"

"No. You might learn too much about the future. That's too big a risk."

"What're you going to do to me? Kill me?"

He looked shocked; he even turned slightly green. "No! I—" He shook his head. "Sorry, sometimes I forget that you're still a pre—a primitive." He shuddered. "If I did something like that, they'd send a kill-capable back to stop me. No, you're safe."

"Oh good," I muttered.

"I'm going to let you go, but I want you to stay away from me. I can't afford to have you interfering, so if I ever see you again, I'll have to erase all your memories of me and everything I've said—as best I can with this breadboard rig, anyway. Because memory's holographic, though, I'll have to cut out a lot."

"I get the picture."

He looked relieved. "Good," he said. "I'm sure you'll be okay." Then everything went black again.

• • •

The first thing I noticed, even before I opened my eyes, was that my left leg hurt like hell, though not badly enough to be broken. I touched the sore spot gingerly, felt bare smooth hard cool skin, and opened my eyes in a hurry. It wasn't my leg, and when I looked along it, it definitely wasn't my body it was attached to. It was Swiftie's. I was . . .

Oh shit.

I had vague memories of being carried, of being faintly surprised that I was strong enough to carry—that my old body was strong enough to carry my—I couldn't see, and it hadn't occurred to me that it wasn't my body. Then falling, a dark dead tree reaching up to grab me like some skeletal hand, then more blackness.

I picked myself up and looked around. I was lying amid a mess of broken branches under the balcony of my apartment; the tree must have broken my fall. Swiftie's bag was underneath me; it contained nothing but some of her clothes (not including the ones I'd given her), but they were better than nothing. I managed to stand, despite the pain in my legs, and staggered away. It didn't seem a good time to stick around. Someone might call the cops, and I didn't think anyone would believe *my* version of events.

I made it across the street and staggered a few blocks away from the apartment before stopping to shelter in a doorway. I caught sight of my reflection in the one-way glass and stared at myself: skinny, pale brown, with small breasts and terrified eyes.

I don't know how long I spent huddled in that doorway; it felt like half the night, but it probably wasn't half an hour. Slowly, I began to recover from the shock.

I had no ice, no home, no WIN—no name, if it came to that— no *anything*, apart from Swiftie's thin clothing. I looked around, and it occurred to me that at least I wasn't lost: I knew the area, and most of the local languages. I actually laughed out loud for a few seconds, but was so startled by the sound that I stopped. I'd never heard Swiftie laugh before, and she/we/I sounded like a sewing machine in dire need of oil.

Okay, I thought. I'd been broke and homeless before—briefly, sure, and many years ago—but I'd survived. I hadn't been female before, but billions of other people had, so I figured it should be bearable, at least. And if the Bodysnatcher could survive a year as Swiftie unprepared, I should last long enough to . . .

What?

I looked at my new face in the mirrored window. Even washed, it was an enigma, a racial witches' brew. Was I Amerindian? Eurasian? Polynesian? Would I get more help in Old Chinatown, North Beach, or Mission? The nearest stripper camps were in Buena Vista Park and Alamo Square, but I didn't want to go to either naked; I couldn't be robbed, except maybe by a gutlegger, but I might be raped. I'd never been much of a fighter, and now I had neither the strength nor the reach that I was used to. Not a good bet.

What about my friends? Nah: None of them would believe me, or even listen long enough to *consider* believing me. I could E-mail them, if I could get a few minutes' access to a com, but the game would be up once they saw me or heard my voice. The change in gender might be explained away, or hidden, but the loss of a quarter meter of height and probably half my mass couldn't be. Maybe later, after they realized that Mike Galloway had changed, I might have a chance, but how long would it take them to notice that I hadn't kept in touch, or for them to call Galloway and not be recognized? A couple of weeks? Even for those who lived in the Bay Area, more likely a couple of months, maybe even a year. Because I rarely stayed in any one place for very long, I'd gotten good at making friends quickly but was lousy at keeping them. My family and my old friends, the ones who knew me best, were scattered far and wide. I hadn't even received Christmas E-cards from most of them. Belinda would probably call me for Christmas, but the Bodysnatcher was probably smart enough to switch the phone onto voice mail and write to her later, when he'd worked out who she was. Walt, my writer friend, who was always ready to listen and would've been easiest to convince, had died of cancer nearly two years ago; like most writers in the United States, he hadn't been able to afford medical insurance. Most of the SF fans I'd known had been Angela's friends; I hadn't been to a con since we split up, and had lost touch with most of them.

First things first. If I was going to survive on the street, I needed some warmer clothes. Now, where was the nearest Salvation Army bin?

· · ·

Running was impossible, and walking agonizing. My new legs were ten or twenty centimeters shorter than they had been and less muscular, my new hips wider, my feet much smaller and so callused that I could barely feel the rain-slick concrete beneath them. To keep my balance, I took small, cautious steps as though I were walking a tightrope, and kept staggering along, searching for somewhere warmer and drier. You don't hesitate on a tightrope.

I was half a block from Gough Street when the troll caught me in its spotlights. I hadn't seen it through the rain; they must have been using infrared. A booming low-pitched voice, like a small earthquake, demanded that I stop.

I did. Those spots can strobe, triggering an epileptic seizure, and trolls are armed with magazine-fed grenade launchers. "NAME?"

I hesitated, then muttered, "Bird." They must have had a shotgun mike trained on me, because they didn't repeat the question. "WIN?"

"No."

A pause, then, "ARE YOU INJURED? YOU SEEM TO BE HAVING TROUBLE WALKING." The voice was still filtered, and utterly impersonal, but it sounded almost gentle, even slightly feminine, confirming my suspicion that these were city cops, *real* cops, not rent-a-cops. I hesitated, unsure of the answer and whether it would help me if they arrested Galloway—and then shook my head.

"WHAT?"

"No," I replied, figuring that they had a stress reader built into the shotgun mike. If so, it must have cleared me, because the lights dimmed until I could see the car behind them.

"TURNING YOURSELF IN?" asked the voice. It sounded vaguely bored; any other emotion was filtered out. I wondered why they were asking—did they think I was stoned? or that I'd rather spend the night in a cell than out on the streets?—then shook my head, and walked, slowly and carefully, into the shadows. Once around the corner and under the cover of an awning, I leaned my shoulders against a wall and tried to relax. I'd almost forgotten what it was to be stopped by cops, and I hadn't had one point a gun at me since the last time I was in Da Vinci Airport in Rome. Maybe I'd been respectable too long.

I stayed there for about ten seconds, then staggered/slithered hastily and painfully—down the last few streets to where I remembered seeing the bin. I listened for snores and ratlike rustles, heard none, and then clambered in. I found three bags of something soft, which I used as pillow, seat, and footrest: It was too dark in there to tell what I was sitting on, but it didn't move of its own volition, or smell any worse than some New York subway stations. I jammed my hands between my aching thighs for warmth, removed them because Swiftie's smooth skinny legs felt so strange, then replaced them. After catching my breath, I searched through the bag at my feet for something I could use as a towel, and made do with a child's sweatshirt.

I'd been running so hard that I'd stopped noticing the cold, and by the time it bit into me, sunlight was sneaking in around the door. I squatted on the floor of the bin and emptied out the bags. They contained mostly kids' clothes, too tiny even for Swiftie, but I found a thin nylon windbreaker, big enough to go over the stuff I was already wearing and almost long enough to cover my butt, with a cantankerous zip and incontinent pockets. I sat there for another few moments, thinking nostalgically of the days of large backyards, women hanging their wet wash out to dry unafraid of thieves or smog—not that it would dry in this weather, with the rain machine-gunning on the sheet metal top of the bin. A moment later, I realized that it wasn't only winter; today was December twenty-fifth, God bless us every one, peace on Earth, plum pudding, fat turkeys, halls decked with boughs of plastic holly (the real stuff was extinct outside nurseries and museums), and shops filled with overpriced toys and guns. This, I thought sourly, is one hell of a way to spend Christmas.

I blinked. Christmas! That was probably why the cops had asked if I was turning myself in. Most prisons served big Christmas dinners, with all the trimmings, and it was not unknown for cops to go hunting for strippers for a few days before, feeding and washing them and letting everyone out by December thirtieth so they'd have enough empty cells for the New Year's Eve crowd. I wondered what the sentence was for streaking these days. Probably pneumonia.

I'd been a vagrant on occasion, sleeping in railway stations and under bridges and once nearly drowning in a storm drain, but had managed to avoid being arrested for it; a police record can make it hard to get a passport. I wondered what sort of record Swiftie might have, where her fingerprints might have been found, and shuddered.

I was pretty sure the Bodysnatcher had been lying about about why he let me live, and probably about everything else, and I didn't think he'd chosen Christmas for humanitarian reasons. It was probably a coincidence: I'd let Swiftie in because it was cold and wet, not even remembering the date. And dumping a corpse over your balcony, even a stripper corpse, tends to upset the cops, and the second floor isn't high enough to make it look like suicide. Of course, he might have taken some slow poison before making the swap, but I doubted it. Cops wouldn't believe a live stripper accusing a citizen, but they might believe a dead one. Assuming they still bother to autopsy suspicious deaths at the state's expense, of course.

I stood and looked out the flap. The rain had slowed to a drizzle, and there was a hint of pink in the clouds. Morning. Christmas morning.

Well, food needn't be a problem, for once: The charities always put on a big Christmas dinner for the homeless too. Tomorrow, of course, it'd be turkey soup, but first I'd have to survive the day. I had clothes, poor as they were; I knew where to find food; I had shelter from the rain. "I got rhythm, I got music," I sang sourly under my breath, "Who could ask for anything—"

Shit. Sometime, somewhere, someone was going to ask for my name again. Should I stick with Swiftie, or—no, better not. Swiftie was someone else. Besides, the Bodysnatcher might not have finished with me, and I sure as hell hadn't finished with him. The only pseudonyms to come to mind were Lewis Carroll, Cordwainer Bird, Heinlein's Anson McDonald, Klaatu's Mr. Carpenter, and Winnie-the-Pooh's Trespassers William, none of which seemed particularly appropriate. Anything like Bird was right out: We'd used that as the pen name when we sold "YesterDei," and the Body-snatcher would probably remember it, and so might the cops. I couldn't think of anything useful to do with Galloway or Mike—except for Nike, the Greek goddess of victory, and I didn't feel particularly victorious— or with my middle name, which I never liked anyway. Nothing too feminine; I wasn't used to thinking of myself as female, and I couldn't guess how long it would take me to learn. So, something androgynous . . . Who was the guy in Greek myth who'd been both male and female at different times? Tiresias, yeah. Too long. Or there was Loki, in Norse myth. He'd turned himself into a mare, so successfully that he managed to get pregnant, but Loki would be a very strange name for a woman. Not much stranger than Cannon, but still noticeable. I considered Lola briefly, and rejected that, too, as much as I'd always liked the song. Japanese mythology was as full of *bishonen*, androgynes, as late-twentieth-century rock, but I couldn't remember any of their names. Maybe I could shorten Tiresias.

I wandered past a number of depressingly soggy parks before I saw a crowd setting up tents and tables outside Saint Mary's Cathedral. A number of strippers were helping; more were sitting in a queue. About half looked like illegals, mostly greenhouse refugees; there were also old winos and junkies and freebasers, younger zapheads, some ex-soldiers with post-traumatic stress or some other syndrome, a few schizophrenics conversing loudly with their personal Gods, and lots of skinny kids who could have been born almost anywhere. I saw one of Swiftie's lovers, the older woman with the scars and floppy boobs, chatting to a young girl wearing a patchwork smock and a mane of improbably red hair. "Swiftie!" she yelled, waving. "Hey, over here."

The man behind them in line snarled, and the woman snarled back. Something appeared from her left sleeve. It looked like one of those long combs for very curly hair. The man moved back slightly, making room for me.

"You're late. Shriek, this is Swiftie. What happened to you?"

I sat down, carefully. "Where's your kit?" she continued, looking at my empty bag. "You get ripped?"

Cautiously, I nodded. She swore in Spanish. "They get it all?" Another nod. She swore again. "Feliz fuckin' Navidad," said Shriek. I managed to smile slightly.

"How many of them did it?"

A telecopter passed overhead, and I waited until it was out of earshot before speaking. "One," I admitted. "Least I only *saw* one. I think I was drugged." They both shook their heads. "Or he hit me up the head. Or both. But I don't think I was meant to get away."

"Gutlegger? Dangergamer? Slave trader?"

"I don't know," I said, improvising furiously. "I can't think too well, or remember much. I—oh, shit—I've forgotten your name."

The woman's eyes widened at that. She sat up and began examining the back of my head. "Can't see any blood; guess it's too soon for a bump." She stared into my eyes. "And your pupils are okay. . . . You *honestly* can't remember?"

"No."

"You remember *your* name?"

"Yeah, but I'm thinking of changing it."

"You think they're looking for you?" asked Shriek.

"Don't know what to think."

The two exchanged glances. "How many fingers'm I holding up?"

"Hah . . . two and a half?"

The woman looked at her mutilated ring finger, and shrugged. "Well, you see okay. Any floating dots or bright lights?"

"No."

"Dizzy?"

"Yeah, a bit."

She nodded. "You call me Mama. Mama Castro. What you going to call yourself now?"

"Tera."

"Terror?"

The man behind me must have been looking interested, because Mama showed him the comb again. The teeth were nails, rusty except for their sharp points. He backed away a little farther. "Well, you're firmer than I am, Terror," she punned. "Or is it Tearer?"

Actually, it was part Tiresias and part *teratos*, or whatever the word is—Greek for "freak" or "monster"—but I didn't think Swiftie would have known that, even if the Bodysnatcher did. "Either way," I replied, "I think I'd better stop sleeping in the same places, too—if I can remember what they are."

"Where'd it happen?"

"The place on Haight. One with the balcony."

She blinked. "What happened? You take someone new up there?"

Would Mama know about Cannon and the others? "It was the guy inside. He opened the window, offered me food and a shower—"

"You trusted a *winner*? Went into his fucking *keep* with nothing more'n a *knife*? And a *man*, too? Jesu, girl, didn't I ever teach you *anything*?"

"I've done it," said Shriek. She sounded slightly sulky. "Sure it's a risk, but you got to take risks sometimes. I never got hurt doing it, and I took some good stuff. Once"—she leaned closer to us and whispered—"I even got a gun—a real gun, an old one, with bullets and all, not just a stinger." Mama looked horrified. "Well, it was safer than letting him keep it," Shriek explained. "I sold it next morning."

Mama, still looking like an abbess who's just found a used condom in the cloister, looked at my head again. "I need a better look at this, and you're going to need some more clothes to get you through the winter." She looked behind her: The queue had grown ten or twenty bodies longer since I arrived, and it was only ten to nine.

"Try Saint Francis's," suggested Shriek. "It's only four blocks, and they let you use the showers—if you don't mind the priest watching through a peephole."

Mama shrugged dismissively. "Hell, no. I used to be a nun. See you soon."

W ere you really a nun?" I asked as Mama peered through my
newly washed hair.

"Uh-huh. Probably before you were born."

"Why're you here?"

"Safer than El Salvador."

"Oh."

"I don't see any blood. How do you feel?"

"A bit better, but . . . disoriented."

Mama nodded. "It shows. You move like you've forgotten how. I
can't find any holes in you, but tranqs don't always leave puncture
marks. What else can't you remember?"

"I . . . don't remember."

"Ask a silly question, you get a silly answer," said Mama, shaking
her head. "You're sure this happened last night?"

"This morning. Yes . . . it was Christmas morning, I know that.
Unless I've missed a *year*."

"No, I saw you a week ago. What day was it yesterday?"

"Wednesday?"

She nodded. "Year?"

"2014."

"When were you born?"

"19 . . . " and I stopped. Mama nodded.

"*Where* were you born?"

I hesitated. "Do *you* know?"

"No. How many kidneys do you have?"

"Two . . . don't I?"

"Hell no—not unless you regrew one."

So the stories about gutleggers buying body parts from strippers, as well as stealing them, weren't just an urban myth. I wondered how much they paid. "You don't talk much like a nun."

"Like I said, that was a long time ago."

"Wouldn't a church here take you? Without a WIN? I mean, El Salvador's a state now, isn't it?"

"Some of the same people are in charge there, and they got long memories. Besides, being a nun isn't much better than this. Let's get you some clothes."

The church didn't have much to offer in the way of clothing except for old T-shirts, but they gave me several of those, and some old army-surplus desert camo pants that were much warmer than Swiftie's ancient and filthy skirt, plus a stained blanket. "Sounds to me like someone's deliberately done a job on your memory," Mama theorized. "Probably tried to cut out something small, and fucked up."

"How?"

She shrugged. "Hypnotism, maybe? Or cutting, but that's not usually *that* thorough. Unless it's some bad new drug."

"Cutting? You mean lobotomy? But there's no scars."

"They go in through the tear duct. Used to take a few seconds with a scalpel; now they use a microlaser. *Much* more efficient."

I shuddered. "But *why?*"

"Maybe you saw something," she suggested a little lamely. "Or someone. Or more likely a gutlegger wanted you alive but brain-dead and didn't finish the job, or someone needed a human guinea pig for something, or maybe someone just has a *very* sick idea of fun."

"Fun?"

"Well, it's the ultimate mind game. There were guardsmen back home, part-time snuff-stars, who would've gotten off on it. Hell, some people get off on watching two half-naked women wrestle in a wading pool full of inedible Jell-O!"

I guess I was supposed to comment, or at least laugh. I didn't. "You've forgotten that too, haven't you?"

"What? I used to . . . ?" I blushed.

"They did do a job on you, didn't they? No, not you: Morningstar. Do you remember the name?"

I shook my head. "I can remember a few faces—like I remembered knowing *yours*—but no names to go with them. Sorry."

"Morningstar's a dirty blonde, about your height, a little more solid. She did a particularly sloppy job of shaving herself a month ago."

"Uh-huh . . . why wouldn't they just have killed me?"

Neither of us had an answer to *that* one, and by now we were back outside Saint Mary's. The line stretched halfway around Jefferson Square, which was studded with enough rent-a-cops for a foot-brawl team, but Shriek still held our place. I wondered how *she* was armed.

There was a radio playing about twenty meters behind us, mostly Christmas carols rehashed with an earthquake beat. Ever since the seventies, I'd been wondering how pop music could possibly get any worse. Well, it had, in time with the recessions getting worse, and I don't think I've ever been so happy to hear a newscast—especially not at Christmas, when even the road toll is made to sound like good news (okay, so it *was* declining, at about the same rate as the number of cars), and viewers were encouraged to feel warm and toasty about the strippers getting their annual good feed. But Santa's never told you that it's the worst day of the year for suicides, has he?

The radio dropped a minor bomb into my musings: Someone had shot up a judo class on Sacramento Street, between ten and eleven the night before. Twenty-one women had been killed. I listened for more details but there were none: There were no witnesses, and the gunman or gunmen had escaped. "Maybe that's what you saw," whispered Mama. "What someone wants you to forget."

I stared at her, horrified, as the newscaster segued into the weather: Blizzards from Maine to Georgia, spaceplane launches held up by snow in Florida, floods reaching new highs in Bangladesh. "Shit, that's not a *mystery*," said Shriek. "It's White Riders, like that restaurant a few weeks ago, and the cops know it but they won't fuckin' say so."

"It wasn't *all* of them," replied Mama. "Someone had to pull the trigger, and the cops have to find that one."

"Why? They all *wanted* to do it, and if anybody *does* get caught, they'll all be his alibi and swear it on their fuckin' Bibles. . . . What do you call that? Conspiracy?"

"Opportunism," I replied absentmindedly. "Riders hate each other too much for conspiracy." The name White Riders was a media invention, rather like Jack the Ripper: It was straight from the Book of Revelation, but suitably reminiscent of the Ku Klux Klan, and it had stuck. Sure, some Apocalyptics had been inciting racist and anti-gay violence for decades now, and the violence happened much too often, but that didn't mean any organization existed. I remembered hearing about the kitchen staff of a Japanese restaurant being gunned down with automatic weapons early in the month, but even though some conspiracy theorists had made a big deal of the fact that it happened on the anniversary of Pearl Harbor, most people assumed the manager had just gotten behind on his loan repayments to the Yakuza or whoever. Even if it was a racist attack, chances that they were connected were slim.

Mama shook her head. "I miss newspapers." She sighed. "Are you old enough to remember cryptic crosswords? Or *the Street Sheet*?" I nodded; Shriek shrugged. "How the hell are you supposed to learn anything about anything from three minutes of sound bites? And how do you keep yourself warm or dry with a radio?"

"Break a window with it and let yourself inside?" suggested Shriek. " 'Sides, what do we need to know? The news never changes."

Mama shrugged. "How old are you, kid? Sixteen?"

"Yeah, *and* I can read. So what? Look, I'm not saying the world doesn't change, but all the changes that matter are so slow, nobody sees them 'til it's too fuckin' late."

She had a point. We hardly ever notice the big picture. I can remember the Apollo program, but that didn't even leave much of a mark on the Moon, much less the Earth—though the computers that made it possible went on to give us the third industrial revolution, the cashless world, and forty percent underemployment. Lots of science-fiction writers in the sixties had guessed that mind drugs would be de rigueur until all human behavior was chemically controlled, but no one imagined the economic and political impact that heroin and coke would have on a dozen countries. The greenhouse effect was predicted in 1938 and mapped out in 1967, and most of us just listened to the weather reports for another twenty years without seeing a pattern, and now a lot of islands were reefs, New Orleans looked more like Venice, America's farmlands were migrating north, and most of the world's military might was being used to watch for greenhouse refugees and send them back home. How much else was happening now that we couldn't see?

"I wasn't anywhere near Chinatown last night," I said. "I was in Haight-Ashbury; I remember *that*."

"Maybe he was the shooter," she suggested. "The winner who lived there. Hell, it was just a guess. Anyway, scuse me; I got to go to the john."

Mama and I spent the night in the Highsore, the long-unfinished skyscraper between Market, Turk, and Jones. The bank that had been building its offices there had lost so much on bad debts that it couldn't afford rent-a-cops, or even a few muteweilers and shhhepherds and someone to throw an occasional sack of kibble over the razor wire; the sign outside had been so heavily graffitied that I could barely make out the Alpha Security logo. There were rumors that the building itself wasn't much healthier than the bank's finances, and in three years, no one had expressed any interest in buying the land. Now there were just four triangular concrete floors and a twenty-two-story column of elevator shafts, sticking up on a corner of the Tenderloin. It had become a stripper enclave with the tacit blessing of the city cops, as long as we brought out our dead.

I've slept in less comfortable squats—it was only slightly worse than an Italian railway station, not much colder than an Amtrak carriage, and beat the hell out of a storm drain—and less private circumstances, but that was when I was male. Long after Mama had drifted off to sleep, I lay there under our shared blankets, wide awake and feeling obscurely threatened, holding on to her for a little extra warmth. A few more windbreaks would have done wonders for the place, but cardboard was too expensive now that most of the forests were gone, and anything more permanent would have been frowned on by the cops.

Shriek had left us at sunset, saying that she was going to cruise the balconies. Mama had been horrified. "After the shooting yesterday? Half the town's ready to blow away shadows!"

Shriek had nodded. "And Saturday, when the shops reopen, they'll sell a thousand guns and a million rounds of ammo, because everybody'll be expecting the governor to crack down. And you know what the hockshops'll pay for a stolen gun then?"

I didn't, nor could I, guess in what currency they'd pay her, but I knew she had a point. Even though stingers and tranq needles were cheap, legal, relatively safe (even a full magazine of tranqs was supposed to be nonlethal for anyone over thirty kilograms), and available in a variety of fashion colors, massacres invariably sparked a hideous rush to buy old-fashioned lethal firearms. The gun shops and manufacturers must make thousands of ice, maybe millions, out of every well-publicized corpse. "And if you're caught with it, that's a felony," Mama responded.

"I'm a minor. And they can't extradite me: I was born here."

Mama looked dubiously at her, and then changed tack. "Look, you can go back to the blood bank next week."

It hadn't worked. I lay there, feeling vaguely sick. Among other things, I disliked taking advantage of Mama. I guess I hadn't done a lot to be proud of in my life, but I'd never actually given a false name to any woman I'd slept with, let alone a false gender. What the hell was I going to do if she wanted sex?

Presumably, lie back and think of . . . well, wherever. England wasn't a particularly pleasant thought anymore: Last I heard, it was the second-worst country in Europe in which to be poor, and one of the ten worst in the world. San Francisco was reputed to be one of the best cities in the U.S.; warmer and drier and farther from the northern ozone hole than Seattle, and more tolerant than almost anywhere else. New Orleans and Miami were okay if you could tread water, and New York was the worst: full of strippers with WIN and ICEcards, even with one or two jobs, who just couldn't afford any accommodation better than tents in the parks and empty lots—when the rent-a-cops weren't tearing down the tents. Of course, Manhattan had been tending that way for thirty years or more, but now it was spreading all the way through the megasprawl, from Boston to Washington. I wondered how Angela tolerated it: I hadn't had anything more communicative than a Christmas E-card from her since the divorce—and not much in the year before it, at that. At least Belinda still wrote two or three times a year; *her* I would miss.

I watched a troll headed down Turk, carefully not pointing its spots in our direction. I fell asleep wondering what *would* happen to a stripper caught with a gun, and was given a dozen different answers in a continuing series of nightmares.

We met our would-be burglar again the next day, at the soup kitchen. Fortunately, she hadn't had any luck.

Mama quizzed me daily, to see what I could remember. She told me she'd been a nursing assistant and had experience dealing with shock victims—though in most of those cases, she admitted, the shocks had been electrical, and administered by Mano Blanco guardsmen. A week later, we had settled into a routine: a shower in the morning, then the public library, lunch at a soup kitchen, back to the library or somewhere else warm and dry. If the weather was bearable, we'd scavenge through bins and Dumpsters for recyclables or discarded food. Most charity and casual work went to the recently homeless—we were considered beyond that sort of help—and begging was rarely worth the effort, not in a cashless world. If we were lucky, we might be given a few cigarettes (as close as we had to legal tender) for posing for tourist snapshots.

I was aware of my new body in a way that I'd never been aware of the old one. Finding public toilets wasn't easy; the city didn't have many that didn't require an ICEcard to open, and those were mostly used as shooting galleries. Businesses were divided between those that advertised RESTROOMS FOR CUSTOMERS ONLY and those that advertised NO RESTROOMS. You could use the facilities at the soup kitchens and some other charities, if you didn't mind standing in a line and occasionally being drafted into mopping the floor, or carrying out a body.

I'd wondered what stripper women did about their periods, and learned, through eavesdropping, indirect questions, and a little logic, that they were usually too malnourished to have them. The only bleeding I did, in that first month, was into a bottle at the blood bank. That was the definition of a month for most strippers, of any sex: the time between visits to the clinic, enforced by the ultraviolet stamp they put on your wrist. If you were lucky, you might spend the whole night in the queue, bored but safe, warm, and dry.

I/Galloway had sold my blood before, of course. The first time, in 1987, I'd desperately needed the twenty dollars to pay the airport tax that my travel agent hadn't warned me about. Now they fed you while you were there, and paid in meal vouchers if you didn't have an ICEcard. It was a long time since I'd been poor enough to eat their food (usually tinned spaghetti, stew, or chili on or over the "use by" date); now, I wolfed it down without even wondering where the "meat" had come from. The meal vouchers bought shelter as well as food; some of the cafés in Old Chinatown let us stay all night, as long as we bought something occasionally. The tea was cheap, and I've had worse.

The news was still full of the dojo massacre. We read the tapes in the library and heard the newscasts in the shops and cafés. There had been at least two gunmen, and more than two guns (the city cops were refusing to commit, themselves): all fully automatic, silenced, and firing caseless ammo. All the victims had been under thirty, all were poor—not stripper poor, but Chinatown poor, even the sensei—and all were identifiably Asian, even the two blondes. Some were fourth- or fifth-generation Americans, while others had married into their citizenship. Seven were waitresses, four students, only eight unemployed; all would be missed by someone.

The why of the massacre was as much a mystery as the who. Sociopaths who fired randomly into crowds had become commonplace last century, but most of them had the good taste to shoot themselves immediately afterwards (I remember one telling journalists he'd kept a bullet for himself, and was only captured alive because it fell out of his pocket). Okay, there had been serial-killer couples, triples (Bonnie and Clyde and whoever they were both sleeping with at the time), and families, but not teams; that smacked of superhero comics, not news. Some people were pointing the finger at the Triads or the Yakuza or the Seoulpa, explaining it away as a case of mistaken identity; others were blaming the northwestern Klans or the Order or the Phinehas Priests; and I heard one ancient crazy at the soup kitchen saying it was someone's way of marking the fiftieth anniversary of the beginning of the Vietnam War.

Barry Shaw—Commissioner Shaw to you, but I once dated his daughter—announced that finding the gunmen was the first priority of the city cops, but everyone seemed to be waiting for the governor to act; she still had relatives living on Sacramento Street who must have known at least one of the victims. You couldn't walk into a shop in Old Chinatown without seeing a petition in favor of stricter gun control, and you were hard put to walk out again without signing it.

On January 5, Governor Song astonished us by proposing a referendum calling for a flat ban on the sale, importing, modifying, or transport of fully automatic weapons, except by the military, and a waiting period and ID check for the purchase of ammunition, magazines, and hand-loading equipment that could be used in automatic weapons. The American National Party, widely believed to be a wholly owned subsidiary of the NRA or vice versa, complained that this was unconstitutional and demanded Song's resignation—but hell, they'd been demanding that every few weeks since her election, and it had become a running gag, even on the street (strippers don't discuss politics much, but shit, politicians don't talk about us, either—at least not when anyone's listening). I wished to hell I could still vote.

Mama dismissed the whole thing as a political stunt, California's equivalent of Kipling's "village that voted that the Earth was flat"—but then, Mama has even less respect for *norteamericano* politics than I do. Twenty years ago, sure, the referendum wouldn't have stood a chance—I remember how long it took the Brady Bill to pass—and Song would have been badly embarrassed, but that was before cheap needlers, with their built-in safeguards, and tranqs. The number of people per capita killed with handguns in the U.S. had been dropping slowly ever since (it was now only about thirty times as high, per capita, as in Canada or Japan, down from nearer a hundred and eighty), and so had the number of rapes—of citizens, anyway. There weren't any figures on stripper rape, but believe me, it happens. A few days later, it almost happened to me.

It was about one A.M., wet and painfully cold, and Mama and I were Dumpster-diving around Hyde Street without much joy. It wasn't a blind alley, but with all the rain, they surrounded us before we noticed them.

There were four of them, too slick for strippers—those were fifty-ice haircuts, if I'd ever seen one, and real leather jackets, as good against needlers as the Kevlar underneath was against bullets—and too young for gutleggers. They stood there and stared for a few moments, then one grinned and reached for something hidden behind his back. If we'd known it was only a knife, we would've run, but we waited too long.

The blade was nearly a foot long, with one edge serrated, and looked very new. The wrist behind it wasn't much thicker than mine, and it was shaking nearly as badly. I'd gone to a few hapkido classes once, during a moment of weakness (okay, so it was three months, long enough to earn my yellow belt; I quit when my girlfriend started dating the sensei), but that was nearly thirty years ago, when I had Galloway's muscle and reach, and I'd had never had to take down a sober opponent in a *fight*. "Can I help you?" I asked as politely as I could, despite almost gagging. Mama crossed herself and began muttering a prayer. They ignored her, but one—not the one with the knife—asked, "You a boy or a girl, streetbeat?"

In the poor light, with my unisex clothes and my body language probably all wrong, it was a reasonable question. "I didn't know you cared," I replied, trying to ignore the sick feeling in my stomach. The others laughed, as I'd hoped: had to stop them thinking as a group. "Can you afford to be that fussy?"

"If we were fussy, we'd have gone to Broadway," replied the largest of them. He seemed genuinely amused. "Looks like you're the best we could do."

"Okay, streetbeat," said Knife. "Give us a look. Pants off."

I glanced at Mama, who still seemed to be praying, then looked back at Knife, smiled, and vomited over his jacket and jeans. He recoiled and swore, and I grabbed the wrist of his knife hand and twisted. He was already badly off balance, which made my job that much easier: I rammed his head into the side of the Dumpster, making a noise like the Rank gong, and stepped on the fallen knife in the same motion. The one nearest Mama, the one who hadn't spoken, reached out to grab her and had his jacket torn by her raking claws.

He was about to yell something when she grabbed his ear and shoved a claw up his nose. "Don't struggle," she whispered. I swooped on the knife while the other two were reaching for theirs, and dropped onto Knife's back.

I guess I've made it sound too easy; believe me, I was nearly shitting myself at the time. If either of them had had guns, I guess Mama and I would both be dead.

Knife tried to roll over and throw me, but I stabbed him in the ass, an inch or two from the groin. He shrieked with pain and fear, pissing himself, and the other two leaped back. Mama let go of her victim's ear and pulled back her claws, and the three of them ran like hell, not looking back until they reached the street. Knife continued to scream and struggle, but he shut up when Mama's claws scraped against his cheek. We kept the knife and the sheath, took his watch and his jacket, and then let him go.

"Where did you learn to fight like that?" I asked Mama as we collapsed against the side of the Dumpster.

"Until a minute ago," she panted, "I didn't know I had. What about you?"

We were too exhausted to walk back to the Highsore, so we spent the rest of the night under a treehouse in a playground. Mama wanted to make love, but I told her I was still feeling too tense. "Two tents?" she punned wearily. "You were lucky to *have* tents. *We* had to sleep in hole in road."

"Lookshury," I replied, in a pretty fair Yorkshire accent. "We were evicted from . . . oh, hell, I don't remember the rest. Good night."

I wanted to keep the jacket, but Mama talked me out of it. It was too good for the streets, a fence would pay two or three hundred ice for it, and another stripper might kill me for that.

Shriek found us a fence: a pawnbroker (surprise, surprise) on Jessie Street with a few authentic-looking leather jackets already hanging on the rack and a showcase of knives and shuriken. She sold guns, too, but not ammunition, though if we'd wanted anything that wasn't in the shop, she would have gotten it for us (at a markup, of course). The jacket bought a Canadian air force greatcoat and a carton of joints, and the survival knife was traded in for a more easily concealed butterfly knife (well, how often was I going to need a compass or a fishing line?). The watch was a cheap digital job, but she gave me an even cheaper penlight in exchange for the studded leatherette band.

I'd had previous experience with barter economies, of course— the only sex I ever actually bought was with a lovely young Russian woman who charged two cans of Coca-Cola for the night, with her father's old KGB badge thrown in as a bonus—but I was astonished by Shriek's knowledge of the going exchange rates, the values of a dozen different brands of cigarettes (marijuana and tobacco), condoms, and other items that now served as cash. It was like watching a pre–ICE Age currency buyer. I gave her two packs of joints as commission, divided the rest of the carton with Mama, and then we headed out to the Mission.

"How long've you been on the streets?" I asked Shriek while Mama was in the shower.

"Three years, maybe four, something like that. But not for much longer."

"Since you were fourteen?"

"Thirteen or fourteen, yeah."

"Why not much longer? You going to join a stable?"

She snorted. "Been in and out of stables for years. They *love* young girls, and it craps on selling my kidney. No, I'm gonna be a citizen."

I was about to laugh, but she seemed perfectly serious. "Going to get married?" In theory, at least, it was still the easiest way to pick up citizenship (hey, it'd worked for Galloway) and an ICEcard. Of course, you had to *stay* married for at least two years to keep it all, and the government still didn't recognize lesbian marriages, even in California.

Shriek shook her head. "I'm nearly seventeen. I've got a California WIN, I was born here, my parents are citizens. . . . Gonna go for genalysis, get an ICEcard they can't touch an' a real job, an' get off the streets." She grinned, showing teeth too even for a stripper's. "Move up to the slums."

I looked at her more closely. She was far more weatherbeaten than the teenage girls I'd grown up with, but she might have been white, a few years ago. Her blood-mud-red hair probably hadn't been washed since November (having it freeze to your scalp isn't fun), but her eyebrows were pale brown, and her eyesight was still good, so she hadn't always been homeless. She spoke English like a second or third language, but she could well have been as WASPy as Galloway (though he was a lapsed Catholic Celt; in his case, it probably stood for White Australian Sexist Pig). "You've got a WIN?"

"Didn't I just say so?"

"So why're you here?"

"Craps on home," she replied flatly, and I shut up.

O'DWYER

I walked down Castro slowly, sticking close to the walls and trying to look in every direction at once. Most of the queers would have died on Day Zero, but I wouldn't want to show my back to any who hadn't. Spinning like some fuckin' ballet dancer, I saw something pop up in a nearby window, and I brought both guns to bear before I could identify it. White male, camo jacket, armed: one of us. There was another soft *clack* on the other side of the street, and I wheeled: The laser sight on the .44 put a dot between another pair of blue eyes, a young woman's. I stood there, waiting, knowing that time was running out for me fast, and then I saw the fuckin' sniper on the second floor, black as leather and aiming what looked like a Galil. I wasn't going to use the Ingram to hit something as small as a window, so I brought the .44 up and blew a lovely big hole in his chest before he could fade. Then I heard a convincing-sounding scream, looked down, and saw that the girl I'd scoped before now had company—a ninja behind her, with a fuckin' tanto pointed at her throat, and someone in front with his back to me, showing Hell's Angels colors on his jacket and greasy black hair down past his fuckin' shoulders. One squeezed-off shot took the top off the ninja's head without any sweat, but the Angel, shit, if I misjudged this one, the bullet would tear right through him and hit the girl. I wasted a few seconds making a decision—probably long enough for a biker to execute a rape and zip himself up again afterwards—and then switched the Ingram to semiautomatic.

"Bang," said Martini. "Time's up."

Shit! I lowered the gun and turned to face him. "What *should* I have done?"

"When?" he asked idly, coming up to check my marksmanship.

I pointed at the Angel and the girl with the .44, resisting the temptation to pull the trigger. "This. There's no clear shot."

Martini looked at the decapitated ninja and nodded. "You think there's always gonna be a clear shot?"

"What should I have done?"

"Whatever you want. Two of them for one girl's not a bad deal. Or you could use something with less penetration—throw a knife, or whatever." An Alpha rent-a-cop appeared in the room with a pile of new cutouts under his arm and replaced the ninja. "Of course, he might be wearing armor under that jacket. You never know—not until you try."

"What would *you* have done?"

"Shot the bastard before he turned around and shot me. I woulda *tried* not to hit the girl, but what use would she be if I was dead?" He slapped me on the back. "Hey, don't let it get you down. I know it's hard to take this Disneyland-type crap seriously. In the real world—"

I nodded. "Copy that. You're testing my marksmanship, not my convictions. Guess I'd better remember that."

"Bullshit," said Martini grimly. "Marksmanship is a conviction, and you better remember *that*. Now go tell MacRae it's his turn. Skye wants us all out of here by sunrise. Move it!"

Skye owned the compound, so you didn't disobey an order from him while you were here, even if he was as crazy as some of us thought. Or maybe because maybe he wasn't. I moved.

6
TERA

Twenty to thirty years ago, when I was Mike Galloway, I couldn't spend three days in the same city without being mistaken for a local. In London or Washington, okay; even in Moscow or Tel Aviv, no big deal; but in *Tokyo*? I guess I have a knack for adapting to my surroundings quickly, learning the appropriate behavior with a minimum of conscious effort. Now, three weeks after being dumped off a balcony into the street, I was just another stripper; I'd almost grown accustomed to my new body, I could walk and even sprint without stumbling, I'd learned the rather rudimentary etiquette of San Francisco stripper society, and I usually remembered which rest room to go to (I coped with *that* one by thinking of it as learning a new language: If you've ever had to choose between *Damen* and *Herren* in a hurry, you'll understand). Even *I* occasionally forgot I'd ever been anyone else, at least during the day. By night, I still dreamed Galloway's dreams, dreams of the sixties and seventies and later decades of travel and rootlessness, but also dreams of work and play, warm beds, good food, of seeing my daughter born, and of being male. I woke every morning cold and hungry and a little disoriented and generally feeling like shit, but so did every stripper in the city, whatever their age or sex or history. I have no idea how the city cops recognized me, but I guess that's their job.

I was walking down Guerrero late one misty morning, on my way to the nearest soup kitchen, alone—Mama had spent the night with Blair, an old lover of hers whom Swiftie hadn't known—and the troll passed me, U-turned slowly in the empty street, and came to a halt a few yards ahead of me.

"NAME?"

Damn. "Bird."

"WIN?"

"No."

A pause, then, "FULL NAME?"

"Theresa Bird," I replied, quickly enough that it sounded like the truth—I hoped.

"ANY OTHER NAMES?"

"Other names?"

"ARE YOU ALSO KNOWN AS TEARER?"

"Tera, yes. Sort of short for Theresa. Why?"

The cop paused again, then said, "GET IN."

"*What?*"

"GET IN." A door in the back popped open.

"Am I under arrest?"

They seemed to consider that. "WE *CAN* ARREST YOU, IF YOU PRE-FER. . . ."

I decided not to push it, and got in. The door closed behind me, and the voice asked, "WHERE WERE YOU GOING?"

"What?"

"WHERE TO? THIS DOESN'T HAVE TO TAKE LONG."

I told them to take me to the kitchen and waited, trying not to notice the stench. At least it was warm in there. "WHAT DO YOU KNOW ABOUT THE SACRAMENTO STREET SHOOTINGS?"

Shit! Mama must have—no, Mama would *never* talk to *any* cops, not even city cops. Shriek? Or someone Shriek had told? "Only what I hear on the newscasts."

"YOU DIDN'T SEE ANYONE IN THE AREA?"

"I wasn't *in* the area: spent the night on a balcony on Haight."

"YOU'RE SURE?"

"Yeah."

"YOU DIDN'T SEE ANYBODY WITH SUBMACHINE GUNS?"

"Not since Da—" I'd been about to say "not since Da Vinci Air-port," but quickly changed it to "da last time someone's bodyguard told me to move along."

There was a pause, then another voice asked, "HAVE YOU EVER HEARD OF THE WITNESS PROTECTION PROGRAM, THERESA?"

"Nah. What is it?"

"IT GIVES WITNESSES A NEW IDENTITY, A NEW HOME, A NEW LIFE... A WIN, A JOB, AN ICECARD."

I stared at the speaker set into the ceiling; I had the strange feeling that I was alone in the troll. Everyone knew the cops used remote-control telecopters, why not remote-control cars, too? "I didn't see anything," I repeated. "I wasn't even near the place."

"YOU'RE SURE?"

"Hey, it's not the sort of thing you'd forget, is it?"

"NO," replied the voice. A few seconds later, the troll stopped, and the door popped open again. "HAVE A NICE DAY."

"Yeah. Sure. Whatever you say."

I was still three blocks from the end of the queue, but I guess that was just as well: No one likes to be seen getting out of a troll.

The idea hit me a few seconds after I sat down. If the Body-snatcher's story was even partially true, if he had come from the future and studied this era, then he should know who'd shot up the dojo. A massacre like that wouldn't just be forgotten.

Okay, maybe he wouldn't know: maybe it'd never been solved. Or if he did, maybe he wouldn't tell me, and maybe I couldn't per-suade him—no fuck that: I'd persuade the bastard, all right. I could offer him a truce: I get a WIN and an ICEcard, and he'd get to keep his body, undamaged. He'd believe me. He'd been in this body, living this life. He'd know how little I had to lose.

I ripped into the stale bread as though I were starving, which I wasn't: I was just in a hurry. I wolfed the soup too quickly to taste it, which was probably just as well, and I was headed out the door just as Mama was coming in. I kissed her quickly, told her I'd see her later, and ran toward Haight. I couldn't get past the facial-recognition programs to break into the apartment without his keys, I couldn't even make him listen to me on the balcony, but he could hardly keep me out of the shop. I knew where the alarms were, and the window controls, and where the needler was hidden—probably better than he did. And hell, if he called my bluff, I could show him what I'd learned in *my* time on the streets (lovely red-tinted visions flickered before my eyes as I ran). Then I could book myself a

Greyhound ticket to Seattle or someplace, and if I stole his keys, I could get into the apartment, take what I could wear and/or carry, and hock as much as I could.

I stopped about a block from the shop and crossed to the far side of the road. None of this would work if he had a customer. I ambled past and looked in the window.

There was a new sign painted under the Galloway's Travels logo, black letters on an orange background: UNDER NEW MANAGEMENT. The woman sitting at the desk was blond, attractive, and utterly unfamiliar.

Part of my brain was thinking, Well, shit, of *course* it's under new management! My feet were smarter; they kept me going, farther down Haight to the apartment. I climbed up onto the balcony like a ninja on amphetamines. The windows were turned to opaque, and probably soundproofed. I swore, dived back over the balcony, and ran through the rain, looking for a phone that I could use without an ICEcard. A sales clerk at a liquor store finally agreed to call the number in exchange for a joint; when she heard the disconnected signal, she returned the joint. I must have looked badly shaken, because she then offered me a light.

The Bodysnatcher had gone, and taken all that remained of Mike Galloway with him.

Mama and I spent the next few nights on Galloway's balcony, enjoying the privacy while we had it. Wrapped around each other like we were, we kind of drifted into lovemaking, starting with a soft, slow kiss, and a little touching that gradually became a little more intense, a little more focused. Making love to her was easy: I did nothing that Galloway hadn't done to a few dozen women and called foreplay. Mama wasn't attractive, even by stripper standards, but that didn't matter as much when I didn't need an erection. Eventually, I realized that there was no such thing as foreplay: Everything we did was love, or sex, or whatever we wanted to call it.

Feeling Mama's fingers in me almost freaked me out: I had barely even touched myself since that morning in the clothing bin, and that had been out of curiosity. She apologized instantly, thinking she'd hurt me—though she assured me that I was lubricated. "Jesu, they *did* hurt you, didn't they?"

At first, I thought she meant the would-be rapists, then I realized she was referring to the memory loss. I tried to smile. "How long's it been since you had a virgin?"

She chuckled. "Jesu, that's a word I haven't *heard* in—hell, I'm not sure I ever heard it in English before. I don't honestly know. I once had an affair with a Sister Maria Perpetua: Does that count?"

I laughed, and we kissed, hard. I was gasping as she began kissing my neck, then my nipples, then the small scar where my left kidney had been. She looked up, her eyes asking for a yes or a no. I nodded.

It wasn't as good as I'd heard sex should be for a woman, but the next night was a little better, and the next night, and the next night . . . and the night after that, there were lights burning in the apartment, and we trudged back to the Highsore to sleep.

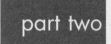

part two

LEX ORBIS

I t was an audi-only call, but aren't they all?

Well, not strictly audi-only: *He* could see *us*. Not very much of us at a time—videphone cameras aren't built for that—but close-ups of the bits he wanted. It made it awkward for us occasionally, but what did he care about that?

Morningstar and I had been in this stable for two or three weeks— since just before the referendum, anyway. Seventy-three percent of voters had asked for tougher firearm laws, which were now being passed, and despite the dire warnings of the Am Nats and the NRA and a few of the rent-a-cop companies, society had not yet collapsed any further—at least it hadn't last time I'd seen it. We didn't get out much.

I don't know when dial-a-fantasy lines were invented, and frankly, I don't give a damn. I know they multiplied like crazy in the eighties and early nineties, presumably as the ultimate form of safe sex; they were first in line when British Telecom started offering videphone services in the nineties, and the AIDS vaccine hadn't noticeably diminished them. Interactive beaver flicks. Live peep shows at home. Wonders of modern technology, huh?

(Okay, so Galloway watched some porn and went to strip clubs occasionally when he was younger, but he/I never actually *fucked* anyone who didn't at least *like* him. At least, I don't think he did— though in retrospect, I do have my doubts about the woman in Moscow.)

Despite my rudimentary but functional Japanese and Mandarin and my instinct for what men like, I probably wouldn't have got the job if Morningstar hadn't insisted. Even with my hair styled and my face (and nipples) painted, I still resembled something censored from the Vietnam War; the madam referred to it kindly as the "victim look." I always played the bottom to Star's top, femme to her domme: She'd shaved her head again, giving herself a twentieth-century dyke look, and I was still finding it difficult to think of myself as female rather than as a man in very convincing drag. In some ways, that made displaying myself easier; it didn't really seem to be my body, especially not below the waist, but I was too busy for much in the way of gender dysphoria. If we filled our quota, we got to live in the room—well, the cubicle, it was almost completely filled by the small and much-abused futon bed, but at least it had a ceiling, four walls, and a door with a bolt—and anything over that bought food and showers and heat and clothes, or paid a little off our deposit. Fortunately, we were busy this morning: It had been Valentine's Day, and a Saturday to boot, so a lot of losers were calling us to vent a little frustration. There were probably long lines at the rifle ranges, too.

The phone rang (a useful anachronism; it woke us when business was slow), and I heard Pauline, the receptionist, purr, "Company, girls."

"What does he want?" asked Star suspiciously. Pauline sounded even more smug than usual.

"It's Roy, your regular. That's all he said."

Oh, *shit!* Star glanced at me, and I shrugged. "We need the ice."

"Good. I'll put him through."

"He gives me the creeps too," confided Star. "I'll try not to hurt. Don't forget to scream."

"I won't," I promised.

If you need to know what happened next, you're as sick as I thought he was. I didn't realized how badly I'd underestimated him until I heard him boast, "I killed a whole pack of slants, a few weeks ago: Don't you wish you'd seen that, Stella?"

"How the hell did you pull that off, lover?" Somehow, Star managed to sound curious rather than incredulous, startled rather than shocked or sickened; fortunately for her, the camera wasn't on her face, but mine. I was glad I couldn't speak at the time, and he probably expected me to look horrified; it was an S&M scene, after all.

"With an MP5," he replied gleefully. "Opened up, and *they* opened up, like the bags of trash they were. On Sacramento Street—a sacrament, get it? Got six of the little whores in a few seconds, running and jumping, but they couldn't get away from me and my buddies. So much for ninja training and all this kung fu ka-ka, right? No match for *real* Americans."

"There's no one like you, lover," said Star optimistically, managing to keep the grimace out of her voice.

"I'm just an ordinary guy," he said, waiting to be contradicted. Star obliged. "You don't sound so ordinary, lover. You sound real big and hard to me."

Normally, you try to string them along as slowly as you can—the stable gets paid by the minute for the call—but Star obviously couldn't take much more of this. I screamed, and the bastard gasped. "Ooh, that sounded good," said Star. "*Real* impressive, lover. Call me again soon, huh?"

There was the click of a disconnection, and then Star rolled off me and doubled up laughing.

"What the *fuck* is so funny?"

"*Men!*" she gasped. "Shit, and I thought *we* were frauds!"

Star always faked her orgasms for the callers: When she *really* came, she laughed, shuddered, banged her head, flailed her arms, and kicked, often hitting hard enough to leave bruises. Two or three orgasms in a row would exhaust her so thoroughly that she'd fall asleep. "You think he was just a fraud?"

"Sure. Like all those jerk-offs who claim to have ten-inch dicks. C'mon, girl, maybe he dreams he did it, maybe he's even sick enough to *believe* he did it, but you know he wouldn't have the *balls*."

"Maybe I don't have your experience with men," I replied dryly. Of course she was probably right—racists and gun nuts from Seattle to San Salvador would have claimed responsibility for the dojo shootings by now, and the city cops had probably stopped counting the false confessions.

On the other hand, if they were prepared to stop and question a stripper solely on the basis of a severely garbled street rumor, they were obviously desperate for even unreliable information. This wasn't an ordinary murder: There were three or four people involved, probably more, and anyone who confessed would have to share the, ah, credit, which would make it much less appealing.

And then I remembered the rapists. While Roy probably didn't have the balls to kill anyone alone, he *might* as part of a pack.

Pauline was far too fat to be a stripper, and I soon learned that she was a citizen with an ICEcard: She'd been doing dial-a-fantasies long before videphones were a problem, and still made the occasional call herself if the guy had a fat fetish or no video pickup. She was paid in ice and was eligible for old-age benefits in a few years, but she lived in a cot next to the switchboard and hadn't decided whether or not to quit her job.

Pauline slept during the day, when business was slowest. So, usually, did Morningstar and I. We could have worked as fluff girls in the TV studio upstairs, but neither of us liked handling men. At about nine A.M., I left Star sleeping and went outside.

The weather was damp and disgusting, and the library was full and humid, almost steamy. It was a pleasant change not to be the shabbiest person there; some of the students looked much worse than I did. I skimmed through the old newstapes, then grabbed a few books on twentieth-century guns. A few minutes later, when I saw my reflection in the powder-room mirror (why do women have to have such tiny bladders?), I realized that I was smiling.

I splashed cold water over my face and tried to calm myself down. Then I headed back to the stable, stopping at a bakery en route.

I'd thought that walking those last six stripper-strewn cold city blocks with a rumbling stomach and a sack of danish was the difficult part of this job, but that was before I tried to bargain with Pauline for Roy's phone number. She obviously thought I was trying to make a private deal with a customer and cheat the stable out of its percentage—not that she objected to that per se, but she sure as shit wasn't going to lose *her* share. "Or is he going to marry you?"

I almost gagged. "*That* creep?"

"Two cartons. In advance. *Straight* cigarettes," she added, her voice like a fried Mars bar. "I don't smoke pot."

Jesus, and I thought *I* was old! "I can't afford *that!* I wouldn't clear that much in a *week*, and I just bought some clothes—"

"Sorry, you're not my size."

"Look, it's nothing the stable would get a percentage from—"

"There's *nothing* these bastards don't take a percentage from," hissed Pauline. "This creep wants to meet you, he comes here and pays admission. He wants to buy your panties, they sell him a pair. He wants a blue movie, even a *snuff* movie, with you in the starring role, they'll do that too, if the price is right."

I heard a door open down the corridor. Star sized up the situation in an instant and asked, "How much do you need?"

"Two cartons of straight cigarettes. I might be able to manage one. . . ."

Star raised an eyebrow, then nodded. Pauline grabbed her pen and wrote the number on my palm. "Have one," Pauline muttered sourly, opening the sack. "You look like a refugee."

"Thanks," I said, and kissed Star. "I'll pay you back as soon as I can," I promised, then walked back outside casually, and then ran like hell to the nearest police station.

It was good to be reminded, occasionally, that city cops still have faces as well as visors. You had to peer through shatterproof glass to see them, as though they were objets d'art or venomous snakes. The desk sergeant looked too fat to wear armor, unless that *was* armor, and old enough to remember the days when most cops didn't. "Can I help you?" he asked, politely but without any curiosity.

"I think I know who shot up the dojo on Sacramento Street."

He looked marginally less bored. "Do you have any evidence?"

"No." The cop grimaced slightly. "There hasn't been any information released about the guns used, has there?"

"So?"

"Was one of them a Heckler and Koch MP5? A silenced nine-millimeter SMG?"

The cop started slightly. I might have been completely wrong, but it obviously wasn't a standard question. "I don't know," he admitted after a few seconds' thought. "Just a minute."

He pressed a button and soundproofed the glass. He even looked down, in case I could read lips (don't I wish). A moment later, a handleless wood-veneer door opened a few meters to his right and the cop said, "You can go in now."

Whatever it was, I was now in it up to my bony knees. I walked toward the door, then stopped when I saw the familiar arches of a metal detector and chemsniffer. There was a shield on the other side, gyrfalcon in hand, and I caught myself wondering if the alarm would sound if he fired through the archway.

After a long, cold moment, the shield stepped back and a rather soft, female voice asked, "Can I take your coat?"

I relaxed slightly, and began unbuttoning the greatcoat; my knife, as she'd guessed, was in the pocket. I rolled the coat into a bundle and held it out at arm's length. The shield stepped through the doorway and took it. Her gun stayed pointed at my feet until she was back beyond the arches; I could feel the desk sergeant watching me, and realized that there had to be a firing port hidden below that window. It might only have been for a stickyfoam gun, but I doubted it. A moment later, the shield nodded, and I walked into the next room.

There was another man inside, in plain clothes, looking down at a monitor. "Name?"

"Theresa Bird."

"WIN?"

"No."

He looked up and nodded. "I'm Sergeant Wazaki. Follow me, please."

I did. Everything was the drab beige of old recycled paint, but it's remarkable how much tidier offices are since multiframes became cheap and paper valuable. Wazaki led me to a cubicle only slightly larger than the toilet on a Greyhound bus, waved at a spare chair, and asked, "What have you got?"

"What?" I sat; he didn't. I could read his badge; it said he spoke Japanese and Spanish, and the other symbols presumably meant something to other cops.

"What are you selling? You told the desk something about a gun."

"I heard someone confess to the murder—well, to being involved. He said he'd shot six of the women with an MP5. Now, no one near the dojo heard any shots, did they? The H and K MP5 3D3—"

"Had a sound suppressor built in; I know. What do *you* know about guns?"

I smiled ingenuously. "I know which is the dangerous end."

"Then you've never used one."

Galloway had had basic training with a handgun once, more than

twenty years ago, and with a needler more recently, but Swiftie probably hadn't. "No."

He nodded. "*Both* ends are dangerous. Anything else that makes
you think this confession is kosher?"

God bless America: Where else would you find a strawberry-blond
half-Japanese who unconsciously speaks Hebrew? "He said that Sacramento Street was deliberately chosen, that the killing was a
sacrament. I haven't heard that before. And he seems the type who
might have done it—or the type to be friendly with men who might
have done it."

"How well do you know him?"

"I know his first name and phone number."

"No surname? No other details?"

"None that aren't on your database. Only the confession."

"Any other witnesses?"

"If absolutely necessary, yes—one, and I'll want protection for her,
too."

Wazaki sighed. "You said you don't know much about guns.
Okay, here's a free introductory lesson. Once upon a time, yes, we
could usually identify the model of gun a bullet had come from by
looking at the markings on the spent cartridges. Rifling marks on the
bullet itself could be matched to a particular gun, if we had the gun,
but the only clues to the make of gun were the class characteristics—
size of the lands and grooves, direction and angle of twist, stuff like
that. If the class characteristics of two makes of gun, say your MP5
and an Uzi, are pretty much the same, we can't learn very much just
from the bullets, particularly if they're badly deformed by hitting
something hard. Then some bright boy had to invent caseless ammunition. No cartridges. Makes ammo much lighter, guns more efficient, and our job just that little bit harder because we often can't
match bullet to gun until we have both, and not always then. We've
been trying to get numbered microbeads put into all ammunition to
make identification easier, but the Am Nats keep blocking that, and
anyway, it wouldn't help with gun owners who hand-load their own
ammo."

"So you don't know whether any of the killers used an MP5?"

"Exactly. We know they all used automatic nine-millimeter par-
abellum weapons modified for caseless ammunition; we can guess

that they used silencers or suppressors; we *know* how many guns were used and which gun shot who, but we're not releasing—"

"Four."

Wazaki paused, then continued, "Not releasing that information; the rifling marks do not match any we have on record—and even rifling marks aren't as distinctive as they used to be, guns are too precisely machined nowadays—and we have not found the guns, but this doesn't mean they haven't been dumped or destroyed."

"What if you searched this guy's place and found the gun?"

"And what if we *don't* find the gun?" he asked, eyebrows raised. "You've given us some good stuff before, Swiftie, but never very much we could *use*—which is why you're still living outside with a knife in your pocket." I tried not to gape. So that was how the Body-snatcher had stayed alive: as a police informant. His knowledge of the future must have made the job easier for him, and that was probably why the city cops had been so interested in talking to me. "Judges don't like to give warrants out just on hearsay," Wazaki continued. "You'd think they had to pay for the paper themselves. So. Where did you hear this confession?"

"No comment. What about geneprinting?"

"They were too damn careful. Every drop of blood and strand of hair we found came from Asians, and most of them from the victims—except for one blond hair, which we took to the ICE, but that turned out to be from one of the investigating team, and he had an alibi. Shit happens. Any other details we could check?"

I thought about that. "He said he shot six of the women: You could check that, I guess, but I don't know what it'd be worth."

"Not a lot. They didn't just spray the room with fire, they *saturated* it. In most cases, we have no way of knowing which bullets were fatal. Can you get anything else out of him?"

I shrugged. "I don't even know his full name."

"Give me what you have," he suggested. "I can database it, see if he has a record at least. It'd help."

"He says his first name is Roy; he could be lying, but I doubt it." Hell, no one likes to be called by someone else's name when they're in bed. "His phone number's 575-07145."

He sat down and keyed that in. "There's an H. R. O'Dwyer at that number . . . Hector Roy. Maybe he doesn't like being called Heck.

Born in Oregon in 'seventy-six, so that'd make him thirty-eight or thirty-nine. Sound like him?"

I shrugged.

"No carry permit or explosives license, no criminal record apart from a few misdemeanors"—he bit his lip, obviously wondering how much to tell me; I was astonished he'd been as indiscreet as he had already—"never been outside the U.S., current driver's license but no car, fingerprints not on record." He picked up a pencil and chewed it. The unchewed end, the one you write with, looked unused; the other was thoroughly mangled. Maybe they flavor the plastic nowadays, the way they used to perfume erasers.

"That's all you have?"

"That's all we're *allowed* to have. You want a dossier, try the Credit Exchange."

He was joking, of course: The ICE never gives away data—or anything else—unless it's to implicate someone who's cheated them. "What sort of misdemeanors?"

"Misuse of telecommunications," he replied blandly. That meant threatening or obscene e-mail or phone calls, or maybe just using a false return address on nuisance e-mail. Maybe Star was right; maybe he was all talk. "Paid his fines, end of story."

"What're you going to do?"

"With this?" Wazaki smiled thinly. "Nothing. We'd need a lot more data. What are *you* going to do?"

T he End," Gary said, sort of soft and slow, as he usually did when
he was beginning, so soft you could almost hear the Wagner he
had playing in the background. He didn't need to speak loud in the
beginning, because everybody was listening hard and the yelling
hadn't started. "Long as I can remember, seems there's always been
somebody saying the End was coming soon. Saying God was coming
soon, the Arks were coming soon, the Star they called Wormwood
was coming soon. Saying the Millennium was coming soon! Saying
all manner of catastrophes were coming soon! Saying . . ."

He paused. He'd been getting louder and faster, and each "soon"
was coming more and more like a scream. Now he said, all soft and
slow again, "And they were right about the Catastrophes, weren't
they? Can somebody say 'Amen'?"

Everybody did, but it was low and sort of soft, and he chuckled.
"Amen to that, oh yeah, because He gives us this day our daily disaster, doesn't He? Blizzards in that great and mighty dragon of a city
in the East, the highest flood ever recorded in one land, the longest
drought in another, and everywhere, crime and sickness and famine
getting worse every day, every single day—can somebody say
'Amen'?"

He smiled as we said it, and then he said, "Some say that the End
is already happening but we haven't noticed. Some say the world
ended near enough to a century ago, oh yeah, a hundred years ago,
at the end of the First World War, and in that century only *they* had
noticed that the world had ended. Now . . ." He paused, to let us
laugh for a while, and then he said, "Now, I don't happen to believe

these people are *right*, exactly, but we got to admit, they have been a *baaaad* hundred years. They've been bad for this country, and what is bad for this country is bad for the *world*—say 'Amen.'

"Now, like I said, I don't believe these people are exactly right, the world hasn't *end*ed, but don't let anyone tell you it hasn't *started* to end. We were a stronger country a century ago. We lived in what the historians call 'splendid isolation,' and we didn't let the sicknesses of all those other countries touch us, oh no, but we went to the wars. We went to Europe, fought our own sort of people, then we went to Japan, and Korea, and Vietnam, and other countries, and other wars, and every time, every single time, we came back a little less healthy. When we came back, we came back with refugees from these countries and these wars. Every time, every single time we went to war and our boys died there, there were less of *us* here, and more of them—say 'Amen'—*BUT!*" and he yelled through the "Amen" that was booming right back at him from the crowd, "BUT THE *WORLD HASN'T ENDED* YET!"

"No," he said when the cheering and the hallelujahs had stopped. "No, not yet, not *just* yet. Like I was saying, we've had the catastrophes, we've even had the Year Two Thousand Come and Gone, but it sure wasn't the *Millennium!* And do you know *WHY?*" He paused for long enough to let people wonder; not long enough to let them answer. "I'm going to tell you *why*.

"Bible says seven seals will open; now, you all know that, I don't have to tell you. It's all in *Revelation*. Chapter Six—right after you see the great throne that's covered with wings and eyes and crystal-clear glass, flashing like lightning and sounding like thunder, and isn't that a wonderful description of a spaceship coming from a man who'd never even seen an electric light before?—and you remember who comes out of the first four seals, oh yeah. They're each 'given authority over one-fourth of the Earth, to kill by means of war, famine, disease, and wild animals.' And the fifth seal, you remember, that contains the souls of the martyrs. Ah, but the sixth seal, when that opens, there's going to be a great earthquake, and the sun's going to turn black and the moon bloodred and the stars fall to Earth and the sky disappear; the kings and the presidents and the generals, the rich and the powerful, they're all going to hide in caves or under rocks—can I hear you say '*AMEN*'?"

He grinned at the mighty roar from the auditorium and continued. "But the sun wasn't black today, was it? No, not any more than *I'm* black! And the moon's not red tonight, either; I saw it on my way in. I look at the sky all the time, oh yeah, and it's still there, and so's all the stars. Now, we've had war and famine and disease, and you may wonder what's happened to all the wild animals, but maybe that time's over or maybe, maybe He meant some other *sort* of wild animal, so maybe the first four seals have been opened, and maybe the fifth seal's been opened, but the *sixth* seal . . .

"Oh, yeah. The sixth seal's not open yet, and we're a long way from being ready for the *seventh* seal, and some people have got tired of waiting, they say it's never *going* to open, we're wasting our *time* watching the sky! They say we'll be waiting *forever*, and the world's going to go on like *this* forever, but whenever I hear somebody say that, I know he *wants* the world to go on like this, I know he's *scared*, because maybe he's not going to be *saved* like you and me—can I hear you say '*AMEN*'?"

This "Amen" was a little quieter than the last one, like he'd started people thinking, and worrying. "Because not everybody's going to be saved, we know that. There's seven billion, nearly eight billion, bodies on this earth, and while most of them you can just *look* at and know *they're* not like us, they're going to die here with the Earth, and there's maybe half a billion who *do* look like us, even if they don't *think* like us, there's not going to be room for all in the Ark"— he grinned—"or in the New World, oh no, oh no.

"*Why* hasn't the sixth seal opened? *Why* hasn't the sun turned black and the sky disappeared? That's what they ask me, and I ask, What would happen if the Arks *did* come tomorrow, and blot out the sun and the sky? Even if they could *see* our cities through the smog, where would they land? Where could they go to find us, and not be besieged by the near-humans?

"We must find a place for them, we must *make* a place for them, and a place for *us*, a place for those *like* us, a place where those with the genes and the vision can *find* us, and a place where the near-humans will not *dare* to go. Until that hour, we will not, we can*not* be saved."

He was spitting the words out now like bullets, like autofire, and hammering on the lectern; suddenly he stopped, and became calm and quiet again. "Oh, yeah, I know, you've heard this before. There have been false prophets, and your faith has been tried—say 'Amen'—and I know you want to ask me, When? I could say, I have *told* you when. When we have taken that step, when we have begun to save *ourselves, that's* when. But, true as it is, it's also easy to say, and most of you have known it for *years*, you've been watching the skies and building your shelters and getting yourselves ready for years, and you want *more*.

"A week from next Tuesday, that's the twenty-fourth, about ten-thirty A.M., there's going to be a quake in Los Angeles. Not the great earthquake, only a three-point-something on the Richter scale—do you know what *Richter* means? It's German for 'judge': You might like to think about that for a moment. . . ."

He grinned broadly. "The L.A. quake is just a warning, and there shouldn't be more than a hundred people killed, all or most of them near-humans; I don't believe there's a hundred *True* Humans in that Godforsaken city." He paused for a few cheers and hallelujahs, then repeated, "*That* quake is just a warning, to give this once great nation one more chance, to give the True Humans *three days* to *rise* and evict all the traitors from Congress and the Senate and the state governments. *Three days* to begin purifying this country, and make a place for the Elite. Not a desert, not a mountainside where nothing can grow, but a shining city that will be *our* city, where other True Humans can find us, where our Creator can find us, and a fit landing place for an Ark . . . because, if Humans do not create such a place, those who are more than Human *will*, even though it means destroying whatever stands there now."

The audience was very quiet. "*If* this warning is not heeded . . .

"If this warning is not heeded, if there is even *one* near-human Khazar or part-human mongrel or white and human-looking but corrupt weak-minded traitor, one atheist or Zionist or pacifist or queer, in *any* position of power in this country, do not expect mercy from the Creator of Worlds. Mercy is not infinite. Patience is not infinite. We True Humans are an endangered species on our own planet, and if we do not *act*, our *time* will not be infinite!

"If this warning is not heeded . . .

"The Greenies tell us the oceans are rising. If this warning is not heeded, *three days* after the Los Angeles quake, they will *see* the oceans rise, as the Egyptians saw the Red Sea rise—and fall about them. If this warning is not heeded, *three days* after the L.A. quake, there will be another quake out in San Francisco, an eight or nine on the Richter scale, and then a great tidal wave will hit the city and wash it clean. The Asians, and the Mud People, and all the queers who like to play in the mud like pigs, they're all going to be washed away just before sunrise and the sun's going to come up on a whole new day, and, let us pray, a *very* different city.

"And *that* won't be the End, oh no, but only the *Beginning* of the End. It's going to be a start, a Sign, but the rest of the cleansing we're gonna have to do ourselves. Can I *hear you say* 'AMEN'!"

He did.

I found O'Dwyer's address in the phonebase. He lived on Missouri Street, in a seventh-floor apartment without a balcony. Every window in the ugly concrete building was opaqued, and probably well soundproofed. Zero percent for charm and aesthetic appeal, but the security was excellent: a ninja couldn't have gotten in without—

Something in my mind went *clunk!* O'Dwyer had said something about "ninja training," and while he likely wouldn't have known a ninja from a geisha, there were probably a few serious martial artists at the Sacramento Street dojo who would be interested in meeting him.

Unfortunately, it was already late afternoon, the rain was becoming heavier. I was a good three klicks from Chinatown, most of it downhill, my legs were tired, and MUNI doesn't consider cigarettes legal tender, so I decided that the dojo could wait until tomorrow and headed back to the stable.

I'm sorry. I am truly sorry.

Roy didn't call that night, and I didn't hear about the shootings until the next morning. It wasn't a dojo this time, but a dormitory in Berkeley; the victims were Asian, the killers armed with autoloaders, and the witnesses—at that time—nonexistent.

I stayed just long enough to hear the end of the newscast; a few seconds later, I was out the door and headed for Chinatown.

I hadn't been to the dojo before; all I knew was that it was on Sacramento, in or very near Chinatown (according to the newstapes), and upstairs from street level. If I'd bothered thinking beforehand, I wouldn't have expected it to be a dojo during the day, either: Any empty space in Old Chinatown was considered almost as precious as it was in Hong Kong. I'd walked through the rain from Bush to Broadway and back twice, without seeing any sign that said Martial Arts Academy in any language I recognized, before this occurred to me.

I sighed, and wandered toward a phone booth (they still had them in Old Chinatown, complete with the fancy tops). There were fifteen screens of martial arts schools of various persuasions listed on yellowpages.com, but none on Sacramento. I looked through the dusty window at the insanely busy street, not really seeing anything, and wondered what the hell to do next. What would they use that kind of space for during the day? A restaurant or café? A film studio? A black market supermarket?

Someone tapped on the glass, bringing me back to earth. I took one last glance at the phonebase, then nodded and stepped out. The woman thanked me—I must not have looked like a stripper—and the door closed between us. I walked away from the booth, feeling less like Superman than I ever had in my life. *Either* life.

Suddenly I stopped, and realized I was looking at a long row of opaque third-story windows. Most of Chinatown is *old*, so old that many of the windows are antique glass, not shatterproofed, soundproofed, or prismatic, with curtains, blinds, and screens giving what privacy they could. Four opaque windows in a row meant four recent replacements, and you couldn't spray a room with autofire without breaking the windows.

The room, when I finally found it, was being used as a massage parlor—a *real* massage parlor, filled with folding tables, paper screens, and fully dressed masseurs and masseuses. There were no signs of the massacre: The walls were hidden by screens, and the floor had been scrubbed to the verge of annihilation. The old woman by the door, whose English wasn't much better than my Cantonese, assumed I was there as a client. I didn't look destitute, as a stripper should, but I didn't look respectable either; kind of half Avon lady, half old dope peddler. We were still banging words together and failing to light any fires when one of the masseurs came to our rescue.

"You wish to work here?" he asked in English.

"No," I replied a little tersely (I can ask for work in seventeen languages, even if I can't always understand the replies). "I have information about the shooting on Christmas Eve. Is there someone here I can speak to?"

He remained impassive—he had the broad face of a sumo wrestler, with features that seemed too heavy to move at all—but his irises widened slightly. "There's me," he suggested.

"What will you do with the information?"

"What do you have?"

"A name . . . and an address."

"Have you been to the cops?"

"Yes."

"What did they say?"

"Insufficient evidence."

The masseur nodded. "What's the name?"

"What are you going to do?"

We stared at each other for a moment, then he asked, "What would you like us to do?"

"I don't know. Get into his apartment and look for the gun, I guess."

"Even if we could do that, do you think he'd still have it? It could be at the bottom of the bay."

I shrugged.

"What's your interest in this?"

That was a difficult one. "I . . . if I'd told you this yesterday, it might have stopped the shooting in Berkeley. Maybe it wouldn't have, maybe there won't be any more, but . . . I don't know."

He nodded again. "What's the name?"

"What are you going to do?"

"I don't know."

We seemed to have reached an impasse. The old woman, who'd been watching us as though we were a tennis match, yawned and closed her eyes.

"Can you come back here at three?" the masseur asked.

"I guess so."

"Good." He bowed, very slightly, without looking away from my face. "May I ask *your* name?"

"Tera."

"I'm Pat Hong. I'll see you at three."

• • •

"Am I doing the right thing?"

To my delight, Mama had arrived at the soup kitchen, without Blair, while I was still in line. I didn't mean that quite the way it sounds. I wasn't jealous of Blair, I just wanted to talk to Mama alone, even though it meant waiting outside in the cold for more than half an hour (line-jumping, and sitting for longer than it took you to eat, were considered felonies for anyone with two working legs).

She was silent for nearly a minute. "What do you think the Asians will do if he *has* the gun?"

"How will they know? He probably has a dozen guns, but only the city cops will be able to identify *the* gun—"

"Do you think they'll wait? Do you think they'll care? They may end up lynching anyone they catch with a machine gun."

"Maybe that's not such a terrible idea, either."

"Maybe." She watched two seagulls fighting over a crust and shook her head: There were still a few winners in the city who would rather feed birds than humans. "But there's a lot of guns out there, and right or wrong, if they start fighting back . . ."

"Did you hear what happened in Berkeley last night?"

"Yes, and I've *seen* people shot, in groups. Have you?"

"No," I admitted. I'd been in Beijing in 1989, teaching English, and had hung around with some of the students in Tiananmen Square, but I'd left town a few days before the shooting started, more by luck than by planning. "What did you do?"

Mama stared past me. I don't know what she was seeing, but it wasn't the Laser Shack across the street. "I refused to kill. That sounds easy, but I *have* had a choice: I've been in situations where I could easily have reached a gun, where the guardsmen were too preoccupied or too damn drunk to have stopped me—"

"But you're armed now."

"Yes, but I bluff, I don't *kill*. While I have these claws, anyone who wants to hurt me risks being hurt himself: Most won't take that risk. Unless he has a gun, of course.

"You've changed a lot since Christmas, girl. You would never have asked me a question like that. You asked questions, sure, all the time, but you never asked for an *opinion*. You seemed even more depressed than you were before, like you were utterly lost."

"Everyone over twelve gets depressed around Christmas."

"Maybe, but you seemed so far down I was worried we were going to bury you where you lay, and it took you a month or more to get back to normal, not that you were ever Pollyanna or anything. And you're less—I don't know—arrogant maybe."

"Anything else?"

"Small things," she said, with a little shrug. "You *give* more when you make love; it's not just that your technique is different, someone might have taught you that, and you still don't relax worth a damn, but . . . You seem *older* in a lot of ways. You always seemed to know more and less than you should, but now, sometimes, you talk like you remember things which happened 'fore you were born, like you've read more and seen more and been further than you could have done, and like you *understand* more. Sometimes, if I can't see you, I could think you were my age. Hell, even your *walk* has changed: You used to walk like an Angeleno, someone who hated walking and had never had to do it before. There's probably a lot more that I can't put my finger on, but that doesn't matter. I haven't stopped loving you; I'm just not sure I *know* you anymore."

"Do you love me as much?"

"Love is love," she said firmly. "You can't have more or less love; it's indivisible, if that's the word I'm after. I could probably *like* you a little more now than I did, when I get to know you again."

I sat there trying to think of something intelligent to say, and Mama put her arms around me. "Do what you feel you have to do."

"I *can't* do nothing. I know, I know, everyone else does—"

"You're not everyone," she replied. I'm at least one more person than you think I am, I thought, and asked, "Where are you living now?"

"In the Highsore. It's too damn cold to sleep out, and I'm too damn old for a stable." She sighed. "How long are you going to stick it out?"

"I don't know."

"Shriek's turning seventeen in a few days, says she's going to get an ICEcard and a place of her own. Maybe she'll let us sleep on the floor."

• • •

Hong and two equally burly companions frisked me, took my knife, and then marched me through a bewildering series of corridors, stairwells, alleyways, and side streets, past antique wooden doors and wallpaper that actually might have been paper, over carpets that would have looked at home on a mammoth, and under fly-speckled low-watt incandescent globes (I had a sneaking suspicion those were illegal) before ushering me into a small, untidy, state-of-the-art office that might have been two meters from the dojo, or two miles, or even two decades. An old man who looked like Fu Manchu's father was hunched behind a computer desk; a beautiful Eurasian woman, who looked to be in her late teens or early twenties, sat on the other, swinging her lovely silk-sheathed legs. When Hong shut the door behind us, the woman looked me up and down, and then turned to the old man. She said a few short words, which didn't sound like any language I knew, and he shuffled over to a battered sideboard and began making tea. "Pat says that you have information about the shootings at the Sacramento Street school," she said in English.

"Yes, but I can't vouch for the source."

The woman smiled. "What do you know?"

"I *don't* know who you are."

The smile remained. "I don't know who you are either. My name is Connie, if that helps."

I recounted O'Dwyer's confession, then the conversation with Sergeant Wazaki, carefully excluding all names. Connie glanced at one of the men behind me, and then back at me. "What do you want, in exchange for his name?"

"Any evidence that I can give the cops."

"Why?"

I looked closely at the woman and decided to try being honest. "They've offered me a new ID, on a Witness Protection Program."

"And what do *we* get?"

"The shootings stop."

"What if they don't?"

"I don't know."

"What if it isn't him?"

"I don't know."

She nodded. "What's the name?"

I hesitated.

"You may as well trust us," she said flatly. "You've already admitted you can't do anything with the information alone."

She was right. "Hector O'Dwyer."

"That wasn't so bad, was it? Sit down; this won't take long. Black tea or green?"

"Black, please."

She turned the terminal on the desk to face her. "Address? Phone number?"

A minute later, the old man handed me a cup of tea, and Connie looked up from the monitor, her expression slightly sour. "Not much. He was in the National Aryan Alliance until it broke up, but he was never charged with anything, and he didn't join any of the splinters. Since then, National Freedom Festivals in 'eleven and 'thirteen, American Aryan Congress last year, and a couple of e-mail offenses." She shrugged. "Might be a useful idiot for someone, but that's about it."

"You keep dossiers on these . . ." I tried to think of an appropriate noun. The three of them looked at each other, but only Hong looked embarrassed.

"Not really," said Connie. "We just . . . hack into the membership lists and dossiers that already exist around the place, and run search programs to see what we can find. These groups are terrible at computer security, and if we keep track of their movements, sometimes we can warn people of their plans—though more often it's useful *after* the fact. The best we can usually do is tell the cops where to look for safe houses, weapons caches, and likely escape routes. It didn't help when the dojo was attacked, even though we'd known that a lot of these thugs had been visiting San Francisco for no apparent reason for a few months beforehand. Most of their support comes from small towns where the jobs have gone, or rural areas where farmers can't afford to pay off their bank loans; not from the big cities, and certainly not from here. It worried us at the time, but there wasn't anything we could do about it; all we can do is keep watching and wait for someone to make a mistake. Most of these groups collapse because someone turns informant, or when their leaders blow themselves up with their own bombs."

"How many are there of you?"

"Doing surveillance? Usually only me, though I swap info with other people from other groups in other cities; the Net has made being nosy a lot faster and cheaper. The only real privacy that exists for anyone anymore is the likelihood that no one's going to bother looking—but of course that's been true for decades, if not forever. Some ultraright and racist groups—Nazi parties, Klans, vigilante gangs, the sort of people the media call White Riders and who usually call themselves Race Warriors—have been using the Net since the early nineteen eighties; it was cheap once they'd bought the hardware, fast, worldwide, difficult to censor, and relatively anonymous. No voices to voiceprint, no fingerprints or postmarks, no magazines or tapes in plain brown wrappers, just names that might or might not be real, and it's almost impossible to trace someone's physical location. They still use it for propaganda and random harassment— you should read the spam we received last week, one of their more outrageous spokesmen predicting earthquakes for L.A. and San Francisco some time next month. . . . Do you read English?"

"Huh? Yeah, sure."

She smiled grimly. "Read this. It went out to a couple hundred newsgroups and mailing lists, from survivalists to UFOnians to gays, a few weeks ago. Some hackers even went and changed links in a lot of sites to go straight to this. I don't know what they'll do when the Earth refuses to move—call it a conspiracy, I guess. They see conspiracies everywhere—they hate the ICE as much as they hate us, or even each other. Hate is what they do best. This is just one of the more *coherent* rants."

I glanced at the screen. It was a plain-text generator, compatible with even the cheapest, most simple e-mail viewer. I looked down at the keyboard and noticed that it was lit up with Chinese ideographs. Rather nervously, I tapped the long black switch nearest my right thumb, and the screen scrolled down without anything exploding.

```
The End
An Address to the Free Assembly of the Human
Nation
February 13, 2015
By Gary Donner
```

Long as I can remember, seems there's always been somebody saying the End was coming soon, saying God was coming soon, the Arks were coming soon, the Star they called Wormwood was coming soon, saying the Millennium was coming soon! Saying all manner of Catastrophes were coming soon!

I read it through twice, then looked up from the monitor, shaking my head. "Who is this idiot?"

"Donner? Minor-league hate merchant," explained Hong. "Used to be a sports commentator, then a right-wing talk-radio host; now he claims he's a prophet. Of course, he didn't *write* this himself, it's not his style at all—his is rather breathless, uses very few long words, and is full of football or boxing clichés. But we don't really know who wrote it for him; I ran it through a text analyzer and it didn't match the style of anyone we know who Donner might be fronting for; he's not attached to any group that we know of."

"Which isn't to say that none has attached itself to him," said the old man. "There are dozens of neo-Nazi parties, Ku Klux Klans, and similar groups competing for membership dollars, and despite all they have in common, none of these groups have ever accepted a single leader over all, or even a single plan. Occasionally, one of the Führers or Grand Dragons or whatever will begin a campaign, hoping the others will follow suit, but fortunately, they never have and pray God they never will."

"Sounds like the Manson family," I muttered. The old man nodded, though his expression was strange; Connie and Hong looked puzzled. "What's a Khazar?" I asked, hoping to distract them.

"A descendant of Cain," replied the old man softly. "Roughly translated, anyone who isn't white. Have you ever heard of Identity Christianity?"

"No."

He sipped at his tea and then said sadly, "It was invented in the nineteenth century, as an attempt to cast the British in the role of the 'Chosen People.' According to the author, the true Jews, Isaac's sons, crossed the Caucasus Mountains into Britain—hence 'Saxons,' Isaac's sons, and 'Caucasians'—and the people then known as Jews were descended from Cain, whose father was said to be Satan, not Adam. American anti-Semites adapted the idea for their own purposes last century, and managed to unite some of the racist groups back in the nineteen eighties; members started going to the same churches, and then the same conventions, subscribing to the same magazines, training in the same compounds . . . and, of course, they discovered the Internet. Groups in different states who previously hadn't been on speaking terms began to form a nationwide network, and the number of groups actually *increased* during this time, thanks largely to recruiting on the Net—though it's difficult to be sure about the actual number of *members*. But even with the Net, these groups never managed to start the race war most of them dreamed of; most of the hate crimes committed in this country in the nineties, foul as they were, were done by a few individuals, most of whom had probably never *heard* of Identity Christianity. If Donner, or his scriptwriter, is referring to Khazars, it's probably an attempt to reach some of the die-hards who still believe in it. You noticed he referred to UFOs, too? That's probably to endear himself to groups like the Silver Shirts, who believe in perfect Aryans returning to Earth in flying saucers. I'm very much afraid that someone—someone with *money*—is trying to unite all these groups again. Of course, this someone is probably more interested in raising money than raising an army, but it is likely that many crimes will be committed in the interim. Whether or not this someone had anything to do with Sacramento Street, I can't say." He sighed. "We can only hope the police catch the people responsible, though they probably won't. The real police don't have the resources any more than we do, and the rent-a-cops only protect their paying clients."

"Or," muttered Pat, "that the bastards accidentally touch off their own ammunition dumps and blow themselves up, as most of their heroes have."

I sat there and digested this. "Okay," I said finally. "Who are *you*?"

There was another long silence while they all looked at each other, then Connie said, "We're teachers."

"You're *what?*"

She repeated it in Mandarin and Korean. "We teach English, computer literacy, martial arts, massage and reiki . . . survival skills."

"To whom?" I asked, then answered myself before anyone else could speak. "Refugees."

"Mostly, yes," said Pat. "We'll teach almost anyone who comes to us, which includes strippers and a lot of hyphenates who can't find work, and we drag out the mats and use the place for a shelter after midnight. But we don't advertise, except by word of mouth, and . . ."

"And the words and the mouths are Chinese."

"Mostly, yes," he repeated. "And if you want to call us racist, go ahead: I suppose we are. These supremacist groups have been concentrating on Asians more and more in recent years. They blame us for the recession, for unemployment, for the heroin trade and other crime, for the greenhouse effect, for wars and genocide and human-rights violations. They do not distinguish between different nationalities; through telescopic sights, I suspect all Asians *do* look much the same." He shrugged. "And so, we look after our own. How many Chinese do you see living on the streets?"

I shrugged. I'd known enough Asians to know that racism isn't just a disease of whites. Traditionally, the Vietnamese hate the Cambodians who hate them right back, the Japanese (who also thought of themselves as "the white race") and Koreans and Indonesians hate almost everyone, and *everyone* hates the Chinese, which is one reason why they're known as "the Jews of Asia." It made at least as much as sense as the French hating the Germans, or the Serbs hating the Croats, or even the Irish hating the Irish, and, speaking as an ex-Australian, I couldn't exactly boast: It was barely fifty years since we repealed the White Australia policy and voted that the aborigines were citizens, not wildlife. And less than twenty years ago, our government was refusing even to apologize for centuries of dispossession and genocide. Jesus, even white Seth Efricens—sorry, I mean South Africans—felt entitled to blast us occasionally for our human-rights record.

The old man sipped at his tea again, then asked, "What are you going to do now?"

"Take this to the cops, if that's okay by you," I replied. He nodded, very slightly. "And then . . . I don't know. It depends on what they do. Maybe I'll come back here."

"If you want to break into this man's apartment, I'm afraid we can't help you," the old man said impassively. "If he owns firearms, his security system is bound to be excellent."

"That wasn't what I had in mind. I used to teach English, in Thailand" (and in China, Japan, Korea, Spain, Mexico, and Turkey, but I didn't think they'd believe *that*). "Maybe *I* could help *you*."

I think he smiled, very slightly. "Perhaps. Thank you for your time. Pat will show you the way out."

Sergeant Wazaki didn't seem particularly happy to see me, or overly impressed with my information, though that might have been partially due to working a weekend shift. "We're not going to get a search warrant—which is what we need—just on hearsay. You've never even *seen* this O'Dwyer: For all you know, he might be a quadriplegic with a big imagination. The White Rider theory isn't that popular in Homicide. They're used to worrying about the maniacs who call themselves Satanists, rather than maniacs who call themselves Christians. And it could just as easily have been a Triad killing, or a street gang—lots of them still use Uzis—or even a group of dangergamers—"

"Why would they shoot up a beginners' judo class?" I asked, shuddering at the idea of dangergamers en masse.

"A mistake. The wrong place, or the wrong time, or maybe they were only after one person and the others were in the way—"

"What about the Japanese restaurant, three weeks before?"

"We haven't any proof that there's a connection. Similar MO and weapons, sure, but the bullets found there don't match the ones found in the dojo."

"And Berkeley?"

"Berkeley's outside my jurisdiction." He reached for his pencil and bit savagely into the end, and I wondered how many serial killers had profited from the rivalry between police precincts (Manson, Bundy, and Jack the Ripper came readily to mind). "And probably different weapons *that* time, too. If it *is* the same people and they have any brains at all, they'll be dumping their guns into the bay after each job and buying new ones."

"Maybe not," I said. "Maybe they collect souvenirs; a lot of thrill killers do, or so I've heard."

Wazaki glared. "Okay, look, I can go and see this O'Dwyer, see if he *could* have done it, if he'll let me talk to him. Without a warrant, I might not get past the lobby, let alone into his apartment."

"What if he doesn't let you in?"

He shrugged. "I'll try to be convincing."

I hadn't taught in a classroom situation for nearly twenty years, and I'd forgotten how exhausting it was and how much fun it wasn't. My first class was made much worse by the bizarre feeling of trying to give birth to a slowly rotating and rather dull chain saw, which I mistook for appendicitis and later realized was my period approaching. The luxury of two (sometimes three) adequate meals a day was taking its toll; my hips no longer resembled a double-bladed ax, my ribs were beginning to disappear, my back was breaking out in pimples, and my breasts were as large as any twelve-year-old girl's or Romanian gymnast's.

I'd lived with women before, when I was Mike Galloway, so I guess I should have recognized the premenstrual symptoms—what Angela had always called the Lady Macbeth blues—but I didn't really grasp that they were happening to *me* until a few days later when I saw the sticky pink bloodstains in my panties. By three o'clock, I was feeling dirty as well as sick, and the cramps were so painful that I could barely walk to the bus stop (Connie, bless her, bought me a MUNI pass, fed me Midol, and lent me a tampon), much less drop in on Wazaki, and by the time I reached the stable, I felt as though I'd thrown myself on a grenade. Pauline dosed me up with more Midol and gave me a sponge to stick up my vagina—she wasn't going to throw me out while I owed her money—and Star made love to me, cutting the gut-wrenching cramps with orgasm after orgasm; she said it always worked for her, and while it didn't feel good, it certainly felt better. Fortunately, it was a slow night (Mondays usually were), and I had enough time between calls to wash myself.

Although teaching English is traditionally done without moans or screams, it didn't occur to me to skip work the next day: I'd been a casual employee or my own boss for most of my previous life, and paid sick leave was something that only happened to other people, so I struggled through two hour-long classes. Not all of my students were Chinese, and I learned a few words of Khmer and Vietnamese, plus a few potentially useful Korean phrases that Galloway had never needed. Pat Hong took me to a good cheap restaurant downstairs (we both received lunch in lieu of wages), told me a little about himself, and invited me on a date. I told him I was a lesbian, and asked if he knew whether Connie was straight. He didn't, but he hoped she was, so we shook hands, wished each other luck, and changed the subject. "Would you like a massage?"

I thought about it for a moment, then shook my head. I've never learned to relax for a male masseur, and most of my body already hurt. "I'd better get home, get some sleep. Some other time?" This wasn't a lie: I was already half asleep, and I dozed for most of the bus ride home. I didn't contact Wazaki again until Wednesday afternoon, and by that time, O'Dwyer had already disappeared.

Disappeared? What the hell do you mean, disappeared?"
Wazaki leaned back in his chair and sighed. "He didn't show up for work or call in sick, he doesn't answer his phone, and he isn't using any water or electricity. I'm trying to get a search warrant for his place, but I still don't have probable cause."

"Shit." No one had to tell me about freedom of movement in the U.S. Long before I was a travel agent I used to drive six or seven hundred klicks a day, delivering deadheads, and I've seen more of the country than God would want to look at. I'd stopped wondering where the Bodysnatcher could have gone, and though O'Dwyer probably wouldn't risk leaving the United States without a good false passport, he might well be in Florida or even Panama. It occurred to me that he might even have gone to Galloway's Travels for a cheap ticket.

Nah. Unless he was seriously stupid, he wouldn't risk using his ICEcard, especially not on a major purchase like an airfare. The ICE would find him inside an hour, if Wazaki could persuade them to fucking well look. Besides, there were at least three other sociopaths in or near town who would hide him (or would they? would he trust them? had they already left?), or he might have a yen to rough it: in the Rockies, in what was left of the forests up in Oregon, or in the desert, like the Manson family. Of course, if he'd read and believed that spiel about the quakes, he might have been planning to leave town anyway. "How long will he have to be gone to count as probable cause?"

"I'll keep trying," he promised. "Two or three days, I guess."

"What's the date today?"

"The twenty-fifth . . . oh, yeah." He grinned. "Assuming the city's still here."

"Ah?"

"Haven't you been watching the news? Some Apocalyptic asshole's predicted a day of natural disasters for Friday. Claims to have predicted the tremor in L.A., too—you okay?"

"No . . . no, not really." I hadn't heard of the L.A. tremor and had completely lost track of the date. Suddenly, I felt horribly clammy, and I suspect I'd turned very pale.

"You want a glass of water? Or coffee? Awful coffee, sure, but—"

"Lots of sugar." Even awful coffee was a luxury not to be refused. I'd almost forgotten that I used to live on the stuff, but hell, that was in another body.

"Sure. Be right back." He paused just long enough to lock me out of the computer, then disappeared into the maze of cubicles and corridors. The coffee was the same paper-bag color as the walls and tasted almost as bad as he'd predicted, but I gulped it down. "Tremor in L.A.?"

"You didn't hear? It wasn't the big one, but a few people were killed, and a few dozen more are still missing. You have friends or family down there?"

I shook my head, and wondered whether I should I tell Wazaki about the spam on the Net. He probably wouldn't believe me: I wouldn't have, under the circumstances. "You were saying you spoke to O'Dwyer. Did you get to meet him?"

"No. He wouldn't let me in. The manager gave me a description— male caucasian, one-seventy-five tall, eighty-five to ninety kilos, heavy build with some beer muscle, hair blond, cut short and receding—the hair, that is—"

"So he's not a quadriplegic?"

"No. No distinguishing features to speak of."

"Where does he work?"

"Why?"

"Has he disappeared like this before? If we can prove that it's uncharacteristic, unprecedented . . . I really think we need to find him soon."

"You think there's going to be another massacre?"

"Yes."

He shrugged. "I'll do what I can. Can you prove that?"

"No, but one more thing . . ."

"Yes?"

"Find out what you can about a man named Michael Byron Galloway."

"You know, I've never been in the *front* seat of a troll before."

Wazaki shrugged without taking his eyes from the road, even though we were on one of the uninhabited freeways and the car was doing all the driving. "We have a ride-along scheme, but it isn't real popular; mostly cops from other cities, journalists, professors . . . a few kids who want to be cops, but there aren't many of those."

"Even with underemployment at—what, forty percent?" The official figures were lower, but they excluded anyone on "workfare" or taking "training courses," anyone doing unpaid "domestic duties," and the homeless.

"Forty-four." He nodded. "But the city's broke—hell, what city isn't?—and the rich prefer hiring rent-a-cops to protect their own turf to paying taxes and protecting everyone. Half the security firms pay better than we do, with less training, less stringent entry requirements, and better working conditions, including no Internal Affairs Department. So who'd want to be a *real* cop and get shot just for doing their job? Sometimes I think that *is* our job," he concluded sourly. "There's just too many guns out there, too many people who think there's a war on—or want one."

I considered asking him why *he'd* become a city cop, and decided it wouldn't be diplomatic. "I thought that needle guns—"

He swore. "Sure, lots of people bought needlers and tranq rounds, but what d'you think they did with their old shotguns and . 38s? They sold 'em, until the prices started dropping so low that they were cheaper'n toys. Of course the manufacturers kept churning the damn things out, too, and the politicians wouldn't do anything about that—that might have cost jobs, which means votes—and the market was still being flooded with imports, AK-47s and Uzis and Strikers."

"And cops started wearing body armor."

"Sure, and so did everyone on the street. Besides, a full-shield suit won't stop a rifle bullet, especially if it's Teflon tipped, and it probably weighs more'n you do. Why d'you think I'm not wearing it now?"

"Because it scares the shit out of people?"

"Yeah, there is that," he replied, nodding, "and I like to think people are less likely to shoot you if they can see your face, if they know you're another human being."

"Even with that cannon on your hip? Why don't you just use stingers?"

Wazaki snorted. "No range, no stopping power, no damn good against armor, and they take a few seconds to work when they *do* work. Besides, with a needler you have to shoot someone just to get their attention, whereas I've never actually had to *use* this, just threaten to. With a falcon, I can even take out a car if I turn the cylinder back; most of us load one APEX round as well as stun rounds."

I tuned out, as I always do when people start discussing the merits of various guns, and watched a zep heading out of SFO. There was a time when I couldn't see a plane, a zep, even a Greyhound bus without wishing I were on it, even if I had no idea where it was going. I'd lost some, though not quite all, of that urge since moving to San Francisco; maybe it wasn't home, whatever that meant, but I felt like a part of it, and would mourn it when it was gone, whether it was by quake, or becoming enveloped by the L.A. megasprawl, or any other disaster.

It had taken Wazaki most of Wednesday afternoon and Thursday morning to get the search warrant, and he obviously had other work to do. Predictions of imminent catastrophe bring out the worst in some people, though not in as many as you might expect (I can still remember the headline of a story about floods in Iowa, from a New York paper: NO LOOTING!). "What's all the hardware for?" I asked when he stopped talking. "Making coffee?"

"What hardware?"

I nodded at the electronics crammed into the dashboard and around the windshield. "Oh, that," he said. "Surveillance."

"Surveying who or what?"

There was an uncomfortable pause, then, "Us, mostly. Some of it's remote-control gear, in case of emergencies, a driver down or whatever. It's what they give us nowadays instead of partners. Who's Galloway?"

"Sorry?"

"Galloway. We have almost nothing on him: no record, no permits. . . . He sold his business and apparently left town about a month ago, and we don't know where he is—except that he hasn't left the country. Not legally, anyway. Any link between him and O'Dwyer?"

"I don't know."

"Doesn't seem likely; his DoI file suggests that he's a burned-out liberal. Did a lot of work for Amnesty and Greenpeace and some aid programs overseas, but that was years ago. I guess he might have become disillusioned enough to change to the other extreme, but it seems unlikely. What do you know about him?"

"What do you know about a guy called Donner?" I evaded. "Gary Donner?"

"The sports commentator?"

I shrugged. I can stay awake during a basketball game (sometimes), and I used to like watching gymnasts until they started making me feel like a cripple, but I'm not exactly a sports fan. "The preacher."

"Might be the same guy. Big? Red hair, beard?"

Galloway wasn't enormous, but he was a few centimeters taller and a few kilos heavier than Wazaki, and size is easy to fake on the screen—and a time traveler might make a name for himself (and a damn sight more money) predicting sports results as well as earthquakes. "Uh-huh."

"What about him?" asked Wazaki as he parked the troll in O'Dwyer's bay.

"Nothing, really; just a hunch. But it's something to look for."

"Sure." He unbuckled his seat belt and checked his gun. "Look, this warrant only covers guns and ammo; even if he's left a signed confession I can't touch it, so I shouldn't be long. Maybe twenty minutes. If he has left any firearms behind, I'll just call Forensics. Don't touch anything."

"I won't."

"I still don't know why you bothered coming along."

"I have to know," I replied simply.

"Sure," he said, and shut the door. I leaned back in the seat and closed my eyes. A few minutes later, the floor jolted sharply, and I was wide awake. *The quake!*

What the fuck to do? I had forty-something stories of apartment block right on top of me. Trolls might be tough, but nothing could withstand that. How far was I from the exit? How many floors down? Would the street actually be any safer?

A few heartbeats later, I noticed that the world had stopped shaking; after a moment's thought, I realized that it had only moved once, a single lurch or jolt. The ceiling had stayed where a ceiling should, and the troll's touch-sensitive car alarm hadn't even whispered. Had it been a quake at all? I thought of calling Wazaki, but his holdie-talkie would be useless in this steel-frame fortress.

I sat there for a few quiet and very long seconds before venturing out of the car and running like hell, following the arrows to the nearest exit. The first sign that something was wrong was a burning book, blowing across my path as I ran into the street. Looking around, I saw more of them, and at least a dozen magazines. I looked up and saw smoke billowing out from the seventh floor.

It took me a few seconds to realize what was wrong with this picture. Those windows were supposed to be bulletproof, burglar-proof, soundproof, and suicide-proof; if smoke was going to pour from anywhere, it should be the air-conditioning vents on the roof. And then I saw the mess of prismatic glass scattered over the street.

I stomped on a fluttering magazine and stared at it; the cover had charred past recognition, but there were pictures of people using firearms (ranging from pistols to full machine guns) on every page I saw. It was probably ten years old or more; paper was too damn expensive for magazines nowadays. More magazines blew away, like burning butterflies, but most of the paperbacks rolled over the pavement slowly enough for me to catch them, extinguish them, and bag them. They might be evidence. Some of them might even be readable. Besides, I've never liked the idea of books being burned. Only Nazis and fundamentalists sank that low. Of course, O'Dwyer had been both, but . . .

A moment later, I finally realized what must have happened to Wazaki, and I threw up all over an antique copy of *Soldier of Fortune* before running toward the foyer.

The inner door was locked, and pounding on the glass had no result. The caretaker, I guessed, had probably been with Wazaki when the bomb had gone off, so regardless of any alarms that'd been triggered, *she* was never going to let me in. I tried the intercom, pressing buttons in random sequences, but no one answered. I swore, took one last useless hapkido kick at the door, and then sprinted back down to the parking garage, hoping that my strategically placed sneaker had prevented that door from closing and locking me out. It had, and to my relief (and amazement), the troll hadn't automatically locked its doors when I'd abandoned it. It didn't even sound any alarms—well, none that I heard—when I let myself in again. I lay back in the seat for a moment, to catch my breath, and silently thanked the gods for my new, younger body. Then I reached for the radio.

"Officer down," I panted. "Missouri Street. Request assistance."

There was a long, agonizing silence followed by a crunchy "Say again?"

"Officer down. Request assist—"

"Who the hell is this?"

"Sergeant Wazaki—"

"You're not Wazaki."

"No; I think Wazaki's dead. There's been an explosion—"

"Who is this?"

"My name's . . . ah . . . Bird. Theresa Bird. I'm an informant. Wazaki had a search warrant, but the place must have been booby-trapped."

"Okay, okay. We'll have someone right there."

"But—" Suddenly the dashboard began lighting up like a Christmas tree on amphetamines; then the troll slowly reversed out of the parking bay. I reached for the door handle, but nothing happened; some automatic or remote-controlled system had locked me in. Oh, fucking wonderful.

The troll drove slowly up to the street and circled the block before heading back to the freeway. It was a ten-minute trip back to the station, probably longer with the troll sticking so closely to the minimum speed, and I soon decided that I'd enjoy it a damn sight more if I didn't watch the road. Instead, I reached into my bag to find out what I'd rescued from O'Dwyer's library.

The thickest book to emerge was a paperback of L. Ron Hubbard's *Battlefield Earth*, which I wouldn't have bothered picking up if the cover hadn't been charred beyond recognition; the next was a 1995 translation of *Mein Kampf*, more thoroughly burned than read; the third was General Sir John Hackett's *The Third World War*; the fourth, *Job*, Robert A. Heinlein's last halfway enjoyable novel. The next two fat handfuls included *Ballistics and the Muzzle-Loading Rifle, Myths of Northern Europe, Hitler's War 1939–42, Still 'Tis Our Ancient Foe*, and six more Heinleins: *Expanded Universe, Farnham's Freehold, Starship Troopers, Tunnel in the Sky, How to Take Back Your Government*, and *The Day After Tomorrow*.

I've always believed that a library is a great indicator of a person's interests and character; what did this tell me about O'Dwyer? Well, about half the books were science fiction, so he obviously dug the stuff. This was probably just a chunk of his library, GO- to IR- or thereabouts, so he knew the alphabet, and he had an orderly sort of mind—and it looked as though he didn't distinguish between fact and fantasy. I was thinking that *that* was scary when, suddenly, the door of a police-station garage closed behind me.

I told the cops the same story the same way three times and refused to repeat it again until they let me call a lawyer.

"You *got* a lawyer, Swiftie?" asked the one who rated a chair. Great, just what I needed: someone who'd known the Bodysnatcher. I'd never had to do this before. It wasn't the first time I'd been stopped and questioned by cops, but back then, I'd usually been able to call a friend of mine on the force instead of a lawyer. More effective, and a hell of a lot cheaper. Another cop, younger and darker, laughed. "Sure, there must be lawyers on the streets."

"Only honest ones," replied the chair man. "Look, Swiftie, you've always talked to us before—"

"Never for free," I reminded him.

"And never about a dead cop. Times change." I didn't reply. "Okay," he said. "Book her: illegal residence, vagrancy, obstruction, leaving the scene of a crime, removing evidence . . . anybody got any other suggestions?"

"Stealing an official vehicle?" said one of the women.

"Sounds good. I hope you're not allergic to kelp, Swiftie."

"Nah," I replied, "but I *do* have a low tolerance for slime."

He grinned. "Okay. Do it, and call the PD's office." Then he turned back to me. "Or is there anything else you want to say?"

" 'What I tell you three times is true,' " I muttered, not expecting them to recognize the quote. None of them did.

My lawyer, Quinn, turned out to be a solidly built redhead with a Texan accent, who must have been quite a knockout some twenty years before. I wondered how she'd avoided being made a judge. I told the story a fourth time for her benefit, and she turned to the chair man, rubbing her forehead. "You're robbing me of my beauty sleep for this crap, Yorick?"

"She's—"

"Bullshit. Just because she's a stripper, and the only witness you have, you think you have to lock her up so you'll know where to find her. Jesus, it's lucky they don't print phone books anymore, or do you still have a couple put aside?" I chuckled, and Quinn and Yorick—both about Galloway's age and obviously old friends and/ or enemies—glanced at me curiously. Beating someone with a phone book was an old cop trick last century, a method of avoiding leaving bruises. I'd never experienced it myself, but then, I used to be white. Nowadays, presumably, cops had other methods of not marking their victims.

"What about the caretaker?" I asked, hoping to distract them. "Isn't *she* a witness?"

"Sure," said Yorick sourly. "She was standing right behind Wazaki when he opened the door. At least *somebody* was. Near as we can tell at this date, the room was gimmicked with a claymore mine; everything behind it was burned, everything in front of it shredded. The woman living on the other side of the hall isn't expected to make it either."

"What about this O'Dwyer?" asked Quinn.

"Can't find him," Yorick replied, his tone suggesting that I wasn't going anywhere until they did.

"Put an ICE trace on him."

"Christ, give me *some* credit, willya? We did that soon as we heard her story."

Quinn smiled at me. "You'd be amazed what they can do when it's a cop who's been killed."

"Personally, I think the bank was worried about the insurance," grumped Yorick. "Anyway, O'Dwyer hasn't used his card since Tuesday afternoon. This doesn't necessarily mean he's dead, but I wouldn't bet against it."

"He might have friends," I reminded them.

"You're sure he wasn't in the apartment?" asked Quinn.

"Forensics would have found *something*, even if he'd been sitting on the bomb. They didn't." Yorick turned to me. "What do you know about these friends?"

"I've already told you—"

"How long do you think they'd hide him?"

"Dead or alive?"

"Alive."

I glanced at Yorick's watch. Ten-thirty-two. I must have been here for nigh on seven hours; no fucking wonder I was tired. "Damned if I know. These guys are worst-case-scenario junkies; back in the eighties and nineties they had compounds, bunkers, underground railways, phony ID factories . . . but that was when Armageddon was big business. How much of this they still have, and how much they're willing to risk for a turkey who rings dial-a-fantasy lines to confess to multiple murders . . ."

"Have you ever met this O'Dwyer?" Quinn asked.

"Nah. Heard his voice, and I'd know it again, but I've never actually seen him."

"Or any of his 'friends'?"

"Nah . . . at least not that I know."

"But you'd be willing to tell a court what you've told us?"

"Sure."

"Do you want protective custody?"

"Not if it's just a euphemism for jail."

She nodded. "What if you were offered a WIN and an ICEcard?"

"Hold on a—" said Yorick, getting to his feet. "I mean, okay, maybe after we find this O'Dwyer, if we find him alive."

"And in the meantime? You don't have a safe house somewhere?"

"Yeah, but the paperwork . . . I'll have to get the captain to authorize it, and she—"

"When?"

"Not before eight."

Quinn glanced at her watch and grimaced. "Do you have somewhere to stay for tonight, Theresa?"

"Sure."

"Hold on a—" Yorick expostulated again, turning slightly red.

"We'll want immunity, too," said Quinn.

"What if the captain says no?" asked Yorick. "What if we catch this asshole O'Dwyer? Where do we find her?"

"You can call me," I suggested. "It's only seven ice a minute."

"Well, gentlemen, I think that's it," said Quinn, standing as Yorick's face turned purple. "Can I drive you anywhere, Theresa?"

It was a quiet morning, until the building started shaking.

Star had been taken out to dinner by a client, or so Pauline told me, and she hadn't returned by the time I fell asleep. The quake broke into the middle of a lucid dream, memories from a few years before; my first thought, when I finally awoke, was that someone had stolen my cock . . . and then I saw the light fixture swinging, heard the doors rattling, felt the bed vibrating, and a more primitive, quicker-acting part of my brain shouted *Earthquake! Get under cover, you idiot!* and I obeyed it. I reached for Star and was horrified to discover that she wasn't there: I wasted a few seconds trying to remember what had happened, and then rolled onto the floor and slid under the bed. It wasn't easy; there couldn't have been more than twenty centimeters clearance, max, and I wasn't as skinny as I had been. I had almost remembered who I was by now, for all the use that was likely to be. I know of nothing so mind-freezingly scary as the feeling that the very earth has betrayed you and that there is no safe place anywhere, you can neither run nor hide nor fight. Even when it's over, there's no sense of relief; you wait for the next one and know that it's going to be worse.

There was an occasional crash and crunch and scream, and a few unidentifiable tearing sounds, but most of the noise was muffled by the futon above me, and nothing came through it or landed on the bed hard enough to bend it. I couldn't smell any smoke or gas, which was the only thing that would have gotten me out from under shelter; even when the shaking stopped, I lay there for nearly a minute, too nervous even to breathe loudly, and then I cautiously poked my head out from underneath the bed to look around. Our only window was the transom into the corridor, and all the electric lights were apparently out; it took my eyes some time to adjust to the near darkness. I felt horribly exposed, half certain that something was going to come crashing down into my face—but nothing did. The walls and ceiling were badly cracked, the teleo was lying in pieces on the bed and floor, the fluorescent light was hanging from the ceiling at a thirty-degree angle, and the sliding door had been shaken out of its frame, but I hadn't been buried alive.

I slid out from under the bed and discovered that I couldn't get the door open by myself; I could hear yells and screams, and sounds that might have been people running, but no matter how much noise I made, no one came to help me. Finally, I aimed a disgusted kick at the door and my heel went straight through it. It took a painful minute or so to extract my foot from the polyboard, and maybe half that to tear at the edges of the hole until I could escape.

The corridor was empty of people, but one of the lighting columns from the studio upstairs had crashed through the ceiling/floor, difficult to pass but not impossible; I lost a little skin getting through, but managed not to dislocate or break any bones. I don't really remember much else until I was standing outside, naked and shivering, and thinking, "Oh, no, not again."

There were dozens of people in the street, maybe hundreds. I could hear voices and see bodies but no faces; it was still about an hour before dawn, the sky was clouded over, and there was a strong smell of smoke in the air. The yells and screams had abated slightly, and it was impossible to tell where they were coming from.

"I see you made it," came a familiar grunt from out in the street. Pauline.

"Yeah, I guess so. Everyone else out?"

There was an almost audible shrug: She didn't know, and presumably didn't give a fuck. "I saw Tiffany and Amber," she replied finally. "It's dark in there; nothing we can do 'til morning."

Let me guess, I thought; None of the others owed you any cigarettes. "Leonie! Mariko! Nastassia!" The yell echoed along the street but no one replied, so I rushed to the door and yelled again. There was no sound from inside. "Did Morningstar get back?"

"Haven't seen her all night. Get away from there; you can't help anybody."

I looked back over my shoulder. "I'm freezing," I said, "and I'm going to get some clothes. Do you know if there's a flashlight anywhere?" I knew there were plenty of candles and matches inside, but there might also be gas leaks.

"No," said another voice, much deeper than Pauline's. Leonie was

standing behind me, a two-meter-tall silhouette against the darkness.
"No," Pauline echoed.

I looked up at Leonie. She shrugged slightly, and then followed
me inside.

Brothels and blue-movie studios are designed for privacy, even
when what is happening inside is legal; if you want to watch, you
pay. The windows in the stable were old, toughened glass, opaque
from both sides; it was worse than being in a cave. Leonie and I made
it as far as the corridor by "looking" with our hands. We stopped
after I brushed against something that toppled and crashed, then we
slowly groped our way back to the street.

"There's a Stop-and-Rob on Juniper," Leonie reminded me. "I
think they have some flashlights. Minis, anyway."

I nodded. That was four blocks of broken field running, if the
streets were passable at all. Lots of people would be panicking, and
some of them would be armed.

I glanced at Pauline, huddled there in her quilts, and remembered
that I was still naked and would have been cold if I hadn't been too
frantic to notice. I turned around to talk to Leonie; she was already
halfway to the corner. When I caught her, she stopped long enough
to hand me her fur jacket, revealing her working clothes—a black
latex corset and garter belt. As the jacket barely reached the tops of
my thighs, I was glad of the darkness. No one whistled, or tried to
stop us; I guess we matched the scenery.

The mini-mart had been a maze even before the quake; now it
was more like an Escher print, though at least it wasn't as dark inside
as the stable had been. "Where were the flashlights?"

"Somewhere near the center, I think," Leonie replied uncertainly.
"They were giving them away with those new rechargeables. . . .
Third aisle back, or fourth . . . near the cassettes."

I carefully picked my way through the rubble, sliding my bare feet
along the floor rather than risk treading down on broken glass or
something worse. My nose told me that some bottles had smashed—
there was the sticky piquancy of cola, the dull tang of soy sauce, the
formaldehyde-ish, funereal reek of cheap whiskey, and other smells
I couldn't identify. We searched the third aisle together, inching

along back to back, without finding the flashlights or even the cassettes.

Suddenly, the shadows around me became sharper and began moving. I turned to look behind me, to see where the light was coming from, and noticed Leonie peering over the top of the shelves. The beam swept across her face, and stopped: I caught a last glimpse of her strong, handsome profile before she tried to duck, too late, and something invisible ripped into her face and out the back of her head.

13

TERA

I stood there for a moment, tasting the blood on my lips, then hit the floor: This didn't seem like a good time to be a hero, or heroine, or whatever. As quietly as I could, I searched through the pockets of Leonie's jacket for her knife, without success. The shadows on the ceiling were shifting, and I could hear things being crunched under heavy boots. His gun had been a damn sight quieter than he was, which meant he wasn't a cop, even a rent-a-cop. A looter? Not that it mattered; whoever or whatever he was, he hadn't given Leonie a chance to surrender.

I glanced at the shelves—hitting him with anything lighter than a piece of furniture would probably just piss him off—but they were solidly bolted to the floor My only chance was to get close enough to him to grab his gun hand, and then—

Disarm him? Die trying, more likely, but surprise was the only advantage I had, and most people are surprised when anyone does something that stupid. I removed my jacket as I crept closer to the end of the aisle; there was just enough light to let me see where I was treading, and he was making more than enough noise for both of us. I got there with a few agonizing seconds to spare, and waited.

The thick tube of the silencer was, as I expected, the first thing to appear; the rest of the gun emerged an instant later. I grabbed his wrist and twisted, while swinging Leonie's jacket toward his face; it wrapped itself around his head quite nicely. He fired blindly, spraying the ceiling and the shelves, and swung the heavy flashlight without connecting. I let go of the jacket and jabbed my fingers into his solar plexus.

His right hand was much stronger than my left, and he didn't release his grip on the gun, even when I rammed my knee into his funny bone. The gun had a magazine nearly as long as my forearm, so there was no percentage in waiting for him to run out of ammo. All I could do was keep it pointed as high as possible and away from me, and put up with being sprayed by crap as the bullets tore up the ceiling and the jars and packets on the shelves opposite. I snatched the half-meter flashlight out of his left hand and cracked him across the head with it, but the bastard still didn't go down. Either I wasn't as strong as I thought, or the jacket protected him, or both.

It looked as though I wasn't going to get this turkey's gun without prying it from his cold, dead fingers, and I won't say the thought didn't appeal to me. He grabbed the jacket with his free hand; as soon as I could see his nose, I smashed the butt of the flashlight into it. He rocked and almost overbalanced; I jabbed at his nose again, and connected with the fingers of his left hand. He grabbed the flash and twisted it from my grasp, shining it into my eyes. I hit out blindly, and the edge of my hand connected with something that yielded. The gun fired, the flashlight fell to the floor, and the gunman followed it.

I stood there, still holding his wrist in case he was playing possum, and then rammed my knee into his face. Nothing happened, so I did it again. Then, with my right hand, I twisted the gun from his hand and threw it over my shoulder. Then I dropped the body, grabbed Leonie's jacket and the flashlight, briefly considered grabbing the guns I knew the manager kept under the counter and decided against it, and got the hell out of there.

I had nearly made it across the road before a bullet smacked into the concrete between my feet: I glanced behind me and saw the gunman in the mini-mart's doorway, trying to draw a bead on me. I grabbed the nearest fence, vaulted over it, and nearly landed on a large dog. We stared at each other silently for a second, and I retreated until my back was against the fence. The dog—an enormous shhhepherd—opened its mouth side and closed it again without removing any part of me, probably trying to bark and forgetting that it lacked vocal cords. It sniffed me, its hackles up, and then opened its mouth again. I kicked it under the jaw, hard enough to shut its mouth with an audible crack. Okay, so that was a stupid thing to do, too: the dog rolled over, backed off for a moment, and then the fence shook and the gunman came flying into the yard. He landed on his knees, heavily, and the shhhepherd swung around to face him. Instinctively, the man raised his pistol; true to its training, the dog went for his gun hand, biting it with an audible crunch. The man yelled and fired, and I stood there for a second wondering which of them to hit with the flashlight. Then I grabbed the top of the fence again, leaped back over to the other side, and ran like hell in the general direction of the stable. No one shot at me again, or if they did, they missed.

It didn't take long to find Nastassia in the ruins of the stable, and when I did, I almost wished I hadn't. Finding Mariko was far more difficult. Like me, she'd hidden under the futon when the quake had started; unlike me, she'd been trapped there and stunned when the ceiling had fallen, but she would probably have survived until the rescue workers arrived, even without my help. At best, I'd saved one life at the expense of another.

I carried her outside wrapped in her quilt; she weighed even less than I did. Pauline merely grunted when she saw us, and I wondered if she'd moved at all since Leonie and I had left. She hadn't even asked what had happened. I hoped she was in shock but I didn't really believe it: She was probably just a selfish, apathetic, ignorant blob. I started wondering what Mike Galloway would have been doing now. Probably drowning, if the tsunami that—

"Where are you going?" Pauline asked as I lay Mariko down beside her.

I don't like losing, and sometimes just breaking even isn't good enough. "I'm going to help someone."

"Who?"

I didn't bother answering: She wouldn't have understood, anyway.

I couldn't get close enough to the Highsore to see what had happened to it, but I did see the crowd that had gathered around, and I noticed the elevator shaft was leaning at an unhealthy angle. The sky was gray, with a hint of pink on the horizon; it looked like becoming one of those overcast days that almost makes you wish it had stayed dark. I stood there and stared for a few seconds, and then turned away. The skyline looked different. I could make out the Transamerica Pyramid, though there didn't seem to be as many other tall buildings as there should have been. But there was no evidence of flooding, so if there had been a tsunami, it hadn't reached this far inland—yet. I only had some Apocalyptic's word that it was going to happen at all, and even if he wasn't crazy or lying, he hadn't been too forthcoming with details.

So where to go now? Wazaki was dead, Star had disappeared, Mama might be on Shriek's balcony in Oakland or under tons of ferrocrete. West was my old life, but that was nothing to do with me anymore. North and east was Old Chinatown, and maybe Connie and/or Pat. Northeast it was. I turned east and started walking.

I've never been a morning person, and nearly every sunrise I've seen was a warning to get some sleep. I'd walked most of a block before I realized that the orange sky should have been in front of me, not behind.

The city was burning. I started to run.

There were three of them in the street just ahead of me—four if you include the victim—and no one else in sight. The three looked fairly young, and were armed with nunchaku and knives. The victim had white hair and looked as though he'd already been badly beaten.

I'd lived in New York long enough to know what to do: nothing. Walk down the next street. It's what I would have done before the change, which is probably why I took a step forward, gripping the flashlight like a baseball bat, and swung at the nearest mugger's head with all my strength. He fell facedown into the street and stayed there.

The other muggers looked up, and the one with the knife started walking toward me slowly, giving me a chance to run. I stepped around the fallen mugger and into the middle of the street.

While I stared at the man with the knife, waiting for him to make his move, I tried to remember what my hapkido teacher had taught me. Legs are useful, he'd said; when your adrenaline's flowing, your legs are stronger than your arms, so run if you can, and kick if you can't. And never hit the hard parts with your fist; hit the soft parts, or use an instrument. Knife rushed at me, too fast for me to parry; I stepped aside, and the knife scratched the sleeve of Leonie's jacket without cutting me. I swung the flashlight, but the mugger ducked underneath my arm and slashed at my thigh. I kicked out with my other leg, sending both of us staggering backwards. He came lurching forward again; I tried to parry his knife and accidentally smashed him across the knuckles. He dropped the knife and I jabbed at his nose with the butt of the flashlight. He stepped back, and then kicked at my gut: It probably would have winded me if I hadn't instinctively tried to protect my groin (*real* females instinctively protect their chests, which is probably what he expected me to do). His sneakered foot connected with the flashlight; he flinched, and I grabbed his ankle with my other hand and twisted. He flipped over, hitting the street headfirst; I dropped his foot and stepped back, waiting for him to get up again. I was still waiting when I heard the nunchaku whistling through the air, and I barely managed to duck. I tried to parry it with the flashlight and received a sickening rap on the knuckles for my efforts.

He kept advancing, and I kept retreating, waiting for him to knock his own teeth out or sprain his own wrist or any of the other things beginners with nunchaku do to themselves. He couldn't have been a beginner: He pelted me with blows, and while I managed to protect my head, ribs, and kidneys, I knew I couldn't possibly beat him. Try kickboxing with an airplane propeller someday if you don't believe me.

I was hoping that the old man had managed to crawl away so that I could turn and run, when a hole the size of a Tokyo hotel room appeared in my assailant's chest and there was a god-awful *blammmmm!* I stood there for a few seconds, wearing his heart on my sleeve, and then doubled over and threw up.

"You okay?" yelled the old man.

"Sure," I croaked. "I always do this when I'm having a good time." I took a deep breath and yelled back, *"Okay!"*

He limped toward me v-e-e-e-r-y slowly, a big revolver in his hand. "You got guts, whoever you are. What's your name?"

"Tera."

He seemed to consider this. "I can't see clearly. Are you a woman?"

I was feeling bad enough to tell him the truth, but I settled for "Last time I looked."

"Where from?"

Jesus, didn't this guy know any *easy* questions? "Why did you have to shoot him?"

He laughed. We were close enough, now, to see each other fairly well. "Self-defense."

I decided not to argue with him—I'd had enough of being shot at—and changed the subject. "This doesn't look like your end of town. What were you doing here?"

He glanced over his shoulder. "Pawnbroker's back there, full of guns. Didn't want 'em to fall into the wrong hands."

"Uh-huh." Were there any *right* hands? "How badly are you hurt?"

"A few bruises. Don't worry about me; I'm a survivor."

"Cuts? Broken bones?" He was close enough now that I could see his face: His left eye was shut, his nose looked as though it'd been broken at some time, and there was a little blood in his beard and mustache, which might have meant anything from a bitten tongue to internal injuries.

He spat onto the street, experimentally, and stared into the dark blob. "A few teeth, maybe."

"What happened to your eye?"

He stopped in midstep and put his hand up to his face. "Shit. Bastard must've popped out."

I stared, and he laughed. "It's okay: I lost it over a year ago. Cheap Taiwanese plastic pistol blew up in my hand, and the slide took my eye out. You live and learn. My name's Skye. *No!*"

He was looking past my shoulder, and I spun around to see a heavyset man, dressed in black stonewashed denim, black leather, and a black ski mask, aiming a bulky submachine gun at my back. "Not her," rasped Skye. "Terror here may just have saved my life."

Heavyset stared at both of us, then laughed. "We are not without honor," said Skye softly. I don't know which of us he was talking to, but the man lowered the muzzle of the gun and stepped back. I stooped, picked up the fallen knife and stuck it into my belt, then turned to face Skye.

"Go," he said. "You have my safe-conduct. Don't forget my name."

I backed away from him, slowly; I didn't trust Heavyset not to shoot me in the back, but I didn't think he'd do it without orders. I made it to the intersection safely, and then turned and ran. For a moment, I was bathed in light; I glanced over my shoulder and saw a large car rolling slowly toward me—then stumbled and fell facefirst into the shadows at the side of the street. Heavyset waved at the car—a dirty, ancient Land Rover festooned with enough spotlights for a disco—and it turned into the street I'd just left and chugged to a halt.

I lay there for a moment, wondering why that gun had looked so familiar. As stealthily as I could, I crept back to the corner and peered around. Skye was supervising as three guys in black carried armloads of firearms out of the pawnshop and into the van. It looked as though they already had dozens of weapons in there, which was a hell of a lot more than four guys would ever need.

Even the most fanatical collector wasn't likely to go out picking up guns immediately after an earthquake; nor were these strippers or ordinary looters looking for trade goods. Someone was raising a fucking *army*.

Maybe my sense of time was still screwed up, but it seemed they stripped the store in a couple of minutes, as quickly as if they'd had a lot of practice, then drove away. I took one last look at the Land Rover, trying to read the license plate, but it was obscured by something black, mud or oil or whatever.

When I was sure they were gone, I returned to the street for another look at the fallen muggers. Nunchaku was obviously beyond any help I could give, but the two knife-artists were probably only stunned.

I was still staring down at them, at the holes in their heads and the blood on the street, when something hit me from behind and everything went very bright, and then very red, and then absolutely and impenetrably black.

15

PETER

The building was still intact (except for Hoddy's place, of course), just like Skye had told us it would be; the old man might be vague about everyday shit sometimes, but I was learning to trust his predictions. The wave hadn't come this far east, or the fire this far south, and most of these new high-rises had been designed for resilience, which probably meant that everything inside had been thrown around like dice in a cup. It'd probably be a hospital or something by midday, which didn't leave us much time. I told Scott to keep out of sight and for fuck's sake let me do the talking, and Hoddy led us to the stairwell.

Adams opened the door for me without more than a few seconds' hesitation, and I pulled the trigger before I could even see her face. Stupid nigger bitch wasn't even wearing any Kevlar. Her husband stared as she doubled up, then he came rushing toward me, so I put a round right into his open mouth. I knew they didn't have any kids, thank Christ (even a girl can fire a needler, and the others didn't have shield suits yet), so I told the others to get their asses inside and shut the goddamn door.

I felt like killing Martini for fucking up his hand, or whatever he'd done to get pulled from the team; *him* I could work with. Scott talks mean, but sometimes he freezes when the shooting starts, and Hoddy can't shoot without shutting his bloody eyes.

The room was a mess but not a disaster, and I found the shield suit at the bottom of the closet. It was too small for any of us, but about the right size for Forster—maybe a little big around the hips and too tight in the crotch, but it'd do well enough. The falcon was locked away in a drawer in the desk, of all the stupid places. We got out of there seven minutes behind schedule, and we still had ten more calls to make.

Hoddy managed to keep a straight face until we got back to the jeep, then he started grinning like a zaphead. Maybe he was getting hooked on cop-killing. I filed the thought for future reference and looked at the map.

I woke slowly and reluctantly, with my head feeling as though it were giving birth. Everything was a dark gray, and the skin around my eyes felt tight and drawn: I eventually realized that I was blind-folded, probably with gaffers' tape. I tried moving my hands and discovered that they were tied to something on either side of my head. After nearly a minute of wriggling around, I determined that I was tied to something fairly soft and slightly mobile, probably a metal-frame bed with a headboard. The room was quiet, almost certainly soundproofed, and it reeked like something old and dead and evil, though that might just have been me.

I moved as much of me as could move and decided that I still had all my limbs, even all my fingers. I couldn't say the same for my clothes (well, Leonie's clothes), but I didn't feel as though I'd been raped. I wasn't gagged, so I tried yelling a little. A few seconds later a door opened behind me, and then slammed shut again.

Some time later—seconds? minutes?—the door opened again, and I felt, rather than heard, someone walk in. "Look," I rasped, "I don't know who you think I am—"

"I have no idea," the someone said—someone female, late twenties to forties, speaking crisp English with a trace of an Asian accent, probably Japanese. "Suppose you tell me?"

"I'm Tera—Theresa Bird. How long have I been here?"

"Two nights."

Ouch: No wonder my mouth was dry. "Where am I?"

"You're in no position to ask questions."

"Yeah, well, forgive me if I don't get up."

She didn't laugh. "What is the last thing you remember?"

"Uh . . . the earthquake. I mean, a few minutes, maybe an hour, after the quake. I was headed for Old Chinatown, and there was this fight, uh, three young guys against one old guy, outside this hockshop. I thought they were looters, mugging him or something, and . . ." I told her the rest of the story as accurately as I could. She seemed to consider it for a few seconds, and then asked, "You hit two of them with a flashlight?"

"One of them. The other I threw, and he must have hit his head."

"Both of them were dead when we arrived. You didn't kill them?"

"I don't *think* I killed them. I guess it's possible—but when I saw them again, they looked like they'd been shot, not just . . . I didn't have a gun, you must *know* I didn't have a gun. . . ."

"We didn't hear any shots."

"Silencers. They . . ." Suddenly, through the fuzz in my head, came two clear memories: The first goon with the bulky SMG, and a picture in a book about guns, an MP5 something-or-other, the sort of gun O'Dwyer'd said was used in the dojo massacre.

The gun that was used in the dojo massacre . . .

I shook my head, as best I could. Of course *that* might be a coincidence, but after half a lifetime of casual work, I know how to tell someone with experience from someone without. The men in black had planned and rehearsed that raid on the hockshop, which meant that they must have been expecting the quake.

"They . . . ?" she prompted.

"I only saw two of them clearly, and one had an MP5, the sort with a silencer built in."

A pause. "Do you know who they were?"

"I can guess. Apocalyptics, Survivalists, White Riders . . . they may even be the ones who shot up the Sacramento Street dojo. From the way they were collecting firearms, I think they're getting some sort of small army together. The old man said his name was Skye. That's all I know."

"Why Chinatown?"

"What?"

"You said you were going to Chinatown. Why?"

"I work there, teaching English. . . . Some of my friends teach there, probably live there. . . . I was hoping to find some of them still alive."

"Names?"

"Pat Hong . . . Connie . . . uh, I don't know her surname, but she gave me my job, she's in charge of *something* . . . that's all I know. Look, can I have something to drink? My throat feels like something died in it."

I felt her start slightly. "Later," she said. "Where are you from?"

"I don't know. I don't remember my parents, or any place other than here. . . . This *is* still San Francisco, isn't it?" The echoes suggested that the two of us were in a normal-sized room, maybe three by three by three, with a solid ceiling and a door that closed—a luxury, in a ruined city.

"How old are you?"

"I don't know. Eighteen? Twenty? Twenty-five? Does it *matter?*"

"Where do you normally live?"

I groaned. "I work nights in a phone-sex stable on Isis Street. Before that, I used to sleep in the Highsore, or on a balcony on Haight, or a dozen other places, most of which are probably underwater by now. How bad is the damage?"

My interrogator was silent for a moment, and then I heard her stand and walk away. I heard the door close, and listened for her breathing, just in case she was still inside but wanted me to think I was alone. After what felt like a minute, I decided that she wasn't there, and began testing my bonds. Whoever had tied me to that bed had known what they were doing, and I soon decided to save my energy. The room seemed to grow slightly darker, but that might have been my imagination.

Finally, the door opened again, and this time two women walked in. My interrogator asked, "Did you know the quake was going to happen?"

"*What?*"

"Did you know the quake was going to happen?"

"I'd heard it predicted, but I didn't believe it. At least I don't think I did. I really don't know."

Something plastic-tasting was placed against my lips, and half a cupful of warm water, or something equally wonderful, was poured into my mouth. I spluttered at first, then gulped it down greedily.

"Where did you hear this?"

"It was on the Net—a spam. Connie showed it to me when I told her about the—" Suddenly, but maybe too late, I shut up.

"About what?"

Oh *shit*. I tried thinking quickly, but my head was hurting too badly.

"About *what?*"

Who the fuck was this woman, anyway? Whose side was she on? It seemed unlikely that an Asian would team up with the Apocalyptics, and even less likely that the Apocalyptics would let her, but she might be a mercenary or . . .

Suddenly there was a gurgling sound, and I realized that she was drinking the water she'd brought me. Pain crawled slowly up my throat and into my mouth, and the urge to say something, *anything*, that might persuade her to let me drink began thumping in my head, drowning out all lesser thoughts. "Water . . ." I rasped.

"What did you tell Connie?"

I cursed her in Korean, and she laughed, and replied in the same language—then repeated the question. "The same thing I told the cops," I replied.

"And what did you tell the cops?"

What difference could it make if I told her? If the women were with the Apocalyptics, they might kill O'Dwyer (which wouldn't cost me any sleep), but there wouldn't be any point in their killing Connie. If they were on Connie's side, they'd know I was telling the truth. If they were cops . . . "Take this fucking thing off my face!"

"What did you tell the cops?"

"I'll tell you when I can see you."

"I can wait all day," she replied. "Can you?"

"You can kill me if you want," I rasped. "I sure as shit can't stop you. But I'm not going to tell you another fucking thing until I can see your face."

The two women walked away from me; there was a hasty, whispered discussion, and then the door opened and closed. One of the women strode back to the bed and ripped the gaffers' tape (and, I suspect, my eyebrows) off my face. "You've got balls," she said in English.

I used to have, I thought, but they wouldn't have helped me in this situation. When I managed to open my eyes and focus, I saw my interrogator standing over me: a short, muscular, not-very-attractive woman wearing a dirty red bathrobe. There was a large knife in her left hand—probably a kitchen knife. "So?"

Haltingly, I told her about O'Dwyer and the dojo massacre. "I can't prove anything—but that doesn't matter. He's murdered a cop, now; they won't let him get away."

"Why didn't you tell us this earlier?"

"I didn't know who you were. I mean, I *still* don't, but I . . ."

She smiled, then picked up the cup of water from the floor and put it to my lips. I glanced around the room but saw nothing to indicate where I was: no windows in sight, no furniture apart from the bed, no light except from a small battery-powered lamp, a heavy-looking self-closing door, no attempt at decoration. A basement somewhere, presumably— or a bunker. "Do you know who *you* are?" my interrogator asked softly.

"What?"

"Where did you learn to fight?"

"Fight?"

"You knocked out two trained fighters and stood up to a third, without even being scratched. What do you call that?"

"I call it luck." She snorted. "Look, I sneaked up behind one and got in one good hit—just like someone did to me. The knife-artist . . . well, isn't it an old saying that the best swordsman in the world isn't scared of the second-best, but the worst?"

"I know the saying, but I don't believe you're *that* bad. Have you ever trained?"

"I took a few hapkido classes, about"—oops, that was probably before Swiftie was born—"six, seven years ago, I guess."

"How did you sneak up on them?"

I could've told her that I studied library science for a semester, but I don't think she would've believed me. "It's a useful skill on the streets. Besides, they were right near the corner: I didn't have to sneak very far."

She looked at me skeptically, then turned and walked out. "Hey!"

"Yes?"

I tugged at the bonds tying my hands to the bed—electric flex wrapped in pillowcases—and asked, "Please?"

"Later." I stared. "There's someone else who wants to see you," she said. "I can bring you some food—and a bedpan, if you need one?"

"Yeah. Thanks."

She walked out, leaving the electric lamp on; in the moment before the door shut behind her, I glimpsed a very large and equally poorly lit room outside. I have no idea how long I waited before the door opened again.

The woman who brought in the bowl of rice was small, blond, and elfin-looking, and she wore an old gi tied with a dark (black?) belt. I didn't recognize her until she was sitting by the bed with the light on her face, and I noticed her blue eyes. "Cannon!"

She started slightly, almost spilling the rice. "Do you remember me?" I continued. "We . . ."

She was silent—so silent, in fact, that I thought I'd made a mistake. "I'm Tera," I said. "I used to call myself Swiftie, but . . . well, I had to change my name. It seemed like a good idea at the time. . . ."

The spoon hovered above my lips: I could talk or eat, but I couldn't do both. "I'm sorry," I said, "but I thought you were someone I knew."

No answer. I decided to eat. A few spoonfuls later, she murmured in Japanese, "Where were you Christmas Day?"

"What? I was . . . I went to Saint Mary's for dinner. Was I supposed to meet you somewhere?"

The baleful look she gave me would have meant yes in any language. "So sorry," I muttered. "I've been having a problem remembering things lately. I think I was hit in the head. Look, wouldn't it be easier for both of us if you untied one of my hands? Just one?"

"Yes, but I can't. Not yet."

"So you *are* going to let me go? Eventually?"

"I think so. Sozu-san is angry that you interfered, and I think she would've been happier if I'd hit you a little harder and killed you outright."

Something about the way she said Sozu-san made it sound like a title rather than a name, but my Japanese vocabulary didn't stretch that far. "*You* hit me?"

"I didn't recognize you," she replied simply. "And you were in the wrong place at the wrong time. If you'd had a gun, I probably *would* have killed you: I knew you weren't Skye, but I guess there must be *some* women in his sick little band."

"Who is Skye?"

Cannon watched me for a moment, then fed me another spoonful of rice. "You really don't know?" I shook my head. "What about Gary Donner?"

I swallowed. "He predicted the quake. That's all I really know."

"I don't know much more; none of us took him seriously before. Donner has a following, mostly thanks to his radio show, but no group affiliation, and he's been careful to keep his hands clean. Skye used to be a Klansman, Grand Cyclops or something, but he's supposed to have given that up when he started running for governor in Arizona with Am Nat backing. Fortunately, it didn't help. Eventually, the Nuts realized that they had a loser and dumped him for a moderate, whatever *that* means when the Nuts say it, though officially he retired because of poor health. He dropped pretty much out of sight—apparently he really *was* sick, and there was even a rumor that he'd shot himself—until last year, when he sold his business and moved to Oregon."

"What sort of business?"

"Private security firm. He 'invented' the shhhepherd—he'd been cross-breeding wolves with Alsatians to get dogs that were big and nasty enough to eat strippers, then removed their larynxes. I don't know whether that's done surgically or by genetic engineering, but he has a patent on them." I nodded; the breed (brand?) was a couple of years old, and already almost as popular as muteweilers. "He took the money from that and branched into selling firearms and surveillance equipment and running a very successful school for rent-a-cops—"

"A private army," I murmured in English.

"What?"

"Just a hunch. What did he do in Oregon?"

"Started again from scratch; a new firm, Alpha Security."

"Why did he move?"

Cannon shrugged. "We don't know. Maybe he was short on ready cash—he had some hospital bills to pay; heart attack, I think—and found that costs were lower up north. Alpha has a reputation for employing and retraining ex-cons, a lot of them hard-core violent types, as guards, and I suspect he's underpaying them. Rumor has it both the state and federal governments pay for their training at his rent-a-cop academy and turn a blind eye to some of the other crap he pulls because he has such a good record of cutting down on recidivism, which keeps prison numbers down." She sighed. "There's also a rumor that he's been running a service for dangergamers—finding victims, providing alibis and native guides, disposing of the bodies, all sold like a package tour—and needed a new hunting ground. Or maybe he'd just made too many enemies in Texas. We really don't know."

"I thought dangergames were just an urban myth, like alligators in the sewers." Dangergamers, named after the frequently remade thriller *The Most Dangerous Game*, supposedly paid to hunt human prey, usually strippers and illegal immigrants who could be made to disappear without being missed. I'd never seen any evidence that dangergamers actually existed, though Mama certainly feared them, and I'd thought the story was just a fable started by frustrated hunters not wealthy enough to get a license for other game. It would be too easy for the service provider to blackmail the clients; the only way for the hunters to remain anonymous would be by using money that the ICE couldn't trace, and even then the risks were enormous.

"Maybe they are," Cannon conceded. "I know no one's ever caught anyone involved with it. Anyway, once in Oregon, Skye opened some new Web sites and newsgroups and mailing lists, some aimed at confirmed Apocalyptics, and others for *potential* Apocalyptics; gun nuts and survivalists and old skinheads and the religious right, of course, but also wargamers, military science-fiction fanatics, UFO-worshipers, gay-bashers, conspiracy junkies. . . . Not all of these are going to become White Riders, or Race Warriors, or whatever he wants to call them, but some will contribute in other ways: ice, information, alibis, sanctuary, or just by spreading rumors and propaganda. And they're not *members* of anything: There's no dues, no uniforms or badges, no names—except for one, which you won't find mentioned anywhere on the Nets."

"Which is?"

"The Apostles," Cannon replied in English, then switched back to

Japanese. "We don't know whether that just means Skye and Donner, or everyone who listens to them, or whether there's actually some real organization. There's a rumor that they're trying to build a pyramid scheme, twelve apostles each recruit and arm twelve apostles, who in turn recruit and arm another twelve, but whether this is a reality or someone's dream, we have no way of knowing."

"There were four gunmen at the dojo."

Cannon shrugged. "So I've heard, and about the same number attacked the Japanese restaurant in Harlan Place and the dorm in Berkeley. And Skye and Donner both had alibis for all three nights; even some of Skye's own followers say he's crazy, but no one thinks he's *stupid*."

"Have you ever heard of a Roy O'Dwyer?"

"Sure. He's wanted for killing a cop. A *nisei* cop, but they're looking for him anyway—or they were, until *this* happened."

"How bad is the damage?"

"Chinatown's . . . well, the fire's out, but there's not much left of it, and what there is looks unsafe. The radio says there are more than a hundred dead, thousands still missing, and maybe half a million homeless—who weren't homeless before, that is. The initial shock was an eight-point-eight on the Richter scale, and there've been two big aftershocks while you've been out; a lot of the hospitals have collapsed, and the rest are dying room only, everything west of Broderick Street was either flooded or buried in mud, the Highsore and most of the freewayvilles have collapsed, there's cracks in some of the dams in Oakland and a piece out of the Golden Gate, no power or phones or water you can trust, the subways have been shut down, there's drowned bison on the streets and boats in the trees."

"*Thousands?*" I gasped as it finally sank in.

Cannon nodded. "There's nearly four thousand winners still missing, last we heard, and no one knows how many strippers were in the Highsore, or the parks, or the tunnels and storm drains." She grimaced. "A dam cracked over in Berkeley, and though they had time to get nearly all of the people out, they're all homeless now too. The army's setting up tents and giving out food and stuff, but you can't get in unless you're a winner: It's supposed to be so they can find the missing sooner, and you can believe that if you like."

"So you've set up your own here."

"What do you mean?"

"That's what this place is, isn't it?"

She scraped the last of the rice out of the bowl. "I have to go. Sozu-san will be in to see you later. Do you want the bedpan?"

I looked at her and tried to smile. "You *know* what I want." Cannon didn't smile back; she just walked out, taking the lamp with her. Damn.

There is only so much you can do when tied to a bed, alone, in a completely dark and rather soundproof room. I tried listening to the voices outside, recognized the rhythm of Japanese with some syllables that were probably English, but was unable to pick out any words.

I passed the time with memory games, silently reciting as much as I could remember of some of my favorite poems: "Jabberwocky," "My Last Duchess," "Monsieur Prudhomme," "The Love Song of J. Alfred Prufrock" (okay, so that one got away), "The Raven," a few haiku and sestinas, *"Die Lorelei,"* "For Anne Gregory." After that, I ran through my internal little black book, which didn't take long— I'm okay with addresses, but I can't remember phone numbers worth a damn, never could. Then I checked on my languages: "Bed" in Japanese is *betto*, in Spanish *la cama*, in Portuguese *a cama*, in Mandarin *chuang*, in Cantonese *chohng*, in Thai *chimdaa*—no, that was Korean; *dtiang* is Thai. "Beautiful," another word I always made a point of learning in any language, is *utsukushii* in Japanese (I always loved the sound of that one; it's difficult to say unless you mean it), *meili* in Mandarin, *hou* in Cantonese, *bella* in Spanish and Italian, *belle* in French, *skoen* in Swedish, *schoen* in German, *suai* in Thai. Suddenly, I realized that I had free-associated into thinking about Angela (with nostalgia, yet). A moment later, I realized that the "me" in those "memories" was Tera, and all the lovemaking was female-to-female. I tried to remember having sex with Angela, but without much success: I could see it happening, see her sitting astride me sliding up and down on a cock, but I couldn't *feel* it anymore, and it didn't turn me on; I gave up voyeurism a long time ago.

I lay there in the darkness, trying hard to think of something else; I may have drifted off to sleep without knowing it, and I have no idea how much time passed before Cannon and Sozu-san returned.

"How are you feeling?" Sozu-san asked, in Cantonese.

"I'm still alive," I replied.

"Good. I'm going to [something] you now. You may not be able to walk [something], but I'd like you to get up as soon as [something]. Okay?"

"I understood *most* of that," I replied, also in Cantonese, then, in English, "You're going to untie me, and you want me to get up and walk as soon as I can? Is that right?"

She nodded, then asked, "What languages do you know?"

"English, Spanish, Japanese . . . pretty good Mandarin, Russian, French, German, a little Cantonese, a little Korean and Thai . . ."

"Khmer? Vietnamese?"

"No . . . only a few words." I watched her face for some flicker of expression, wondering just what I was confessing to. She merely grunted softly and untied my left hand, then stood back. I was obviously meant to do the rest myself, and I tried to free my right hand, but without success; the knot was too complex, and I'd never been a Boy Scout. About a minute later she untied it for me, and then stood back again. I sat up slowly and carefully, then went to work on the bonds on my feet. Using both hands, I managed to free myself after a few minutes, feeling that I'd failed some sort of test. I flexed my legs cautiously until I felt strength seeping back into them, and then slid off the bed and stood. Cannon and Sozu-san stepped back slightly, but said nothing.

I managed one rather shaky lap of the bed, being careful not to venture too near the door. On my second pass, Cannon stepped slightly closer to me, then kicked my legs out from underneath me. When I tried to stand, she grabbed my left wrist and threw me onto my back. Sozu-san's knife reappeared in her hand, and the next thing I knew, the point was a millimeter away from my throat. I lay as still as possible, too scared to even *breathe* violently.

"*Who are you?*" asked Sozu-san again, in Japanese.

"What?"

"*Who are you?*"

"I . . . who do you want me to be?" The knife touched my skin. "I'm Tera—I told you that. I used to be called Swiftie."

Sozu-san glanced at Cannon. "No," Cannon said. "The walk is all wrong—it's kind of familiar, but it's not Swiftie. The accent is different, and the rhythm of her speech—and Swiftie didn't know Cantonese."

"She might have learned. . . . Is that all?"

"Oh, the body's hers, right down to the scars, but it's not *her*. I couldn't have taken *her* out with one kick, not like that. I'm not even sure you could."

Sozu-san shrugged, and then barked a few syllables at me. They might have been Vietnamese or Khmer, or Lao, or Burmese, or Grand High Martian. I didn't respond. Then she muttered something unrecognizable in what sounded like Korean. "How long have you been Tera?" she asked in English.

I glanced at Cannon. "Since Christmas morning."

"And before that?"

"I was known as Swiftie."

"No," said Cannon. "Try again."

I stared, and then realization hit me hard enough to leave me speechless for a moment. The Bodysnatcher may have been trapped in Swiftie's body for months or even years, but someone else had owned it before him, someone else had died in that alley—and *someone* must have known her, must have noticed the changes that time around.

I looked into Cannon's eyes. So, she'd known all *three* of me: Tera, Swiftie, and—

"My name was Mike Galloway," I said. "Swiftie . . . stole my body." And I told them the story, as best I could.

M artini was about to smash his right fist into his left palm, the way he'd always done when he was pissed, then he suddenly remembered that he didn't really have a right fist anymore. "Fuckit, Gary, you shoulda told us about this *before!* Taking guns is one thing, but jewelry and other shit . . . We're supposed to be *stopping* looters. Why didn't you tell us?"

"You didn't need to *know* earlier," Gary thundered. "Are you losing your nerve, Tyrone?"

Skye, who was sitting in the corner between two of his big fucking dogs, swiveled his chair and looked at Martini, who turned away from that accusing one-eyed stare, caught between it and Gary's fury. I don't think Martini would've bothered answering a question like that from anybody else (or let them use his Christian name, which he hated), and I'm not sure any of the rest of us could've answered honestly. Whoever had planned this, Gary or Skye or both of them together, had been smarter than I ever would've guessed; none of us could back out now—except maybe Martini. He'd helped plan everything, sure, but *he* hadn't killed any cops.

"You know he's not," said Scott, calmly stroking his beard like it was a guitar or some sort of pet. "None of us are. It's just . . . I mean . . . executions are one thing, the dangergames and the gutlegging gave us money when we needed it, but *theft* is—"

"How did you get *your* shield suit, Scott?" I asked softly. He flushed.

"Rocky's right," said Skye, smiling. "Desperate times require desperate measures. We have weapons to buy, special weapons. Heavy weapons, state of the art, hideously expensive, but *necessary* if we want to match our enemies' strength, so we need ice. Besides, it's not *theft*; we're reclaiming stolen property. A lot of this gold was stolen from Fort Knox, back before the ICE Age; stolen from Americans, from *us*. If the slants hadn't made cash illegal, we could pay this with good honest American cash—you do remember cash, don't you, Scott? Sure, I still have some, most of us do, and it will be worth something again, but right now nobody else *wants* it, not even our friends in the army." He stroked his beard. "And heroes have stolen from their enemies before. Jason stole the Golden Fleece, the Greeks looted Troy, the Nazis collected art treasures by the kiloton, the Bruder Schweigen robbed armored cars. It's an honorable tradition." He turned to Martini. "And we're sending you back to the Barracks to relieve Mitch."

Martini sat up straight. "Fuckit, I didn't mean—"

"The rest of you can go," said Gary. "Not you, Rocky. Ron . . ."

Martini waited until there was only the four of us in the room before exploding again. "Why *me*, for fuck's sake?"

"I'm not sure you've fully recovered yet," Gary said with surprising softness. "Right now, you're more useful there than here."

"And *somebody* has to feed the dogs," said Skye, with a straight face. Martini glared, and his arm jerked as though he were going to give Skye the finger—then stopped as he remembered his missing hand. Gary hammered on the table. "And I trust you out of my sight," he continued. "I can't say that for everybody."

Martini quieted down and nodded curtly. Gary dismissed him, and he stomped away, slamming the door behind him.

"*Can* we trust him?" he asked Skye.

The old man shrugged. "I'm not sure we can *rely* on him anymore. I think he's lost a lot more than his hand, but he's not the traitor."

"Who, then?"

Another shrug. Sometimes I couldn't tell whether he was being secretive or whether he just hated admitting there might be something he didn't know or might've forgotten, but lately he'd been getting even more mysterious than usual. "*I* don't trust O'Dwyer," I volunteered, "and Scott talks too much, even when he's sober."

"I don't blame you," said Skye, "but we need Scott, and Hoddy still has his uses. No, I suspect the traitor has yet to appear."

"But he *will* appear?"

"Treachery is inevitable." said Skye with a gleam in his eye and a smile that would scare the shit out of most men. "One can only be ready for it. The readiness is all."

That," said Sozu-san, "is the most preposterous story I've ever heard. Are you sure you don't want to change any of it?"

I didn't think I could shrug without cutting my own throat, so I merely grimaced. "I'd *love* to change the past, but I can't change the story."

Sozu-san didn't even smile. "Why the hell couldn't you have hit her a little harder?" she asked Cannon.

"I believe her—or him," replied Cannon, to my amazement. "I don't know if any of *Swiftie's* story was true, but . . . this isn't Swiftie. I've seen her change like this *before*, remember? And you saw her walk; she moves like someone who's had a lot of practice, but also like she's used to needing a lot more room, someone taller and wider and heavier, and she slouches like someone who's spent a lot of years behind a desk. And I can't think of a better explanation; can you?"

Sozu-san scowled and switched to Japanese. "You knew this—Galloway?"

"Not like Swiftie did. To me, he was just this guy who let us make love on his balcony; I don't think he even watched. And he gave us food and coffee sometimes, and some clothes once."

"A winner," Sozu-san sneered, "and white." She stood and the knife disappeared into her sleeve. "We've wasted too much on him already. Get rid of him."

"*She* can help us. She told us about O'Dwyer, taught English at the dojo, she's worked in hospitals and refugee camps, she can still fight—"

"*He* isn't your sensei," the older woman said with what sounded like an attempt at gentleness. I looked at Cannon, and guessed that her sensei had taught her much more than whatever martial art she had a black belt in. "And if his story is true, he's a waste of a body; he hasn't any loyalty to anyone or anything. Let him fend for himself."

"We've decided to let you go," said Cannon three nights later. "We can't afford to keep feeding you, so we held a kind of trial; sorry you weren't invited." She looked rueful. "We have a rule that anyone who votes for the death penalty has to be prepared to carry out the sentence, so people who aren't sure tend to give the benefit of the doubt. A majority voted to let you leave, as long as we made sure that you couldn't find your way back. No one voted to let you stay; not even me. It wouldn't have been safe. For you. Some of the people you . . . the people who were shot by Skye's friends, have family here." I nodded; something in her expression told me that the decision not to have me killed had been very close. "I wish we could find Connie," she murmured, producing a roll of gaffer tape, "or Pat Hong, but we can't. I'm sorry . . . what should I call you?"

"Tera, I guess. Mike Galloway was someone else; even I can't remember him very well anymore. Who was"—I glanced down at my body—"before Swiftie? Your sensei?"

"Oh, she was always called Swiftie, on the streets—she was fast, very fast. She called herself Naja, which was what Sozu-san called her . . . but Naja's dead now, isn't she?"

"So Swiftie said. Was Sozu-san *her* sensei?"

"A long time ago; Swiftie became much better than her. How did you know?"

"I'm a teacher myself," I replied. "I recognize the signs. Naja—that was Swiftie's name here?" *Naja* meant "cobra" in Hindi or Bengali or some Indian language, and I thought it was the name for the genus, but that was all I knew.

"It was her name for herself." She cut a strip of tape and placed it over my eyes. I looked at her face for as long as I could. "I'm so sorry about this," she said as she helped me to my feet. It occurred to me, suddenly, that I might have been wrong about her name—not Cannon, the gun, but Kannon, the Japanese Goddess of Mercy. She was best known for exposing herself to some male god in order to make him laugh, hence the Japanese expression "going to see Kannon," going to see a strip show.

"What's so funny?"

Kannon. Stripper. "Never mind." He who laughs last didn't get the joke in the first place.

I've always had a pretty fair sense of direction, but Kannon led me around so many corners and over so many heaps of rubble that by the time she stopped, I had no idea where I'd been. The usual nonvisual cues no longer worked; the city sounded and smelled too different. There were some hills, ups and downs, but they weren't murderous, and I don't remember any stairways or tunnels. "Count to twenty slowly, and then remove the tape," Kannon whispered maybe half an hour later, and kissed me quickly. "*Sayonara*—and good luck."

"Thanks," I said, but there was no reply, not even an audible footfall.

Helping search through the rubble of the Highsore for bodies was probably the second worst job I'd ever had, but they gave us three war-surplus meals a day, an occasional change of clothes, a place to stay after curfew and a cot under cover to sleep on, and they didn't ask too many embarrassing questions.

I'd been working there for four days when I noticed one of the cops who'd helped interrogate me after Wazaki's death, the young African American whose name I hadn't caught. He didn't recognize me, and didn't seem happy to know me when I introduced myself. I probed gently and learned that he hadn't lost any loved ones in the quake because he hadn't had any to lose; he just hated being homeless. "Flood and fire damage, too; they say it'll take at least six months to repair," he grumped, "and nothing's ever finished on time or under budget. Half of the stations are unusable, too, the computers and phone lines are still down, power's rationed, we've got to organize everything with pens and paper, and there's a lot of us missing or in the hospital or maybe even dead, I don't know. Bloody nightmare."

"What about Yorick?"

"Lieutenant York to you, and what about him?"

"Is he okay?"

"Sure, you couldn't kill that bastard without leveling the bloody city. Internal Affairs've tried three times, and he just walked away. Why'd you ask?"

"Just conversation. With Wazaki dead, he's the only cop I know by name." I looked around at the shield suits. "I'd thought the National Guard would be running things by now."

"They're around. They dropped a whole shitload of engineers and signals corps down at SFO, night after the quake. Cleared a few runways, set up a new control tower, and got the first planeload of evacs out by noon the next day."

"Evacs?"

"Didn't you know? They brought planes in from all over, and took 'em out as soon as they were full. I hear there's nearly two million already bugged out, maybe more." He shrugged. "Of course, they were all citizens, could prove who they were, and they had friends or families to go to, or enough ice to get by. Most of 'em, anyhow. But there was no reason for 'em to stay here; most of the businesses are shutting down, at least in the short term, so the jobs are gone, though they'll probably start coming back after all the bodies are recovered and the insurance companies pay up. Lucky they shut down all the nuclear plants on the fault, or we'd *all* have to go." He stared at the rubble. "I wonder if your friend O'Dwyer got out. It wouldn't have been easy. Maybe we'll find him under that shit, or drowned in a ditch somewhere. Something to look forward to, hey?"

"He wasn't my friend, and I wouldn't know him if I saw him. Just his voice."

"Me neither, but I guess his dental rec"—he glanced at the rubble—"uh, geneprint's all we need. You don't really think he could've cooked up another ID, do you? Not nowadays?"

"I don't know." I was fairly sure he hadn't gone any farther than Oregon, and I suspected he was still in town, dead or alive. If that many people had left, there'd be plenty of places to hide. "How bad has the looting been?"

"There's been some, but not as much as you'd expect—never is, 'cept after a riot. Or a blackout. I guess quakes are just too scary."

"What about guns?"

"Huh?" I gave him the *Reader's Digest* version of the story about Skye and company looting the hockshop. He considered this, then asked, "You really think they *knew* the quake was coming?"

"Yes." The tsunami hadn't been anywhere near as bad as Donner had predicted; it had thrown a lot of mud and a few boats a few blocks, drowned some bison in Golden Gate Park and animals in the zoo, but it had petered out before it reached Haight-Ashbury, and probably helped put out a few fires when the gas lines had ruptured. Most of the "flood damage" was actually caused by liquefication—the soil turning to mud, causing buildings to sink. Otherwise, the prediction had been dead on.

The shield shook his head. "Can we just say that they were *ready* for an emergency?" I was silent. "Look, when I was a boy, back in the nineteen eighties, every idiot claimed to know when the *world* was going to end. Even the President told us we might be the last generation, and I gotta give him credit for trying. My folks believed him, like they believed Oral Roberts when he claimed that God would kill him if he didn't get more money. They believed the televangelists when they predicted the rapture for 1997 because it was six millennia after 4004 B.C. and Christ was born in 4 B.C., then 1998 because it was three times 666, then 1999 because of Nostradamus, then 2000 because of the millennium bug. They were a little dubious by 2001, and getting pretty skeptical by 2002. Point is, if you keep predicting a disaster and you don't get bogged down in details, you're probably going to be right *eventually*. Okay, so you read this crap on the Net a few days beforehand, but how do you know they haven't been crying wolf and changing the dates every week?"

I shrugged. I wasn't convinced. "But I'll tell 'em about the guns," he continued. "Y'know, it's a pity you're not a citizen. You'd make a good cop." I think he meant it as a compliment.

A week after the quake, when we'd almost given up hope of finding any more survivors, I saw Tiffany in the line for breakfast. She told me that she had a job cleaning bedpans in the improvised hospital in the Moscone Center, where her "patients" included Mariko and Commissioner Shaw (rumor had it he'd had a heart attack but was refusing to leave the city), and that Pauline had already flown out and was hoping for work in a retirement home. I told her what had happened to Leonie and asked if she'd seen Star.

"Not since she went out, night before the quake. Maybe she flew out too."

"She was a winner?"

She laughed. "Used to be a fuckin' shield. She never tell you?"

"No." I knew a little of Tiff's history—she was born in Mexico, and had been an exotic dancer until her silicon-stuffed breasts had ruined her back—but none of Star's.

"Been married, too," she said vaguely. "Think she's even got a kid, somewhere."

"Did you see the guy who took her out?" I fished, hoping against hope that it wasn't O'Dwyer.

"I got a glimpse," she admitted. "Tall, blond, nice buns, looked enough like Star to be her brother or something . . . either that or he was there to make a tape. Most of *my* clients look more like Danny DeVito."

"Did you hear his name?"

"Peter. And I think he was another shield."

I blinked. "What?"

"Well, she acted like she knew him, and he had a gun in his armpit—big gun, not just a stinger—and a smaller one in an ankle holster. And he walked like a shield . . . and he didn't look around, like he didn't want to see something. And his hair was real short and sort of . . . uniform, *capisce*? Like he was either a cop or gay? And he didn't act gay."

I nodded. "But you don't know where they went?"

"They said they were going to eat; that's all I heard." She glanced around the room, made sure that everyone was too busy eating to listen in, and said quietly, "You think they're going to send us home when this is over?"

"I don't know."

"I guess if they do, *I* can always walk back. Where you from?"

"It's that bad in Mexico?" I evaded. I'd taught English in Mazatlán, but that had been nearly thirty years ago and I'd been obscenely wealthy by local standards. Tiffany responded by making some gagging sounds.

I caught up with Johnson—the city cop—later in the day, while I was sifting through the rubble at the Highsore in the hope of finding something that would help ID some of our dead. He confirmed that the plan was to start repatriating the illegals by the end of the month, and finish by summer, when the evacuees were expected to start returning home. "But whether or not they'll be able to make that sort of schedule is anybody's guess. You want to stay, huh?" I nodded. "I hear they're going to finish tearing down the freeways, and their plans for the Tenderloin and Chinatown are pretty radical. The urban planners've been waiting for a quake like this for *years*. And I hear that the navy is thinking of shutting down its facilities here if they're too badly damaged, and moving its people down to San Diego or up to Seattle, and the air force may do the same. Oh, by the way, I passed on that story of yours. Seems you were right. Lot of gun shops, pawnbrokers, even some private collections, been stripped down to the last round of ammo. Looters walked right past computers, cameras, teleos, all sorts of good gear, just took the firearms—oh, and some jewelry, though that was probably some other gang."

I shrugged. "Jewelry's easy to carry, and if you know real from fake . . ."

"Yeah, I guess so." He hesitated, then added, "They found some bodies, too, with holes in them. Looked like nine-mil autofire. They took 'em up to Sacramento for autopsy. I asked them to let me know what they found."

"Thanks."

They let him know, all right. They let me know, too, at four in the morning. I thought it was just a nightmare, until I saw Kannon.

The Guard caught her out after curfew," Johnson explained, before he realized how that sounded. She'd just come out of surgery, and we were standing beside her gurney in the corridor while they tried to find somewhere else to put her. "*They* didn't shoot her," he added hastily. "They were doing a patrol, checking the damage from that aftershock last night. She was already badly wounded—she started running away when she saw the jeep, but she'd lost a lot of blood, even though she'd been bandaged pretty well, and they caught her. . . ." He rubbed the sleep out of his eyes. "I heard she broke the wrist of the first man to grab her, but that can't be right; he musta fallen or something. Anyway, she hasn't told us a goddamn thing. Shock, I guess.

"They searched the area, found dozens of bodies—last I heard, they still hadn't finished counting—in the car-park under some office block. Some were still alive, some were just in shock, a few were looking after the others, but most of 'em were badly shot up. From the look of it, whoever did it—and there must have been a bunch of the bastards—just kept shooting until they ran out of ammo."

He glanced down at Kannon's face. "I hear they were all Asian—the bodies, I mean. Sound familiar?"

They made space in the makeshift hospital by turning a tiny office, barely two meters square, into a private room, and I lay on the migraine-blue Brillo carpet near Kannon's cot and waited for her to speak. She remained utterly silent until Johnson left the room just after sunrise, and then she rolled over, reached down and grabbed my hands, and pulled me toward her, kissing me so hard I winced, until she remembered who I was, or wasn't, and pulled away slightly. I didn't let her go. "It's okay," I said, in Japanese—not for privacy (we were the only people in the room), but because it seemed to be her favorite language.

"Why did they bring you? Are you . . . ?"

"I'm the only one who can identify O'Dwyer," I replied. "At least I hope I can. The gunmen—did you see them?"

"I didn't see their faces. Any of their faces. They were . . . they wore . . ." She covered her face and eyes with her hands.

"Ski masks?" She shook her head. "Hoods? Helmets?"

"Shield suits," she whispered. "Ten of them, wearing shield suits . . . We thought they were cops, but they had SMGs, all silenced. They just opened fire and sprayed the room, I don't think they'd been expecting so *many* of us, but they killed as many as they could before they turned and ran."

"You're sure they were shield suits? Not just fakes?"

"They were armored; they stopped knives." She began crying, very quietly, and I held on as firmly as I could until her shaking subsided. "I don't know if they were real cops, but when I saw the jeep and all those guns, I just . . . Well, what would you have done?"

"The same, but not as well; I don't have the skill."

Kannon leaned back to look into my face, forcing me to loosen my grip. "Yes, you do," she whispered.

"Naja did," I corrected her. "You beat the living crap out of me, remember? Okay, I sometimes wish I was Naja—anyone you could love so much would have to be a . . . I don't know, but I'm not. I'm just a forty-nine-year-old bum who got transplanted into the body of—"

"The *body* has the skill," she said. "You can use it, as you did the night of the quake. You have to—have you ever heard of *wu wei*?"

"No."

"Pity. I don't think I can explain it. I wish Sozu-san were here, she . . ." and she started crying again. I kissed her eyes and licked the tears away. She pulled me closer to her. The doona had already slid down to her waist, and she kicked it until it was bunched up around her knees, so that we were separated by nothing but her thin hospital gown and my T-shirt and jeans. I could feel her nipples rubbing against mine as she started kissing my face; our tongues touched fleetingly, and suddenly it felt as though we were flowing into each other, becoming one organism. Kannon unbuckled my jeans with one hand, while the other stroked my neck. A moment later, we were locked together, smooth thighs slickslipsliding over moist labia, one perfect fluid rhythm, heart-rhythm harmony pulsing and pleasuring, allconsuming alldevouring lips and tongues and teeth and fingers and nipples and clits all blended together, sweet sharp salt whimpering whispering sobbing crying. . . .

I felt years dissolve, I felt Galloway (who?) diminish and disappear, I felt young and alive and strong, strong enough to leap over a moving car or swim forever never drowning or walk through a wall kicking and screaming and—

I was . . .

I was I was.

Johnson was waiting outside when I finally emerged. "She awake?" he asked, pointedly not meeting my eye or looking at my damp jeans.

"Yes."

"Should I get her some breakfast?"

"I'll go."

He nodded. "Shower's 'round the corner, if you want one."

"Thanks." I walked down the corridor, still floating slightly, then stopped. "Have the others said anything?"

He shrugged. "I haven't heard."

"I wouldn't hold your breath," I said. "We may be looking for cops."

The hot shower must have been invented by a woman; if it'd been a man he'd be famous, and deservedly so. Whoever she was, she's probably brought more pleasure into more lives than Jesus Christ and Walt Disney together. Luckily, the hospital's solar water heater and purifier had survived the quake (though the pressure left something to be desired), and the spray felt like it was washing what remained of Mike Galloway away.

I'd given my clothes to a candy striper (do they still call them that?) to take to the laundry, which left me nothing to wear but a thin robe and my spare panties; chilly, but good enough for breakfast in a hospital. The canteen looked like something out of *Alien*, which put you in the right frame of mind for the food.

"What did you mean about looking for cops?" asked Johnson, grimacing as he sipped at his coffee. I told him the rest of the story between mouthfuls of synthetic scrambled eggs. His expression became even more sour; when I was finished, he shook his head. "They weren't *city* cops. No way on earth."

Meaning that they *might* have been rent-a-cops; I knew there was animosity between the city cops and private security guards, but I kept forgetting how intense it was. "Where would they get the shield suits?"

"Fakes. From a film company or something." He didn't sound convinced, and I certainly wasn't. I'd worked as an extra in half a dozen countries, and in my experience, film companies hired real cops, city cops, to play cops whenever they could; not only did they look like and know how to act like cops, they brought their own uniforms and guns (and sometimes even their trolls), provided security free, and prevented anyone getting parking tickets. "They were armored."

"Stuntmen, then."

I shrugged. "What happens to old shield suits? When a cop retires or something?"

"They're recycled, given to the rookies. The only *real* shield suits in the city either belong to cops or are locked away in stores. Same with the falcons. They must've been fakes."

"They weren't using falcons," I said. "They weren't trying to bring anyone in alive. . . . You're saying that if the suits *were* real, they must've come from serving cops."

Johnson looked into his coffee. "*If* they were real. We don't know, and I don't think . . . And they weren't cops, they couldn't have been; we're too goddamn *busy*. Okay, maybe one or two cops could have got away long enough, maybe there's one or two that badly twisted, but not *ten*. That'd take so much organization. . . . It just couldn't be done."

"Someone at stores?"

"Uh . . . okay, possible, but real risky, especially now. I'd bet against it. Maybe the factories stockpiled a few that never get registered, or are listed as spare parts or something."

He was reaching, and he knew it. "What about *dead* cops?"

"What?"

"What if the suits were taken from dead cops?"

Johnson swallowed the dregs of his coffee, looking sour. "How? You can't kill a shield without putting a hole in his suit."

"What if he's not wearing it at the time?"

He thought about this for a moment. "Okay, everybody knows one cop, maybe you could get two or three suits that way if you weren't worried about the fit, but not *ten*."

"Personnel records?"

Johnson snorted. "You'd have to be a hell of a hacker—and all the computers have been down since the quake. No way."

I had a disturbing early-morning sort of feeling that there was something important that I just couldn't put my mental finger on. I tried to think. "How big was the aftershock last night?"

"Five-point-something, I think. Some of the temporary buildings collapsed, and there were a few injuries, but I haven't heard of any casualties."

"And what time?"

"Don't tell me you slept through it? About ten-thirty, eleven . . . I can find out exactly, if you want. Why?"

I wish I could say that I was astonished, or incredulous, or even horrified, and I wish like hell I'd been *wrong*. "They knew the aftershock was going to happen," I said as soon as I saw the report. "Kannon says they got out maybe five minutes before. Okay, she wasn't wearing a watch, and shock does nasty things to your time sense, but even if it was an *hour*—"

"It's not evidence," said Johnson.

"They were ready for the big quake; a few minutes later, they were out looting for firearms. They had the whole thing planned. Then, last night, they waltz into a makeshift shelter and start shooting, killing dozens of people just before *another* shock, when the rescue and medical services are going to be stretched to breaking point and everyone's too busy to look for them. It has to be the same people."

Johnson shook his head. "And you still think they're cops, too?"

"I never said that. Maybe one of them is, or used to be: I don't know. But don't try to tell me there's no such thing as a racist cop."

He grunted. "What do you want to do?"

"I want to go to Skye's compound up in Oregon with a warrant for O'Dwyer. Even if he's not there, we get a chance to search the place."

Johnson stared at me, turning slightly red. "Anything else? A few nukes, maybe?"

"Nah, that won't be necessary. Why, do you have some spares?" Johnson said nothing. "What's wrong?"

"You want to pull a troll and a couple of cops off duty for a wild goose chase during an ongoing emergency? You got any evidence?"

"How many dead bodies do you fucking well *need*?"

Johnson took a deep breath and said softly. "Even if you're right about O'Dwyer, girl—and I think you probably are, but what the hell is *my* opinion worth?—no one's going to give us that sort of fishing license when you haven't even seen the bastard . . . or any of the bastards, apart from Skye, if that *was* Skye." He shrugged. "And if you're thinking of asking Yorick, save your breath. He'll say the same, but not so politely. Now you know how *we* feel nearly every day. Sorry."

The next day, they decided that Kannon was going to live and sent me back to work and the tents. The corpses we were finding now were crushed almost (but not quite) beyond any recognition, and smelled even worse than they looked. Most of the other refugees knew that the job was nearly over, and they were working as slowly as possible, hoping to delay their extradition. Two mornings later, when I was sitting in the canteen drinking breakfast and feeling like Dante in Hell, I felt something tap me on the shoulder and heard someone whisper in my ear. "There he is. That's him."

I recognized the voice as Tiffany's and raised my head slightly until we were looking in the same direction. "There who is?"

"Him! See? The blond guy talking with the guards. There, near the urn."

"Okay. I see him. Who is he?"

"The shield. The one that came for Star."

I gagged and nearly spilled my coffee trying not to stare at the guy. I could see why Tiffany had picked him for a cop. He had the smile, the slight swagger, the haircut—even a shave. He was wearing a bulky down jacket (the sort that went out with fur coats and jungle camo), but he still had the slightly lopsided look of a man who carries a heavy pistol on his forearm most of the day.

Tiffany was watching him closely, but so were many of the women in the mess: He looked a little like Flash Gordon, a little like a Hitler Jugend recruiting poster, and a lot like the half-witted phys ed major my first fiancée left me for. No one that handsome should ever be trusted. "You're sure it's him?" I murmured.

Tiffany waited until the guy had turned away from us, and then nodded. "Sure."

"Okay. Can you go up to him, ask him if he knows where Star is?"

She hesitated; leaving an unfinished meal on the table was risky. "Can't you?"

"He doesn't know me," I replied. I wanted to keep it that way too, but I didn't say that. "What should I say, that I was Star's lover? She might not want him to know. Besides, he might get the wrong idea— or the guards might—and I don't *like* men."

"Okay, okay . . . watch my plate for me?"

"Sure."

She sashayed over as best she could (not easy with her back) and broke into the conversation with all the subtlety of a dinosaur at a creationists' convention. I wasn't able to hear any of the conversation, but I didn't need to: The blond faked being taken aback, then faked innocence, then became vehement, and then walked out. Interestingly enough, the guardsmen didn't seem to be backing him up, and Tiffany hung around and talked to them for a few minutes before walking back to the table; she even blew one of them a kiss. She sat down and took a spoonful of beans, and I said, "Don't tell me. He never saw Star, he never even came *near* the stable."

She nodded, chewed hastily, and then swallowed. "He's a lying pig."

"I guessed that."

"Funny thing is," she said, spooning another load of beans into her mouth, "the other guys, the guards . . ." She ruminated for a few seconds. "Some of them know him from the reserves. Funny thing is . . ."

"Yeah?"

"It's like they all knew different people. One of them said this guy—his name's Peter Bright—was a real lady-killer"—I suspect I shuddered—"but they never *seen* him with any woman, he just looks like the type. One of the others said he was gay, mostly for the same reason. One of them said he was real religious. You know what *I* think? *I* think it's all bullshit, rumors, and none of them knows him at *all*."

"You're probably right," I said glumly. "Peter Bright, huh?"

"Peter Bright, huh?" Johnson thought for a moment, stirring his coffee as though it might improve the taste. "Works over at Union Street?"

"Does he?"

"Well, that's the only Peter Bright *I* know on the force, and I don't know him well."

"Blond? Blue eyes? Early thirties? Looks like Flash Gordon?"

"Who?"

"Never mind."

Johnson sipped his coffee cautiously. "He's blond," he said. "I've never noticed his eyes; he usually wears shades, when he's not suited up. Why?"

"A friend of mine disappeared on the evening of the quake. I think he was the last person to see her, but he denies it."

"Working girl?"

I nodded. "Ex-cop, or so I hear."

Johnson blinked. "You know her name?"

"Stella . . . I think."

"Stella Chapman?"

"I don't know."

"When was she dismissed?"

"I don't know that either. She was blond, about my height but a few kilos heavier, midthirties . . ."

Johnson took a sip of his coffee, nearly put his eye out with the spoon, and flinched, spilling the tepid crap down his shirt. "Oh, hell."

"You knew her?"

"I knew a Stella Chapman," he admitted, brushing at his shirtfront and spreading the stain. "She wasn't actually a cop—she worked in the computer section for a while, about four years ago. You say she was a . . ."

"We worked in a stable. Strictly videphone sex," I assured him: it didn't seem smart to mention the Jell-O wrestling, or to say we were also lovers.

Johnson shook his head, his expression bleak, then looked up. "Sounds like it's dangerous to know you," he said.

I shrugged. "Look, there may be an innocent explanation. I've heard Bright's religious, he might—" Johnson looked sour. "What's wrong?"

"Oh, I guess he might be *religious*," said Johnson, "if it's some sort of fringe group, Scientologists or Mormons or one of those twenty-cent New Wave outfits, UFOs or crystals or something, but he's no *Christian*."

I shrugged. I was raised as Catholic, but I'd never been religious (thank Goddess) and I knew better than to argue with anyone who is. "I was going to say, he might just be trying to hide the fact that he went on a date with a sex worker. I don't even remember him being a client of ours. I just want to know that Star's okay. Can you check to see if she's flown out?"

"I should be able to." He grimaced. "Phone porn, huh?"

I nodded. "It's a living—well, it was. How big is the force, nowadays?"

He stared at me, eyebrows raised. "What? Why?"

"You seem to know everyone, at least slightly. So does Yorick. That suggests it's pretty small."

"Minuscule, more like," he grumped. "Rent-a-cops outnumber us nearly twenty to one, last I heard. We're just a little better equipped and a damn sight better trained—unless you count a felony record as training. That's why I don't believe your idea about cops—or even ex-cops—being behind those shootings. Rent-a-cops, now, that's different. You're right: We all know each other too well, we all get transferred occasionally, work with different partners—they say it prevents corruption. And we all have to go through psych tests, polygraphs, that sort of crap, all the time. And, okay, most of us are white, and yeah, some of them are racists but . . . hell, we're not stupid. Ten Nazi cops, or Klansmen, or whatever they are, they'd get *noticed.* One guy might slip up once a year, well, nobody remembers it, but ten people make ten times as many mistakes as one, at least; they're ten times as noisy, they have ten times as many girlfriends and drink ten times as much."

I nodded. " 'Three can keep a secret, if two of them are dead.' "

"Huh?"

"Ben Franklin."

He looked at me strangely; I kept forgetting to play the uneducated young refugee, especially when I was tired. "You're probably right," I said.

"I probably am," he agreed. "I'll see if I can find out what happened to Stella. Try and stay out of trouble, okay?"

I was sharing my tent with three women and two young girls, all of them straight. It had been nearly a week since that morning with Kannon, and I was horny as hell. I was lying there waiting for them all to go to sleep so I could masturbate when I heard a vaguely familiar giggle outside. Tiffany. I should've guessed why she was smiling and bouncing at dinner. Nice to know *someone* was going to get laid tonight. I stared at the soggy canvas, frustrated, and wondered where they'd found to enjoy their interlude. Because of her bad back, Tiffany would insist on a mattress, at the very least, as well as warmth, shelter from the rain, and privacy. Had they found an empty tent? Or something more luxurious?

I closed my eyes and squirmed until I managed to convince myself that I wasn't really spying on them, that I just wanted to know where I could take Kannon when they released her tomorrow. That rationalization must have taken me all of two seconds; then I was up and into my jeans and boots and gliding toward the tent flap. I peered out cautiously; the rain had slowed down to a thin and silent drizzle, barely more than a cold and translucent moist mist, but Tiffany and her partner were still hurrying as fast as the mud would let them, never looking back.

I blinked. The man was wearing a full shield suit, complete with gyrfalcon on his forearm and stunstick and Mag-Lite in his belt. Obviously, the cops would have a few comfortable hideaways, and an excuse to be out after curfew. I tried to convince myself that it couldn't be Peter Bright—Tiffany was often hornier than she was smart, but she couldn't possibly have been *that* stupid—and failed. Bright was good-looking, if you liked men, and obviously had some charm. I faded back into the flap of the tent as the shield glanced over his shoulder, then watched him unlock the door of a prefab plastic first-aid shed. I hesitated, then half dashed, half slid over the muddy grass toward the shed.

There was a crack between the door and the jamb nearly half a centimeter wide; I put my eye to it, and then moved back until I could focus. All I needed to see was the man's face, enough to reassure me that it wasn't Bright; I promised myself that I'd return to my tent as soon as he'd removed his helmet. I kept repeating that promise, silently, as Tiffany sat on the trundle-bed and struggled to pull her sweatshirt up over her head, revealing a bra like both halves of the Hindenberg; I barely noticed the shield grabbing his stunstick until he'd touched it to her neck.

Tiffany twitched, and then crashed backwards onto the bed before he could catch her. The shield, still fully suited and masked, returned his stunstick to his belt, and then reached for the pillow on the bed. I slid my knife out of my sleeve—only a cheap steak knife stolen from the hospital canteen, but it'd been a long time since I'd felt comfortable without one—and tried to force the lock.

The shield's right hand slid back into sight, now brandishing a knife almost as long as my forearm. He placed the pillow over Tiffany's right breast, and then stabbed down into it, as both the lock and my steak knife snapped.

He spun around wildly, and I pulled the door open and faced him, a target he couldn't possibly miss. I felt a horrible wet warmth between my thighs, and realized I'd pissed myself with fear. I stood there, frozen, and waited to die.

The shield regarded me uncertainly. He must have been terrified of making a noise (who in their right mind would muffle a *knife*?), and maybe he hoped that I'd just go away quietly and let him escape. Instead, I took an unsteady step forward.

Slowly, he let go of the knife, and brought his right hand up until his shaking fingers were pointing at my chest; then the gyrfalcon whipped forward out of its holster and into his hand. He flinched slightly, and then fumbled with his thumb along the top of the butt, where the hammer would have been on an old-fashioned slug-thrower. I was close enough to kick at his hand, but I knew it wouldn't do me any good; even an idiot couldn't lose a pistol that was tethered to his forearm with memory flex.

We continued to stare at each other, and then he found the switch and flicked it, and I saw the cylinder revolve, heard it click into place. Maybe I could dodge; maybe if the rocket hit my hand, the shock wouldn't carry far enough to stun me—

"Tera?"

The whisper sounded like a shot in the tiny shed, and we both jumped. Tiffany had pulled her sweatshirt down far enough to see past it, and was staring blearily at me as she groped for the hilt of the knife. I was about to scream at her to stop, the blade must be slowing the bleeding; maybe I *did* scream, but none of us heard it, because the shield wheeled around and fired at her head at point-blank range. I grabbed at his arm—an instant too late.

He continued his spin, throwing me into the wall, and then rammed his armored elbow into my ribs. I kicked at his knee with all my strength, and only succeeded in hurting my foot. I couldn't see his face, much less his eyes, so I concentrated on his gun; at that range, it looked like an empty missile silo. There was nothing to stop him from firing again, and I—

22

O'DWYER

The infra showed a heat source in between the trees, but I didn't shoot, just in case it was one of us; there weren't enough suits for the recruits. I walked through the woods as quietly as I could, but I trod on a branch and nearly went ass-over—bitch must've set up a trap—and fired a burst out of the Ingram as I fell. So much for stealth. There was this lot of silence, and I propped myself up on my elbows and tracked around for the heat source. It was there, but it looked fainter and smaller. I wolf-howled, and someone from that direction howled back. Damn.

I picked myself up and waited until they appeared: two new recruits with M-16s. One of them asked, "Any luck, sir?"

"Nah. Haven't even seen her. Monkey-bitch's probably up some tree somewhere."

"Think the dogs'll find her?"

"If we don't get her first." I put a fresh clip into the Ingram. "If we do, they can have what's left."

The little chickenshits glanced at each other, and the talker said, "Martini told us that she was to be brought in alive."

"If possible," I corrected. "Come on." I turned around too fast and was glad I was wearing the helmet so they couldn't see me wince. The bitch had really known how to kick.

"Martini told us to patrol the fence."

I snorted. "Even if she could find it, she couldn't get over the fuckin' thing."

"I thought she was a ninja. . . ."

The kid was really starting to get on my nerves. "Okay, you go, if you want to miss the fun. But cover each other's backs. We wouldn't want her to get your guns." They stared at each other uncertainly as I stomped deeper into the woods. The bitch shouldn't have been that hard to find. Sure, it was dark, but I hadn't given her that much of a head start, and she was barely one step above a stripper, probably hadn't seen more than a hundred trees in her fucking life. Wish I'd made her bleed; would've made it easier for the dogs.

The talkie buzzed, and I grabbed it. "Squirrel here."

"This is Snake. There's been shooting reported in your area."

Martini. Fuck. "Uh . . . it wasn't her."

"Just as well for you."

"You'd rather she escaped?"

"It wouldn't be an issue if you hadn't untied her, fuckwit! A leash. Jesus. How sick can you get?"

"I hope," I said dangerously, "that you don't think I'd do that to a *white* woman."

"Why the fuck did you have to do anything to this one?"

"We were *supposed* to rape her. And humiliate her. Skye's orders. If he didn't want her to escape, why the fuck didn't he blind her like the rest?"

"Don't try to think; you'll hurt your head. My guess is he wants her to draw us a map, or lead us somewhere. Or maybe someone's been talking and Skye wants her to recognize him, point the bastard out. Did you ever think of that?"

There was this heavy shitty feeling in my guts; maybe the bitch had ruptured my kidney with that kick, but I didn't think that was it.

"We'll find her."

"You'd better. And when you have, I'm sending you back to the city."

"But—Skye's orders . . ."

"Skye's orders put me in charge," Martini gloated, "and that gives me the power to send you back in the next car. Think yourself lucky that killing you'd be bad for morale—but not as bad as that slanty-eyed bitch getting out of here and talking. Do you understand me, Hoddy?"

I nodded silently and switched the select on the Ingram back to single shot. "Copy that. Yeah, I understand."

The first thing I saw when the blackness went away was Kannon's beautiful face. Maybe I wasn't dead after all. Then I remembered Tiffany, and threw up all over my pillow.

"You got hit with a stunstick," Johnson explained as Kannon brought me a new pillow. "Full strength. You've been out for more'n a day."

"I forgot his left hand," I said, wondering why he hadn't killed me.

"Huh? Oh, okay."

"Now do you believe me?"

"What'm I supposed to believe?"

"He was a shield. He shot Tiff"—I retched, but there was nothing left to vomit—"he shot her with a falcon. And he was wearing a shield suit."

"We saw the suit," said Johnson. "People came running as soon as they heard the falcon fire; a few saw him running out of the shed, but they didn't realize what was happening until it was too late. He must have panicked and run, not realizing you were still alive." He was silent for a moment. "We had to call in the bomb squad to remove the rocket from your friend's eye: It hadn't hit anything hard enough to detonate it." I blinked, and he shook his head. "There wasn't anything we could do for her. The knife wouldn't have killed her—it only broke a rib and barely scratched her heart, would you believe; that pillow and her implant might have saved her, if that'd been all we had to worry about, but being shot in the face like that . . ."

I nodded and wished like hell he'd just go away. "Yorick will want to talk to you," he continued. "Did you see his face at all?"

"No, he never removed his helmet, but . . . it was Peter Bright." Johnson shook his head, his expression sad. "Wasn't it?"

"He's got an unshakable alibi. Seven of them, even."

"Who?"

"Me," he replied dourly. "And six guardsmen. We were on patrol last night, all night. I wanted to keep an eye on him, so I asked to be assigned with him, and . . ." He shrugged. "Do you have any idea who else it might have been?"

"No," I said sourly. "Did Tiffany say anything?"

"No; she never regained consciousness. We're checking every cop's falcon to see if it's been fired, but I haven't heard any results."

I glanced over at Kannon. "Am I allowed to walk?"

She nodded. "You can lean on me."

Best offer I'd had in days. "Where's the shower? I'd like to clean up a little."

There was clean linen on the bed when we returned and a different guard (female) on the door. Kannon and I curled up on the cot together; it was a tight fit, but neither of us minded.

"We've residue-tested the falcon of every cop in the city," said Yorick as soon as the door had slammed shut behind him (why can't cops ever begin a conversation with hello, like normal people?). "And if you think that was easy in this mess . . ."

"Lieutenant York. Nice to see you. Take a seat," I added, a second too late. He glanced at Kannon, who looked back neutrally and wiggled slightly nearer to me.

"We've got everyone who's used their gun in the past forty-eight hours, *and* their partners, making full reports," Yorick continued after a moment's pause. "This bastard is wasting so much of our time—"

"He *wasted* a friend of mine," I snapped back.

"Save your breath," suggested Kannon. "He's just worried about the missing guns."

I watched them glaring at each other and asked, "Have you two met?"

"Not that I remember," growled Yorick.

"The lieutenant has a reputation," replied Kannon. "But don't let

me interrupt. Pretend I'm not here; pretend none of us exist at all.
You always have before."

"There are guns missing?" I asked.

"Yeah," Yorick admitted sourly. "And suits."

"How many?"

"Eight," he replied eventually. "That we've found so far; there may
be more. The falcons aren't really a problem; none of the cops carried
any reloads. Oh, you can buy the rockets on the black market, but
they cost more'n an AK-47. That's for APEX; I don't think anybody
bothers selling taser rounds."

"Apex?"

"*Armor-piercing explosives*. What they used on—your friend."

I nodded. "That's military hardware. What're cops doing with it?"

"Stopping traffic," he replied blandly. "It'll blow the engine out of
a car. And there's always the chance that some asshole in war-surplus
armor is going to go on a rampage. Most cops put one APEX in the
cylinder, sometimes two, just in case. You can revolve the cylinder
backwards if you press the safety and squeeze the trigger. I never
heard of anyone ever getting mixed up; ninety percent of cops never
even fire one after they finish basic. They're not really that effective
against soft targets, anyway, especially at close range; almost never
detonate, unless they hit bone."

I thought of Tiffany and then blinked. Soft targets. "Do you know
why the killer stuck the knife through a pillow before stabbing her?"

"Oh, that. It's an old knife-pistol, Chinese army surplus. The hilt's
like an old cloverleaf derringer, fires four small-caliber bullets—four
or five millimeter, I think. Does zero damage—well, not zero, precisely, but you get the idea."

I nodded. I'd seen a similar weapon in the ninja museum at In-
ayama, a flintlock disguised as a sheath knife. Great for inspiring
paranoia, I thought, but not much use as a weapon.

"They were probably trying to make it look like a Triad killing,"
Yorick continued. "Of course we still don't know that it wasn't, but
a lot of those knife-pistols were bought by survivalists, too. A knife
that fires bullets, a pistol that looks like a knife and can still kill when
it's out of ammo . . ."

"There's no way to trace it?"

Yorick shrugged. "Nah, not really. We've sent it up to the forensics at Sacramento, but I wouldn't get your hopes too high, not unless it's already been used to kill somebody else."

I shuddered; that was cold comfort if I ever heard it. "So what do we do?"

"Well, if either of you had bags to pack, I'd tell you to pack them," he replied. "We're flying you out soon as you can walk. Top priority. Where the hell are the two of you from, anyway?"

Kannon stared at me, her blue eyes wide with alarm. "We're *witnesses*, for Christ's sake!" I shouted.

"Yeah? Who can you identify?" He shook his head. "All you know is a name, and all you were able to do with that was lead a cop into a death trap. Forget it. You'll be safer somewhere else, anyway."

"What if we don't cooperate?"

"You'll be geneprinted. Even if you sneaked in here, there'll be records of you somewhere—"

"You think everyone was born in a hospital?" retorted Kannon.

Yorick stared at her. I think he was genuinely amazed that we didn't want to go home; I wondered where the hell *he* was from. "Hey, look, we'll send both of you to the same place, if there's any way we can." We didn't answer, and he backed out of the room. We lay there silently for nearly a minute, just holding each other, and then I whispered, "Where are you from?"

"L.A."

"Huh? I mean, I can see why you don't want to go back there, but—"

"Well, not L.A. exactly," she said. "I grew up in a . . . I guess you'd call it a commune. Out in the desert, near Coyote Lake. They grew a little grass, before it became legal, and a lot of refugees lived there, but mostly they didn't want to be part of what they called the ICE-world. Anyway, one of the things they didn't believe in and couldn't afford was hospitals, so I never had a WIN or an ICEcard.

"I don't know who my father was. We weren't separatists; most of the women were bisexual and there were always a few men around—some stayed, some didn't—but the women ran the place, and they didn't believe in patrilineal descent. I knew my mother, and that was supposed to be enough. She was a blue-eyed blonde; they called her Bast, and she wouldn't talk about where *she* was from, but I think she was South African." She pronounced it "Seth Efriken."

"Sozu-san used to say my father was at least half Japanese, but I think she said that about everyone she liked."

"What happened to the commune?"

She grimaced. "We were living too close to some weapons-testing ground for our own good. I don't know whether someone'd flown over and seen the plantation, or whether we had someone with us who had a good reason for being on the run. Maybe they just had an accident with one of their germ bombs or something, and wanted to evacuate the area before anyone found out. They didn't tell us shit, even when it was over. Anyway, one night this helicopter landed near the house and a pack of storm troopers with rifles came pouring out. We might've been okay if one of the men hadn't had a shotgun.

"We'd had trouble before with biker gangs, and we'd dug ditches, built traps, and that sort of shit all around the place, straight out of *Seven Samurai*. Most of the women knew judo or aikido or kempo, and some of them had *athames*—ritual daggers—and could use them. There were axes and hatchets and machetes around the place; we'd been able to look after ourselves okay. Maybe this guy was on the run, like I said, or maybe he'd just appointed himself perimeter guard; he may not even have recognized the chopper for what it was. I heard it, but it landed on the wrong side of the house, and all I saw was these guys in helmets with rifles, so I can't really say I blame him for shooting.

"Of course, the soldiers were wearing armor and the shotgun didn't stop anyone, but it gave them an excuse to start shooting back. The house wasn't that solidly built on that side—we'd rebuilt some of the walls with pressed earth blocks—but the others were still wood, and pretty rotten wood too. I don't know how many people were injured, how many killed. They told me my mother was dead and that's why they were putting me in an orphanage, but I also heard she was in jail, or in an asylum." She shrugged. "Anyway, that was eleven years ago. She probably *is* dead now.

"I escaped and came here. I was about nine, I think; we didn't have any calendars, either, except for an Aztec one that no one could really understand. I've been a stripper ever since."

"Do you know where I came from? Did Naja ever say?"

"Not really. I think it was Thailand, or Burma, or maybe Cambodia; I think her parents brought her with them, and sold her to pay for their tickets. There used to be quite a market for children in the West. Not just for adoption; they needed them for kiddie porn, prostitution, gutlegging—some say there were Satanists in California buying babies for human sacrifice, but that's probably just a myth. Of course that was in the days when the dollar was mighty and most Asian currencies, especially the baht, were wastepaper, and the Coast Guard wasn't using spy satellites to watch out for illegal immigrants. Some parents were paid, usually in heroin, and some were told that their babies were going to be adopted by rich Americans and gave them up willingly; after all, they were only girls." She grimaced. "Now it's supposed to be a buyers' market: Infertility treatments are better and surrogacy easier, so fewer people want to adopt; there are more refugees than ever before, and so many Chinese girls being sold, though that'll probably change when sex-selection treatments become cheaper. Anyway, you survived, and you're probably better off without some of those memories." She stroked my hair and kissed my neck. "I have a few I wish I could give away."

I remembered the Bodysnatcher and shuddered. "What'll they do if they can't deport us?"

I felt her shrug. "I don't know. They can't afford to jail all the refugees; there's only so much work that can be done by convict labor, only so much kelp needs cutting, and even that only postpones the problem—they'll have to let us out someday. They could send a few of us up to Alaska to plant trees, but no more, not until they've built some more housing, and that's still a short-term solution and a very long-term investment."

"How do you know all this?"

"Connie told me—before the quake; I haven't seen her since. She's one of the best hackers in the city. The Republicans have been paying her to spy on the Am Nats and the Democrats, the Democrats have been paying her to spy on the Nats and the Republicans, and she's been selling it all to the Greens at a discount. They're all worried about the homeless, scared they're going to be the big issue next election. Unfortunately, none of them have any good ideas, or none that they can sell.

"It's not that people are scared *for* the homeless, any more than most Seth Efriken whites were ever scared *for* the blacks. They're scared *of* them. They're worried about how much they're having to pay security guards to prevent the homeless from sleeping on their balconies or stealing their garbage. They're worried about knives and clubs and garrotes, and firearms that might have been scavenged from trash cans or bartered for sex. They're worried about their children cutting themselves on the razor wire, or being eaten by their muteweilers. They're worried about their property values decreasing. And they're terrified that the next riot might reach *their* neighborhood, instead of being stuck downtown." She grimaced. "On the other hand, they don't want to be the Nazis or the Khmer Rouge; they do have consciences, if not compassion. Have you forgotten thinking like that—winner?"

I lay there silently. "Is that why you hate Yorick?" I asked finally. "Because he's a winner?"

"Nah. He's a pig—I don't mean he's a cop, that's his job, but he's a *pig*. He was promoted to the rape squad a few years ago, and his arrest record dropped to the lowest in the city. He just didn't take it seriously. They kicked him back to Homicide, and he became a champion again. Pig."

"You think he'll . . . ?"

Kannon hesitated. "I don't know. I think he still wants something from you."

"Yeah," I replied. "My head. He's going to blame me for Wazaki's death until someone finds O'Dwyer." I stared at the ceiling. "Probably me."

"Do you know where he is?"

"No," I replied, "but I'll bet Bright does."

I stood in the center of the room and waited. I'd chosen the location carefully; it had been one of my favorite dim sum places back when I was still Mike Galloway, and was far enough west to have escaped the Chinatown fires. It was on the second floor, up a straight and slightly creaky staircase from the muddy street, and there were windows (but no fire escapes) behind me and to my left. If I ended up trapped, it was my own stupid fault. I'd walked past it often enough to be sure that it wouldn't be reopening in a hurry, though the mass-produced decor didn't look much worse for a little earthquake damage. The tables wouldn't stop any bullets or rockets but they provided plenty of visual cover, and I was able to hide half a dozen sharp kitchen knives under some strategically placed chairs.

I'd waited for four days, thinking and planning and learning, before siccing Kannon on Bright. I told her to tell him to tell O'Dwyer that "Lee" needed to see him, and when and where, and not to let on that she wasn't Lee (I'd almost forgotten that O'Dwyer didn't know my *nom de voyage*, or Star's; to him, we'd always been Lee and Stella). Bright probably knew me by sight, but he didn't know Kannon; there was no reason for him not to associate the message with me, no reason I could see not to pass it on—unless O'Dwyer was dead, of course, or had fled the city, or I was entirely wrong and there was no link at all between the two.

I was wearing too-small bitten-off jeans and an old ballistic jacket with worn-out Velcro, and nothing underneath; it hung open, showing the edges of my areolae. It wouldn't save me from many bullets, but it might distract O'Dwyer from looking too closely at my pockets and sleeves. I hadn't been able to find or make much in the way of weapons, and without the advantage of surprise, I—

I heard a footfall on the stairs; someone heavy, trying to be quiet. As I'd expected, he was about an hour early, which is why I'd been *three* hours early. I waited.

The first thing to appear was the muzzle of a gyrfalcon. It was followed by the rest of the gun, then an armored arm, and then a helmeted head (probably in descending order of usefulness). I kept my right (empty) hand in plain sight, above the table; I knew that an ordinary knife wouldn't cut through a shield suit, but there were weak spots, joints, where I could stab with some effect. The sides of the chest. The backs of the knees. The armpits. The waist. A slightly familiar voice (I thought) asked, "Lee?"

"Roy?"

"You alone?"

"As agreed. You?"

There was a moment's silence, then he stepped into the room and looked around. "Yeah. What the hell's so all-fired important that we had to—" he began, then stopped when I opened my left hand, showing him the cassette. He stared, and then asked stupidly, "What the fuck is that?"

"It's a tape of our last conversation," I lied. "I thought the cops might be interested, but I'd rather sell to the highest bidder." I kept my voice low, forcing him to step closer to hear me. The gun was wavering between my hand (held well away from my body) and my chest. If Yorick was right, at that range, the impact wouldn't be enough to detonate the warhead on an APEX round. I might even survive, if he hit my hand or foot. "And no, it's not the only copy," I added.

"You didn't tape that call," he said uncertainly, taking another step away from the doorway. "The stable—"

"Oh, we wouldn't blackmail a regular customer," I told him, "but one of our girls was murdered last year. Since then, we've taped all the calls. The sicko ones like yours we kept for at least a month. So *what am I bid?*"

I imagine his face turned an unpleasant white behind that visor. "What the fuck do you want?"

"Where is Stella?"

Hesitation. "Is that all?"

"You know?"

"Maybe. Maybe I can find out." Even hidden by a helmet, with his voice filtered by a microphone and speaker, he was about as inscrutable as a neon sign.

"Is she still alive?"

He was trying to think, probably working on a lie. Slowly, the penny dropped and the gun stopped wavering. "What the fuck do I care about the tape? I've killed *cops!* They must be looking for me already. What difference is *that* going to make?"

"To the cops, none at all. But you didn't shoot up the dojo alone, did you? What're your *friends* going to do when they hear you blabbed the whole thing into a cassette recorder? Isn't that why you came here alone?"

Hesitation.

"Lucky for you they won't let you out on bail, I guess; you'll probably be safer in prison. Or can the Apostles get you there, too?"

No answer, but I could feel him wince. "So," I said. "Where's Stella? I already know Bright took her—*where* did he take her? And why? And put the gun down, for Christ's sake. Killing me won't help you."

"It won't do anything for you, either," he replied thickly. "Way you tell it, my best chance is to get out of here while I can."

I shrugged, showing him just a little more flesh. "You can get out without your friends to help you? I've met some of them, and they didn't strike me as the forgiving sort. If I were you, O'Dwyer, I'd be praying that whoever comes through that door next is a *real* cop."

The gun didn't waver. "Then I guess I'm fucked either way."

"There's a first time for everything," I replied, before I could stop myself.

"Huh?"

"Nothing." I wondered whether making him angry was a good idea. He'd probably try to rape me instead of (or at least before) shooting me, and that would mean removing some of his armor. But he stared at me blankly for a moment, and then took a step closer, pointing the falcon at my face. "Is that what you think, huh? That I've never fucked a woman? You think I'm just a queer or something? Well let me tell you, I've fucked your Stella, and fucked her *proper—*

no more slanty-eyed dykes for her." I heard a slight creak; someone was climbing the stairs. "We've all fucked her; how do you like that? And when I get back, I'm going to—" Another creak, loud enough for O'Dwyer to hear over his own ranting; he stopped and turned around slowly, bringing the gun to bear on the doorway.

"You bitch," he whispered, as though the intruder couldn't have heard him from the street. "You set me up, you fuckin' bitch." I don't know how long we stayed frozen like that, but suddenly, before I could react (and what the fuck could I have *done*, anyway?) O'Dwyer ran to the doorway and fired. I heard the roar of the rocket, the thud of the impact as it hit something hard, and a hollow blast, followed by the sound of something heavy rolling down the stairs to the accompaniment of O'Dwyer's shrieks of laughter. I bowed my head slightly, hoping that it had only been another Apostle instead of a cop or guardsman, and reached into my right jacket pocket. O'Dwyer turned around, still laughing loudly, and waved the gun in my general direction. "*Now* what?" he yelled. "Got any *more* tricks up your slanty cunt? Bring 'em on! *Bring 'em on!*" I smiled and threw the paint bomb with all my strength. It hit him squarely in the forehead, covering his entire faceplate in shit-colored quick-drying paint. With the same motion, I hit the floor and rolled. The rocket missed me by at least a meter and hit the wall without exploding.

Johnson had told me that shield-suit visors were coated with the same nonstick layers they used for subway car windows, so I probably didn't have much time. On the other hand, if Yorick was right (and that wasn't something I felt like betting my life on), O'Dwyer didn't have many rockets, either. I stood cautiously, then picked up a chair and threw it across the room. It hit another stack of chairs, knocking it over, and O'Dwyer spun around so fast that he staggered, almost falling. Then he drew himself up to his full height and released his grip on the falcon. The memory flex flexed, returning the falcon to its forearm holster, while O'Dwyer fumbled with the pockets on his belt.

I should have guessed he'd have a backup gun, but I hadn't expected it to be so small that I had to bite my lip to stop myself laughing. O'Dwyer tilted his head, as though listening for something; he obviously hadn't recovered his bearings from that near-fall, and had no idea where I was. I walked as silently as possible toward the bar where I'd hidden the stickyfoam gun, as he drew his flashlight with his left hand and began flailing about with it like a blind man with a sawed-off cane. Unfortunately, he didn't move away from the doorway. I saw him freeze and listen again, then swipe at the air with the flashlight without connecting with anything except the walls. Then he returned the flashlight to its belt loop and brought a hand up to his faceplate. Wiping it only seemed to smear the paint.

He stood there pondering for nearly a minute, then turned to face the corner. I sneaked toward the bar as quickly as I could, but the stickyfoam gun was still just out of my reach when O'Dwyer turned around, his visor up, and brought the gun to bear. He was red-faced and sweating profusely, and looked even more scared than I felt; for a moment I wondered which of us he intended to shoot. We stared at each other, and then he began to laugh again.

"Oh, shut up," I snapped. He stopped and looked as though I'd slapped him. Then he laughed again.

"What's the matter?" he croaked between giggles. "Don't you *want* to know where Stella is? Don't you want to know what we're doing to her? Don't you want to know what we're going to do to *all* of you? You're going to *listen* to me, cunt, and then you're going to beg me to kill you."

"You want to kill me?" I took a step closer, then another. It was probably a stupid thing to do, but it was safer than going for the bulky foam gun, and I was too steamed to cower any longer. "Then kill me. Even an asshole like you couldn't miss from *this* range." I was speaking slowly, and I lowered my voice as I neared. He seemed to be having trouble focusing, which was fine by me. "Here. I'll make it even easier for you." I reached out and grabbed his right hand—and then forced it back in the direction it wasn't meant to go. He screamed and squeezed the trigger, and the bullet smacked into the Kevlar below my right shoulder an instant before the pistol hit the floor.

Armored, he was nearly twice as heavy as I was, and maybe half as agile. I twisted his arm behind his back, emptied his falcon, removed the stunstick and handcuffs from his belt, propelled him ungently toward the doorway, and cuffed him to the rail at the top of the stairs, where he had a good view of his latest victim.

"I'm going for the cops," I panted. "Try not to get killed before I get back, okay?"

They charged O'Dwyer with the murders of Bright and Wazaki and the caretaker, and with arson in the first degree, but not with the massacre at the dojo, or with Tiffany's murder. They already had enough to execute him twice, and no matter what sort of bargain they offered, he wouldn't name his accomplices. "Even if he did, it'd be the word of one murderer against three or four," Yorick explained. "We'd need independent witnesses, or hard evidence—the guns, at least—just to get an indictment."

"The guns are probably at the bottom of the bay."

"Maybe," said Yorick with a shrug. "But we've matched some bullets from the dojo, the dorm in Berkeley, and the restaurant on Harlan Place; it looks as though they were hand-loaded by the same equipment. Some of the rifling marks match, too; one gun was used at all three killings. I won't tell you any more than that—we may need it as a polygraph key—but I think some of them like their guns too much to throw them away; they don't make many like that anymore."

I considered that. "Where did O'Dwyer get the shield suit and the falcon?"

"They were issued to cops who've died since the quake," he said grimly. "And so were the rockets we retrieved from the restaurant, *and* the one we pulled out of your friend Tiffany. But he's claiming that he bought them, or stole them, from the cop-killers, and at the moment we can't prove he didn't. We haven't even asked him, officially; we're still waiting for some better evidence to turn up. If he gets off for killing Bright—which is unlikely—we'll charge him with the other murders, but we can't mention them at this trial; it's prejudicial. But we *will* mention them at the penalty phase; we're asking for death."

"No!"

He blinked. "Huh? You don't think he deserves it?"

"If he dies, you may never find the others!"

Yorick shrugged. "If we get him death, he'll appeal, and he may try to bargain. Juries don't like executing anybody if they know his accomplices have gotten away; they don't think it's fair." I suspect I looked dubious. "Okay, so it's a gamble," he admitted. "What else can we do? Besides, don't you think he *deserves* to die?"

I grimaced. Maybe some people—serial killers, some politicians, tobacco company execs, the builders of Chernobyl and Bhopal, and assorted other multiple murderers—*do* deserve to die just as painfully as their victims died, but I've been firmly against the death penalty for as long as I can remember. Cops and attorneys have a vested interest in securing convictions, especially for murders, and judges and juries are fallible and sometimes prejudiced, and they convict innocent people too damn often. I remembered Gandalf's advice to Frodo: If you can't give life to those who deserve it, be very careful about dispensing death. I don't know whether Yorick took my grimace as agreement, but he let the matter rest.

I was the star witness, of course, protected by one-way glass and a voice-distorting speaker the whole time. The county courthouse in San Francisco was still being repaired, so they moved the whole circus to Sacramento and locked Kannon and me in a motel room with all the character and charm of a fiberglass coffin. We spent most of our time in bed, sleeping and relaxing and fucking and laughing at the porn on the teleo. We drank hot strong coffee and cold filtered water and all the different flavors of soda in the fridge, and we took deliciously hot freshwater showers and then dried ourselves on warm clean soft towels. And she taught me a little about *wu wei* and *chi* and Tao, and how I'd been able to use Naja's skill and O'Dwyer's strength to break O'Dwyer's wrist. "Don't think about it; thought is too slow. The power isn't in your mind, it's in your nerves—Naja's nerves. It's part of your nature."

O'Dwyer pleaded not guilty to the first charge, the murder of

Wazaki and the caretaker, claiming that the Constitution gave a citizen the right to protect his home in his absence. By his logic, Wazaki was an intruder, a trespasser, and if anyone had murdered him, I had. He admitted to shooting Bright, but claimed that I'd tricked him into believing that the cops were coming for him and weren't going to take him alive. His lawyer tried to keep him off the stand, and not to cringe visibly during his testimony; I heard that he tried to plead the charges down to manslaughter, reckless endangerment, and possessing explosives, but the DA hadn't bought it.

They brought me in to testify on the second day, and kept me there until the fifth, mostly because O'Dwyer's lawyer stood up and objected at least once a minute. The judge allowed me to mention the existence of the warrant, indicating that Wazaki was *not* trespassing, but not the charge. I wasn't even permitted to describe the circumstances under which O'Dwyer had told me about the guns. Apart from that, both lawyers pretty well left me alone; the defense didn't ask me about my work in the stable, or anything else that might discredit me as a witness (I guess it reflected badly on O'Dwyer; I'm sure some of the jurors must have called a phone-sex service or watched porno at some time, but none of them would ever have admitted it or hesitated to condemn someone else for it), and the prosecution didn't seem to be exerting herself at all.

The courtroom was packed, and very few of the spectators looked like members of the Roy O'Dwyer Fan Club; most of them, I suspect, were Wazaki's colleagues or family. But I noticed Skye, sitting silently at the back of the audience and staring cyclopically at my window; I don't remember him looking at O'Dwyer at all. He was flanked by two ridiculously muscular men, both thirtyish and both dressed in leather jackets, black acid-wash Levi's, and cowboy boots (Skye was wearing a slate-gray business suit with a blue shirt and regimental tie). The man on his left was dark and rather stocky, with a war-surplus crewcut and a prosthetic right hand; the man on his right was a red-bearded behemoth at least two meters tall, who I was sure I'd seen before . . . somewhere. After an hour of trying to place him, I wrote a note to Yorick, warning him that there were Apocalyptics in the courtroom. He merely looked bored.

"You should've seen them before we made them leave their fancy dress outside," he said. "We got Klansmen, Militia, California Rangers, five different Nazi parties—"

"And Skye."

"Yeah, I heard about your run-in with Skye. Unfortunately, we never found any of those, uh, bodies, and O'Dwyer doesn't even admit to having *heard* of him, so it'd just be your word against his again." He shrugged. I tried to remember Donner's prophetic spiel; had that mentioned Skye? Connie might know—but she'd disappeared too. Damn.

"Who're the bookends?"

Yorick stared at me. "I don't know the guy on the left, but you mean to tell me you don't know Gary Donner? Used to do sports news on Channel Six?"

"I don't—" I began, and then froze. I knew that Donner had predicted the quake, and I'd heard that he had red hair and a beard. The Bodysnatcher knew the future, and Galloway had red hair and a beard; a little injudicious use of Occam's razor had led me to the conclusion that Donner was Galloway, or the Bodysnatcher, or both. And I'd been wrong. The Bodysnatcher had disappeared again.

part three

REX ORBIS

26

TERA

It had been a generally shitty week, especially at work, which made the weekend that much more precious. Riding the Metro home, I toyed with the idea of staying in bed until Monday . . . and finally rejected it. It had taken me more than a year to get this far.

We ate dinner—fried tofu, noodles, and kelp salad—in silence (you *can* buy meat in the northeastern sprawl, but not on an honest person's salary, especially not if you also have to buy enough antidepressants to raise the *Titanic*). Kannon—I'd become accustomed to thinking of myself as Terri, but could never think of her as Karen, despite nearly a year's practice and all our coaching from the Witness Protection Program's people—had already made it clear that she didn't want me to go, and I had made it equally clear that I was going, and she went off to her class without even kissing me good-bye; I think she would have broken something if she had. I pity anyone who crossed her path on her way to the dojo. Even the strippers. Especially the men. She'd been on the streets much longer than I had and had never known the nine-to-five sort of routine, and she was still finding it difficult to adjust—but she also enjoyed the material comfort and security, and kept telling me that my curiosity was putting us in danger. I think she wanted to forget that I'd ever been white and male, and wanted me to forget it too, which was impossible. I waited until she was gone before calling for a cab, then showered and changed. I didn't bother with makeup; Star had occasionally tried to teach me the rudiments of cosmetic use, but without much success.

From the outside, the Greyhound was a twentieth-century relic, heartbreakingly familiar, but the gas tanks had been replaced by fuel cells, the new windows were prismatic and soundproofed, the computer probably knew the route better than the driver, and the seats were shabby but slightly more comfortable than I remembered (though maybe that was because I was thirty centimeters shorter). Nothing else had changed, except the landscape we drove through. Bus stations are usually in the ugliest part of town, and Washington has never been a beautiful city even when the weather was good (JFK once described it as "a blend of northern charm and southern efficiency"), but the ancient burned-out buildings outside looked more desolate—and more dangerous—than the quake-shattered ruins I'd left behind. I really missed San Francisco; why couldn't more cities be that beautiful? How much would it cost?

Philadelphia looked cleaner, if nothing else. It had never been one of my favorite cities when I was Galloway, mainly because of a shortage of cheap places to sleep, but no city with seven universities is completely without charm. My taxi driver was a UPenn graduate (I wish that astonished me), and she took me on a grand tour of the University District at my expense—necessitated, she said, by the maze of one-way streets.

The Danforth Institute was a renovated ancient stone-walled farmhouse a few blocks from the universities. "I'm Terri Lock," I told the gateposts as the taxi driver ran my ICEcard through the meter. "Dr. Rice is expecting me."

There was a moment's silence, then the gates swung open uninvitingly. " 'Abandon hope, all ye who enter by me,' " I muttered, and walked in. The gates shut behind me with a soft clang.

It was warm inside, with none of the antiseptic smell that I remembered hospitals having when I was a kid, but I still found myself shivering uncontrollably. The nurse at the reception desk was pretty, in an efficient sort of way. "Dr. Rice is—"

"She'll be right out," she said with a hospital-issue smile.

"Thank you."

Dr. Rice turned out to be a stocky, leathery, gray-haired woman with a big voice, masculine stride, and firm handshake—a hybrid of Jewish grandmother and Abrams tank. She didn't waste time with small talk. "You're sure you want to see him?"

If this was an example of her bedside manner, no wonder she

worked with comatose patients. "I wouldn't have come all this way if I didn't."

"Okay. We checked with his daughter; she had no objections. . . . Where did you say you knew him from, again?"

"He was a friend of my mother's, originally, in Bangkok; he taught English there." This was consistent with the "legend" the Witness Protection Program and I had contrived. "We were pen pals, though he was lousy at writing letters, and I looked him up when I came to America. I lost track of him after he left San Francisco, but I met someone who knew his daughter's address, and she told me he was here."

Rice clicked her teeth. "Did she say what'd happened to him?"

"She told me he'd collapsed and was in a cryptogenic coma."

"That's right. The EEG shows some activity, but he doesn't respond to anything we've tried."

"Have you tried other languages? He speaks—he *used* to speak—Japanese, Spanish, Mandarin, French, Russian, and German, and a little Thai. And English, of course."

"We've tried a few of those," said Rice after a moment's thought. "He doesn't respond to any sounds, or any other cues—smells, for example. There's no apparent physical damage to the brain itself, so it's not a stroke. We did a lumbar punch, and his CSF is normal, so if it's a toxin, it obviously breaks down very quickly after doing . . . well, whatever it does. Did. What do you know about his lifestyle?"

"Well, he didn't use drugs, at least not when I knew him, and he hardly ever drank: There was a history of alcoholism in his family, and he was scared he might have the genes. He's lived alone since his divorce, oh, probably ten years ago now. Most of the women he met were buying airline tickets, which made it kind of hard to form any lasting relationships. What sort of details are you looking for?"

"I really don't know. I've never seen a case quite like this one."

"Do you know when this happened?"

"Not exactly; he lived alone, and he might have been unconscious for nearly a week before anyone started worrying about him. But judging from the condition he was in when they brought him in, I'd say"—she consulted the chart she was carrying—"the first week of March. Probably sometime on the fourth or fifth."

Sixteen months ago, and about a week after San Francisco quake. "And he was living in Minneapolis?"

"Yes."

I nodded. Maybe the quake had changed the future so that the Bodysnatcher no longer existed, had killed an ancestor of his or something. Or maybe some less drastic change that had prevented him choosing Galloway, or from landing in Swiftie's body by mistake. Or maybe his mind had returned to its own time, or just into a younger and healthier body, leaving Galloway here; maybe he'd planned something to destroy the body and it'd failed, or maybe he hadn't bothered. After all, what did I know about time travel and braintaping? About as much as a dolphin knows about fishing nets. Rice opened a door and looked in, then shut the door quietly. "Are you sure you want to do this?"

I shrugged. It seemed unlikely that my old body was going to answer any of my questions, however much I felt like beating information out of it byte by byte. Consciously, of course, I realized that the body wasn't the person; neither of us was the Bodysnatcher anymore, and I wasn't sure that either of us was really Mike Galloway anymore, either. "Yes," I said. "Maybe he'll recognize my voice."

"He hasn't recognized anyone else," Rice said guardedly. "Not even his wife or daughter."

"Ex-wife," I said automatically, and wondered how they'd persuaded Angela to make the trip. I don't believe Galloway could have done it himself, but maybe she wanted to see him dead, or helpless. "What about his parents?"

"His father is dead; we've contacted his mother, and she can't afford—"

"*Dead?*"

"Yes," said Rice. "He died last December. A stroke."

I stared, and realized, to my horror, that I was crying. Partly for my father, partly because the Witness Protection Program had forbidden me to contact him and I'd never had a chance to say goodbye, but mostly for Galloway and how isolated, how alone, he'd been—*I'd* been. "I'd still like to see him," I said gruffly, wiping my eyes with a tissue.

Rice shrugged and opened the door. Galloway—the body—was lying on the bed, breathing slowly; he reminded me, absurdly, of the

Sleeping Beauty waxwork in Madame Tussaud's, the one you keep expecting to wake up. My—*his*—hair had been shaven off and allowed to grow back, and there was more gray in it than I remembered. They'd gotten rid of my beard, too, for the first time in nearly thirty years; I'd forgotten what that chin looked like. The room had the subdued pastel cheeriness of a psych ward, but the bed was obviously a hospital bed, the nightstand full of medtech, and the chairs cheap government issue.

"Hi, Mike," I said as cheerfully as I could manage. "Do you remember me?" No response.

Dr. Rice left me alone with the body for half an hour, and I spoke to him in every language I knew. "Do you remember Swiftie?" I asked. Do you remember the apartment on Haight? San Francisco? Vancouver? Perth? London? Paris? Munich? Tokyo? Bangkok? Hong Kong? Ankara? Eilat? Mazatlán? Remember driving deadheads proofreading picking fruit fishing for squid working as an extra a tour guide an orderly at a refugee camp your wedding your divorce the birth of your daughter? Do you remember *anything*? Jesus, do I have to do all this remembering *myself*?

No answer. The Bodysnatcher had gone again, and I didn't even know where to begin looking for him.

M y first action after shutting the door of my hotel room behind me was to jack my notebook in and send a reply to my anonymous informant: OK, you were right.

There was no mail until two days later, by which time I was back at work and Kannon/Karen and I had more or less made up. I was an interpreter-cum-data-shuffler for the Immigration and Naturalization Service, which would have been a depressing job anywhere but was made much worse by having to live in Washington, where strippers lived within screaming distance of the White House, drums of toxic waste had to be labeled INEDIBLE, and black men were three times more likely to go to jail than get into college. I spent all my time at a terminal and a videphone and rarely *saw* a scrap of paper, but unfortunately, regulations said I had to turn up to work at a desk for a year before applying to telecommute or qualifying for a cubicle. The message was anonymous, as always, and read only: Can we talk? Text only?

OK

Did you see Galloway?

I suspect I shuddered, but no one noticed; as long as I looked busy and answered the phone when it rang, I was just another piece of office equipment. Yes. Still in a coma; no change.

I know.

Who are you?

Later. I need your help.

What sort of help?

Finding people. Stopping Skye.

Skye?

Can you come back to San Francisco?

No.

It's important. You and I may be the only ones who know about Skye.

Know what?

Silence. Hesitation? Then a picture appeared, a head-and-shoulders shot of a pretty Asian woman against a blank background, rather like a passport photo but too bland to be real—airbrushed or some cybernetic equivalent, or maybe wholly computer generated. Recognize her?

No.

Could it be Connie Chen?

Connie? I looked more closely, wondering where the picture had come from. The obvious answer hit me a moment later. Reconstruction?

Yes.

She's dead, then?

Another pause, then, This woman's dead. No positive ID.

Quake?

Shot.

I stared at the picture. Connie dead? When?

Last year. Spring, probably March. She was found in Rogue River, naked, three entry wounds in her back. The body was badly decomposed, so as I said, no positive ID yet.

Dental records?

Lost in the quake, if there were any, and most of her bottom teeth were missing or broken. That probably wasn't postmortem. Her fingerprints aren't on record either. The picture's just a reproduction, based on the skull. There are other women missing who it might be.

I backtracked a little.

Where's Rogue River?

Oregon. Just south of Skye's property, where he breeds his dogs and trains his goons. But we can't

prove anything: plenty of guns in that part of the
country. Survivalist territory.

Oh, great. I looked at the picture again. It might have been Connie,
but darken the skin and it might just as easily have been me. I can't
make a positive ID from this, I typed, and I can't come
West to see the body. Have you asked Pat Hong?

He's dead.

Even though I'd pretty much expected it, that hit me harder than
my father's death had. Discovered a year ago. No suspicious
circumstances. Sorry.

The quake?

Yes.

I tried to remember the name of the old man in Chinatown, but
I had only met him once and wasn't sure we'd ever been introduced.
Besides, I wasn't entirely sure I could trust my anonymous informant.
If you won't tell me who you are, can you at least tell
me who you work for?

Missing Persons.

At least that made sense. You're obviously better at finding people than I am, I replied. What can I do?

There was a long pause, then When are you from?

When? I stared at the screen, decided that had to be a typo. Not
that it mattered; telling him where I was from (assuming he didn't
know) was dangerous enough. You first, I typed, after a pause of
my own, and waited for a reply.

243. You?

I stared at that number, trying to make sense of it. I knew there
was more than one calendar, of course: It was year twenty-five fifty-
something of the Buddhist Era, fourteen twenty-something A.H. for
Muslims, and well into the sixth millennium A.M. for Hebrews. Shin-
toists counted from the ascension of each emperor of Japan, and the
Taiwanese from the founding of the republic. "243" could mean anything, or nothing; it might even have been a typo, one digit missing.
I continued to stare, and then typed, I can't tell you until I
know who you are

Later or earlier?

I continued to stare at the monitor, then opened another window
and called up the Science Fiction Library and ordered a copy of

"YesterDei," the story Swiftie had written. A few seconds later, there was a click as my informant logged off.

"YesterDei" was set in the year 237 of the New Calendar, which began with the settling of Mars, probably later this century; none of Earth's old religions had traveled well, and soon the New Calendar was being used on Earth, for convenience, as well as on the collectively wealthier and more powerful Outer Worlds. Most of Earth's nations were no longer economic or military entities, but their names were still rallying cries for fanatics and terrorists. Faster-than-light travel was still impossible, our only contact with other intelligent life was a centuries-old message that we couldn't decipher, and though we'd discovered and settled three Earthlike planets in other solar systems, and sent robot probes out in search of more, even the Outer Worlds were reluctant to build more of the great sleeper ships needed to travel between the stars. Time travel *was* possible, but only to the late twentieth and early twenty-first centuries—and only if you didn't mind stealing someone's corpse at the moment of death. As I said, it was a pretty bleak scenario.

Of course my anonymous correspondent might simply have been spinning out a fantasy based on "YesterDei," but I doubted it. Not just because it was a rather obscure story, its fifteen minutes of fame long past, but because it should not have been possible for him (or her; who was I to make assumptions about gender?) to discover any link between the story and Terri Lock. First, he'd need to have blown the Witness Protection Program's records wide open, and then done the same with the financial records of the publisher, which were probably more heavily protected (did you ever hear about the family on Witness Protection who were given consecutive Social Security numbers, despite their ages? Well, so did a lot of other people. Even if it was only an urban myth, it didn't exactly inspire confidence).

I stared at the monitor and suddenly remembered an Isaac Asimov novel, *The End of Eternity*, in which a time traveler had been trapped in the early twentieth century and tried to draw attention to himself in a way that only his contemporaries would notice. He put a classified ad in a newspaper, the text shaped like a mushroom cloud, with the first letter of each line spelling A-T-O-M—years before the Manhattan Project. Putting some sort of coded message in a story, in an archive on the Net, was a pretty good twenty-first-century equivalent. It would be hard to be sure of selling the story, but maybe it had been plagiarized from some near-future award winner—and the delay between writing and publication might not matter if you were sending a message to the future. What would you think if a story published in, say, 1955, had the first man on the moon, a Neil Armstrong, saying, "That's one small step for a man, one giant leap for mankind"? Or a near-disastrous *Apollo 13*? Neither would raise any eyebrows for at least a decade. The rest of the story—or maybe the author's bio on the title page—could contain the other clues, obvious with hindsight, but invisible to me.

I suddenly remembered that something very like that had happened, at least once; there was a successful novel about an unsinkable ship named *Titan*, with too few lifeboats, hitting an iceberg on her maiden voyage across the Atlantic. It was published several years before the *Titanic* was built, and the title, aptly enough, was *Futility*, but that was probably just a coincidence—at least, I was mostly sure it was.

I scanned "YesterDei" again, thinking, Help me, help me, I'm trapped in 2014. . . . I speak your language. . . . Please send money.

What was it Dorothy Parker had screamed from her office window? "Get me out of here, I'm as sane as you are"?

I waited another week to hear from my unknown informant, without success. I tried return mail, but the sysop told me that there was no such address. I read "YesterDei" over and over, searching for clues, finding nothing, then studied the transcript of our conversations. Whoever he was, he was concerned about—perhaps obsessed with—"stopping Skye," so I decided to learn what I could about Skye.

I'd met the man but had never heard his first name, which made it difficult to conduct a search. What had Kannon told me about him? He'd achieved some high rank in one of the Ku Klux Klans, run for governor for the Am Nats and lost, then sold everything and moved to Oregon, where he'd started up a private security firm that might or might not have had a sideline selling package tours for wanna-be murderers. None of the Klans' Web pages were likely to give detailed biographies of their former officers, and I'd never found a dangergames site, but a search for gubernatorial candidates named Skye seemed to be a good place to start. I came up dry, but expanded the search to other electoral races, and found an Alfred Dean Skye, born December 1965, who'd run for the legislature in Arizona in 2006 and 2010; the photo looked enough like the man I remembered from the courtroom to keep me interested.

He'd received twelve percent of the vote the first time he ran, seven percent the second time, not a bad showing by Am Nat standards, but not good, though the incumbent had been popular and Skye had no experience in government. The few quotes attributed to him didn't read well on the screen and wouldn't have sounded much better—but this was six years ago; he'd had time since to learn how to write speeches. He rigidly followed the Am Nat line of law and order, small government (I've never quite figured out how those two go together), low taxes, states' rights, and a freeze on immigration; while he said nothing that a Klansman would have disagreed with, he managed to avoid sounding like an absolute fanatic. The only biographical information about him, apart from his business dealings, was a mention of three years' service with a volunteer border patrol in Texas. Unusually, none of the other candidates had bothered running any negative publicity on him either time. The last mention of him with an Arizona dateline was in September 2013, when it was blandly reported that the former political candidate had been wounded on a firing range, but that there were no suspicious circumstances, no reason to doubt his story that his pistol had exploded. They commented that this was the second time Skye had been rushed to a hospital that year, and wondered, tongue-in-cheek, if he was about to retire from politics due to poor health. Maybe he had; he didn't even rate a mention during the 2014 campaign. So far, so boring.

I ran a search on his full name under the news database and found a hundred and fourteen references, seven flagged for photo. I called up the most recent of these and saw a picture of him at a fund-raiser in Hollywood for rebuilding San Francisco. In the same photo were Gary Donner and his wife, Sophie, a stunning Nordic-looking blonde in a dress that made her look attractively top-heavy. I stared at this picture for more than a minute, trying to remember where I'd seen that woman before, then zoomed in on her face and neck. The makeup and jewelry made it difficult to be sure, but without the distracting details of the elaborate hairstyle, expensive dress, and eye-catching display of cleavage, the woman looked enough like Morningstar to be her sister, even her twin. Unfortunately, there was no mention of her maiden name.

I zoomed out again, and read the body text that accompanied the picture. Skye's rent-a-cop firm was Alpha Security, Inc., and its logo, a dark blue alpha within a gold five-pointed lawman's badge, was one I'd seen too often when I was a stripper. It promised armed response, and meant it. The text went on to say that Alpha had been awarded a three-year contract for civilian police services for San Francisco. Just what you need to make you feel better, I thought sourly; the inmates have taken over the fucking asylum. I wondered how many looters, and suspected looters, they'd shot already.

It was easy to guess how Skye had done it, if he really *was* from the future (or had some contact with it); history would have told him what the minimum bid would be, and he could have undercut them easily, especially if many of his rent-a-cops were volunteers, not mercenaries. Unlike many of his staff, he had no criminal record, nothing to prove that he was not a "fit and proper person." I ran a search for Alpha's Web site, which boasted of its resources: more than fourteen hundred men trained under their unusually stringent program (stringent for a rent-a-cop firm, at least; the full course ran for one hundred days, though there was a twelve-day crash course that they claimed was popular with employees of other companies), more than two hundred dogs (mostly shhhepherds), riot vehicles (number unspecified, but only one was pictured), telecopters (ditto), and trained horse police (four pictured: Skye and three unidentified women). No specific mention of weaponry, though the complete training course had two hundred hours of armed combat and only sixty of unarmed, and gyrfalcons and fully automatic weapons were theoretically unavailable to civilians. Nervously, I called up as much San Francisco news as I could find, hoping for a picture of some of Skye's rent-a-cops, but the Web was strangely silent on the subject. The site gave no biographical information on Skye, not even mentioning his time with the patrol, which puzzled me—I would have thought a man in that sort of business would want to boast of a military record, or at least some police experience. Even more strangely, he had no Web page of his own that I could find, so I continued reading the news clippings. Nothing very informative, or even scandalous; again, no one even seemed to speculate on his private life or his past. I guess if I had an army and a detailed knowledge of the present as history, I could arrange that sort of secrecy too. I gave up, placed a bookmark in the collection of newsbites, and went back to work.

I scanned the news stories that mentioned Skye, but none of them were particularly informative. There was no connection at all to any of his associates except for the one photo of himself and Donner, and that looked as though it might have been a casual meeting. A glance at the photo confirmed it; it was obviously unposed, and Donner seemed more interested in his new wife's cleavage than in Skye. I was looking at this when I remembered Sherlock Holmes's lesson of the guard dog that didn't bark (one day I'm going to have to reread those stories and find which one it came from). Why didn't the dog bark? Why were there no other names linked to Skye's? A man with that much money and power must have had, if not friends, then at least a few business associates.

To confirm this, I ran a search for any articles or photos that included both Skye and Donner. Nothing but that one photo. Damn.

Having nowhere else to start looking, I ran another search for Donner. This proved much more fruitful; not only did he have a personal Web site and two fan sites, he rated a page of his own on Nutwatch. The news stories about him started back in 2000, when he won a football scholarship to the University of Oregon. His own Web site confirmed this but was short on details of his football career. The sports pages filled in some of these blanks; He'd become known as "Thunderhead" Donner because of a vile temper, which seemed to infect most other players within about five meters of him. Even when he hadn't been the first to land a blow, he'd often been penalized for racial slurs and other insults. His captain was described as using him "like a tac nuke; the only safety measure is not to be there when he goes off." Away from the football field and pressure, he was consistently referred to as charming, likable, popular. He apparently dropped out of college (no one on any of the sites ever accused him of being smart), and after a couple of years working on his family's fishing boat out of San Francisco, he reemerged from obscurity at the '08 Olympics, where he won the silver in the hammer throw. Partly on the strength of this, and despite or because of a tendency toward colorful language and strong (if hilariously ill-informed) political views, he began a new career as a sports commentator on television and radio. He acquired a small cult following, and first attracted the attention of Nutwatch.

Nutwatch was a Web site that listed the most egregiously idiotic statements made by public figures from Aristotle to the present (its icon showed Newt Gingrich hunting a rather Daliesque giraffe). Donner's page was short, with most of the howlers made during his time as a radio talk-show host. Few of them resembled the speech in which he'd predicted the quakes, but he'd obviously had time to prepare that—or, more probably, someone else had. On that subject Nutwatch was silent.

Donner failed to qualify for the 2012 Olympiad, and his career in talk radio began and ended in 2013, probably because he had too much competition; would-be successors to Rush Limbaugh were a deutschmark a dozen. He also lost his job on Channel 6 to a good-looking young black man, and as no one seemed to want his endorsement for their products (hammer throwers aren't much of a market), he opened a bar in Oakland and bought into a few sporting-goods stores. In the past year, though, Donner had been slowly emerging from obscurity because of a knack for picking winners—just football, boxing, and the Winter Olympics, but I guess anything else would have looked suspicious.

There was no link in any of the sites to Skye or his company, and only a brief mention of Donner's wedding, again with no information about his wife except for her first name, and an interesting wedding photo on one of the fan sites. It showed a handsome young man standing on the other side of Sophie Donner, and gave his name as Alan Mueller, identifying him as (a) an athlete from Germany, and (b) her son by a previous marriage.

The nineteen-year-old Mueller, according to the news stories about him, was indeed an athlete, another Olympic medalist, winning silver in the biathlon as well as scoring well in several rifle, pistol, and archery events; he had narrowly missed qualifying in fencing, and was expected to do better in 2020. The wedding was held a week after the winter games and had received a little hype; Olympic winner reunited with long-lost mother, that sort of thing. All very boring, except for the bio, which gave his mother's name as Sophie, Sophia—and Sophia Stella.

Finding a marriage certificate for Sophia Stella Chapman and Jon Mueller took most of my lunch break; I was lucky it'd happened in the U.S. and that I'd made a good guess at the year. Alan was born barely five months after the wedding. Finding a date for the divorce was more difficult and tracking the Muellers after that beyond me, but at some time Jon Mueller, an architect, returned to Germany with his son. The newsbites said he'd died in 2014, never having been reunited with his wife. I looked at the photo of Donner's wife again, trying hard not to believe it. Granted that Tiffany had seen Peter Bright take Star out on the evening of the quake, the idea of her marrying Donner was—

Bright was dead. Tiffany was dead. O'Dwyer was nearly dead and not expected to live, having been attacked in prison within a week of getting out of solitary, not that the Witness Protection people would let me near him anyway. Unless I could get in touch with my informant at Missing Persons, I was going to have to speak to Star myself.

"Y ou're out of your mind," said Kannon.

I shrugged. It occurred to me that the problem was that I was actually out of my *body*, not my mind, but this didn't seem a good time to say so. "I have to know," I said.

"And there isn't any other way for you to find out? What about videphone?"

"Service to San Francisco hasn't been restored yet. Audi only, and that's unreliable."

She snorted. "So your ex-cop ex-girlfriend marries a white racist pig. I'm glad this astonishes you, because it doesn't even *surprise* me. A lot of Europeans talk the good talk, but most of the time that's all it is. When it comes to the crunch, nearly everyone sticks with their own kind."

"Does that include me?" I was sorry as soon as I'd asked.

"You're going to her, aren't you?" she snapped, then sighed. "No. Yes. If it doesn't, it's because you've learned the hard way who your people are. If it does, it's because sometimes you forget. I'm sorry. But I suspect that when it comes to getting married, sex matters a lot more to most people than politics."

I shook my head. She might have been right—look at Romeo and Juliet—but I couldn't believe that about Morningstar. "If she recognizes you," she said, "the Witness Protection people will wash their hands of you. And me."

"Yeah, I know." Shit. Maybe she was right about there being some other way, someone else who knew Star well enough that she'd know, just by seeing her, whether anything was wrong.

Shriek had been living in Oakland when the quake had hit and
had since moved to Reno, but I couldn't remember whether she knew
Star or not. Mama Castro did, but she was working in a women's
refuge in Santa Fe and would probably find it difficult to get away.
I wasn't supposed to contact either of them anyway, but I knew I
could trust Mama.

"Are you going to go?" asked Kannon.

"Not if I can find another way," I evaded.

"It's not as though she was in any danger."

That was hard to believe, though she was probably right about
that, too. "I'll get dinner," I said.

"Morningstar?" said Mama. "No, the last I heard was that you
said she'd disappeared. Mind you, I think the only reason she
would've tried to contact me is if she were looking for you. Are you
sure this woman is her?"

"No," I answered, and explained what I knew. Mama listened carefully; I wished I could see her face, but the refuge was strapped for
funds and had just an old-fashioned audi-only phone.

"Could they just be using her name?" she asked after a long silence.
"Trying to hide someone else?"

"A refugee? The—" I was about to say "the Apostles," but remembered that Mama didn't know about Skye. "These people?"

"Not a refugee, necessarily," she said. "A criminal, maybe. Some
woman who's supposed to be dead?"

"It's possible, I guess, but she . . ." She looks like Star, I thought, but
I realized how little that meant nowadays. This woman, whoever she
was, had obviously had her body sculpted, so why not her face? And
you don't need fingerprints or a genescan for a marriage license. And
her son had accepted her—but he probably hadn't seen her at all since
he was two years old. "Okay, it's possible, but how do I *know*?"

"You've got me there," replied Mama. "Of course, if you're sure
that Morningstar wouldn't have done anything like this, then it's
fairly simple; she isn't her."

I shook my head. "She might have done it for reasons I haven't
thought of. She used to be a cop; what if she's working undercover
to infiltrate the . . . group?"

"That's pretty far-fetched," said Mama uncertainly.

"I agree, it is, but is it any more so than the idea of Star marrying a Nazi?"

She was silent again, for several seconds, then asked, "What are you going to do?"

There are at least a dozen, and probably a hundred, services on the Net that claim to be able to find the addresses of celebrities, from fantasy writers to politicians to retired porn stars, price depending on the amount of hacking necessary. Home addresses are, of course, the most expensive. I hesitated before asking for Donner's address, and told myself that if he lived in the Bay Area, then the risks were just too great. But my query gave me a choice of addresses: one in California, one in Colorado, and one in Oregon. I paid for all three, plus phone numbers.

The California address turned out to be in San Jose, far enough from San Francisco that I might get away with it, close enough to be convenient for Donner. I waited until the office was empty (not difficult with the cutbacks), and prepared a speech, glad to be able to use my job as an alibi. I planned to claim that someone had miskeyed the date when Alan Mueller had entered the country and that we needed to confirm it. I called San Jose, and the house computer there told me that no one was home at present, but it could transfer me if I wished. I hesitated, then agreed.

Stella answered the phone, looking beautiful in a disturbingly artificial way. "Donner residence, hello?"

"Star?" My mouth felt dry, woolly; my speech was forgotten.

A slight double take, then, "I'm sorry?"

I tried again. "Sophie?"

"Yes, this is Sophie Donner. Who's speaking, please?" There was no recognition in her eyes, and her body language was wrong. I took a deep breath, preparing to launch into my speech, and began, "My name is Lee, and I'm sorry to call you at home, but I need your help."

"Yes?" Coldly.

I looked at her again, but it was plain that she didn't recognize my name or my face. Without thinking I asked, "When are you from?"

That obviously hit home; her eyes widened, and she opened her mouth to speak, then shut it again. "I need your help," I repeated more urgently. I looked past her, noticing a wall of what looked like real wooden planks. "I . . . there's a problem. I can't explain it over the phone like this; I'll have to see you. . . . Where are you? Leadville?" She nodded quickly. Maybe Mueller was catching up on his skiing. "I'll be there soon. Bye." And I hung up, hoping she wouldn't use callback to find me. She didn't.

I stared at my screen saver—a sunset over Olympus Mons, filmed by one of the Mars Rovers—and sighed. Colorado. Two days by bus or train, one by zep, and I still had no idea of what to do when I arrived.

I sent a message to Missing Persons, saying simply, I may have information on Stella Chapman, missing since quake, and waited two days for a reply. When there was no reply, I booked a zep to Denver for Friday night and made love to Kannon as though it were the last time. Her expression when she left for work the next morning suggested that maybe it was.

I packed a bag—toiletries, enough T-shirts and underwear and antidepressants for a week, the palmtop, CDs of the complete Travis McGee novels, *Sandman* comics and Beethoven symphonies, the sound tracks to *The War for the Oaks* and *The Untouchables*, and a new Glock needler and my old plasteel butterfly knife—and caught the shuttle to the airport. Despite my nervousness and the silent treatment from Kannon, I felt surprisingly good—almost euphoric—when the zep took off, and not just because I was out of the airport. I was traveling in the style I'd become accustomed to last century: the backpacker, the overeducated bum with an ICEcard, a Walkman, and enough to read. For the first time in many years, I felt at home.

The café had a stunning view of Mount Massive, which was probably why the cappuccino cost almost as much as my standby zep seat. The deterrent effect of the prices and the brilliantly engineered acoustics of the booth gave us the privacy for our conversation. Security was guaranteed by the layout; we could be seen by the waiters, but not by any passersby. "You said you needed help," said Star/Sophie.

"I do. Something went wrong; I'm in the wrong body, and the brain . . . there's so much I can't remember. I can't even remember why I'm supposed to be here, I just know that this wasn't part of the plan."

"How do you know?"

"I'm *male*," I croaked. "This body . . ."

She raised an eyebrow. Her makeup was movie-star perfect, but with an element of movie-star unreality. "I can see how an Asian might be useful," she said softly, "but no, if you were male . . . Alpha wouldn't have made a mistake like that."

I nodded. "I don't remember who I was supposed to be, but someone must have made a mistake with the time of death, and I found myself in this body instead, on a slab in the back of a van. I think gutleggers had taken her and flat-lined her, then left her, figuring she—I—couldn't just walk away." I grinned bleakly. "Fortunately, that's just what I did . . . but I didn't get very far. I came to again in a hospital, and they told me who I was supposed to be, took me home. . . . They were scared there was brain damage, and I think they're right. But I remember some things, fragments. . . ."

She nodded. "Alpha's been worried about the possible effects of neural damage on taping, but it's not easy doing experiments, though that's something he wants to try now he's here-now. How did you find me?"

"Yours was one of the names I could remember, and Donner's, and when I saw a picture of you together . . ."

"Lucky you got me," she said. "Do you remember when you're from?"

I shrugged. "237, I think. At least I remember the date; it might be when I was born or . . . I don't know."

Her mouth tightened into a thin line. "Upwhen from me, I'm afraid. You'll need to speak to Alpha."

"Alpha's here?"

"What? No, he's in San Francisco, probably at the bunker." She finished her coffee. "You'd better come home with me; we'll contact him later."

"Donner's not here," Sophie/Star said with what sounded like relief as she drove the armored BMW into the garage, "but Alan will be back sometime tonight, so you'll have to be careful around him; we've told him almost nothing, and he's going to wonder why you're here."

"What'll you tell him?"

She shrugged. "That you have information we need; he won't like it, but it should be enough. He has nothing personal against Asians, it's just politics. What would you rather I called you, by the way?"

"Just Lee," I replied as the garage door closed quietly behind us.

"Okay." She led the way from the garage to a sitting room with a view even better than the café's. Sophie/Star collapsed onto a sofa and stared at the ceiling—one of the few surfaces not adorned with weapons or trophies. "God, I hate this century. I know they say this soy stuff is supposed to be safe, but it's still wrapped in a plastic bag; I feel like I'm smuggling toxic waste in my chest. How long have you been here?"

"Nearly a year now. You?"

"Three months. Is this butchery really the best body-sculptors can do here?"

"I'm afraid so."

She shook her head. "My nipples feel like rubber, and I keep expecting my spine to snap. And the *clothes*." She unbuttoned her blouse, unfastened her bra. "What can you remember about your life upwhen? Who were you? What did you do?"

I knelt beside her. Having no idea what else to do or say, I whispered "This," and kissed her on the lips. Her eyes widened, and her mouth opened, our tongues touched, and then she pushed me away, gently but firmly. "No," she growled. "I won't say I'm not tempted, but it's too risky." She buttoned her blouse again while I retreated to a nearby chair. "Okay, so you were male. Are you *sure* you're from 237?"

"Not absolutely. Why?"

"Hmm. I don't know, you just seem . . . familiar. I shouldn't have let you do that, but—God, you'd think that these primitives would know *something* to make up for the tech they don't have. You wonder why they *bothered* overpopulating the planet. And have you tried one of their vibrators? About as erotic as cleaning your teeth." She shook her head. "And Gary is like . . . like he was in a hurry to finish before a football game starts, in a rush to get somewhere that isn't really worth going to. How do pre-women ever put up with it?"

Prewomen? I shrugged. "When you've been told for most of your life that there's only one item on the menu, and you can't even have very much of that . . . ." She looked puzzled by my metaphor, then laughed. I'd always suspected that was how the future would view us—either with laughter, or with puzzled disgust.

"Alpha did warn me about presex," she said wistfully, "though I wish he'd told me more. But my mission is to keep Gary in line by keeping him happy, and that means pandering to his ego for as long as he's useful." She sighed and glanced at a large and remarkably ugly wooden clock near the hallway that led to the bedrooms. "Sometimes I wish I hadn't let Alpha talk me into it, but it's good to be useful."

"Yes."

"I'll tell Alpha about you, but there probably won't be much he can do without taking you to the bunker or the camp; there's no hardware here, and he'll probably need to do a complete scan. What he'll do after that . . ." She shrugged and I looked away, pretending to be interested in the clock. "Are you hungry?" she asked. "I don't *believe* the stuff they have to do just to make food in this century."

Mueller returned home just after we'd started eating, and while he was obviously taken aback to find a dark-skinned Asian woman in his house eating microwaved lasagne with his mother, he wasn't overtly hostile or even rude. He didn't seem entirely sure how to talk to Sophie either, though his English was at least as good as hers, and after passing through the kitchen (a real twentieth-century kitchen, not just a kitchenette) and sitting room twice, he disappeared into his room. Sophie and I spent most of the evening watching the reruns on the *Star Trek* channel; she laughed at nearly everything except the jokes, and I soon found myself joining in. She gave me a quick kiss before I went to bed at about two A.M., and I lay there in the guest room and wondered what the hell I was going to do now. Sleep eluded me, so I keyed what little I'd learned into the palmtop and e-mailed it to Kannon, reread "YesterDei" to see how it matched what Sophie had told me about upwhen, then started rereading *The Green Ripper* in the hope that it might inspire me to some heroic gesture that wasn't entirely pointless. McGee and Meyer had just left the funeral service when I heard a tentative knock on the door.

I'd made sure my needler was where I could reach it, but I wasn't sure how much use it would be—the magazine only held ten tranqs and couldn't be reloaded without special tools, the house was too isolated and too well soundproofed for the sonic alarm to be heard by anyone outside, and the mountains would probably block the radio alarm. "Yes?" I replied softly.

The door opened, and Sophie stepped in and closed it behind her quickly but quietly. She wore a negligee that Donner had almost certainly bought her—the snow queen look, all white lace and fake fur trim. We looked at each other for a moment, and then I shut down the palmtop and placed it on the nightstand. The negligee fell to the floor an instant later.

Before I could speak, she said, "Never tell anybody about this. Not even Alpha. Agreed?"

"Agreed," I said. The body-sculpting made her look like a por- nographic parody of the Morningstar I'd known, but I discovered an instant later that she still tasted the same.

She was a greedy lover, but not inconsiderate or unskilled, even without the technical support that she must have been accustomed to. She was obviously used to male partners, but she knew what she liked and was good at guessing what I'd enjoy. I don't know whether it was Sophie I was pleasing, or Star's body remembering me, and after a few minutes the sex took over and nothing else seemed to matter.

I don't know how late it was when Sophie left the bed and wrapped the negligee around herself again. I noticed, with some alarm, small bruises already forming on her body, visible despite her post-orgasmic flush. I'd been careful not to bite her neck or anywhere else that might be on public display, but if Donner returned home . . . I wondered if she'd been trained in the use of twenty-first-century cosmetics, and tried to remember where she'd bitten me. She looked at me, her expression unreadable, then walked out quietly.

We were both subdued, unsure of what to say, at breakfast the next morning, even after Mueller left. There'd been no reply from Alpha (Skye?), and I didn't want to ask Sophie for too many details of their plans. I tried scanning Donner's library for information, but it wasn't remotely as interesting as O'Dwyer's had been. Most of what I found was about sports, fishing, or guns; politics and religion were obviously mere sidelines. Not a single print book, not even a comic. There wasn't even a Bible, unless it was on the hard drive of his computer. There were a few post-Holocaust movies in his film col- lection, including *Red Dawn*, but there was also *Pink Floyd—The Wall* (hardly a pro-Nazi movie, though I suppose some viewers might not have noticed), and no *The Birth of a Nation* or *Triumph of the Will*.

The only music discs were a few head-banger albums that would have been cut when he was in his teens, *The Wall* again, and a pristine boxed set of Wagner, probably a gift. "Looking for something to read?" Sophie asked as she walked in.

"I guess the library's at one of his other houses," I replied.

She shrugged. "He doesn't read much. Alpha used to give him books on politics and history in the hope that he'd read them, but I don't know what he did with them; probably just gave them away. Scott keeps giving him trashy science fiction, and he reads some of those, but he prefers twodees—*movies*. Alpha didn't choose him for his brains."

"Who's Scott?"

"Another nobody," she replied, grimacing. "He's written a few books, and he has a small following that Alpha thinks might be useful. Edits some of the publicity material, and wants to write our history when this is all over."

When *what* was all over? Sophie sat at the terminal and read her mail while I continued to browse the shelves. "They'll be here to-morrow night," she said, "or maybe Tuesday morning. They're buy-ing some weapons and can't leave."

"I thought they already had guns."

"Must be special weapons," she said vaguely. "Prebombs or some-thing. Alpha doesn't tell me very much that Gary isn't supposed to know, in case I let something slip. Maybe he'll tell you, I don't know, or maybe it's in one of those memories you lost. I hope he can do something about restoring them without . . ."

I blinked, and then grimaced. Without reconfiguring my brain entirely, wiping out all the memories he didn't need—*my* memories? Assuming, of course, that he believed *any* of my story?

"That doesn't leave us much time," said Sophie quietly, turning away from the computer. I nearly asked "Much time for what?" but her expression—bedroom eyes, if ever I saw a pair—answered the question for me.

We fucked (there wasn't even enough affection between us to call it making love, except for what I felt for what remained of Mor-ningstar) for the rest of the day, until about an hour before Mueller came home. She taught me a few tricks that probably hadn't been

invented yet, and I taught her a few that had apparently been forgotten, but otherwise, it was like playing a very good X-rated virtual-
reality game with a home movie of an old lover. I suddenly caught
myself wondering how Kannon felt when *we* made love, knowing
that my body had once been Naja's but my mind had been a white
male's. Try explaining *that* one to a marriage counselor sometime.
Can you say "doomed relationship"?

I tried to get Sophie to talk about herself and the world she'd
known, but she didn't tell me much that was useful; I gained a picture of an Earth in decline, balkanized by old strifes and surrounded
by a loose but powerful alliance of other human worlds, but I'd
guessed that much from "YesterDei." It was distinctly reminiscent of
Germany between the World Wars, or the South at the time the Ku
Klux Klan was born. Alpha, of course, was from a few years farther
upwhen and Sophie knew little about his era, but she assumed it
was similar or even worse. Maybe he had some grand vision of creating a political force that would enable Earth to dominate the Outer
Worlds, or maybe he was just tired of feeling like a loser and wanted
an empire of his own, however primitive it might be. I suppose the
same might be said of Hitler, and Stalin, and Vlad the Impaler, and
hundreds of others who'd left bloody footprints across history.
Whether the race war was part of Alpha's master plan, a heartfelt
passion, or just an easy way of attracting and uniting twenty-first-
century thugs, Sophie didn't say. The Earth of her time belonged to
the poor and uneducated (who I gathered enjoyed more material
comfort than the twentieth-century poor and uneducated, and in
some ways more than the twentieth-century rich), to a small inbred
aristocracy whose wealth and power would mean nothing offworld,
and to all others unable or unwilling to emigrate. Inevitably, many
of the poor were African or Asian or South American, though Sophie
didn't seem to bear them any particular ill will. She was more reluctant to discuss the offworlders, and I wondered whether she'd ever
met one. Of course, if they only came to Earth as tourists or advisers,
as she implied, I could understand some of her hatred.

I looked around the house trying to plan an escape route; the
security system seemed designed to keep people out, not in, but there
were alarms on all the windows and doors, and we were a long walk
from any town unless I stole one of Donner's cars, and that seemed

even more risky. I'd never driven a snowmobile, and skiing was right out. Besides, I hadn't learned enough yet.

Dinner that night was even more awkward, with Mueller seeming even more resentful. I went to bed early, and Sophie joined me a little after midnight, assuring me that Mueller, a morning person, was already asleep. The sex was good, but not as good as it had been; my dislike of Sophie's politics was beginning to eclipse the old love I associated with the body and face she wore. She left an hour or so later, and I rolled over and was trying to sleep when I heard the yelling. Mueller. Shit.

I should've stayed where I was, and maybe I would've done so if I hadn't heard the slap. I ran out the door, not even bothering with a robe. Sophie stood in the hallway, between Mueller and me. She had her back to me, but when she turned to look at me, I saw a handprint, outlined in red, across her face. Mueller was dressed in jeans and a University of Heidelberg sweatshirt, but he didn't seem to be armed; he glared past Sophie, then pushed past her and hissed, "And as for you, you slant-cunt dyke, I'm—"

He was standing less than a meter away when he raised his hand, and the next thing I knew, he was bent over before me, his right arm twisted behind his back. Naja's reflexes must have taken over again. He swore long and loudly in German (it's a good language for it), and I asked in the same language, "How many good fingers does an archer need, shithead?"

He lashed out with an elbow, but I was ready for that; I dodged it easily and broke his little finger in the same instant. "Wrong," I said. "Just two and a thumb." I looked up at Sophie, who was plainly terrified. "Now, are you going to be a good boy?" I emphasized the point with a knee to his balls—not hard, just as a warning. He grunted, then swore again.

The urge to kill him was very strong; maybe that was Naja's influence, but I doubted it. Alternatively, we could lock him outside, but in this weather that would probably kill him anyway. I looked at Sophie. "What should I do with him?" I asked in English.

"Let him go," she whimpered.

"Not until he promises to behave."

"He'll behave," she said a little more confidently. "When Gary sees what he's done—"

"What *I've* done?" snarled Mueller. "What about what *you've* done?" Sophie shook her head. "Do you really think he doesn't know?"

He looked up suddenly; maybe I was imagining it, but he seemed to be trembling. "Do you think I could keep a secret from him?" Sophie continued. "Didn't you know there are cameras in every room in this house?"

If it was a bluff—and I was prepared to bet it was—then it was a brilliant one. I was still tempted to drop him over a cliff, but when I released my grip on his arm, he merely staggered away from me. He straightened up, and then walked past Sophie toward his room, careful not to brush against her.

"I'm glad that worked," I whispered as I walked closer to her. The mark on her face was fading; if Mueller was luckier than he deserved to be, it wouldn't even bruise. "But I think I'd better get out of here anyway, wait somewhere for Alpha to come and pick me up."

"Where? Why?"

"I don't think Alan's going to give up that easily," I said. "He won't dare do anything more to you, but I'm . . . anyway, if you give me a lift down to town, I can wait for a bus to Denver, then catch a zep, call you when I've found a place to stay."

She looked uncertain. "I can lock my room, keep him out, you can stay with me—we can't keep him from telling Gary now, but if I can tell Alpha first . . ."

"Who is Gary likely to believe? Were you telling the truth about the cameras?"

"Of course not. If they *were* there, I'd have shut them off first. No, he'll believe Alpha."

"You're sure?"

"Well . . . fairly sure. He might suspect. He's like that—"

"You said he had a temper. Is he likely to hurt you?"

"No . . . I don't think so. You he might . . ." She hesitated, then shrugged. "Maybe it *would* be better if you weren't here. He'll believe Alpha before he believes Alan, but he'll believe Alan before he believes you. How long will it take you to get dressed and pack?"

Five minutes later, I walked out of my room and into the hallway, trying hard not to smile. Mueller was waiting for me at the front door. The device in his hand looked so bizarre I didn't even recognize it as a target pistol until he shot me in the chest.

I woke to find myself back in Donner's guest room, or another room exactly like it; the only thing that was different was a large, heavily bearded man in a dark gray greatcoat watching me intently and pointing what I couldn't help but recognize as a gun—a Schmeisser, one of those submachine guns you always see Nazis carrying in World War II movies—at the ceiling. I could see his face clearly, which meant that he didn't expect me ever to describe him to anyone. Shit. My chest was bandaged, my hands and feet gaffer-taped to the bed, and there was more tape covering my mouth; it would have been easy for them to have blindfolded me. I opened my mouth to try to speak, and the gun came down quickly to point at my head. "The boss told me you weren't to talk to anybody but him," he said. "Stay here; I'll go get him."

That might have been meant as a joke; his mustache hid his mouth, making it difficult to tell whether he was smiling. I merely nodded and he walked out, the gun pointed at the ceiling again. I glanced around the room as best I could; there was no sign of my palmtop or my bag. A moment later Skye walked in, followed by a younger, heavily built man with a five-o'clock shadow and government-issue crew cut. Both wore bomber jackets, black jeans, and black gloves, and both were armed, Skye with a large knife, Shadow with an even larger automatic pistol. As soon as the door was shut, Skye reached down and tore the tape off my face ungently. I looked at the weapons and resisted the urge to scream out.

Skye looked as though he were about to speak, then he peered at my face intently and hesitated. "I've seen you before, haven't I?" I didn't reply, and Shadow raised his pistol to hit me across the face, but Skye shook his head. "Look, if you're who I think you are, I'll let you live." Shadow stared at him blankly. "*Where* have I seen you?" asked Skye. "You . . . your hair was darker, and longer; your face . . . thinner, I think, but I didn't get a good look at you then. Where?"

I swallowed. "San Francisco," I said thickly. "Chinatown."

Shadow laughed, but Skye held up a hand—the one without the knife. "When?"

"The quake."

"And your name?"

Jesus, what name had I given then? "Tera."

He nodded. "Yeah, that was it." He turned to Shadow. "We can't kill her."

"*What?*"

"She saved my life that night. Before your time. I owe her."

"You're shitting me," said Shadow. Skye shook his head. "Can we—"

Skye looked at me. "Mueller shot you with a .22. You have a broken rib, but he missed your heart; maybe he wanted you to die slowly." I nodded weakly. "Or maybe you managed to duck. Lucky for you it was only a single-shot pistol and Sophie knows how to patch a wound. That's one hell of a tale you told her—is Tera really your name?"

"Is Skye yours?" I replied. "Or should I call you Alpha?"

"Alpha's just the name of my company," he said smoothly. "*One* of my companies. If Sophie's referred to me as Alpha, it's because I sometimes have to make decisions as though I were Alpha Security, put its interests before my own. . . . I've had a lot of responsibility thrust upon me. What's your *real* name?" I was silent; if he was going to lie to me, I didn't see any reason to tell him any truths. "Lee?" he prompted. "That's what you told Sophie."

I glanced at Shadow, then turned back to Skye. "I'll tell you, but not him."

"There's nothing you can say in front of me that you can't say in front of him," said Skye.

"Oh?" I looked at Shadow again. "When are *you* from?" I asked.

He flinched and turned to Skye, who replied, "I know what you told Sophie, but I also know that your story is impossible. Now, what *is* your name?"

"And who are you working for?" asked Shadow. "Who sent you?"

He was obviously rattled, even if Skye wasn't. "Upwhen from Sophie?" I asked.

"I've sworn not to kill you," said Skye, "but I *can* hurt you. Now *what is your fucking name?*"

He hadn't really lost his temper, but there was a distinct dent in his cool. I took a deep breath and answered, "Some people call me Lee."

"Lee who, or who Lee? Look, I assure you, we *will* find out."

"Lee Bird."

There was a moment's silence, and then Skye nodded. "Now, that wasn't so difficult, was it?"

I looked at his face—his expression was strange, unreadable—and then at Shadow's. He seemed to have bought it. "Your turn," I said.

"Ve vill ask ze questions," said Skye in an outrageous German accent. "Do you need a drink, Lee?"

"Yes, please."

Skye nodded, then turned to Shadow. "I'll be back in a minute. Watch her."

It felt like much more than a minute—at least five, probably ten—before I looked at Shadow and asked, "If you're the only one he trusts, we may be seeing a lot of each other. What should I call you?"

He hesitated, then shrugged. "Ron."

"I don't mean to pry, but your right hand . . . that's a prosthetic, isn't it?"

He looked at my hands, still firmly tied to the bed, and nodded. "Pretechnology," I said. "Must be tough." No reply. "What happened to it?"

He didn't speak. A moment later, Skye walked in, carrying a 49ers insulated mug in his left hand, a palmtop in his right. "Ah, room service," I muttered as he closed the door behind him. Ron's mouth quirked in what might have been the ancestor of a smile. Skye put the straw to my lips and let me drink—it tasted like plain tap water, but I hadn't been expecting champagne—then took the mug away.

"Well, I thought your name was familiar," he said, "so I've just done some checking. Did you write a story called 'YesterDei'?"

I hesitated, then nodded. "Co-wrote it. Did you read it?"

"A while ago. A friend pointed it out to me. Interesting setting; I'll have to read it again."

"It seemed a good way of calling for help."

"Help?" He raised an eyebrow. "Whose help? What sort of help?"

"Yours, of course. I'd lost a lot of memory—I think this brain was damaged—but I knew I wasn't here alone"—Skye looked skeptical, so I changed my tack slightly—"and I thought that if no one here noticed it, someone upwhen might and—"

"And do what?"

"I don't know. As I said, there are holes in my memory—"

"And even bigger holes in your story." Skye grunted. "Co-wrote with who?"

"Whom," I corrected automatically. How easy would it be for them to check where the payment for the story had gone? "A man named Mike Galloway."

"Why?"

I shrugged. "Mostly . . ." No, saying that it was to cover my tracks didn't make sense if I *wanted* someone to find me, did it? "Because I'd never written anything before, knew nothing about it—hadn't even read any of the zines we tried to sell it to later. Galloway was an old science-fiction fan who'd done some writing. He thought of the title and changed the ending and a lot of the language, but all the ideas were mine."

"What did you tell him?"

"Galloway? That I'd split the money with him if he wurped and submitted it for me. I don't think he expected me to write anything, let alone finish it, so he agreed."

"Where did you know him from?"

"I was working in a phone-sex stable and he was one of my regulars. He seemed harmless enough, so I let him take me out to dinner a few times."

"And where is he now?"

I must have hesitated. "I don't know. He stopped calling, and I think he left San Francisco before the quake, but where he went—"

They looked at each other. "You're lying," said Skye flatly. "Where is this Galloway?"

"I don't *know*," I repeated. "I tried looking for him on 411.com once, but there was no listing. The shop he said he ran closed months before the quake. Maybe that wasn't really his name, or maybe he's dead—he was in his fifties and in pretty shitty shape. Or maybe he committed suicide. He must have been pretty fucking lonely if I was the only woman he could find to talk to, but if he did, I'd rather not know. Okay?"

Skye stared at me, his expression sour. "We can come back to that. Do you have anything to support this bullshit story about being from the future?"

I looked at Ron and smiled. "*He* believes me." Ron almost blushed.

"He's a soldier," replied Skye smoothly. "Soldiers are trained to believe bullshit. You have to convince *me*."

I shook my head. "I've nothing material, nothing but memories and not many of those. I don't even remember who I was supposed to be in this time." I repeated the story about waking up on a slab as I'd told it to Sophie. Skye listened without interrupting, then shook his head.

"Supposing that any of what you've said is true," he said, "what do you want me to do? Restore your memory? I suspect that even *if* I had the know-how and the hardware, I'd have to erase what memory you have now first. I think that would violate my oath not to kill you. What do you think?"

"You're probably right."

"And you strike me as a survivor type—which I mean as a compliment, in case you were wondering. Or do you just want somebody to—what did you call it?—play your braintape into a male body?" He looked me up and down. "Then what would we do with that body that wouldn't violate my oath?" He sat back in the chair and rubbed his chin, and a smile spread slowly across his face. "I think I've heard enough."

He obviously wanted me to ask what he was going to do, but I didn't give him the satisfaction, and the room was silent for more than a minute. "There's nothing else we can do here," Skye said finally. "As soon as Sophie says you're well enough to travel, we'll be on our way."

"Where to?" I asked, looking at Ron rather than Skye. "Oregon?"

Ron didn't even flinch. "Maybe," said Skye. "Later." And he walked out.

He returned a few minutes later with Sophie, and they examined my wound, which was smaller than I'd expected. I was wondering how they'd managed to bring any medical technology with them, then realized how much "medical technology" many of us carry in our heads that would be a godsend to an earlier century—ideas like sanitation, vaccination, aseptic technique, anesthesia, mouth-to-mouth resuscitation (which we ignorant Europeans could've learned from the Australian aborigines if we'd been paying attention), CPR, diets to prevent beri-beri and scurvy, and the knowledge that mosquitoes carry malaria and fleas bubonic plague. Even advising them to clean their teeth occasionally, that burning ghettos full of Jews didn't prevent the Black Death, or that tight corsets and silicon injections were bad for women, could have reduced the grand total of human misery. Of course, you'd make more *money* with the formulas for gunpowder, napalm, and mustard gas.

"Well, can she travel?" asked Skye. Sophie hesitated, and he added, "I swore an oath not to kill her."

Sophie nodded, her face carefully blank. "I'd better come with you—"

"No."

"How long do you want her to live?" she snapped, flushing suddenly. "She has a punctured lung; will it violate your oath if she drowns in her own blood tomorrow? Take me with you, or leave her here for a few days, or get a *real* healer."

Skye brooded for a moment, then turned on his heel. "Pack your things; be ready in an hour."

Donner was waiting outside the room as Skye and Greatcoat ushered me out, one holding each arm. My feet were untied, but my hands were cuffed behind my back and my mouth taped shut. Donner took a step toward us, then drew back his hand to slap me across the face; I dodged right, then left, and the blow missed me and smashed into the side of Skye's head. Skye's plastic eye rolled across the floor, and then I planted one foot and kicked Donner in the groin. He was too startled at having slapped his boss to try to dodge, and he folded up very neatly when my foot connected. I then kicked back into Skye's knee and he overbalanced, bringing the three of us down onto the floor in a heap. I fumbled behind me for the pistol on Skye's belt, without success; Greatcoat wouldn't let go of my arm, even when I head-butted him in the nose. Skye was yelling for Ron, who came running in from the sitting room with Mueller hot on his heels, both of them brandishing pistols. Mueller took aim at my chest, and Ron elbowed him in the gut, then sapped him with the butt of his gun. He smiled at me, then drew a bead on my neck, and I realized the muzzle of his gun was too narrow for a firearm; it was a needler, probably loaded with tranqs. It fired silently and I felt the slight sting as the dart hit me in the neck. Everything went blurry, and then black, and that's why I don't remember the trip back to San Francisco.

The first time I had a general anesthetic, as a kid, the changeover from consciousness to blackness was so sudden that it felt as though I'd simply disappeared. Since then, I'd often hoped that death would be like that, instantly ceasing to exist, like turning off a light switch. Tranq needles don't act that quickly, though the sensations of losing and regaining consciousness are uncomfortable and disorienting without actually being painful. The best thing I can say about them, though, is that they beat the hell out of being shot with a firearm.

It was dark when I came to, much darker than any room I'd ever been in. The floor was cold and level, the wall I felt when I reached out was cold and smooth, and the lack of echoes suggested that I was in a rather small and soundproof chamber. I stood and reached up until I could touch the ceiling—higher than two meters, less than three—then fumbled my way around in the dark, trying to take the measure of my domain. It was tiny, a little more than three paces long and two wide; there was a chemical toilet, a sagging cot that might have been comfortable in Tutankhamen's day, a wall and door of depressingly solid metal bars, a stink of fear and depression and old dust, and a lot of darkness. And me, and no clothes that I could find except for my bandages, and no antidepressants. Great.

I have no idea how many hours, or days, I spent in that darkness waiting to see or hear something; I tried using my pulse as a timer for a few minutes, but soon lost count, and it seemed pretty unproductive anyway. I tried sit-ups and push-ups until I was exhausted, then the same sort of memory exercises I'd used when Sozu-san had held me captive; reciting poetry, recalling different words and expressions in different languages, reconstructing wheres and whens of first times with various lovers. It soon became clear that I wasn't going anywhere in a hurry, nor was the darkness, and before long I was remembering *last* times with various lovers, which is a much less pleasant way to pass a few hours, even when the last times were also the first times. I've never been a great fan of one-night stands, and most of mine were genuine attempts to start relationships, even the ones at youth hostels and science-fiction conventions. At least I would've sworn so at the time. I think I remembered all the names correctly, though the chronology was dubious. When I'd milked that of all the pleasure I could get from it, I tried reciting *Hamlet*, improvising when I became stuck, then started on *The Importance of Being Earnest*. Even allowing for the bits I had to fudge, *Hamlet* is at least three and a half hours long, and *Earnest* maybe half that, but the light levels didn't seem to be changing at all. I tried singing aloud, in the hopes that someone would complain, maybe even call the cops. Nothing.

My mouth was becoming dry, and I tried to remember how long a person was supposed to be able to last without water. That wasn't a pleasant thought either, so I went back to making lists. The cats I'd lived with. What I'd eaten in my favorite restaurants in my favorite cities. The best hundred movies I'd ever seen. The best hundred books. The Travis McGee novels, in order of publication. The *Flashman* novels and the Miles Vorkosigan adventures, ditto. The seventy-nine episodes of classic *Star Trek*. The Apollo astronauts. My recipe for spaghetti bolognese from the time when I could afford meat. If this was Skye's idea of keeping me alive, his sense of humor stank on ice.

I suspect I drifted in and out of sleep several times; I was definitely asleep, and dreaming of teppanyaki squid, when I heard the metallic creak of the door opening. I looked up and saw two large flashlights being held by tall shadows. "Good evening," said Skye.

I tried to spit but my mouth was too dry. "If you say so," I croaked. "How long have I been here?"

"In here? Not long."

I nodded. "I gather this is part of your bunker?"

"Bunker?"

"I don't know, maybe it was something Sophie said." I looked at the wall behind me; it was a pale institutional green, except for a band of very dark green near the floor, and a patch of rough bare concrete where something had probably been removed. It was vaguely familiar, but I wasn't quite awake enough to place it. "Sensory deprivation? Pretty crude interrogation method, isn't it, even for a pre?"

"I'm sorry about that," replied Skye offhandedly. "We don't take many prisoners." It was meant as a threat, but I was sure it was also a lie.

"If this is the way you treat them," I said, "you don't deserve any." Secondhand Oscar Wilde, but better than nothing. "If I don't get something to drink soon . . ."

The other shadow—Ron?—threw something at me, and I caught it without wondering whether I should. It turned out to be a collapsible bottle filled with what weighed and sloshed like cool water. "Thank you," I said, found the cap, twisted it off, and drank. It tasted like water too, and if it wasn't, so what?

"You're very trusting," said Skye.

Too late, it occurred to me that there might be worse things in water than mere poison. Truth drugs, maybe? Though there was no such thing in 2016, Skye might have synthesized something . . . or was he just trying to psych me out? "I don't have a lot to lose."

"No," said Skye. "Can you walk, or do we carry you? I need hardly warn you what will happen if you try another stunt like the one you pulled in Colorado. Were you trying to escape or was that just a suicide attempt?" I shrugged. "Well, you won't be escaping from here," he said, "and we're not going to kill you, but we have some very interesting methods of hurting you if you fuck up. So, can you walk?"

"Yes," I said, and stood. I looked around me, and suddenly guessed where we were; I used to be a travel agent, after all, and I was supposed to know tourist attractions. Alcatraz. An isolation cell in . . . what was it? D Block. The Hole, as the inmates used to call it. "Where are we going?"

They hustled me along to another cell two doors down, one with an identical paint job but better lighting. It looked like a twenty-first-century version of Frankenstein's lab, with an untidy hedge of electronics—most of it probably scavenged from high-school science storerooms and Laser Shacks—surrounding a heavy table fitted with restraints. "Lie detector?" I asked.

"Something like that," said Skye. "On the bed, please."

I looked at his face, realized what was happening, and suddenly felt very cold; if I hadn't been dehydrated, I probably would have pissed myself. "It's a braintaper, isn't it?"

"On the bed," repeated Skye curtly.

"What're you going to do?"

Skye sighed, while Ron tapped his flashlight on his palm like a baton. "Most of your story is obviously crap," said Skye. "But you know a lot that you shouldn't, and we need to know who told you. Don't worry, we're not going to erase or overwrite anything, just take a tape for study."

"Study?" I looked at them and realized there was no way of getting past them, and nowhere to run to if I did. I didn't believe for a minute that I could swim to San Francisco, and even if I did, Alpha would probably pick me up almost instantly. I remembered the story of the only man known to have escaped from Alcatraz alive; they found him hanging on to the Golden Gate bridge, suffering from hypothermia and cardiac arrest. After a brief stay in a prison hospital, they shipped him back to Alcatraz. Some fucking escape. I lay down on the table and Ron strapped my wrists and ankles to the table legs while Skye placed a helmet on my head. "Don't worry," he said. "This won't hurt a bit," and I saw him smile for an instant before something covered my eyes. "That'll come later."

"Why couldn't you do this while I was asleep?" I muttered as Ron bound me to the table with another belt around my waist.

Silence from my captors, then "Quicker this way. The important stuff gets buried while you're unconscious. Now, where did you hear about braintaping? You don't have to answer aloud; it's the thought that counts." He rattled off more questions, and I tried not to think of the answers, distracting myself again with poetry and old memories. I don't know if it worked—probably not, especially when a question took me completely off guard—but it passed the time, and it helped to feel that I wasn't cooperating.

After a few hours, Skye removed the apparatus from my head. "I'll be back if these aren't any good," he promised.

"And you're just going to leave me here like this?"

"More or less," he said, with a quick glance at my body. "But don't worry, I'll send somebody in to keep you company."

The camo-clad wild-eyed man who walked in a few minutes later was leaner and younger-looking than most of Skye's cronies, and handsome in a way that was almost pretty; more like a racehorse than a warhorse. Give him a pair of Ray-Bans and he might have had a career as a model, but there was something unnerving about his eyes, worse even than Skye's; they were deep-set and shadowed, and they moved too fast, as though they were utterly independent of his face and body. When he saw me—strapped to the table, naked, and spread-eagled—they brightened slightly and the corners of his mouth twitched into what might have been a smile, but his gaze didn't stay on me for long, and it never reached my face. He shut the door behind him after scanning every square inch of the room, extracted a condom from a jacket pocket, and unfastened his webbing belt.

"Does your boss know you're here?" I asked.

"He knows everything," he replied, with a hint of a giggle. "Sees everything, hears everything. There are cameras, microphones, everywhere. We both know what you did with Gary's wife, too, and we're going to teach you the error of your ways." He reached over and squeezed my nipples, pulling and twisting hard enough to hurt, but I didn't make a sound. "Jesus, what miserable little tits." His pants were around his booted ankles now, and he shuffled closer to the table. He unwrapped the condom as though it were an IQ test, and rolled it onto his erection, his hands now moving almost as quickly as his eyes. I kept talking, partly in the hope that he'd realize I was a human being rather than a collection of body parts, partly to distract myself. He pulled me down the table so that my vagina was near the edge and pushed into me awkwardly. I yelled with the pain, but that only seemed to encourage him, so I tried to stop, but he was beyond hearing me. He kept up a monologue about lesbians, how much he hated them and what they needed and what should be done to them, and then, after what might have been a few seconds or a few minutes, pulled out and raised my ass clear of the table so he could force his cock into my anus. He obviously expected this to be easier than it was, so if he knew anything about sex at all, he'd learned it from watching videos. This time I yelled simply because I was unable not to; the shame would come later, but all that mattered then was the pain. I retched, and if my stomach hadn't been empty, I would have vomited.

It was over before I'd stopped yelling; he was carefully removing the condom, befouled on the outside by blood and shit and on the inside by him. There was no pleasure in his expression, and no post-coital *tristesse*; just more hatred, and what might have been resent-ment, maybe even shame. The monologue wound down slowly while he wrapped the filthy condom in a tissue and dropped it in a trash can, then pulled up his pants and fumbled with his belt buckle, obviously reluctant to get it dirty. "Was it good for you too, bitch?" he sneered as he walked backwards to the door, still not looking at my face. "I'll see you again soon. Maybe tomorrow."

I was dehydrated, but I managed to summon enough saliva to spit on him. I missed his face, hitting his jacket instead. He turned pale and swore at me, then smiled coldly. "Tomorrow," he said. "Be seeing you."

Ron came in a few hours later, to unstrap me and guide me back to my cell. There was a cold-light stick there, good for another hour or so of greenish glow, another bottle of water, a plastic plate of franks and beans and a plastic spoon. My period had started, so I was bleeding from my vagina as well as my anus; I cleaned myself up as best I could with toilet paper and a little water, then realized I'd been crying, which was enough to set me off again. When I'd finished, I took advantage of the light to examine the cell. The peep-hole in the door was blocked by what I suspected was a low-resolution infrared camera, so I blocked it further with wadded toilet paper, then sat below it and ate, wondering how long it would take Skye to read my braintape and what he'd learn from it. I bent and twisted the light stick, halfheartedly trying to open it so that I could drink the cyanide inside, but it was too tough for my teeth and I didn't have anything that could be used as a knife. I kept at it long after the light had faded, because it was something to do, something with a hope in hell of distracting me from what had just been done to me. I didn't want to sleep because I didn't want to dream.

. . .

I was still huddled in that corner, half asleep and shivering fit-
fully, when the door opened. I rolled aside and—still not quite
awake—into a defensive crouch. If it was the rapist back for more,
I was going to make him pay for it.

Instead it was Ron, alone for once, with another tray and another
light stick. "Breakfast," he said.

"Where's Skye?"

"Busy. Do you want this or not?"

I thanked him, stood slowly, and took it. It was more canned
food—dinosaur macaroni in a cheesy sauce—and bottled water.
"What about . . . ?" I tried to think of some name foul enough for
the rapist and failed. Ron blinked, then nodded. "Don't worry about
him."

"He's dead?" I wasn't sure whether I sounded eager or disap-
pointed.

Ron shook his head, then tapped his ear; the room was bugged,
and I suspected the sick fuck was listening. "He's around, but cooperate and he won't be a problem. Try to escape, like you did in
Colorado, and he'll be back. *Capisce*?"

"Yeah." I took a step away from him. "That is one sick puppy.
When is he from?"

"Now, but Skye trusts him," which implied that he didn't. "He's
useful, good at what he does."

"Is he an Apostle, or do you have to be at least half human?"

Ron glared at me, which wasn't much of an answer, and walked
out. I was left alone for another day, or maybe only half a day, before
he returned with another plate—tinned chili—and collected the
empties. I tried asking him the date, but he didn't reply. "I just
thought while I was in San Francisco, I'd hate to miss the Folsom
Street Fair."

He glared again. "What makes you think you're in San Francisco?"
I shrugged. "Anyway, that crowd isn't coming back. Most of them've
moved up to Seattle."

"Pity. What about the jazz festival?" He grunted and walked out.

The next time the door opened Skye walked in, a flashlight/lantern
in one hand and a pistol in the other. The door shut behind him and
he leaned against it. "Mr. Galloway, I presume?"

I didn't budge. Skye sighed. "Look, I've seen some strange brain-tapes in my time, but yours was so damn chaotic that once we'd gotten through everything, I still didn't believe most of it. I thought maybe you had a mess of—what do they call them now? dissociative personalities?—in that head of yours. Maybe, just maybe, some of these could survive a swap-hop; maybe the upwhen personality could be merged into one or more of them. That would've been one explanation—I didn't like it, but it was possible."

"Aren't you worried about who might be listening?" I asked, looking up at the ceiling.

Skye stared, then laughed. "Oh, him. I told him to go grab some coffee, and made sure he did. I could've waited for him to get some sleep, but he doesn't do a lot of that. Cooperate, and I'll keep him away from you; hit me again, and I'll hold you down while he goes to work. Anyway, that's some set of memories you've got, Mr. Galloway."

"I'm not Galloway." Way too late for Galloway.

"Maybe not, maybe not anymore," he said smoothly, sitting on the end of the cot. "I haven't sorted out all of the memories—how many languages do you *know?*—but there's too damn many of them for a woman your age, and a lot of them belong to a man who thinks of himself as Michael Galloway. I did some checking up on Mr. Galloway and found his body, and that's when things started to make sense. So, somebody taped Galloway's brain and did a pretty good job of flat-lining yours, then . . . but you know all of this. What I couldn't find out was *who* and *why.*"

"Believe me," I said, "I don't know the answer to either question, and I'm at least as curious as you are."

Skye looked at me for a long time, then nodded. "I believe you, Mr. Galloway. I can assure you it wasn't anyone *I* sent back to this time, but there are other travelers. Not many—it's a one-way trip, at least in my time, unless you know how to build a braintaper—but I suppose you may have encountered one. The story you told me about landing in the wrong body is also possible, though I've never known it to happen, and as for what happened to Galloway's body . . . that's very strange." He shrugged. "What worries me, though, is why a traveler would choose this time and city, and why he'd take such care to leave you alive; maybe I'm just a suspicious old man, but it seems to me that he might have come here to try to stop me. Maybe he even left some memory implanted in you to help him—a command to kill me, perhaps."

"Then why did I save your life in Chinatown?"

"A fair question, and one which I can't answer—which is why *you're* still alive. But you can see my problem. For instance, who or what led you to Sophie? And why did you run the risk?"

"I recognized her from a photo," I said. "We used to be lovers—before she was Sophie Donner. I had to know what had happened to her, why she married a neo-Nazi pig—"

Skye shook his head. "Gary's not a pig. Part goat and part bull, maybe, but not a pig. Nor is he a Nazi. He gets angry and he likes to spout off, but he doesn't hate for very long. He wouldn't normally have gotten mixed up in something this big or nasty, but he had some gambling debts, and I helped him pay them and turned things around for him. It's just that the people who follow him—"

"Are really following you."

A shrug. "Well, yes, but I'm not a Nazi either."

"You were a Cyclops in the Klan."

For a moment he looked genuinely bewildered, as though he'd completely forgotten this, and he hesitated before saying, "Well, that was a long time ago."

"Before you—swap-hopped, I think you called it?"

Another shrug. "As I said, you can see my problem. You know too much, and too little. If I let you see the big picture, it's possible that you could be of use to us, but I really don't believe I can trust you. You attach too much importance to the names, the labels: Klan, Nazi, White Riders, Order, Phinehas Priests, Freemen, Militia . . ."

"Apostles."

"Where did you hear *that* one?" I didn't answer. "Not important. Look, think of it as party politics. You're an intelligent . . . uh, person. You know there's less difference between the Democrats and the Republicans than there is between Coke and Pepsi; they're all just brand names, but names that still attract loyalty, names that people will recognize and buy. I needed that sort of brand-name recognition, that's all."

"For what?"

"I can't tell you. I need these people, and I need the city. You and Sophie were lovers?"

"She wasn't Sophie until you flat-lined her," I snapped. "Her name was Stella. Why did you have to pick *her*?"

"I didn't; Bright did. He remembered her from her days with the police and linked her to Mueller, who he thought would be useful to us; he's the golden boy of the Military Sports Group, one of the German neo-Nazi gangs. And you should be glad; she would have been killed in the quake if we hadn't."

"And that's an excuse?"

He shrugged. "You became lovers again; that's intriguing. Maybe that old theory about gay genes is true and braintapes can't override the genes. Or maybe it's residual memory that the tapes don't touch—in the cerebellum, maybe. Instincts. Habits. What do *you* think?"

"I think your friend the rapist *belongs* on this rock," I snapped, "and that means you do too, and I hope you both die here."

Skye looked at me, his expression sad, and nodded. "As I said, cooperate with me and I'll keep him away from you. If you're very helpful, I may even be able to find you a cell with some light. I'll see you later, Galloway."

If they were feeding me daily, then two days passed before I saw Skye again. His tone and expression were sour; I guess scanning through braintapes is a frustrating exercise. I wanted to ask him how he distinguished memories from dreams or fantasies, but I didn't like my chances of getting an answer that meant anything. He asked me a few questions that I guess weren't readily apparent from the tapes, like who I was working for and where I'd learned to fight well enough to cripple Mueller. He didn't seem to know that I'd been the one who turned O'Dwyer in or inadvertently led Bright into an ambush, and I wasn't eager to tell him. I told him again that I wasn't working for anyone and had had only a few hapkido lessons decades before. He seemed skeptical about that, but there must not have been anything in the braintapes to contradict it. "And when you took on those thugs in Chinatown—was that real, or just a setup?"

"Setup?"

"To win my confidence."

I shook my head, incredulous. "One of them nearly killed me; the others—you shot them, didn't you?"

"Just to be sure. Sorry, but paranoia is an occupational hazard in this line of work. It's easy to know who my enemies are; the problem is not knowing which of them might be dangerous. The liberals are harmless, the strippers are too disorganized to be anything more than a nuisance, most of the gays and the Asians have already retreated from the city . . . but I find it hard to believe that you're not getting help from *somebody*, even if you don't know it. If it's nobody from your time, maybe they're from further upwhen or . . ." He shrugged.

"Why would they wait this long? Why wasn't someone, a kill-capable, waiting with a sniper rifle when you checked out of the hospital?"

"Kill-capables are rare in my time," he replied. "I may be the only one they've sent back. And they may not have been able to find a suitable host; we need undamaged flat-liners, who are also rare, and we need to know the *exact* time and place of their clinical death, and that sort of data isn't easy to come by. That's why we're not fighting World War Two. It was in that story you wrote, remember?"

" 'YesterDei'? I didn't know if that part of it was true."

"Most of it is true," said Skye, "but truth changes. Who was it who said, 'Who controls the past, controls the future'?"

"George Orwell," I replied. "*Nineteen Eighty-Four*. He also wrote, 'If you want to imagine the future, imagine a booted foot stamping on a human face—forever.' Is that true too?"

Skye stood. "Possibly, but I shouldn't let it worry you, Mr. Galloway. You won't be seeing very much of it."

S kye returned another three meals later, alone as usual, and this
time his expression was more than sour; there were rage and
uncertainty and urgency in the mix, plus other emotions I couldn't
read. "You say you're working alone," he thundered as soon as the
door closed behind him.

"Yes."

"Then why is somebody offering us a hostage exchange?"

"What? *What?*"

He glowered at me, obviously undecided as to whether to believe
me. I was equally unsure whether to believe him; the only people I
knew who'd given me *any* help were the teachers, a few city cops,
and Missing Persons, and I couldn't imagine any of them rescuing
me, or even knowing I was here. "Who?" I asked weakly.

"I don't know," he rumbled. "Whoever it was has two of my best
men, and he offered to exchange you for them. Actually, you were
his second choice, so don't flatter yourself. But I'm to hand you over
at sunrise tomorrow, or he says we'll find them in a Dumpster with
their genitals cut off and sewn into each other's mouths."

I tried to whistle but couldn't quite manage it. "Someone's taken
lessons from the KGB."

"Somebody you know?" he growled.

"No one I *want* to know," I assured him. I thought of adding that
my encounters with the KGB had been purely social, but decided
this wasn't a good time to rely on his sense of humor. "What're you
going to do?"

"Try to decide just how dangerous you are," he said. "Why he wants you, what makes you worth two of my best, and how he knows you're here."

I wasn't sure I liked this any more than Skye did. "Who was his first choice?" The old man glared at me, and I shut up. He mused for nearly a minute, then looked up into the darkness; I wondered who was listening in. "Look, I need those men," he said gloomily. "I can't let them die like that. You, on the other hand . . . ." He stood.

"So you've decided?"

"No," he said. "I don't have to decide until sunrise."

"What time is it now?"

Maybe he was distracted; he actually looked at his watch and answered. "Five to twelve."

"Noon?"

"Midnight," and the door slammed shut between us.

I tried to sleep, and maybe I did, but I doubt it; in a few hours I'd either be free or, more probably, dead. Of course, I knew nothing about the intentions of my anonymous benefactor, either; for all I could tell, it was Donner and Mueller out for revenge. The mere fact that someone knew that I was a hostage suggested that there was a traitor, or at least a leak, in Skye's operation—a cheering thought, but not one that made it any easier to sleep.

I know I was awake when the door opened and Skye walked in again, closing the door behind him. "Well, I'm going to let you go," he said. "I don't know what's going on, but I don't have any more time. I promise you that if you ever fall into our hands again, you'll regret it."

"I believe you."

He nodded. "And you can pass that on to whoever's behind this. This is my city now, and it's only the first of many. We're going to spread north from here, then east, nonviolently if possible, but we *are* armed. Bit by bit, we're going to take back enough of this country for us to live in." There was a gleam in his good eye that I hadn't seen before. Fanaticism? Desperation? Paranoia?

"Us?"

"Look, you saw what happened last century," he said. "We're about the same age. . . . After Kennedy came and went and everything stopped making sense. People, American people, started demanding their rights. I don't just mean women and blacks; some men, white men, thought they had a right not to go to war just because they didn't want to. Then Nixon got caught, and there was a series of other disasters: Roe versus Wade; we lost Vietnam, we lost Iran; there was AIDS and crack; the air was poison, the rain acid, the sun could kill you; you couldn't trust the government or the military and then you had the Bakkers and the others; you couldn't even trust the Church, it seemed there was nothing left to believe in, nobody to follow, no values, no order. The Millennium was coming, and there were two sorts of American left, the ones who believed in nothing and the ones who'd believe in *anything*. And the Millennium came and the Apocalypse didn't happen, and there were all these zombies wandering around looking for order—"

"Which you've provided?"

Skye shrugged. "Look, Galloway . . . ever since the nineteen sixties white men have had everything taken away from them; they've been told they have no souls, no jobs, no future, no right to bear arms, no reason to feel proud, none of the things their fathers should have been able to give them, no country, nothing but a shitload of guilt. Many believed it and are now completely useless. Well, I'm going to give them somewhere to live where they can enjoy their rights again, give them their pride and their jobs and their future back, and maybe their souls as well. Some people used to think we could recapture the whole country, but even if that was ever true, it's now too late—but give us a few years, and we can take the Northwest with a minimum of force, northern California, Oregon, Idaho, Washington State, Montana, keep them white and maybe avoid a race war. I don't expect you to share our values, and I won't ask you to, but I will ask that those who *don't*, find somewhere else to live."

There was something strange about his expression, as though he were reading a prepared speech that he didn't entirely believe—but maybe that was his eye, which always gave him a slightly evasive look, or maybe he'd said all this too often before to convey any passion anymore. His "vision" didn't justify murder, but perhaps it helped explain a few. "The Sacramento Street massacre—"

"Was meant as a warning, yes, like the other shootings, but mostly as a test for the participants. I wouldn't allow anyone into the Apostles until they were blooded."

"Male bonding?"

He looked as though he was about to spit. "I needed to know who I could rely on, and who might be a traitor, a plant."

"And if people ignore these warnings and don't leave, what then?" I asked. "Death camps?"

"Of course not; we have something much more efficient. Do you remember the Rajneeshi, Galloway? They gained control of a county in Oregon by moving enough voters in to take over the local government, which is the way we plan to do it. . . . Of course, if that failed, they were ready to poison the water supply. Your tapes suggest you were a science-fiction reader; do you know a book called *The Day After Tomorrow*?"

"I think I read it, about thirty years ago," I replied. "Early Robert Heinlein, right? China invades the U.S., but is beaten by a weapon that only kills Chinese."

"We have that weapon."

"You're shitting me," I said, though I wasn't sure that he was.

"It's not as neat as Heinlein's, and it's much slower—a bioweapon, not a ray. A cocktail of bioweapons, actually—some effective against blacks, some against Asians, a few others, all transmitted by air, but all harmless to genetically pure whites. The mongrels will just have to take their chances."

I suspect I looked skeptical, but Skye smiled, the glint in his eye brighter. "We didn't make this ourselves; we don't have the facilities for something like that. We bought it from the army."

"*What?*"

"Well, from a disgruntled employee or two at one of their biochemical weapon labs. I don't know how long ago they made it, or what they've done to test it; it was probably meant for use in China and Africa, not locally, though they say the military has to be ready for every contingency.

"Tell your friends we have it, by all means; tell them to get out of our country as fast as they can, or die here. Now, shall we go?"

W hen they peeled the gaffer tape from my eyes, I was standing
in thick fog on the world's most beautiful bridge, with the
sun shining over my shoulder. The two overmuscled men who
pushed me toward the other car wore urban camo fatigues, SWAT
body armor and old-fashioned police riot helmets with the visors
down. Twenty meters away stood five other men: two in track pants,
T-shirts (one stenciled with ALCATRAZ SWIMMING TEAM, the other
marked with a pink triangle and OUT LOUD), and handcuffs, and three
behind them in bomber jackets, jeans, black gloves, and plastic Hal-
loween horror masks—Yoda, Frankenstein's Monster, and the Mad
Hatter—so I was the only one naked. I took as good a look at the
unmasked men as the fog permitted, until the three trick-or-treaters
stepped back from their hostages and I was shoved toward them.
Yoda asked, "You okay? Can you walk?"

The accent sounded Hispanic. "I think so." He and the Hatter
looked at each other, then the Hatter nodded. "Let's go," he said.
The Apostles had already walked back to their car; maybe they had
heavier weapons than their pistols in the trunk, maybe not, but I
kept glancing over my shoulder, expecting the Apostles to shoot us.
"What's up?" asked Yoda.

I told him and he laughed. "Too scared of snipers."

I looked at the woods ahead and nodded. Of course, that meant
the Apostles would have snipers of their own back on the San Francisco side. The Monster removed his jacket and handed it to me; his
arms were pale and downed with light brown hair. The jacket was
warm and, though it wasn't long enough to cover my crotch, it had

a hard plate, presumably Kevlar, that covered the heart and made me feel a little less vulnerable. Despite myself, though, I continued to look back.

The car was an old limo, plush and comfortable, that had almost certainly belonged to a car service or an undertaker. Yoda sat up front while the Monster and the Hatter sat in the seat facing me, their pistols still politely holstered. We drove north, and the masks came off as soon as we were clear of the bridge. The Hatter looked Vietnamese; Yoda was black with an army-surplus haircut and mustache; and the Monster had a dark blond ponytail and green eyes and looked vaguely familiar. He had a faint Canadian accent, and a few seconds later I placed him: I'd seen him play Edmund in *King Lear* in Golden Gate Park back . . . Jesus, was it really less than two years ago?

"Do you need food? Something to drink? A doctor?"

"How about a tampon and a pair of pants?"

There was an embarrassed silence, then Yoda passed me a box of tissues. "Best we can do for now, I'm afraid."

I thanked him. "You're not going to blindfold me or anything?"

"Not unless you really want us to," replied the blond, obviously amused. "Relax. My name's Colin, by the way."

"Lee," I said automatically, then paused. "Or Terri. Or Tera. I've had to change names a few times. Where are we going?"

"Point Reyes."

They seemed trusting enough, perhaps too trusting. "How did you know they had me?"

Colin shrugged. "I don't know; we're just . . . the guys they sent to pick you up."

"Well, thanks for risking your butts."

"Hey, the way we hear it, you walked into Donner's house, kicked him in the balls, crippled his son, and seduced his wife. You're lucky to be in one piece."

There didn't seem to be much point in correcting the chronology, so I asked, "Who were the two you just handed over?"

"Forster and Fratinelli—Skye's lawyer and his demolitions specialist. You don't know them?"

"No."

"They're among his more reputable associates." The driver snorted. "Okay, visible associates," Colin conceded. "Fratinelli's sold a lot of explosives to the militias and a lot of other nuts, but no one's ever been able to prove anything, even when stuff that's been used to blow up hospitals and churches has been traced back to him. He also writes a lot of do-it-yourself manuals and puts them up on the Web occasionally. He ran for office a couple of times in Idaho, as an Independent when he couldn't get an endorsement from the Am Nats, spent a lot on television spots, but had a small problem: Even the people who agreed with him, and there's a lot of those in Idaho, just didn't *like* him. Then he won the contract to blow up any unsafe buildings in town; Skye probably leaked the other bids so he could undercut them. I don't know how far back they go, or what Skye's offered him."

"And Forster?"

"Hot young lawyer," said Colin. "Too damn ambitious and impatient for his own good. Skye's probably offered to make him his attorney general or something. No criminal record, not much politics, but what he must know about Skye's plans . . ."

"Did you interrogate them?"

"The boss probably did, but we didn't hold them long—too scared that Skye was going to start reprisals against people in town, not that there's many left of those."

"What's happening?"

"A lot of them have left or are leaving; they don't like Skye's idea of law'n'order, or some of the people he's bringing in to enforce it. Some of the uniforms you'll see around town are scary—okay, they're funny too, especially the kilts, but they're scary if you know what they mean. And strippers seem to be disappearing, though I don't know where they're going—rumor has it Skye's rounding some of them up and taking them up to Oregon to straighten them out."

"He's turning them into security guards?"

Colin shrugged. "That's the story. He does seem to be taking the younger, healthier men—white men anyway. I've heard stories that some of them have come back wearing Alpha uniforms, but I haven't seen it myself." I remembered what Skye had said about the Rajneeshi and their trick of stacking the vote up in Oregon by bringing the homeless up to their ranch; was he trying something similar? A moment later, it occurred to me that he might want them for spare parts—or to flat-line so he could bring in more of his cronies from upwhen. "I haven't been back since what he did to the Castro," said Colin.

"The Castro? What did he do?"

"A pack of his thugs—not his security troops, another pack of thugs from out of state, his troops were nowhere to be seen—went through the place, tearing down every rainbow and Leather Pride flag, breaking every window they could. . . . Of course, most of them wouldn't break, so they kicked the doors in and threw in firebombs. Except for the bookshops; they dragged all the books out into the street and set fire to them there before torching the shops. It was just like something out of Nazi Germany."

I nodded. "Kristallnacht: the Night of Broken Glass. The Brownshirts went around smashing the windows of Jewish homes and shops and burning Jewish books. Skye must be a history buff."

Colin looked at me bleakly. "Home," said the driver as we parked near the old youth hostel. "What do you need first?"

"A shower and some clothes," I suggested hopefully.

"No problem. Have you eaten?"

There were people emerging from the building and walking toward the car. I shrugged. "Yes, but I don't know how recently."

"Okay. Yoshiko will look after you," said Colin, nodding toward a plump Japanese woman, "and the boss wants to talk to you when you're ready."

A shower, a quick examination by a medic, a large bowl of noodles, and two cups of coffee later, Yoshiko ushered me into a small room where three people—a man who looked to be well into his seventies or beyond, and two middle-aged women, one Asian, the other a redhead—sat around an old round wooden table. Yoshiko closed the door behind me, and the redhead looked up at me, her expression carefully neutral. It was Quinn, my one-time defense attorney. I glanced at the other woman and recognized Sozu-san. "We can't go on meeting like this," I murmured.

"No," she replied sourly. "You still seem to be landing on your feet. We were hoping to spring Connie Chen, but they said they didn't have her, and you were the best we could do."

There wasn't much I could say to that; sometimes my continued survival astonished me, too. I looked at the old man and realized I'd seen him before, too, in the small office in Chinatown where I'd first met the delectable Connie. We nodded to each other, and I sat down and hoped my knees would stop shaking. The triumvirate looked like judge, prosecutor, and counsel for the defense, but they might just as easily have been judge, jury, and executioner. "Is this my trial?" I asked.

Quinn blinked, obviously startled, then laughed. "Hell, no. We're on the same side. This is just a debriefing; the boss chose us because we'd met you before. We want to know what you can tell us about the Apostles."

I hesitated, then sat, and told them about my conversations with Skye. They nodded at different points, and jotted down a few notes, then Quinn said, "Move back in the story. What were you doing in Donner's house—apart from sleeping with his wife?"

"Finding out what I could."

"You were taking one hell of a chance. Why?"

I looked at Sozu-san. "I know *you've* heard of braintaping, but how much do the others know?"

She looked back at me, her expression sour. "I've heard your story before, yes, or have you changed it again?"

"No, but I know more of it now than I did then, and while I can't make you believe any of it, Skye *does*. Skye believes he's from the future too, so does Donner's wife, so does at least one of his associates, a guy with a prosthetic hand. Now maybe we're *all* crazy, but I think Skye has some hardware that doesn't belong in this time, and he knew when and how hard the earthquake would hit and where he'd be safe; that's how he was able to plan those raids on all the gun shops in town, and his attack on your shelter"—I nodded to Sozu-san—"which I'm glad to see you survived. But whether he's from the future or whether that's just a big lie, some science-fantasy vision of the Apocalypse he uses to keep the Apostles following him, he says he has bioweapons which only kill Asians and Africans, and he intends to use them if the city isn't evacuated."

"Do you believe him?" asked the old man.

I had to think about that one. "Not entirely. I'm not a biologist, but I know what's happened when new diseases have hit societies that haven't built up an immunity to them, what happened to the Native Americans or the Aboriginal Australians . . . but those were first-contact situations. The overlap of immune factors among the races in America is too great for something like that to work now; AIDS showed how quickly diseases can spread and what sort of borders it can ignore. In fact, if the army has or had a bioweapon to use on Asia or Africa, as Skye said, it's almost certainly designed to take advantage of the high percentage of HIV on those continents, and the cost and general unavailability of medical care, rather than any sort of racial differences. Even if you had a disease that was transmitted by, say, sushi, it would still hit thousands of whites as well as Japanese."

"But not many of Skye's followers."

I shrugged. "Maybe not." I knew that at least one Australian neo-Nazi group that specialized in torching foreign restaurants still bought a lot of Chinese takeout. "But I can remember when people thought AIDS was just a disease of gays, before they realized it could be transmitted by dirty needles, blood transfusions, sloppy surgical technique, breast-milk, and old-fashioned unprotected hetero sex. It was never the sort of magic bullet Skye is talking about. That's just not possible anymore; we're all standing too close together for that sort of accuracy."

"You think he's bluffing?"

I shrugged. "Probably, but I wouldn't want to bet too heavily on it. He may be lying, to us or to his own people or both, or he may have been lied to. He may be insane—genuinely insane, a paranoid schizophrenic who forgets his medication occasionally; he certainly gives that impression." I shrugged. "Or he may have a bioweapon, but maybe it doesn't work, or maybe it only works if he locks his enemies into ghettos with strict apartheid and keeps them there until they die of whatever cause, or maybe it kills everyone regardless of race. I just don't know."

There was a long pause, and then the debriefing continued. They showed me a collection of photographs, asking me who I recognized. Ron was Tyrone Martini, one of the few Apostles who'd seen combat in a recognized war—in his case, as a sergeant in Desert Storm. Since being demobbed he was rumored to have served in a mercenary in later clashes, and with various state militias, but the group had no proof of this. Greatcoat was Walter "Wolfgang" Wirth, leader of a pack known as the Winter Wolves, European Apocalyptics who prided themselves on being more Nazi than the Nazis; they blacklisted anyone whose ancestors were born south of the Alps or east of the Oder. And the rapist was Michel "Mitch" Dupont, who'd received communications training in the navy and briefly held a private investigator's license in Seattle before being charged with two rapes. He'd been acquitted of those but had been found guilty of a swag of lesser charges, mostly invasion of privacy and weapons. Since then, he'd been selling surveillance equipment and other spy-tech over the Web.

We talked until well after dark, without even stopping for meals, and when Quinn began yawning I finally asked, "What are you going to do?"

"What?" asked Sozu-san.

"You have all this information about Skye and the Apostles now," I said. "You had plenty before, and now you know their plans. What are *your* plans? What're you going to do?"

"We don't know their plans," replied Sozu-san stiffly. "You admitted that Skye was probably bluffing—"

"Does that matter? How many people has he killed already? Too many. He—"

"What do you recommend?" asked Quinn softly. "Assassination?" I shrugged. "We don't want him to become a martyr, and besides, who would replace him? And how many of us would he kill as a reprisal?"

I sighed. "I've met a few of his so-called Apostles, and none of them have his brains or his drive or his . . . vision, I guess. It may be tunnel vision, but it isn't shortsighted; he has a long-term plan, but I get the impression that none of the others know all of the details. I don't say they're not dangerous, but they're much *less* dangerous. I think Skye's carefully surrounded himself with subordinates who aren't leaders, aren't any threat to him, and whose first meeting without his presence will probably turn into a bloodbath."

"That's a hell of a chance to take," said Sozu-san, "and not your decision to make. Besides, Skye hardly ever leaves Alcatraz anymore, so he's not exactly an easy target. Our only hope would be to infiltrate his staff at the bunker, and they're all white males, and I don't know what sort of screening process they have to go through—"

"But you've tried?"

"Of course we've tried," replied Quinn. "Six men, and none of them have ever reported back. They're almost certainly dead, and I hate to think how much information Skye might have gotten from them. We can't afford to take that sort of risk again; if Skye finds out exactly where we are, he can wipe us out easily."

I leaned back in my chair. It seemed unlikely that Skye would have the time to braintape every volunteer who came forward, but maybe these men had given themselves away somehow. "Who's really in charge here? Who makes the difficult decisions?"

There was an uncomfortable silence. "It's safer if we don't tell you that," replied Quinn eventually.

Safer for whom? "Will you pass on my recommendations?"

"That's why we're recording this interview."

"That's not enough."

The old man sighed. "What do you want us to do? Try to recapture the city by force? Even if we had enough people, we don't have enough guns, and they do, they always did."

I was sitting under a great old tree outside the hostel looking through the branches at the stars; I wasn't sure I was ready to sleep inside again just yet. It must have been long after midnight when someone—Colin, the actor—found me. "You okay?" he asked.

I shook my head. "Why are you here?"

"Quinn was worried about you. You're free to go—I'll give you a lift if you want one—but no one knew where you were."

"I meant, why are you still *here?* Hovering around San Francisco like a condor, waiting for the top predators to finish feeding, when you know they won't leave anything . . ." To my horror, I discovered that I was crying. He sat down and put an arm over my shoulder.

"Just me, or all of us?"

"Either." I sniffed.

"I can't speak for anyone else, but this is my home."

I looked at him dubiously. "Where are you from?"

"Ottawa, originally, but so what? Where's *your* home?"

I shrugged. " 'I am the cat who walks by himself, and all places are alike to me.' That's what I used to think, anyway; they were sure starting to *look* alike. Okay, there were still a lot of beautiful houses in San Francisco, and the parks, people loved the place and *cared* about it . . . but it's the people, not the place. Any city *could* be like this."

"Then why aren't they?"

"I don't know. I guess it's the people, again. That's why I hate the idea of giving this city to Skye without some sort of fight."

"Is that what you think we're doing?"

"That's what it sounded like when I was talking to the troika in there."

Colin shook his head. "We haven't given up."

"You can think of a nonviolent way to fight this abomination? That's been tried before. Appeasement, passive resistance . . . they don't work against monsters, and these people have chosen to be monsters."

"What would you recommend?" he asked coolly.

I grimaced. "I don't know. If there were a way to revoke Alpha's contract . . . has any of this gotten back to Washington?"

"I don't know. I'm sure some of it has, but Skye has been careful to pick on people who don't normally go to the cops, or who most cops won't listen to when they do. And don't underestimate the power of intimidation—he's strongest in San Francisco, but he has friends and contacts everywhere. I suspect someone's giving him the ice for bribery, as well—and don't forget, it's an election year, candidates are desperate for ice, and law and order's usually a popular issue. Meanwhile, he's telling Washington that while the state of emergency has lasted longer than expected but there's been almost no looting, he's received no complaints about the behavior of his police and no reports of rape or assault, and that the rebuilding is proceeding pretty much on schedule and under budget. The government cares more about that than they do about a few strippers, or even a few hundred, and I suspect they'd rather not know all the details. And what happens if Washington *does* try to replace him? Do you think he'll go quietly?"

"No. I guess it's too late for that. Isn't hindsight wonderful? Pity we can't change the past." I yawned, then nearly bit my tongue. Maybe we *could* change the past. "Your boss . . ."

"Yes?"

"Tell me about him. Or is it her?"

Colin shook his head. "Can't do that, I'm afraid. Security. But he'll probably want to talk to you tomorrow; you'd better get some sleep."

I spent most of that morning dreaming of the Apostles' kristall-nacht, the burning and looting and rape of the city, my city. Every book-burning thug had Dupont's face; every woman they hauled onto a pyre had Sophie's body, though the faces kept changing. Connie. Tiffany. Morningstar. Leonie. Kannon. Mama. I was glad when Yoshiko finally woke me. "The boss wants to see you," she said, "whenever you're ready."

I nodded, managed to shower and dress myself and keep down a cup of tea before letting her guide me into a tiny and untidy office that had obviously once belonged to the hostel manager. I hadn't expected the Boss to be anyone I knew, even slightly, but I was beyond being astonished; the man behind the desk had aged considerably, grown a beard, and lost some bulk since I'd dated his daughter a few years before, but he was still recognizably Barry Shaw. I sat down on the other side of the desk and said, "Good morning, Commissioner."

He shook his head. "Not anymore, I'm afraid. What would you rather I call you? Terri Lock? Lee? Tera? Mike?"

I shrugged. "Lee, I guess. What do I call you? Boss? Chief?"

"Well, you've been calling me Missing Persons, but that's a little formal; just call me Barry."

"*You're* Missing Persons?"

"That's my job, officially. I tried to convince the governor not to accept Alpha's bid, but there wasn't much ice coming in for disaster relief, the government's worried about the deficit and the insurance companies are crying poor, and she didn't really have much choice. I wanted to stay and supervise the police, but they invalided me out—something to do with having been clinically dead," he said sourly. "So I came here to investigate some of the reports that were getting out of San Francisco—especially the reports of the homeless being dragged up to Oregon and coming back as Alpha troops, or not coming back at all. Unfortunately, I'd need evidence of a mass grave or something equally gruesome before Washington would do anything, and even then—hell, most of the people they're killing are refugees, or as the Am Nats and a lot of others would say, illegal immigrants. They don't vote, a lot of them don't even have ICEcards, and most politicians don't care if they live or die. Why do you think they've been in favor of privatizing police forces all over the country?"

"Because it saves money?"

"No, it doesn't," he growled. "It saves on salaries by cutting staff levels, but the savings go into directors' fees and higher pay for the CEOs, who then make large donations to the political parties. How much do you think Skye kicks back from Alpha? The main reason privatization is popular with governments is that it's a way of dodging responsibility. So if essential services aren't being provided, if hospitals are turning people away, ambulances are arriving too late, prisoners are being brutalized, rent-a-cops are shooting strippers, hey, that's not the *government*'s fault, is it? And the government can't interfere with private enterprise, can it? So we need even more damning evidence to get them to act."

"And you don't have any?"

He shook his head. "No, and even if I did, the best that's likely to happen is that Washington will send in the National Guard, and then we'll have a bloodbath. Skye will say that he needs more men to prevent vigilantism, and they'll probably just give him more ice. Not that he needs it; he can cover his losses from what he makes on the Stock Exchange."

"Is that where the ice for . . . this, comes from?"

"Most of it. He's also receiving donations from some of his supporters—or from blackmail—but most of it's from playing the market."

"When are you from?" I asked. "I know you told me, but I've forgotten."

"243," he said. "Nearly two years after Skye."

"You knew Skye, what do you call it, upwhen?"

Another nod. "Oh, yes; we were colleagues. He came back here to try to destroy these groups, but something's gone wrong. I suspect he's become insane."

D estroy them," I repeated numbly.

"Effectively. He was going to unite the different groups by turning Donner into a prophet and creating this great apocalyptic vision, the coming race war with God on the side of the white man, nine parts Revelation and one Ragnarok, then take them all up to Oregon or somewhere for war games and a conference . . . and, meanwhile compile dossiers on all of them to give to the media and the FBI, and ultimately disappear with their funds, make sure that everyone blamed someone else, and let them fight it out with live ammunition a safe distance from any innocent bystanders. It wouldn't disable all of the groups permanently, but it would certainly weaken them . . . and though I can't tell you very much about the future, you cannot imagine how important that is for the future of life on this planet—and not just human life. Do you understand?"

"Not really. Why are you both here, now? Why not Germany in the nineteen twenties, or . . ." The answer occurred to me as soon as I'd said it, but Barry explained anyway.

"Swap-hopping—the transfer of braintapes back through time— is the only means of time travel that's available to us, and it requires a flat-lined but undamaged brain and a viable body at this end. Just as important, it requires exact knowledge of the physical location of that body, and the time that brain activity ceases. Finding hosts earlier than the late twentieth century . . ." He shrugged. "Maybe societies further upwhen from us will discover a way around this, maybe they've been manipulating history further downwhen, I don't know— though personally, I doubt it. Of course, if you're prepared to deliberately flat-line brains when you arrive, you can bring back as many people as you have bodies for."

"Which Skye is doing."

"Yes, though I don't know how extensively, and I'm not sure why; as I said, I think he's insane. The laws upwhen prohibit the use of braintapes to create multiple versions of the same person, and there are no exceptions made, even for swap-hopping. The man upwhen who became Skye—call him Alpha—had to agree to his own body being flat-lined before his tape was swap-hopped, as did I. The only way I can go home is to have myself braintaped here, have this body flat-lined and destroyed, and have the tape stored to play back into my own body after the appropriate length of time—say a year, if I spend a year here."

"They keep your body? How?"

"I can't tell you that."

"Suspended animation? Or do they clone you a new one?"

"They can do either, and more. Lee, I *cannot* tell you any more than is strictly necessary; it's not that I don't trust you, but we're trying to control the future, not introduce more random variables. Incredibly small events can have enormous repercussions. Have you ever heard of a butterfly effect?"

"Sure. Squash a butterfly in the Cretaceous, and you change the political climate in twenty-first-century America. Ray Bradbury, 'A Sound of Thunder.' "

He smiled. "Close enough. Now, I don't know why Alpha went insane; maybe there are residual memories in the brain that swap-hopping doesn't overwrite and some part of him is still the original Skye, or maybe it was physical damage done when a gun blew up in his face and sent fragments into his brain . . ."

"Or maybe he's just been corrupted by power," I suggested. "He's kill-capable, isn't he?"

"Where did you hear—?"

"The Bodysnatcher, originally. Skye said he was maybe the only one from his time sent back here."

Barry rubbed a hand across his forehead. "Yes, he's kill-capable, which by the standards of my time, his time, means he's technically insane already, but he still shouldn't be capable of anything like *this*."

I shrugged. "Maybe he's started enjoying the role he's playing too much to stop . . . or maybe he's become psychotic from spending all his time among primitives like us and not being able to tell anyone who he is."

"That's possible, but I won't know until I talk to him."

"Can you prevent Alpha from being sent back? Send messages to be opened before he leaves, warning him of what will happen?"

"I have," he said. "Maybe it'll work. Maybe there's another time line where he doesn't go back at all, and the future remains as it would have been, but in that time line *I* didn't go back, and I didn't send the message, and we're not having this conversation. Do you understand? Say I *could* have gone back and persuaded Hitler to stay out of politics. That might prevent the Holocaust and save many millions of lives in *one* time line, and maybe in that time line, rockets and computers and A-bombs would've been developed much later, the state of Israel would never have been formed . . . and my ancestors wouldn't have met, and so I wouldn't have been born.

"If there was only *one* time line, the paradoxes would almost certainly prevent time travel being discovered at all. Instead, you never change your own past; by the act of traveling back, you create another copy of the past and change *that*."

I took a deep breath. "I *think* I understood that, but don't ask me to repeat it. One more question: You're the one who told me where to find Galloway's body . . . what happened to the Bodysnatcher? Was he trying to go home? And whose side was he on?"

"Not mine; he was a swap-hopper a few years downwhen from Alpha, here to invest money in some basic research, and yes, he's gone home. That's all I can tell you about *him*. But Galloway's body . . . I persuaded him to go to the trouble of leaving it intact, because I thought you might want it back someday. I have a proposition for you."

It was nearly a minute before I'd recovered from the shock sufficiently to speak coherently. "Proposition?"

"I need someone to infiltrate the Apostles. I think Galloway could do it."

I took a deep breath. "I'm going to have to think about this. . . . What sort of shape is he in, physically? I've seen him, but his legs must be . . ."

"There's been muscle wasting, yes," he admitted. "We have medication that can go some way towards fixing that very quickly, but it has side effects that would shorten your life span. It's against the law, but I thought that if we revived Galloway's body for long enough for you to write a will, bequeathing nearly everything to Terri Lock, and then do this job, you could have your business and your old life back, plus the extra life span. Or would you rather be male?"

"Oh, Jesus . . . I don't know." How many people have ever had to make *that* decision in a hurry? "I'm just getting used to being . . . me. What about my—uh, Galloway's—brain? Is it damaged?"

"It's fine. There's a program running in it now—not a self-aware one, something more like a . . . what do they call it? Disk Doctor? We can switch it off with the correct stimulus, erase it, and play a braintape in without any difficulty."

"You said the medication would shorten my life span. By how much?"

"The medication's just a muscle restorer, plus painkillers; it's something we used to use on astronauts who'd been in microgravity too long. You'd age faster for as long as it was in your system, but you'd also heal faster and need to eat more. It pushes your blood pressure and heart rate up, but not dangerously; if you had any cancers, they'd metastasize faster too, but you don't. There are no other side effects, you don't move faster, or think faster, and you should be able to sleep normally after a few days. The alternative is spending a year or more in a wheelchair, and we don't have that sort of time. You'll still need to do *some* therapy to regain your sense of balance, of course, but you'll need to be walking—preferably running—by the end of the month."

"Why me? You have other white males in your group, and at least one of them's a better actor than I am."

He smiled politely. "If you mean Colin, I've had to talk him out of volunteering. I know a little about your background, Mike, and I think you'd be perfect for this job. You're a survivor, a pragmatist, but you'll also put your life on the line when you think something else is more important. You're not scared of taking risks, and these people admire that. I know you can fight when you need to, you don't freeze or panic, you've had some training with pistols and first aid, and you're not squeamish. You're good at languages; you know

German, and though most of these thugs only know *Heil Hitler!* and *Mein Kampf*, some of the Nazi groups speak German amongst themselves on the assumption that it's a secret code. You've worked with your back as well your brains; you can pass for a local almost everywhere, fit in almost anywhere; you did a damn fine job of disappearing when you were in the Witness Protection Program. You even fooled Donner's wife, and O'Dwyer, and confused the hell out of Skye. And you were a science-fiction fan—"

I held up two fingers. "How do you know all this? And—that was years ago, and so what?"

"To answer your first question, I became interested in you the first time you told Sozu-san your story, and started doing some research. As for the second, have you ever heard of Scott MacRae?"

"No."

He shrugged. "No reason you should, I guess; he had a few short stories published in magazines and anthologies, but his best-known book was printed by a vanity press and parts of it were probably written by Skye, but it has a following, just as *The John Franklin Letters* and *The Turner Diaries* did in their day." I nodded; I'd never read either book, but I knew a little about *The Turner Diaries*, which had supposedly inspired Timothy McVeigh and John William King and others. "McRae's a UFO fanatic and conspiracy-theory junkie; he went from believing *The X-Files* was gospel to joining the Silver Shirts and waiting for the supermen from outer space to save the white race, though he gave that up soon after his first story was published and he had an argument with some of his fellow fanatics. The way he tells it, it was a literary or scientific discussion that turned nasty, but it sounds more like a thinly disguised leadership challenge. Anyway, it caused quite a split in the ranks; Peter Bright left at about the same time.

"MacRae maintained some links with a few Nazi groups but didn't join any of them; instead, he turned to science-fiction fandom and tried to start a group of his own. He succeeded in a small way, mainly by giving away free beer to minors. He's far to the right of even the genre's self-proclaimed fascists. I don't know how he found the Apostles—probably on the Internet—but lately he's written some of Donner's speeches, designed Web sites and bulletin boards for different groups, that sort of thing. But as I said, MacRae has a small following of his own, and he's still actively recruiting at science-fiction conventions and on the Net. He'll be at a convention in two weeks, ArmaCon; that's how I want to infiltrate the Apostles."

"By my attaching myself to a loser like that?"

"MacRae tends towards paranoia and megalomania; he only trusts people who seem to want to follow him. Skye has probably been flattering him, and he may even have told him a heavily edited version of the history of the next few centuries. MacRae is also a talker, even when he's sober. I think we can persuade him to take us back to San Francisco with him—and from there, I hope Alcatraz."

"We? Us?"

He nodded. "You don't think I'd ask you to do this alone. It's almost certainly a suicide mission; *that's* why I won't let anyone else volunteer. If *you* die, you have another body, another chance at life. If *I* die, they play my most recent tape back into my body and I'm home."

"And if we do get to Alcatraz? What then?"

"I can speak to Skye. Maybe I can find out what it is he's trying to do."

"You're not going to kill him?"

"Not if there's an alternative," he said sadly.

"Are you kill-capable too?"

"That's what they told me when they briefed me," he said sadly. "I don't really know; I wasn't trained as a killer. Skye and I both came here to try for a peaceful solution to . . . certain problems. If there isn't a peaceful solution—and it may already be too late for one—then I'll kill him, if I can, and he and I can *both* go home.

"Of course, if he kills me first, feel free to do whatever you think is necessary," he continued, his tone bleak. "I find it difficult to care how many of them you kill; I can't help remembering that all of these people were dead long before I was born, and all of you, even the most civilized and enlightened, seem as crude and barbaric and *wrong* to me as the Crusaders or Conquistadores would to you. It's difficult to feel compassion for many of you when you do, or at least condone, so much that will be considered unspeakable even a century from now. So if you survive me, rely on your own judgment; do as you think best."

34
MIKE

Barry Shaw had given me twenty-four hours in which to make my decision, but he couldn't have had many doubts about the outcome; I hadn't even asked him what would happen if I said no. He probably would have just let me go home to Kannon, sure that no one would believe my story if I ever told it. The next morning he braintaped me, and a day later I woke up in my old body again.

It felt stranger than I'd expected. I'd lost muscle mass, of course, but I still weighed much more than I had as Terri, and all that bulk was poorly balanced on two very weak legs. "I wouldn't try rushing it if I were you," said Barry as he packed his braintaper back into its cases. "Let the bureaucracy take its course when they find you've come to, then disappear as soon as they let you out; we still have nine days left until ArmaCon."

I looked around at the pastel walls and realized that I was still in the Danforth Institute. "Where's . . . ?" The sound of my old voice reasonating through my skull startled me so badly that I couldn't finish the sentence.

"Terri? She went back home to Washington to patch things up with your girlfriend, and to wait for the doctor here to call; she'll be in to visit you in a day or two, unless you change your mind about that." I hesitated, then shook my head. It felt strange enough knowing that there there was another me—well, another person with my memories—wandering around, without having to see her. Terri, the other me, probably felt the same. "Is that no, you haven't changed your mind," asked Skye, "or no, you don't want to see her?"

"Both. I don't want to see her, and I haven't changed my mind."

I tried to grin, though it probably looked ghastly; the muscles in my face didn't seem to be working very well either, and had probably relaxed into a scowl. I certainly didn't want her—me?—to see me this weak, this old, but I knew that was ridiculous. "My body, yes, but not my mind."

"Okay." He glanced at his watch. "I'd better get this gear out of here; the night nurse could wake up at any time. I can't visit you, of course, but I'll see you in a few days. Hope you're feeling better then."

"Yeah." I closed my eyes, thinking, Good night Terri Lock, wherever you are.

The physical examinations seemed endless, but they mostly con-firmed that I was in better shape physically than I had any right to expect, and they brought in a teleo so I could watch while I did my exercises, which were agonizing. I pretended to be interested in the news that I was supposed have missed, but I spent most of the time binge-watching as many of Galloway's favorite old movies as were showing, most of them on the Sci-Fi Channel. *2001. Dr. Strangelove. The Day the Earth Stood Still. The Forever War. Raiders of the Lost Ark. Have Space Suit, Will Travel. The War for the Oaks. Casablanca. Kagemusha. The Seven Samurai. Lethal Weapon 2.* Branagh's *Hamlet. Unforgiven.*

Dr. Corby, a NASA researcher studying hibernation and cryogenic suspension, had discovered treatments· to prevent the shrinkage of ligaments and minimize muscle atrophy during long periods of inactivity, and had been delighted to be given me as a guinea pig. To take my mind off the pain, we discussed NASA's glory days before it had been privatized into oblivion. "There will come a day," she said, "when Earth is as insignificant in human affairs as Spain or England are now, and we will look as silly and trivial as characters in a Jane Austen novel. Our reasons for going to the moon were bad enough, but how are they going to understand why we didn't stay there? It's as though Columbus had discovered America and come back and said, 'Well, you can't go west to India, there's a couple of continents in the way, we'll just have to keep sailing around Africa.' "

" 'I have now mapped this land so thoroughly, no one ever need go there again.' "

"What?"

"Something some explorer—I think it was Sturt—once said of Australia. The Aborigines might have been much happier if no one had; the Tasmanians certainly would have been."

Corby nodded. "I'd like to think we're more civilized now than we were then, but even if we're not, I think the only alien cultures we'll encounter in the solar system will be the sort you keep in petri dishes. And if we meet someone from outside the solar system, it'll be our turn to be the primitives."

I blinked. Primitives . . . "Do you think that'll happen?"

"One day, yes, but don't ask me when. Well, Mr. Galloway, you should be up and walking sometime next year, though I'd advise against football or too much dancing."

"Thanks; I've never enjoyed either."

She grinned. "Glad to be of service, then. Look after yourself, you hear?"

I looked up at Terri from my hospital bed, astonished at just how good she looked. Not quite beautiful, but strong, young, confident, healthy.

"How does it feel to be male again?"

I groaned. "Flabby. Old. And confusing, especially the memories of . . . you know. Dupont. I mean, I look down at this body and I know it didn't happen to *me*, but it did; I have the memories."

Terri nodded. "I had the same sort of problem for the first few weeks, even with the *good* memories. I could almost envy you, your being able to distance yourself from that one. When do you get out?"

"I've asked to be discharged to outpatient status as soon as I can use a wheelchair and they can finish the paperwork. Apparently the Bodysnatcher had enough insurance to cover my bills here, and has left me some money besides. Quite a lot, in fact, though that'll be yours soon."

"You're still going through with it, then?"

"Yes. We made a deal." She looked at me dubiously. "It's a man thing," I said dryly. She grimaced. "Okay, not funny. But I *do* owe him. He's given me back everything the Bodysnatcher took, plus maybe another thirty years of life, plus a chance to make a positive difference to the future, something I didn't think I'd ever have. So take the money and do what you like. Travel. Open another bucket shop somewhere. Have a kid or two, if you like, or just make sure Belinda is okay." I smiled thinly. "She's coming around this afternoon. I could introduce you."

"Do you think that's a good idea?"

"I don't know. Probably not. But do *something*; don't just sit around in an apartment too scared to go out. Okay?"

"Okay." And then she leaned over the bed and kissed me. I held on to her with all the strength I had, and then let her go.

There's a wonderful Heinlein story, "All You Zombies," in which a male time traveler meets a younger female version of himself. Eventually, curiosity and temptation become too much, and he seduces her. Terri and I broke off the kiss, stared into each other's eyes, then shook our heads simultaneously. "I'd better go," she said.

"Yeah," I said thickly, wondering whether she was remembering the same story. "Yeah, maybe you should. Give my love to Kannon."

part four

NEX URBIS

A rmaCon was a small convention best known for its weapons policy; whereas most cons restricted the carrying of weapons to masquerades, ArmaCon made it a requirement of membership that all attendees wear at least one weapon—replica, toy, or authentic—at all times. Their definition of "weapon" was loose enough that you could get away with carrying a Swiss Army knife or an unloaded water pistol, but most of its members seemed to favor handguns, foot-long Rambo-type survival knives, or small swords. Barry had a telescoping baton clipped to his belt and had given me two canes, one a .22 pistol, one a swordstick, both used to support my weight. He'd disguised himself by dyeing his silver-blond hair black and gray, growing a beard and mustache, and hiding his pale blue eyes behind dark brown contacts and horn-rim glasses. We were both wearing jeans, cowboy boots, and T-shirts; mine emblazoned with the Dirty Pair, still my favorite anime characters, while Barry's depicted Frank Miller's *Dark Knight*, a sixty-year-old Batman with a tomboy Robin. As I'd hoped, it made us inconspicuous, as most of the attendees were dressed similarly; there was some camo visible, but even with air-conditioning on full blast, Vegas in August is too hot for much in the way of battle dress. ArmaCon had to find hotels in states where weapons laws were lax, which usually meant Nevada, Texas, or Florida. This time around, they'd booked four small function rooms in one of the dingier casino/hotels.

The male-to-female ratio was even higher than I remembered from other cons I'd attended, though the average weight of the attendees was about par; fans over twenty-five tend to obesity as well as bad eyesight and male-pattern baldness. There were some men who looked as though they might be soldiers, or at least reserves, but most were probably clerks or computer geeks or students. The dealers' room, however, was something else, with a table of weapons for every one of books, comics, or T-shirts. There were more knives and whips than there were real guns, though one comics dealer was selling silver bullets, and a video and movie poster shop also sold overpriced replica phasers and blasters. Another stall offered women's handbags with built-in holsters, and clocks, twins to the one I'd seen in Donner's home, with space for a concealed revolver. There was no sign of MacRae. "Are you sure he's here?" I asked Barry.

"He will be. What should we do until then?"

I took the program booklet out of my bag and studied it without much enthusiasm. The highlight of the morning's video schedule was *The Terminator*, but that was followed by the sequel, and the downward trend continued until hitting its nadir with *Cyborg*. The panel discussions weren't particularly inspiring either, but I saw MacRae listed in an item immediately after the lunch break, a discussion on "Are Post-Holocaust Stories Obsolete?"

"Angela once told me an old rule of running conventions," I murmured. "The more entertainment the host city has to offer, the less effort you have to put into programming. Maybe they want us to gamble."

"Maybe that's where MacRae is."

"He's a gambler?"

"Not particularly, but if you look like you're gambling, the waitresses keep bringing you free drinks. Shall we try the poker machines?"

I glanced at the program again and nodded. "Why not?"

Recognizing MacRae was easy; he had the longest beard I've ever seen outside of a Tolkien calendar, almost long enough to tuck in his Sam Browne belt. He wore black stone-washed jeans, a vest with enough pockets for a troop of kangaroos, and a white drawstring shirt; the hilt of a knife protruded from one walking boot. I watched as he slowly fed tokens into a slot machine. A well-proportioned and mildly pretty waitress brought him a glass half filled with ice cubes; he took it without even glancing at her, and had drained it before she'd gone twenty meters. I picked a machine nearly opposite his and fished in my pocket for tokens; he glanced at me without curiosity and put the glass on the floor. Close up, he bore a faint resemblance to Skye, plus a few kilos and minus ten years or so; maybe they were related, or maybe it was a case of pets and owners coming to look like each other. I didn't much care.

The waitress returned a few minutes later, to ask what we were drinking; I asked for a Coke, Barry ordered a Guinness, and MacRae looked up, smiling for the first time. "What he's having," he muttered. When the waitress had disappeared with his glass, he asked, "You two here for the con?"

"Uh-huh."

"You don't drink?"

I fed the machine and pulled the lever. Nothing. "Not this early in the day."

"You're going to try to get through this con sober? You're a brave man. You"—he turned to Barry—"on the other hand, have exquisite taste. Scott MacRae."

"Harry Burns."

"You wrote *Final Tourney*?" I asked. MacRae blinked slowly, then nodded.

"Yeah. You read it?"

"I work in a bookstore," I replied. "People keep asking for it. Where can I get some copies? There aren't any in the dealers' room."

"I have a few," he said. "How many do you want?"

"Ten, maybe. It's only a small store—mostly used, though I buy new stuff that I think people are going to like."

"What's it called?"

"The Book Cellar," and I handed him a business card.

"So you'd be Michael Ryan? Austin, Texas. That's not a Texan accent; where are you from?"

"Massachusetts."

"Get tired of living in a socialist country?"

"Too damn expensive," I said, "and too crowded. No room to breathe."

"Ain't that the truth. And you, Mr. Burns? Where do you call home?"

"Chicago, originally."

"I thought so. I was born there myself; the ruin of a fine city, not that I have much use for cities anymore. What d'you do for a crust?"

"Work for Boeing, in Seattle."

MacRae chuckled. "Why'd you leave Chicago?"

"Looking for a job."

"Uh-huh. Reason I ask is . . . you ever read any Sherlock Holmes?"

"Some, when I was in junior high."

"You know how he can tell what a man does just from the way he walks? Well, something about you says 'cop.' Am I right?"

"You have a problem with cops?" asked Barry heavily. They looked at each other for a few seconds; MacRae was the first to blink.

"Not unless you're here to give me a ticket," he said with a little laugh. "But am I right?"

"I *was* a cop, a long time ago," Barry replied. "In Chicago. Now I do security work at Boeing. Satisfied?"

MacRae looked away. "Sorry, didn't know it was a sore subject. So, what brings you all the way down here?"

Barry shrugged. "Ah, you know. I'm on vacation, and it's nice to go to a con without any of the usual bullshit politics; no feminist panels, no gay panels, no 'Why is SF so white?' panels, just SF the way I like it, nuts-and-bolts action adventure."

MacRae fed another token into the machine and pulled the lever. The waitress returned with our drinks, and he took a long, slow sip of his. "Mr. Ryan?" he said, when he emerged.

"Yes?"

"I have a few copies of *Final Tourney* in my room. I'm having a party tonight; if you want to come along, I can sell you a few then. Room two-oh-nine, after eleven. You're both welcome, of course."

Barry had provided me with perfectly forged ID, including an ICEcard; the Book Cellar, in case MacRae was sufficiently paranoid to check, belonged to an old friend of mine, who'd confirm that a Mike Ryan worked there if asked (and I'd only had to buy five hundred ice' worth of books and discs from him). We spent the day and the evening sitting through panels and the occasional movie, eating at the buffet, and catching the shows at the Luxor and Treasure Island. Vegas had never been one of my favorite cities; it reminded me too much of the island in *Pinocchio*, the one where the boys are turned into donkeys. The money wasted there (unless you considered the Mafia a worthy cause, of course) would . . . what? House and feed the homeless maybe? Or build and maintain a base on the moon? Pay for schoolbooks for kids and hospital care for the sick? Maybe if the IRS owned Vegas, they could help the needy and give the rest of us a tax break into the bargain, but that'd be communism, or immorality, or something. Besides, they'd probably just use it to build bigger bombs and subsidize tobacco farmers, right?

"What's wrong?" Barry asked as I picked at a shrimp cocktail.

"Just wondering what Vegas was like upwhen. Is it still . . . like this?"

"I can't tell you that."

"Is the world still being run by economists, or have you gone back to reading the entrails of geese instead?"

"Mike—"

"Are there still strippers? People starving, people homeless? Refugees? Disease? Death?"

"Death, yes," he replied. "People still die. The others, I really can't—"

I shook my head. "I'm not asking for investment advice. I just need to know whether the future I'm helping to preserve is worth saving."

Barry sighed. "If you want generalities, then no, there is no one starving or homeless: we can feed everyone adequately, and though you would probably not like the food, I lost quite a lot of weight before I recovered from my squeamishness about some of the things people in this century eat. Nearly all of us live in a degree of material comfort that, in many ways, exceeds anything your wealthiest contemporaries could dream of—and that includes the health care. But I doubt you would enjoy my world; standards of beauty have changed vastly, sex has changed, our ideas of fun, and love, and work, and socially acceptable behavior . . . all have changed in ways you might never imagine. That much I can tell you."

"*Sex* has changed?"

"Attitudes to it have changed more than the act, though even that has . . . I can't tell you any more." He seemed amused and condescending and sympathetic all at once, but mostly amused. I decided to change the subject. "Are we alone in the universe?"

He hesitated. "If you mean alien life, no; life is plentiful. We've found it on planets and moons in this solar system, and on planets in other solar systems. But if you mean *intelligent* alien life, maybe. We've received signals that seem to be of intelligent origin, but they're centuries old, we've yet to decipher them, and the race that sent them may not know about us yet—the message wasn't transmitted by radio, and we don't know if they use it. We have no way of sending a message at faster than light, or a vehicle at more than a half of that speed, so it may be centuries before we know what they look like—if they still exist. We don't even know their name for themselves; we usually just call them the Primes, because they were our first contact and their message began with a series of prime numbers, or Setians after the SETI program, or the Xenes, or simply the Aliens. I'm sorry."

I nodded. "What about travel? Is that still done, or is it all robot probes and virtual reality?"

He smiled sourly. "No. Freedom for humans to travel is one of the things we came here trying to preserve."

"Are you human?"

He blinked, then laughed. "Yes, Mike. Quite human; I was born on Earth, and have lived most of my life here. And that's all I can tell you." And that's all he *did* tell me, for the rest of the day.

Final Tourney was a thin paperback with a cheaply printed black-and-white cover, showing a wobbly chessboard where a white knight, a bishop (looking suspiciously like a hooded Klansman) and a king (topped with a Maltese cross) threatened an androgynous and vaguely oriental black queen. A second glance revealed that the squares were the northwestern states. The price was even scarier, but it was Shaw's ice (don't ask me where it came from; how do you forge ice?), so I bought ten copies. I suspect MacRae had more in his case—I'd seen him trying to sell them to the book merchants in the dealers' room—but I didn't want to seem too eager.

The party was small, as Barry had predicted; the two of us, MacRae, a couple from Oklahoma who seemed to have modeled themselves on the survivalists in the *Tremors* films and who stuck around for an hour arguing with MacRae about the politics in the Niven-Pournelle collaborations (MacRae claimed to have stopped reading them after he'd learned that Steven Barnes was black), and a few others who would drift in, grab a beer, listen in on the conversations for a minute or two, and then drift out again. Many of them looked to be under drinking age; the Oklahoman woman kept watching them, and when one fanboy with breath like a kidney preserved in formaldehyde left clutching three cans, she turned to MacRae and said, "I think you'd better keep an eye on these kids; I'll swear that one isn't sixteen yet."

"Oh, great," said MacRae to her husband. "You two call yourselves Libertarians, and now she wants me to card everybody who comes in? You want another?"

The man shrugged. "It's your money, and it's your ass if their folks catch 'em drunk. And no, thank you kindly, but we better be going."

"Hey," said MacRae, "we gotta catch 'em young, you understand that, don't you?" The Oklahomans didn't reply, and I glanced around the room; he didn't seem to have caught anyone but us, but I didn't say anything either. "I mean, that's what it's all for. Our kids. Making a better world for our kids."

I wondered how much evil had been done by how many people in the name of their kids. Maybe as much as had been done in the name of God; maybe even more. "Good night, y'all," said the woman as the two of them walked out. MacRae swore softly, then turned to me. "You got kids, Mike?"

"One," I said. "Daughter. She's nineteen."

"Then you understand. How about you, Harry?"

"Two boys."

"They gonna follow in your footsteps?"

"Not if I can help it."

"Why not?"

"Why would I want them to be cops? It's a shitty job, and dangerous, and what does it get you? You get spat on, shat on, shot at, and for what? Cruddy pay when you're not suspended, a little pension if you live so long, lousy hours doing stupid paperwork, you work with the scum of the earth, and fuck, my old man got more respect when he came home from 'Nam than cops do now."

"That why you quit?"

Barry shrugged. "What do you mean, quit? They left me twisting in the wind; I was lucky not to do any jail time."

"What happened?"

"Shot a couple of scumbags. Someone claimed to be a witness, said they hadn't been armed, said I'd planted a gun on one of them."

"What about your partner?"

"Didn't have one. Cutbacks. Every city's had cutbacks; people prefer rent-a-cops, and hate paying taxes. Half our trolls are on remote control most of the time."

"Were they black?"

"Who?"

"The scumbags you shot."

"What's that got to do with it? Yeah, they were black."

"And the witness?"

"Yeah, her too."

MacRae nodded and poured himself another whiskey. "What if you could get a job as a real cop in a city where cops are still respected?"

Barry stared at him blearily. "Let me guess. I go to Kansas and wait for a tornado to blow me over the rainbow."

"No, just a city where the government—the city government, not the Washington weaklings—is still in control."

"I thought you were a Libertarian."

"Me? Fuck, no. Have you ever heard of the Aryan Nation?" Barry shrugged; I nodded. "Well, we've taken a city and we're making it our own. No blacks, no spics, no slants, no Jews, no queers, no race traitors. Heaven on Earth."

"Where?" I asked.

"The Northwest."

"Why not Texas?" I asked. "We've got lots of guns, lots of pretty women . . ."

"Too much sun, not enough water, and you're too close to Mexico," MacRae replied grimly. "Read some history. Civilization only survives in northern latitudes, cold climates; people get too lazy and too stupid when the weather's warm. The jungle takes over. Before you know it, they have to dress up like Arabs just to keep their brains from overheating, they're eating shellfish and catfish and all sorts of shit, buying slaves to do the work, sleeping with their sisters, sacrificing their babies. Don't get me wrong, some of my best friends are southerners, but look what's happened to their corner of the world. Besides, there's all these Russian tanks down in Mexico, just ready to invade. . . . No, we need to start from a position of strength; Texas will just have to wait."

"Where in the Northwest?" asked Barry. "I haven't noticed things changing in Seattle—not for the better, anyway."

"We haven't got to Seattle yet," said MacRae, "but we will. Five years, tops; not as quickly as it says in there"—he nodded at the stack of copies of *Final Tourney*—"but that's dramatic license. The first thing is for everyone to stand up and be counted. Eight days from now, we want half a million men, more if we can get 'em, for a big torchlight rally, then we clean up the city and make it ours forever."

"What city?"

"Sin City," he said, smiling. "San Francisco. That quake was a godsend; I mean, who's going to give a fuck what happens in Oregon or Idaho? It wouldn't even make the news; people'd just laugh it off. But taking San Francisco and renaming it, *that's* going to tell the world we're here and we're not to be fucked with.

"But we need more people. Frankly, I don't think we've got more'n a tenth of that half million yet, and we've invited everybody who wants what we want. A lot of them talk the talk, but they won't walk the walk—not yet. What about you two? You want to see a city where law and order isn't just a black comedy?"

"Well, it sounds good," Barry replied. "Let me think about it."

"Come and see it before you decide," MacRae suggested. "Cops got it made there. Pay's not so great yet, but the fringe benefits make up for it. We've bought a lot of real estate dirt cheap—they sell or we tear it down—and we use it for housing our own people. We own a few good hotels, plus a lot of fancy houses in Pacific Heights, one of the ritzy neighborhoods—of course, most of those go to officers, but get on the payroll and you can buy your own place at a bargain price, if you like. Bring your own guns and twelve armed men and you can be a corporal. They do the same, they become corporals and you're a sergeant."

"How many do you need to become a lieutenant?"

MacRae grinned. "We don't have lieutenants. You go straight from top sergeant to captain."

Barry considered this. "Eight days . . . next Saturday night . . . I'll still be on vacation. Quitting my job, moving my family, it's a big decision. Can I turn up for this rally and decide after that?"

The grin became a shade more feral. "If you don't mind getting trampled in the rush. What about you, Mike?"

"I don't know; I've never been a cop."

"Can you shoot?"

"A handgun, yes."

"You haven't been a clerk all your life, then?"

"No."

"What else can you do?"

I took a mouthful of beer without grimacing (the United States may have beaten Australia into space, but we were light-years ahead of them when it came to breweries), and recited, " 'I can keep honest counsel, ride, run, mar a curious tale in telling it, and deliver a plain message bluntly. That which ordinary men are fit for, I am qualified in; and the best of me is diligence.' "

MacRae looked blank for a second or so. "*Macbeth*?" he ventured.

"*King Lear*."

"You were an actor?"

I nodded. "And a teacher, a trucker, an interpreter, a paramedic, and a bartender."

"Always a useful skill. You ever seen combat?"

"No."

"Would you like to?"

I stared, then laughed. "In San Francisco?"

"Like I said, we need more people. Turn up for the rally, bring a gun and some ammo, or we can sell you some, and you're deputized. Ever wanted to be a founding father?"

I remembered Ronald Reagan comparing the Nicaraguan Contra thugs to the founding fathers, though maybe he'd meant the Mafia's founding fathers or some similar group. "Never really thought about it."

"Read the book, then think about it. You have a few days to decide, but if you turn up before Friday, I can introduce you to the chief." He shook his head. "Half a million armed white men, marching together through their own city. Won't that be a sight worth seeing?"

We drove north into San Francisco on the Thursday morning in an old Chevy Electra and, as MacRae had suggested, headed for City Hall. The Castro looked as empty and bullet-scarred as an old Hollywood back lot, most of the buildings along Market had been torn down or boarded up, the Tenderloin had been razed, and the baby-shit brown of recycled paint was everywhere. United Nations Plaza had been torn up, the movie theaters and video shops and peep shows had been torn down, and the Highsore was a hole in the ground, without even a marker. The chessboards outside Hallidie Plaza remained, but there was no one playing. If I hadn't seen the Transamerica Pyramid giving me the finger, I wouldn't have been sure what city I was in.

Every second or third corner north of 24th Street boasted a pair of armed guards in mismatched uniforms: urban camo, desert camo, forest camo, Alpha Security ultramarine, Nazi dress uniforms in field gray or SS black, khaki fatigues almost invisible against the recycled paint, Klan robes, bomber jackets, loud plaid lumberjack shirts, aviator sunglasses and berets and boots and Sam Browne belts and a shitload of guns: shotguns, submachine guns, assault rifles, and at least one pistol and knife apiece. I saw very few pedestrians who weren't wearing some quasi-military costume, but their nervous expressions were uniform enough. None of them looked wealthy, but they didn't dress like strippers, either. I wondered what the Apostles had done to Old Chinatown, but Barry assured me that I was happier not seeing it.

"How many people have come back? Apart from the ones who Skye invited."

"The best estimates, for the city and Berkeley . . . about a third of them; certainly less than half. Oakland and San Mateo County, where the damage wasn't so bad, maybe two-thirds. The hospitals are almost fully staffed, and the universities are supposed to be reopening next month; the seismologists are there already, of course. But every building in Chinatown and the Tenderloin has been condemned or leveled, and so have a lot of the Castro and Haight-Ashbury, and the military bases have been closed; the government wanted to make some cuts, and they decided it wasn't worth rebuilding them. Same with a lot of the businesses, and most of their workers have gone with them. The tourists haven't come back, because there's not much to see; there aren't enough lines open for everyone who wants to telecommute yet; so unless you're connected with demolitions or construction in some way, there isn't much work going. Most of the disaster-relief money was spent on evacuating and relocating people, and not much has gone into rebuilding the city; it's an election year, remember, and the President doesn't want to spend any more than he has to on long-term projects unless it creates jobs. The architects and town planners are still arguing about what should be built in the areas that've been razed and how quakeproof to make them. How much of this is Skye's doing, I don't know."

"How do you expect we'll get in to see Skye when he's got this many people around him?"

"MacRae is one of the Apostles, the original inner circle, even if he's still a few bodies short of making captain. I think we can persuade him to get us close. After that . . ." He shrugged.

"So who are the Apostles? Are there twelve of them?"

"There were, at one time; Peter Bright was one, and he hasn't been replaced, and the same is probably true of Roy O'Dwyer. That leaves Donner, Skye, Martini, MacRae, Dupont, Fratinelli, Forster, Jarvet, Dale, and Larsen. Most of them don't matter now; this army does. Donner might be able to keep them all together without Skye, but not for long."

I looked up and down Market Street; the vacant lots gave it the appearance of a jaw with missing teeth. A small party of Nazis was walking toward a large party of Klansmen a block ahead of us. "There's not going to be another quake, is there?"

"Not in the near future, though the seismologists don't know that. Why?"

"Just an idea. Maybe Skye's still following part of his original game plan: getting the racist right to pour all their money into a city which then slides into the sea."

Barry smiled. "His original plan was more devious. He was going to funnel most their money into legitimate investments, but ones that won't pay off for decades—medical research, alternative energy sources, others that will need zero-g manufacturing to be practical, that sort of thing."

The groups of Nazis and Klansmen met outside where the High-sore had once been, both obviously unwilling to yield ground. After several seconds, both packs snaked into single file, stepped to their respective rights, and slid past each other. It was like something out of *West Side Story*, and I almost laughed. "Do you think a peaceful solution is still possible?"

"Maybe, but I won't know until I speak to Skye." He looked around, obviously worried. "Keep an eye out for a parking spot. I don't think your legs are up to coping with a long walk yet, especially not on these hills."

I nodded. Whatever medical miracles Barry had been able to perform hadn't entirely restored my strength or my balance; I'd stupidly tried a hook kick after only two days of walking without the canes, and fallen on my ass. What the hell; if it came down to a fight, they all had guns, and hapkido would be about as much use as origami.

There were two armed men—one burly and white-bearded and wearing the symbol of the disbanded Afrikaner Resistance Movement on his brassard, the other a sunburned skinhead in a white T-shirt and ripped jeans—sitting casually on a bench outside City Hall. The South African intercepted us a few steps from the doorway. "Cen I help you os?" he asked, his gun pointed in the general direction of my aching feet.

"Scott MacRae told us to come here," I replied, careful not to mimic his accent. The gun had a bore like a shotgun and a rotary magazine like a cartoonist's impression of a tommy-gun. "He's expecting us."

He smiled, showing cheap false teeth, and glanced at our guns. Barry had a sawed-off shotgun on one hip, a ten-millimeter Glock on the other; he'd issued me a U.S. Army Beretta, similar to the one I'd trained with years before but loaded with a large clip of caseless ammo and capable of nearly three seconds of autofire. I'd spent a few hours on a target range getting used to it; I could cope with the recoil from single shots and still hit a man-sized target at fifty feet if I used the laser sight, but that was all. "Welcome to the party. Glad you could make it."

The man at the desk wore a drab gray business suit with a discreet swastika cloisonne pin and a less subtle shoulder holster; he informed us that MacRae was busy, but he'd leave a message telling him we were here. In the meantime, after we'd made our accommodation arrangements and handed over any cameras, mobile phones, or computers, if we'd like to make ourselves useful putting up posters and banners along the route the march would take on Saturday night . . .

As suggested, we volunteered to help out, and were assigned partners. Mine was a scrawny acne-scarred thirtyish corporal from the National Socialist American Worker's Party or National Socialist White American Party or something of that ilk; he only mentioned it once, not being a talker, and names were beginning to blur on me by the time night fell and I returned to my hotel—an old dump on O'Farrell—exhausted. Judging from the lights, the big expensive hotels were already filled, and I wondered how close Skye had come to gathering his half-million men.

In exchange for our work, we were given a token exchangeable for dinner and a beer at one of their mess halls. I ate at a bar near my hotel, hoping to find Barry, and listened to a mixed group arguing, mostly amiably, about the new name for the city. One group was in favor of Fort Streeter, while some strong southern accents suggested naming it after Klan founder Nathan Bedford Forrest. There seemed to be no women anywhere, and I mentioned this to the barman.

"Place isn't safe for women yet," he said softly. "Or kids. Donner's asked for them to be kept out of town until next week; doesn't want any of them hurt on Saturday night."

"Do they have *their* women here?" I asked casually.

The barman shrugged. "Maybe, but they'll be somewhere safe— the bunker, probably. Why?"

I glanced at the other drinkers, some of whom were warbling "The Green Berets," which I hadn't heard since I was a kid. "Well, with all the wine and the song . . ."

He laughed politely. "I'm afraid I can't help you. Everybody's been told to stay away from the locals until further notice, and that means the women especially."

I nodded. "Do you know Scott MacRae?"

"Only by reputation. I've never met the man. Why?"

"He asked me here; do you know where he fits into the hierarchy?"

A shrug. "I'm not into politics."

"Very wise of you, I'm sure." I tipped him and walked back to my room. There was a message from Barry. MacRae had called him, and told him that if we wanted to be deputized in time for Saturday, we could do the tests tomorrow morning, just turn up at the Presidio by seven.

"Are you going?" I asked when we met a few minutes later.

"Yes. Are you?"

"I don't know if I'd pass the physical."

"It may be our only chance to meet Skye."

I sighed "Okay. I'll try."

I walked down the Castro cautiously, heard/saw movement in a window to my left, and managed to assume a shooter's stance and draw a bead on the target without falling over. It was a cutout of a movie ninja, his hood adorned with chain mail and open to show a yellow face and black slanted eyes. I put the cross from the laser sight between those eyes, braced myself against the recoil, squeezed the trigger, and managed to hit him in the neck, almost decapitating him. There was another *clack!* as another target spun around, this time on the roof of the Don't Panic shop. Another caricature, a Zulu with an assegai and shield. This time I actually managed to hit his face.

The interview had been easy, the first-aid and computer literacy tests rudimentary, the psych tests would almost certainly be ignored if they were ever marked, and the physical hadn't been particularly rigorous—they'd merely blinked at my pulse and blood pressure, probably because many of the other wanna-bes were in even worse shape than I was—though the unarmed combat workout had certainly been painful. Ron Martini had been our instructor until the late afternoon, when we'd gone to a shooting range to demonstrate our skill with a pistol and Alan Mueller had taken over. I kept expecting them to recognize me, or at least to notice how nervous I was; maybe they put it down to buck fever. Then we were subjected to something to prepare us for the everyday lot of policemen and soldiers everywhere—sitting around waiting for something to happen—while small groups were sent out for a final test on their combat simulator. The sun was setting by the time Mueller picked me and three other guys and drove us to the Castro.

Another *clack!*, and the sheet of plastic obscuring another window fell away, showing a young woman—barely more than a girl—tied to a bullet-pocked support pillar, a ball-gag in her mouth. She had long dark hair, but I couldn't see her face well enough to know whether she was black or white, much less make out her expression, but she was struggling far too violently to be a mannequin. There was another *clack!* behind me, and I spun around in time to see a cutout of a hook-nosed Israeli soldier in a bright blue UN helmet, an Uzi pointed at my ass. I switched the Beretta to full auto, braced myself, and fired a burst up his body, from groin to nose. Then, wobbling more than a little, I slowly turned back to the girl in the window, switched the selector back to single shot, and stared.

"Time's up, Ryan," said Mueller, ambling down the street toward me. "And one target left. What, you out of ammo?"

I was, but I had another clip. I considered lying, decided against it, considered telling him that I couldn't see the girl well enough to know whether she was meant to be a target or an ally, and ended up telling the truth. "I'm not going to shoot an unarmed woman," I said, "especially not one who's tied up. Is that the test?"

"She's black," said Mueller, peered at her for a moment, then shrugged. "Black enough, anyway. We're running low on targets."

"I don't give a fuck."

"What if I make it an order?" He tapped his captain's bars self-importantly.

"I still wouldn't give a fuck; I'm *not* going to shoot her. Untie her hands, give her your gun, and we'll see what happens, but otherwise—"

"How fucking stupid do you think I am?" He handed me his pistol, a long-barreled Luger. "This isn't just some game. Shoot the bitch, and that *is* an order."

I stood there, a gun in each hand, and envisioned myself putting a bullet into each kneecap (trying, anyway) and then two into his head. I enjoyed this fantasy for a fraction of a second, then kicked him in the balls as hard as I could. He folded up, and I cracked him behind the ear with the butt of the Beretta. As soon as he hit the ground I had the muzzles of both pistols touching his head. We stayed like that approximately forever, and then I remembered to breathe again. I backed away from him on rubber legs, dropped the Luger out of his reach, and holstered the Beretta. "You want her dead, hero, you kill her yourself."

"And what will you do? Shoot me? They'll have you hunted down."

"Shoot you? Hell, no. I want you alive, so you can back up my story when I tell everyone how you were whipped by a fifty-year-old cadet."

He glared up into my face and saw that I was serious. "Asshole," he muttered.

"I'm going to walk back to the car," I said, hoping that my legs would get me there without buckling beneath me. "Shall I tell the next guy to come on through?"

The story must have gotten around by the time I saw Barry at breakfast. "Do you know what they're saying about you?" he murmured.

"No," I said through a mouthful of cornflakes. "That I wouldn't shoot an unarmed girl? That I disobeyed a direct order? Or that I took out an Olympic medalist half my age?"

"Unfortunately no one saw that, and Mueller isn't talking. But opinion's divided. Nobody likes the fact that you refused an order, but not shooting a woman, especially when you only had Mueller's word for it that she wasn't white . . . some of the guys admire that. They don't all hate women—oh, most do, but there's enough with mothers or daughters or sisters or wives who say you did the right thing and like to think they'd have done the same. So Skye's decided not to have you shot as an example."

"That's a relief."

He left it at that until we were in the car on our way to the Presidio, where the march was scheduled to begin. "You didn't save that woman, Mike. You know that, don't you?" I nodded. I hadn't wanted to think about it, but I'd known. "The next man through gut-shot her so she wouldn't die too quickly. The next . . . you don't want to know. But she still died."

"What did you do?"

"My first shot missed," he said softly. "My second . . . I killed her as quickly and painlessly as possible. What was the alternative? Kill Mueller and the others in the car? This is too important."

So he *was* kill-capable, after all. "The end justifies the means?"

"One death instead of billions? I think so, yes."

I wanted to spit. "You don't think we're real, do you? Not real, or not really human. Jesus, you're as bad as Skye."

"Maybe. Are we real to you? Your descendants? Your future?"

"Forget I spoke."

"No," said Shaw. "I can't." He sighed. "Do you want to hear some good news?"

"Sure."

"I was listening to a few people talking about you last night, and it seems Martini, or someone, has decided that you passed your tests. You've been deputized into Alpha Security."

"Hoo-fuckin'-ray."

"As punishment, however," he continued, "you're going to miss out on tomorrow's rally. They're putting you on guard duty instead." I shrugged.

"At the bunker," he continued, suddenly grinning. "At Alcatraz. So I told one of the sergeants that if this was true and they were going to punish you, they'd better give me the same damn punishment. Do you think they'll fall for it?"

The ferry that took us to Alcatraz was the *Harbor Emperor*, with a figurehead of Norton I—an irony I suspect he would have appreciated. Joshua Norton was a bankrupt merchant who one day in 1859 sent a letter to the *San Francisco Bulletin* proclaiming himself Emperor of the United States, Norton the First. A week later he announced that he'd deposed President Buchanan and abolished the Congress for corruption, and then appointed himself Protector of Mexico as well. When the Civil War broke out a couple of years later, he ordered an end to hostilities; unfortunately, neither side listened. He lived in a rooming house and spent the afternoons inspecting the drains and making sure that streetcars were running on time; he was arrested for vagrancy once by some rookie and received a personal apology from the chief of police and the city council. He died in 1880, his funeral procession was two miles long, and his obituary read, in part, "Emperor Norton killed nobody, robbed nobody, and deprived nobody of his country, which is more than can be said for most fellows in his trade." I wondered what he and Skye would have said to each other if they'd ever met.

There were only ten of us on the ferry, seven men and three women; I recognized Wolfgang Wirth, who was unconsciously chewing on a fingernail, and Martini, but none of the others. Alcatraz looked much the same as it had before the quake, but some vandal had painted over the INDIANS WELCOME INDIAN LAND graffito on the old barracks. We were led to a small arsenal in the former rangers' office, where a sour-looking cigar-smoking sergeant with a gut like a sack of manure issued us M-16s, canteens of water, baseball caps, and brassards. "You the guys pulling double duty, huh?"

"Yeah." I looked at the urn of coffee; he nodded, so I helped myself to a cup. It tasted worse than it smelled, but I'd expected that.

"That's 'Yes, *sir.*'"

"Yes, *sir.*"

"You're going to miss one hell of a party," he said.

"You mean the rally?"

"Nah, after that. Gonna clean up the city; anybody who hasn't got the message by now's going to be dead meat by sunrise." He puffed on his cigar. "Berkeley and Oakland too."

"So what's going to be left here to guard? Sir?"

He peered at me through the smoke. "Just the women; Skye wants them out of danger. Say, aren't you the one wouldn't shoot that girl?"

I was about to answer when the door behind him opened and Dupont walked out. He wore the same camo outfit I remembered, with a long knife and a huge revolver on his belt. I saw computers and teleos and what looked like military radio gear behind him. He glanced at us without curiosity, helped himself to a coffee, grimaced, and walked back into his lair. "Yes, sir," I replied. "That was me."

"Well, around here, when we give you an order you obey it. No exceptions and no excuses. You got that?"

"Yes, sir."

"I don't like the kid much either, okay," he said, dropping his voice slightly, "but we can't go pistol-whipping each other every time we have a disagreement. Need every man we got. Now get your scrawny ass up that fuckin' tower." I nodded, and he turned to Barry. "What about you? Whose shitlist were you on?"

"It was my idea to come here," Barry replied. "Sir. I feel responsible for him."

"You his brother or something?"

"Brother-in-law. Poor fool married my sister."

The sergeant looked him up and down, considered saying something, and changed his mind. "Okay. Get up there, make sure no one steals the place."

"Is Skye here?" I asked. "Sir?"

He took his cigar out of his mouth and stared at me, then nodded. "Yeah, so you better watch yourselves. Okay?"

· · ·

"So what do we do now?" I asked as I examined the emblem on the red brassard—a white cross, formed by two bolts of lightning, on a black disc.

"We wait," Barry replied.

"For what? You think Skye's going to invite us in for a drink?"

He nodded toward the cell house on the other side of the barracks. "Do you know *where* he is in there?"

"No, but he's in there."

"How do you know?"

"That's where Martini and Wirth went; who else would they have gone to see?"

"The women, maybe?" Barry shrugged. "But you're probably right."

I looked around the island, at the mostly ruined buildings and the overgrown gardens and the nesting sites for birds, and then along San Francisco's shore to the Golden Gate Bridge. "I can't figure out why he's here at all," I said softly. "On Alcatraz. Wouldn't he be just as safe in a bunker in the Presidio—safer, even?"

"Maybe, but this is one hell of a symbol. It could be to the Aryan Nation what Masada is to Israel. Do you know what the Nazis are calling the island now? Ragna Rock."

Ragnarok. Destruction of the Powers. Twilight of the Gods. The last battle from Norse mythology. The Apocalypse. "Was it part of his original plan? The island, I mean, not Armageddon."

"No. It was all going to happen at his camp in Oregon."

"How large is that camp?"

"I don't know. Why?"

"Could it accommodate half a million?"

"I doubt it. If they brought their own tents, and dug their own latrines, you might squeeze fifty thousand in there for a few days. . . ." He was silent for a moment. "You think he decided he'd underestimated the size of the problem?"

"I think it's possible, but it doesn't mean he's on our side." I shrugged. "So, do we go in, or do we wait for him to leave for the rally? It's quarter past four now, and the speeches start at eight. He'll be gone before it gets dark."

"Wait until the next boat has come and gone."

"You're still hoping for a peaceful solution, aren't you?"

"Yes."

"Have you thought of one?"

"Not yet. Ask me again after I've spoken to him."

"Why do you care?" I asked. "I know why *I* care, but why do you? We're only disgusting primitives, and we've been dead for centuries anyway."

"The more people die tonight, the more it changes the future," he replied. "Unpredictably, and probably for the worse. Do you ever play pool?"

"I used to. Do you?"

"Sometimes. What I'm trying to do is like a trick shot in pool— not a terribly efficient way of moving a particular ball into a particular pocket, but that's the way the game is played."

"Whereas Skye is shaking the table and hoping the balls fall into the right holes in the right order?"

"Ask me that after I've spoken to him," he repeated. I guess I should have expected that.

The next ferry docked less than an hour later, bearing more women and two men wearing Alpha Security caps and lightning-cross brassards over different paramilitary uniforms. It was met by a much larger party, all male and heavily armed and eager to get on board, including the cigar smoker from the office. Barry watched the incoming party tromp up the path to the cell house, while I watched the sergeant salute us sarcastically from the deck. We waited another ten minutes, and then Barry nodded. "How are your legs?"

"They hurt a little when I put my weight on them, but not too badly."

"Can you make it up the path?"

I looked at it; it was about two hundred meters, with a slope of less than ten degrees. "Sure."

"Good. Where do you suggest we start looking?"

"For Skye? The braintaper was in a cell in D Block, but the only spaces on maps of the place that are big enough for a war room and structurally sound are the dining hall, the library, the shower block, and the band practice room. I can't imagine anyone staying in one of the D Block cells voluntarily for very long. Where do you want to start?"

"Let's try the dining hall." He reached into a pocket of his jacket and removed two metal cylinders, handing me the smaller one. I peered at it for a second before recognizing it as a silencer. "Should be good for one clip, maybe two, on single shot," Skye muttered. "Autofire will wreck it. Ready?"

We made it up the winding path and into the cell house without being challenged—there were neither guards nor any obvious cameras—and halfway down Broadway, the corridor between B and C Blocks, before Fratinelli and Alan Mueller walked around a corner less than five meters in front of us.

"Who told you to come up here?" Mueller snarled. He was carrying a long-barreled Luger target pistol and wearing black leather pants and a bomber jacket. Fratinelli wore an Alpha Security uniform with a webbing belt festooned with grenades and other gear. I tried to brazen it out, being as polite as possible in the hope that they wouldn't attract attention by shouting. "We pulled double guard duty—sir."

"That isn't what I asked, fuckhead. If you're on guard duty, what are you doing up here in the cell house? And who's watching the dock?"

"Dupont," I said, after both Barry and I had hesitated too long. "He told us to come up here to grab some food." Too late, it occurred to me that I *should* have said he'd given me an urgent message for Skye; he probably wouldn't have believed that, either, but at least we would have found out where he was.

"Both of you at once?" Mueller shook his head and turned to Barry. "You can go; I'll sort this out with Dupont later. *You*, on the other hand . . ." He drew his Luger, pointed it at the ceiling. "You and I have a score to settle."

"This is stupid," I said softly, as Fratinelli looked at him uncertainly. "We're on the same side, for Christ's sake." I had the Beretta drawn, but it was pointed at the floor between Fratinelli and myself. I heard Barry back away, then I heard what sounded like an old-fashioned pop-top can being opened, and a small red hole appeared beside Mueller's nose. Fratinelli reached for his own pistol, and I raised mine and placed the cross from the laser sight on his forehead—and hesitated. I'd never shot anyone before, and my fingers seemed to have frozen. Mueller put a hand to his face and fired at

Barry, the shot ringing out clearly. I heard something clatter against the bars behind me, and I threw myself down onto the floor, shut my eyes, and squeezed the trigger again and again. Something whizzed over my head, and I opened my eyes. Something on Fratinelli's belt must have been hit by a bullet, because his left side was on fire. As I watched, horrified, he dropped to the floor and rolled on the concrete, trying to extinguish the fire while he fumbled with his buckle. Mueller shrieked and recoiled away from him, and Barry shot him in the face. He bounced off the bars behind him and fell onto Fratinelli, who was still feebly rolling around on the floor, leaving bloody smears on the concrete.

I rolled over to look at Barry, who was standing behind me, his pistol in his left hand, his right arm jetting blood from just below the shoulder. Then someone else came hurtling around the corner, and before I could bring my gun to bear, his Schmeisser was pointed at Barry's back. "Drop it!" he barked. "Both of you!"

It was Wolfgang Wirth. I put the Beretta down, carefully, and raised my hands.

"What gives?" Wirth asked. "Who are you? What happened here?"

"It was Mueller," I said. "He was going to shoot me, and . . ." Two men appeared at the Times Square end of the corridor, and Wirth snapped an order to them to get a fire extinguisher, a blanket, *something*. I suspected it was too late—Fratinelli had stopped moving, and though his uniform was too dark to show that he'd been bleeding, the bloodstained floor suggested that he'd been hit by more than one bullet—but both Barry and Sophie had performed medical miracles on me, so maybe he wasn't beyond all help. Wirth stared at me as though trying to remember where he'd seen me before, then shook his head. "Jesus, I don't know. Skye can decide what to do with you. Get up, and keep your hands on your heads. *Move!*"

"These man have been shot; they're going to bleed to death—"

Wirth swore in German, unimaginatively. "Looks to me like the one on the floor is already gone, and this one shot a superior officer. That's an automatic death sentence in this man's army. Are you going to move, or do you want to die where you are?"

We moved, Barry trying to hold his wound closed with his right hand. Wirth ordered us along Broadway and into D Block, then down the stairs into the band practice room. Skye was sitting behind

a huge antique desk and flanked by two huge gray-brown shhhepherds. The desk was strewn with yellowing papers and dominated
by a laptop microframe and a black enamel statue of a bird that
served as a paperweight. The room was otherwise empty, apart from
a midsized safe, three chairs, two teleos, a gun rack, a cot, a suitcase,
some maps on the walls, and Martini, who was cleaning a machine
pistol. Skye seemed predictably annoyed by the interruption, and
glared at us with his good eye. "Yes?"

"Sir, these two—"

"Adam," said Barry. Martini sat up, his face pale, and Skye leaned
back in his chair, his expression unreadable.

"Who are you?"

"Adam," Barry repeated, and then started into a language I'd never
heard before. I glanced at Martini, who seemed riveted, and then
down at the papers on the desk. *They* at least were in a language I
recognized: Russian. There was a print scanner attached to the microframe, and while I couldn't see the screen, I guessed that Skye
had been using the com to translate the documents.

Skye began speaking, apparently in the same language as Barry,
but more slowly, with a different rhythm. A few of his words sounded
like English, though with the wrong syllables stressed—no, with
equal stress on each syllable, like Japanese—and I started listening
more carefully, wondering if I could trust either of them.

A dam, there isn't much time," I said in Unilish, hoping the sound of his name and his native language would reach the old Adam, that there was something of him still to be reached. "This thing you've started . . . you know what they're going to do tonight? They're going to kill everyone in the city who doesn't meet their ridiculous standards; they've already killed hundreds. This wasn't in our plan. *What are you doing?*"

He stared at me, one eye blank, the other . . . confused. "Jean? Is it you?"

"Yes. What are you doing? What happened to the plan?"

He blinked, then tried to smile. "You need help, Jean; you're going to bleed to death if you don't get that arm seen to. I have a healer here—Ron!" he barked in English. "Get Sophie, tell her to bring her kit." Martini stared at me, his expression grim, and Adam snapped, "Now! That's an order!"

He glared, and then obeyed. "Now we can talk," said Adam. "I've swap-hopped ten people—or is it eleven?—but he was one of the first. We needn't worry about Wirth; he can't understand us. Can your man?"

"Galloway? No. Please, Adam . . . the plan? You were going to destroy these groups, not give them their own city, their own nation. *What are you doing?*"

"It's a funny thing about plans," Adam replied. "They have a saying in this century, 'No plan survives contact with the enemy.' It's a good saying; I wish we'd remembered it. You've seen the enemy, haven't you, Jean?"

I hesitated. Who did he mean? The fanatics he'd gathered together? HumanGenesis? Or the Outer Worlds? "The Offworlders aren't our enemy, Adam," I said. "We fired on them first—or HumanGenesis did. That's what you came here to prevent. Do you remember?"

"I remember," Adam replied, his eye flashing. "I forget things occasionally, more than I used to . . . my head hurts, and sometimes I black out, but I can still remember why I'm here. I'm here to stop HumanGenesis being formed, or at least from arming themselves— right? I *thought* I could do that with trickery, without killing anybody, but there's too *many* of them, and in this century, guns are so cheap and explosives so easy to make. . . . Knowing who they are might not be enough. Keeping them poor might not be enough. Making them look foolish might not be enough. But bringing all of them together like this, with their guns, I made sure they brought as many of their guns as they could carry—" He paused for breath.

"You're going to make them fight each other?" I asked.

"Barry," murmured Galloway in English. "I hate to interrupt, but this . . . this looks like the technical data for a nuke."

I suddenly felt very cold. "What?"

"My Russian is rusty," he said, tapping the paper, "but I think this says one kiloton. That's what—eight Hiroshima bombs? How much are they charging you for this?" he asked Adam. "Two cans of Coca-Cola?"

I stared at him, then at Adam. "You have this bomb, don't you?" I asked in Unilish.

"Fratinelli bought it," he muttered. "He had the contacts. He doesn't know what I'm doing with it, and the others think I have a bioweapon."

"What *are* you doing with it?"

He made a ghastly attempt at a smile. "It's a nuclear bomb, Jean, what they call a suitcase bomb; it has very few uses apart from destroying buildings and killing large numbers of people. I've put it in the Presidio, and it will be detonated tonight, when everyone is gathered outside. The blast zone is small, it will level much of the park, damage surrounding buildings and maybe part of the bridge but not much more, start a small firestorm; the radiation will be a problem, but we should be safe here if we go to one of the isolation cells."

"It's in the Presidio?" whispered Galloway.

I suddenly wondered how much of our conversation Galloway had been able to understand. The vocabulary of Unilish has roots in American English, and someone with Galloway's feel for languages might have understood one word in five, maybe even one in three. He'd obviously understood some of the names.

"Hey, Wolfgang," said Galloway, more loudly. "You know how you reenacted Kristallnacht a few weeks ago? I think you're about to reenact the Night of the Long Knives—and you're going to be the Brownshirts. Your *Führer* here has set you up. You've just marched into the ovens, *nicht wahr?*"

Wirth snapped something in what I presume was German, and Galloway turned to Adam. "I'm right, aren't I? That's why you sent Martini out of the room, so he doesn't overhear any of this."

"Adam," I pleaded, "you can't do this."

Adam shook his head. "You've seen these primitives, Jean," he said in Unilish. "Do you think they can be reasoned with? They're *worse* than the HumanGenesis fanatics; they kill each other over things that matter no more than a tissue type or astrological sign. They murder healers and put bombs in hospitals. They lie to their children, and the things they do to women are monstrous. . . . It's too late, Jean," he said, with remarkable gentleness. "I *have* done it; the timer is already set. It will detonate at eight-fifteen."

Automatically, I glanced at my watch: five-forty-one. "Can you deactivate it?"

"I don't know."

"Who would know?"

"Fratinelli might."

"If he just said what I think he said, then we're screwed," said Galloway grimly. "Fratinelli's already dead."

"Right," snapped Wirth, who was standing on Adam's blind side. "Skye . . . is there a bomb or isn't there?" He drew back the bolt of his submachine gun and pointed it at Adam, who didn't even flinch. Silently, suddenly, both dogs leaped at Wirth, as they'd obviously been trained to do if someone turned a gun on their master. With a howl of fear and rage—mostly fear—Wirth squeezed the trigger and sprayed the room with bullets as he shot at one dog and then the other, and everything between them—including Adam. A bullet ric-

ocheted from somewhere and hit me in the back, where I was protected by Kevlar; another in the thigh, where I wasn't. The impact
knocked me over onto the desk, scattering papers and knocking the
pre-computer to the floor.

I looked up into Adam's face, and both his eyes stared back at me
sightlessly. His head lolled on the bloody ruin of his neck; a bullet
had passed straight through his throat, tearing through both the ca-
rotid and his spine. I rolled over the desk, trying to get behind it and
out of Wirth's sight; my leg and arm protested, but I managed. I
heard footsteps, someone running toward us, and more shots . . .
and then the shooting stopped, and I heard someone running away.

I raised my head, cautiously. There was no sign of Galloway, or
of Wirth, but the dogs lay on the floor, one shot through the head
and immobile, the other through the back and still twitching. "Mike?"
I said.

"Here," said a voice from the other side of the desk.

"Are you okay? Can you walk?"

"No. Maybe. I don't think he got me anywhere I wasn't armored.
Just a second." He reached for the edge of the desk and pulled himself to his feet, his face gray. "No, everything still works, though my
leg—"

"Where's Wirth?"

"Didn't the dogs—" He looked around. "No, no sign of him. He
must have—"

"Get after him!"

"What?"

"Wirth! Stop him!"

He stared at me. "What the fuck is happening?"

"What do you think will happen if he gets to the communications
center? What if the Apostles find that bomb? They have two hours
to defuse it, or to move it. What if they take it to Oakland, or Berkeley, or San Jose?"

He hesitated, then nodded, his expression grim. "Is Skye dead?"

"Yes! Shot in the neck. He was blindsided, didn't even try to
dodge."

He seemed stunned by the idea that Skye might be as mortal as
anyone else, but snapped out of it after only a second. "Does he have
a gun? I may need it."

I looked at the body and noticed an automatic in a shoulder holster. I plucked it out and slid it across the desk, then handed him my sawed-off shotgun as well. Galloway grabbed both and nodded. "Are you any good with coms? Primitive ones?"

"Pretty good."

"See if you can get anything useful out of this one," he said, and ran out of the room.

I saw Martini's body just a few meters from the doorway; Wirth must have shot him without even giving him time to draw his gun. I ran down Broadway and saw the bodies of the two young men in Alpha uniforms who'd escorted us to Skye's office. There was no one else in sight, no one to help or hinder me. I staggered out of the cell house as quickly as I could, keeping an eye out for Wolfgang. I made it to the steps and down onto the path unscathed, and ran a little farther before noticing a flurry of birds over the guardhouse near the dock. Something had disturbed them, and it wasn't difficult to guess what. There was no way I could hit a moving target at that range with an unfamiliar pistol, or catch up with him by sticking to the path, so I scrambled down the bluff, ran, scrambled, walked, and peered around the corner of the repair shop in time to see Wolfgang disappear into the rangers' office. I checked the pistol, a SIG-Sauer nine millimeter, making sure that it was loaded and the safety off, then ran as fast as my ancient and abused legs would let me. The birds, ravens and gulls, scattered about me as I tottered along.

I heard Wolfgang long before I saw him; he was yelling. "—nuke, he said. We've walked right into a trap!"

There was a moment of relative quiet, and I sidled closer to the door, trying to stay out of sight and *very* glad there was no one in the guard tower. Dupont muttered something that I didn't quite hear, and Wolfgang snarled, "It's the Night of the Long Knives all over again, and he thinks you and me are the SA, the Brownshirts. You can believe it or not, but I'm calling the Wolves and getting them the fuck out of here."

"The Brownshirts were a bunch of fucking queers," said Dupont sullenly. "If Skye's planning a purge—"

"He's got a fuckin' *nuke*," Wolfgang howled. "In the Presidio. It's not just a purge, it's Armageddon; old One-Eye's gone berserk. Are you going to help me or am I going to have to kill you, too?"

I crept into the office, hoping I'd remembered the layout correctly and wishing I had one of Fratinelli's grenades. The shotgun would have to do. Wolfgang was probably standing in the doorway to the communications center, with his back to me I pocketed the SIG-Sauer and yelled "Drop the gun!" as I swung around through the doorway to the office, holding the shotgun with one hand and the door frame with the other in case my legs decided not to support me.

Wolfgang was there, almost exactly as I'd hoped, but he didn't drop the Schmeisser; maybe *he'd* gone berserk, because he spun around and fired. I heard at least four shots, and I know at least one of them was mine because the recoil sent me staggering backwards out of the room. The next thing I knew, I was lying on the floor, my left leg feeling like a pillar of fire. I looked up, and saw Wolfgang lying less than a meter away, half of his head missing. I glanced at the shotgun; both barrels were smoking. Dupont was standing over Wolfgang's body, a dark stain spreading across the front of his camo pants. I tried to stand, and realized that I'd been grazed just below the hip; any other shots Wolfgang had fired had apparently missed. Dupont fumbled for the big revolver he wore at his hip and walked toward me, whimpering, "What's going on?"

"He shot Skye," I said, "and Martini. They're dead. Look, there's a first-aid kit somewhere; can you help me?"

He glanced around nervously, then his eyes started to gleam. "And you've just avenged them. You're going to be a hero."

"If you say so. Right now I'd rather just be alive." He was standing close enough that I could see the knife on his belt. Maybe it was a coincidence, maybe not, but it looked suspiciously like the knife-pistol that had killed Tiffany. And I had to stop word of the nuke reaching the crowd at the Presidio.

"I always wanted to be a hero," said Dupont dreamily, a smile creeping across his pretty face as he tugged the revolver out of its holster. He was standing right over me now, and I swung my good leg up and smashed my boot into his groin. It ruined his aim and distracted him long enough for me to grab my own pistol and shoot first. I started firing before I'd even pulled it out of my pocket and my first shot missed, but the next hit him in the shoulder, making him drop the revolver. I kept shooting until the clip was empty, missing him more often than not, or hitting armor, but one shot went through his cheek, narrowly missing his eye, and another creased his ear. He staggered backwards until he collapsed against the wall, his eyes glazed with shock, but still very much alive. I dropped the SIG-Sauer and crawled over to where his revolver—a big Colt Python—was lying. He turned to watch me, his eyes barely managing to track. I picked up the revolver and pointed it squarely at his face.

"Was it good for you, too?" I yelled. I gave him a second or two to think about it, and when he opened his mouth to reply, I fired.

I sat there for a few seconds, or maybe it was a few minutes. "So much for peaceful solutions," I muttered, hauled myself to my feet as best I could, and lurched into the office in search of the first-aid kit. I swallowed the puny little painkillers inside, bandaged my leg and put my thigh in an inflatable splint, and dragged myself back up toward the cell house, wishing I'd brought my canes. Even my good leg was still badly atrophied from the time I'd spent in a coma, and despite Barry's wonder drugs, it was giving me hell from the running and climbing I'd been doing. By the time I'd emerged from the tunnel, less than a quarter of the way to the building, I was wishing that he'd played my braintape into a healthier body.

I'd taken another three agonizing steps before I realized that maybe there *was* a peaceful solution, and one that might have a better chance of success. Not for this time line—it was much too late for that—but for another. If I could just get back to Barry before either of us bled to death.

"Freeze!"

A woman's voice. I looked up to see Sophie walking cautiously around the bend ahead. "Help!" I yelled. "Sophie, please . . ."

"Lose the gun first," she said, advancing slowly, a machine pistol trained on me. "Who are you?"

"I'm Lee," I said, dropping the revolver. Splattered with blood from half a dozen people and staggering as though I were wearing weighted boots, I probably looked like something from a horror movie. "They found me a male body, but it's kind of damaged. . . ." I collapsed onto the path, and she came running toward me.

Barry had blacked out, but he still had a faint pulse, so we did what we could to patch him up. Even with Sophie's upwhen healing skills it was a slow job, and all she could do for me was do a better job of bandaging and give me a stronger painkiller. "He'll die unless we get him to a hospital; if I call the ferry—"

I shook my head. "The hospitals won't be safe, even for us. What did Skye tell you was going to happen tonight?"

"Well, the rally, of course, and then a . . . the word he used was *blitzkrieg*. San Francisco, Berkeley, Oakland, all the way up to Point Reyes, but he was worried about what Washington might do to retaliate. That's why he's turned some of the cells in D Block into a fallout shelter, in case we're bombed."

Jesus, this guy lied more than I did—either that, or he really was so crazy he didn't even know when he was telling the truth. "Is there anything you can do to bring him around?"

"Are you serious?"

"I need some answers. Is there anyone else here from upwhen?"

Sophie shook her head. "They're all at the Presidio, ready for the rally."

I stared at my watch. Three past seven; shit. "Do you remember when you were swap-hopped?"

"Yes, but . . ."

"Do you remember the exact time and place?"

"No, but there was a letter for me with all the data—"

"A *letter*?"

"A hard copy." She nodded. "Good paper, very impressive. From a law firm."

"Do you remember the name?"

She thought for a moment. "Verdi, Sculley and Ord. Why?"

"Thanks. Now, what can you do to bring him around?"

She muttered something in the same language that Skye and Barry had spoken, then fished something out of the first-aid kit. She injected it into Barry's neck and sat back. "Should take about ten minutes."

"Okay. See if you can find Fratinelli and help him, but don't waste too much time—then get all of the women and go to the shelter." The walls and doors should be thick enough to keep most of the radiation out at this distance. "Stay there until someone you know and trust tells you it's safe to come out. Okay?"

"What about you?"

"I'll join you there later. *Go!*"

I was looking through the files in Skye's laptop—Barry had stayed conscious long enough to prevent the security programs from locking me out—when Barry opened his eyes. "Mike?" he said weakly.

I nodded. "We have less than an hour before the bomb goes off," I said, spitting out the words hastily, "and I have an idea that might just save a few thousand lives next time you try this, but I have to know why you're doing it."

"I told you—"

"You told me you were trying to save life on Earth, and something about freedom of travel. I need to know more. You and Skye were both sent here to stop these fanatics. What happens if you fail?"

"We try again," he said softly. "We had several alternative plans—none as likely to succeed as this one, of course."

That didn't sound too reassuring. "Why? What do they do? Steal a better bomb and destroy the entire Earth?"

Barry stared. "No, they . . . well, yes, I . . ." He took a deep breath. "They form their own enclave and declare themselves an independent nation, killing hundreds in the process and leaving thousands homeless. The enclave is only small, but they defend its borders fiercely; they are well armed, and because their population remains low, every man is raised to be kill-capable.

"After the nations that *you* know have collapsed or become irrelevant, the inhabitants of the enclave, the heirs of these fanatics become the extremist arm of HumanGenesis, one of the most powerful political groups on Earth. HumanGenesis as a whole isn't racist as you'd understand it, but genetic engineering . . . let's just say that race becomes more a matter of choice for most people. But HumanGenesis *is* fiercely xenophobic and isolationist, and many of its members believe that humans from the Outer Worlds—especially those outside the solar system—are either aliens or in league with them. Earth, they proclaimed, was for the Earthborn; visitors were not welcome. Many Offworlders, though, still wanted to see Earth for themselves, even if it meant coping with the gravity and weeks or years of travel; after all, most of them still thought of it as their home, too. The man you call the Bodysnatcher would have known all of this, but after he was swap-hopped, HumanGenesis delivered an ultimatum for all Offworlders to leave the planet or be killed, and when this was ignored, they sent kill-capables with pocket nukes to sites where they knew Offworlders were plentiful: universities, mostly, and museums, and world heritage areas and other historic sites."

I stared at him, horrified. "And the orbital elevator, of course," he continued. "All of the bombs came from the enclave; we're less sure about the bombers, some of whom were probably lied to about their mission. It was all supposed to be coordinated down to the second, but some of the bombers were spotted by security, and a few were early, and the alarm was raised. . . ." He paused. "Still, nineteen of them were detonated at or near their targets.

"Millions were killed, but many offworlders survived, and the Outer Worlds began coordinating a rescue mission. The extremists warned of more violence if they were permitted to land, and governments on Earth began hunting down HumanGenesis members, most of whom had thought the ultimatum was merely a bluff. Anyone with pale skin or blond hair was regarded with the utmost suspicion, HumanGenesis supporter or not. Other governments preferred to blame older enemies, and several went to war.

"The Offworlders were more forgiving than I think I would have been; after rescuing as many of their people as they could, they simply announced that they would break all contact with Earth for a period of fifty standard years. Unfortunately, this doesn't stop the wars, which soon escalate."

"But if none of you can kill . . ."

"None of us?" He stared at me, his expression bleak. "Even in my time, there are always a few of us—and with weapons that can kill millions and require only one man to program a computer, a few of us is all it takes."

"*You?*"

He looked startled, even shocked. "No! Nor Adam—the man you called Skye. We'd never killed anyone before we came here." He shuddered. "More than a billion had died by the time I left, and we can't expect any help from the Offworlders."

I shuddered. "What if you could swap-hop your own people into Skye's sick little crew, maybe take it over from the inside, make him stick to his original plan, disarm the Apostles instead of wiping them out? If you knew exactly when and where he's flat-lined Martini and Star and the homeless to provide hosts for his own thugs . . ."

"You have this data?" he said, a hint of hope in his voice.

"No, but I know where he keeps it. It's a law firm. Can you infiltrate them, get the data that way?"

His eyes gleamed faintly. "We can try."

"Is it more likely to work than Skye's solution?"

"Oh, yes. Trying to put an end to hatred and xenophobia with a massacre . . . Skye may have believed it would work, but I don't, and I'm still not sure he was entirely sane. The smaller the changes we make to the time line, the more easily we can control them; what he's done was a desperate act, but as long as we can create *one* time line in which the attack on the Offworlders is avoided, there's still hope."

"Uh-huh. Look, the communications center still seems to be running; if you give me an address, I'll send all the data I have, plus what's in Skye's computer here, to them."

Barry nodded. "Get me something to write on." I grabbed a pen and a spec sheet for the bomb off Skye's desk.

"Is there anything else I can do for you?" I asked as he scribbled away. "If I can get you back to Point Reyes—do you have a braintaper back there?"

"We'd never make it. This is more important." I took the scrap of paper and he grabbed my hand. "It was good working with you, Mike. Your descendants would be proud of you, if they knew you. Good-bye."

I staggered out of the cell house again, cradling the laptop in my arms, and staggered back down the path. I was lurching around the first bend when I saw the ferry headed for the dock; it was close enough that I might only have a few seconds' grace. I swore, and then lurched along as quickly as I could, hoping to get to the office before anyone questioned me. I was unarmed, and I hadn't noticed any weapons in the office, except for Wolfgang's Schmeisser—probably empty—and Dupont's revolver and knife-pistol. I hurried down the path, doing my best to ignore the pain in my legs—the drugs Sophie had given me helped, but they couldn't stop all feeling without leaving me unable to walk—and made sure that when I fell, I fell onto my back so that the laptop wouldn't be damaged, even if it meant hitting my head. My right leg felt like a broken lump of wood by the time I reached the office, but at least I made it without hearing any shots fired.

The gulls and ravens were already picking at Wolfgang and Dupont's bodies; they scattered when I paused to pick up Dupont's revolver, but soon regrouped. I staggered into the communications center, collapsed onto the chair with a sigh of relief, hooked the laptop up to a modem, then created a text file and keyed in the name of the law firm and a quick note explaining the services they performed for Skye. I was about to send it to the two addresses Barry had given me, and to Terri Lock's (it's always a good idea to have a backup) when I heard the birds scatter again and a familiar voice bellowed, "What the fuck's happened here?"

I turned around and saw MacRae standing near the bodies, his pistol pointed at the ground. Behind him were a half dozen men in different uniforms, all of them strangers. I opened the file manager and selected all the text files on the hard drive, and MacRae burst into the office and yelled "Freeze!"

Fuck. "Hi, Scott," I said as casually as I could. "We've had an outbreak of rabies. Wolfgang went mad."

He looked back at the uniformed corpses—the faces were no longer recognizable, thanks to the birds—then back at me. "And who's that with him? Dupont?"

"Uh-huh. Wolfgang shot him, so I'm doing his job. Skye asked me to e-mail these files for him." I moved all the files into the Outgoing Mail tray and was moving the cursor to Send when I felt something cold, hard, and circular press against the back of my skull, just where it met the top of my spine.

"Get up," said MacRae. "Hands behind your head. I'm not letting you touch anything until I've cleared it with Skye." I didn't move.

"And where *is* Skye? And Mueller and Martini? They're supposed to be waiting here; we're running late."

"Still up at the cell house." I stared at the screen; all I needed to do was move the mouse slightly and click it, or press the Enter key— and it might even have been worth it, but for the possibility that MacRae would think of hitting Cancel. I considered grabbing the gun and decided against it; I could hear too many other people running around outside. Moving slowly, I locked my fingers together behind my head and stood, wincing as I put too much weight on my right leg. "I don't think they'll be coming down, either," I said. "I think they're all dead," I informed him. "Skye, Martini, Dupont, Fratinelli, Mueller, Wirth, Harry Burns . . . only the women are still alive."

"*All* of them? *How?*"

I was wondering if my leg would bear my weight long enough for me to make a back kick, and if so, how much good it would do me, when it occurred to me that I'd sunk to their level, depending on violence as a first resort. I was outnumbered and outgunned; they enjoyed violence more than I did, had had more practice, were better at it. What could I do that they couldn't do? Speak seven languages? It wasn't going to help here. Teach English? Proofread? Pick fruit? Act? Mar a curious tale in telling it, and deliver a plain message bluntly?

What had Skye said about Martini? "Soldiers are trained to believe bullshit." If these fanatics believed themselves to be Aryan supermen, if they believed that people like Connie and Wazaki and Mama Castro were evil or inferior, they could believe almost *anything*, as long as it fitted their worldview and didn't contain any uncomfortable new ideas. And Barry had told me that MacRae tended toward paranoia and megalomania, but he could be flattered, and he trusted people who seemed to want to follow him.

"Wolfgang shot most of them," I said truthfully. "At least I know he shot Skye, and Harry, and the dogs; I didn't see him shoot Martini or Dupont or the others—"

"The *dogs?* Jesus. *Why?*"

"He pulled a gun on Skye and the dogs attacked him, and he pulled the trigger. I don't think he meant to shoot Harry, he may not even have meant to shoot Skye, but he said something about the

Night of the Long Knives. He . . . Skye . . ." I took a deep breath. "He thought that Skye was planning to wipe out his people, the Winter Wolves, so he shot him. I think the others just got in his way." I thought furiously, sticking as close to the truth as I dared. "I think he shot Dupont to stop him sending a message—"

"The message you're trying to send now?"

MacRae sounded as though he might be buying it. If I could just persuade him to let me e-mail the files, I didn't care what happened after that. "I think so. I *know* it's urgent."

"Uh-huh." He backed up slightly and glanced over his shoulder for an instant, but the gun—a Colt .45—remained pointed at the back of my head. "Okay, somebody's gone up to the cell house. Until they come back, you don't move, understood?"

"Yes."

"Why didn't Wirth shoot you?"

"He did; you think this thing on my leg is a love bite?"

"Don't get smart. Who killed him?"

"I did." He grunted. "He had the drop on the others, but I had a gun in my hand. Shotgun. Point-blank range. And he may've been out of ammo, or maybe his gun jammed; he'd been using it like a garden hose." I shut up. Liars usually talk more than they have to, and it's actually harder to lie convincingly to someone who can't see your face.

"You know you're admitting to shooting a superior officer? That carries the death penalty."

"Yes. I'd just seen him shoot *his* superior officer."

Another grunt. "But you weren't acting under orders, were you?" He sounded less skeptical, almost respectful.

"Yes," I said firmly. "I'd been ordered to send this message, and I knew it was urgent."

He hesitated. "Did he say anything else? Skye, I mean."

I shook my head. "He took it in the neck. Died instantly."

"Before that."

"He was talking about the rally tonight."

"He wanted it to go ahead?"

It *had* to go ahead. "Absolutely," I said, fairly sure that it was true. "He knew there'd be casualties tonight, in the blitz; he wouldn't want you to stop just because he's one of them. He must have had contingency plans for"—I suddenly realized what it was that MacRae wanted to hear—"for the Apostles carrying on without him. Or Martini, or Dupont, or Fratinelli, or Mueller. You and Donner and Forster will have to take over." MacRae muttered something. "The men will follow Donner, but someone will still have to tell him what to say, write his speeches, act as his adviser."

"Did Skye say that?"

"No, it's just—"

"If I want your opinion, I'll have it tattooed on your skin and turned into a lampshade." He tried to sound tough, but it was obvious he'd liked what I'd said. "Do you know what that message you're supposed to send is? Or where it's going?"

"He didn't tell me. I thought it might be a list of the suspected traitors—"

"What did I just say about opinions?" he said, but there was even less force in it this time. He didn't speak again for nearly ten minutes, while men in different uniforms ran madly around the island and I tried to stand at brace without putting any of my weight on my bad leg. Finally, I heard someone come running up to him. "Skye's dead, sir," he panted. "I found Martini, too, and Fratinelli, and Mueller, and three other men I didn't recognize—recruits in Alpha Security uniforms. The women are hiding in one of the isolation cells, and they say they won't come out until someone they know tells them the shooting's stopped."

MacRae swore, but not for very long. "Skye wanted them to stay here tonight anyway, said it was safer. And we're running late. . . . Right. I guess that makes me the ranking officer here. Rudy, take a detail, get the bodies into the boat. We're going to have some martyrs at this rally: That should get people stirred up, if nothing else does. And when we get back, assign two men to watch every one of Wolfgang's, just in case it *is* treason."

"Sir!" he barked. "Yes, sir." He clicked his heels, walked toward the harbor, and started shouting orders.

"Right," said MacRae, and sighed. "I don't like your story, Ryan, but there's nobody alive who can contradict you and there's fuck-all I can do about it now. I don't have time to read that message, but if Skye's last order was that he wanted it sent, I guess—" He corrected himself sharply. "Carry on."

"Sir," I said, managing to keep the glee out of my voice. "Yes, sir!" I grabbed the desk with one hand to prevent myself from falling over, then moved the mouse, clicked on the Send button, and watched as it started copying and mailing the files from the laptop hard drive. Good. Good. I didn't look away until it told me the transfer was completed.

"Don't think you're out of the shit yet," MacRae warned me when I turned around. He glared at my leg. "You're in no shape to march, anyway, and I'm still not sure I trust you enough to give you a weapon, but as a white man and a soldier, you're entitled to a fair trial, and we're running late. Fleischer!" I held my breath. "Take this man and lock him in one of the cells in the Hole; Forster can interrogate him tomorrow." I stared at him, incredulously, then nodded. "And haul ass!" MacRae barked at his men. "Half an hour from now, we're going to be making history!"

40

MIKE

I was in the cell for three days before anyone came to rescue us, and even then they were wearing radiation-proof suits. They flew us to a military hospital in San Diego, and performed a shitload of tests and kept us there for weeks while the investigation continued; we were never formally arrested, but I can't think of a better description.

The women had fared better than I had, as far as the radiation damage went; their cell had been specifically prepared for use as a fallout shelter, with air filters and other equipment that had gone a long way to convince the investigators that Skye had been responsible for bombing the city. The team up at Point Reyes had done their best to warn people in the city about the blitzkrieg, and while too many had ignored them, or disbelieved them, or chosen to barricade themselves in their homes rather than fleeing the city for the night as they'd been advised to, they'd managed to save a few thousand lives that way. The worst damage was confined to Presidio Park; anyone out in the open would have been killed instantly by the blast. Most of the housing affected by the firestorm belonged to the Apostles; Skye had planned well, in that regard. Many firefighters, most of them volunteers, suffered badly from radiation damage, and I know some died, but I don't believe the rumors about them being buried in lead-lined coffins.

Emergency teams arrived before sunrise, with chelating drugs for anyone who might have been exposed, though they couldn't save the eyesight of those who'd looked at the fireball. Martial law was declared, and the entire city north of Hayes was evacuated (again) for a few months before rebuilding began in earnest; by this time, my hair, which had fallen out, was beginning to grow back. Unfortunately, the cancer in my bones was growing faster, apparently helped on by Barry's wonder drugs. Shortly after this, they discharged me to a civilian hospital, having finally decided not to charge me with anything, and let me have unrestricted access to the Net again. The anonymous e-mails arrived the next day.

The first message read, simply, CONTACT MADE NO ATTACK THANK YOU, no signature, no return address, nothing to say whether the peaceful solution had been tried. The second was longer.

```
Mike,
    They promised me they'd send this to you when
it was over, whatever "it" turned out to be; I
felt I owed you an explanation.
    I know you've sometimes wished you could go
back and change the past. Well, I was offered
that chance; I can't give you too many details,
but they asked what I was prepared to do to pre-
vent the genocide and the partition, and they
gave me some idea of what was involved, and
. . . well, I volunteered.
    I hope everything turned out okay, and I'm
sorry I couldn't tell you any of this before.
                        Sincerely,
                        Michael Byron Galloway
                        December 20, 2034
```

I had time to read the message twice before the picture in one corner, a butterfly, came to life. It ate the text and disappeared, leaving me with a blank screen.

I t wasn't much of a funeral, but then, I've never wanted a fancy one.

Mike lasted fifteen months after the San Francisco blast before the cancer killed him, which was more than Kannon and I managed as a couple. She stayed in Washington, while I went back to Australia rather than face another winter in the Northeast. I backpacked my way around the country, meeting people and picking fruit, then drove a taxi in Broome for a few weeks before returning to the U.S. I spent a month working at the Book Cellar, but Austin had become too much like L.A. to be bearable any longer than that. It soon became obvious that Mike wasn't going to make it to the end of the year, despite Sophie's care, and I asked if he wanted me to take over the shop. He said if I was interested, he'd open another branch office in any city of my choice, but he didn't want me hanging around to watch him die. "I don't know," I said. "I've thought about it, but if there's enough money, I'd like to go to school, get a degree."

"And then what? Go back to teaching?"

"Maybe. I can bullshit in eleven languages; that must be of some use to someone. Maybe I can get a job as an interpreter."

"Who for?"

"I don't know. The UN, maybe."

He looked at me skeptically. "Think you can stand the corruption?"

"For a while, maybe. Hey, I infiltrated the Apostles, didn't I?"

"Yes, and looked what happened to them!"

We held the wake three months later, in Galloway's ground-floor apartment in Berkeley, where Sophie had been living toward the end. He'd tried to will it to her, but as Donner's widow she had much more ice than we did, so it went to me. We sat around and drank— Kannon; Sophie; Mama; Shriek; Colin; Belinda; her husband, Kevin, and their wife, Crystal; a few friends Mike had made that I hadn't met before; even Angela—and then, when we were drunk enough, we caught the BART into San Francisco and a trolley up to Fisherman's Wharf, then stood on the pier and stared out toward the Rock. The *Harbor Emperor* pulled in while we were waiting; Kannon glanced toward it, then told me not to look. Inevitably, I did.

There were four skinheads, the eldest maybe twenty-one, all wearing double-breasted charcoal-colored greatcoats with the crossed thunderbolt symbol of the Apostles on their sleeves: neo-Nazis on a pilgrimage. Sophie, who'd also turned to stare, stiffened and paled with anger, and I grabbed her arm.

"Jesus," she said, "the things I could tell them about their heroes."

"They wouldn't listen," I said.

"Killed by their own weapons and their stupidity, and what did they accomplish, apart from their own martyrdom? Nothing. Nothing but ashes."

The four had looked up and stared at us, and one of the youngest muttered something and snickered.

"They're only boys," said Mama soothingly, "and when they grow up, they'll only be men, and what do men know about life anyway?"

Thirty years later, I still haven't thought of a good answer to that question.

ABOUT THE AUTHOR

STEPHEN DEDMAN'S award-nominated short fiction has appeared in most major genre magazines, including *The Magazine of Fantasy and Science Fiction*, *Asimov's*, and *SF Age*, and in such highly regarded anthologies as *Little Deaths*, *The Year's Best Fantasy and Horror*, *Dreaming Down-Under*, and *Centaurus*. He lives in Perth, Australia, and is currently working on a sequel to his Stoker Award–nominated first novel, *The Art of Arrow Cutting*.